THE BOY FROM
CHERNY YAR

THE BOY FROM CHERNY YAR

BLIND OBEDIENCE

VOLUME 1

RICHARD ANASTASIUS DICKSON

TATE PUBLISHING
AND ENTERPRISES, LLC

Published by Tate Publishing & Enterprises, LLC
127 E. Trade Center Terrace | Mustang, Oklahoma 73064 USA
1.888.361.9473 | www.tatepublishing.com

Tate Publishing is committed to excellence in the publishing industry. The company reflects the philosophy established by the founders, based on Psalm 68:11,
"The Lord gave the word and great was the company of those who published it."

Book design copyright © 2015 by Tate Publishing, LLC. All rights reserved.
Cover design by Rodrigo Adolfo
Interior design by Jomel Pepito

Published in the United States of America
ISBN: 978-1-63306-580-2
Fiction / Action & Adventure
14.11.27

DRAMATIS PERSONAE

Tatar Characters (all names in Turkish or other Turkic variants):

Akilli Khan (Reasonable)

Chieftain of the Kubanshyi Nogay Tatars dwelling at Falaka Sopasi (or the Birches); uncle of Tambor by marriage to Kibar (gentle), deceased sister of Yerinde. Married to Ayla, former slave; father of Altan (Dawn), Mehtap, and Pembesi.

Bashina (Alone)

Elder warrior of the Sopasi tribe. Trainer of Tambor and the tribe in general. Replaced by Kokochu.

Chabuk (Swift)

Third son of Dalgali and Yerinde; Nogay warrior. Married to Eda; father of Kirbash, born at same hour as Misha.

Dikkatli/Kattu (Studious)

Known as Kattu; firstborn of Dalgali and Yerinde and elder brother of Tambor; married to Marwa, a Muslim girl from Astrakhan.

Dalgali (Restless)

Tambor's father; a well-respected trader or merchant of the tribe. Married to Yerinde, Tambor's mother. Concubines (wives) are Natasha, Hawa, and a third, Katya.

Dalgin (Stargazer)

Son of Dalgali and Natasha; Nogay warrior, musician and bard, and chanter.

Married to Livvy, Nissim's sister. Father of Rachel (deceased) and Leah, born around the same time as Misha. Father of Fanasi (Athanasius), born later.

Dilaver (Courageous)

Squire to Tambor, son of Chief Umut, given to Tambor for training by grandfather Onur at the Three Yurts. Married to Burca (Fragrant) . Father of Kan (Soul) and other children; older brother of Erali.

Ender (Very rare)

One of Dalgali's herdsmen. Killed at battle of the Kalmyks. Tambor promised to bring up his sons, Emre and Emin. Wife, Esen.

Erali (Brave)

Squire to Nissim, younger brother of Dilaver, son of Chief Umut, given to Tambor for training by Grandfather Onur at the Three Yurts. Married to Kelebek (Butterfly), cousin of Burca; from one of the Nogay tribes of Azerbaijan.

Esen (the Wind)

Widow of Ender and close friend of Katya, who taught her farming and bee-keeping.

Eda (Well-mannered)

Eldest child; wife of Chabuk; mother of Kirbash (Whip) and other children.

Emre (Friend)

Eldest son and one of the first cadets. Tambor's squire. Both warrior and horseman.

Emin (Trustworthy)

Second son and one of the first cadets. Nissim's squire. Both warrior and horseman.

Faysal (Judge, Arabic)

First son of Lord Selim, chief of Muslim clan; lead warrior of Selim's clan.

Havva (Eve)

Third wife (second concubine) of Dalgali, Mother of Tolga, who was killed at Trabzon. Baptized at Sopasi by Father John. Mother of Irina, who was married to Naveed. Mother of Olga, who was married to Alexei.

Hazir (Ready and willing)

One of the two captains in the Mikhailov campaign. His men destroyed the Garrison. Lost his brother there. Adopted his brother's son, Kiymetli. Accompanied Tambor to Trabzon. One of Tambor's chief advisers. Married to Ruxsar (Yezidi woman). Had daughters, Pinar (Spring) and Hazan (Fall).

Katya

Ekaterina Milanova Sokrovitsyn. Married to Daruvenko and widowed. Russian Boyar (princess) taken by Tambor from Mikhailov at its destruction, given to Dalgali as concubine, later Tambor's mistress and covert mother of his sons Misha and Theodore (Tolga). God Mother to Marta.

Kokochu

Kalmyk warrior and nobleman, expelled from Kalmykia after running the gauntlet, welcomed by Tambor on the Trabzon mission, became training master at Sopasi.

Koray (Ember moon)

Cousin to Tambor; son of Yerinde's half brother Haluk (pleasant)—Derman was their father. Married Kader (fate) from the Lake community. He fought at Mikhailov, battled the Kalmyks at the Volga, and fought the Persians at the Caspian.

Kiymetli (Valued)

Nephew of Hazir; his father died at Mikhailov. Accompanied troop to Trabzon. Baptized at same time as Tolga. One of the first cadets; Nissim's squire. Married to Lyuba, Natasha's daughter; had a son, Grigory (Grisha). Called Vnouk (grandson by Officer Grigory's family). Sworn brother to Zargo.

Lazim (Needful)

The tribe's elderly shaman. Died when Tambor returned from Trabzon. Replaced by Yavuz, son of Bulut.

Lev (Levent)

Originally Dilaver's slave, given to Katya who freed him. Stayed to work in her farm.

Mehtap (Moonlight, baptized as Marta, Marfa in Russian)

Daughter of Akilli Khan and one-time slave; Married to Nissim after he reached warrior status. Mother of Petya and others.

Metin (Strong)

Fourth son of Dalgali and Yerinde; married Yeter of Chief Resmi' tribe after year's service.

Misha (Michael, the archangel)

Son of Katya and Tambor (assumed to be Dalgali's son), stayed with Katya after the demise of the Cherny Yar officers. Nogay warrior and elder brother of Tolga.

Moussa (Moses in Arabic)
Ethiopian eunuch, former slave in Trabzon; helped in the escape of Anna Maria and Livy. Becomes Yurt master of the cadets.

Natasha (Natalia: Nativity of Christ)
Second wife (first concubine) of Dalgali. Russian (Cossack) lady; mother of Dalgin and Zachary (killed while fighting the Persians). Daughters Natalia married Zargo and Lyuba married Kiymetli (son Grigory).

Nissim (Onesimus: Greek, Useful)
One-time (Greek) slave of Tambor; Nogay warrior; companion and sworn brother to Tambor; son of Athanasius of Nicomedia. Married to Mehtap, daughter of the khan named Marta in baptism. Peter (Petya) and Sultana, son and daughter of Nissim and Marta, born around the same time as Tamara and Misha.

Selim (Safe in Arabic)
One of the Lords of Falaka Sopasi, Muslim clan; father of Faysal.

Tambor (Drum)
Hero of novel; warrior and lord of the Kubanshyi Nogay Tatars; son of Dalgali and nephew of Akilli Khan Father of Misha and Theodore (Tolga) by Katya (officially sons of Dalgali); Tural and Salime by Simge, Tambor's concubine; and others.

Tetik (alert, awake)
Son of Tutumlu, a steward of Dalgali. Wounded at Mikhailov; Timov amputated his wrist and saved the arm. Expert at falconry. Accompanied Dalgali with his father traveling in birds of prey. Accompanied mission to Trabzon.

Theodore (Gift of God, known as Tolga, after Tambor's deceased brother)
Nogay warrior and second son of Katya and Tambor (assumed to be Dalgali's son), stayed with Katya after the demise of the Cherny Yar officers.

Timov (Timotheus, "honoring God")
Younger brother of Nissim, servant of Tambor, and eventually merchant and treasurer of Tambor's subtribe. Godfather to Tamara and Misha.

Tolga (Helmet), Baptized as Theodore (Gift of God),
Son of Dalgali and Havva. Half brother of Tambor. Fought the Kalmyks at the Volga and the Turks at Trabzon. There fatally wounded, baptized and buried near Trabzon. Officer Grigory is Godfather.

Tutumlu (Thrifty, Prudent)

Dalgali's chief steward with the caravan. Father of Tetik.

Usta (Expert)

One of the two captains in the Mikhailov campaign. Destroyed the wharf area. Led the Blue Raiders against the Volga Kalmyks. Father of Coskun (New boy), one of the first cadets.

Uyari (Warning)

Female shaman or wise woman and assistant to Lazim. Chief midwife of community. Went to Mikhailov with Tambor. Sister to Matushka Meryem and brother Evgeny.

Yavuz (Stern, Grim)

Young shaman replaced Lazim after he died. Son of Bulut, shaman of The Lakes.

Yerinde (Appropriate)

Only acknowledged wife of Dalgali and mother of Dikkatli, Tambor, Chabuk, and Metin (sons) and Vermek (daughter).

The Original Cadet Class

The Lions

Nissim's Team

1. Kiymetli, first squire
2. Jyrgal, Tambor's half brother
3. Pishana, Persian
4. Feofil, Father John's son; replaced by Serik, of the horsemen
5. Yakup, of Selim's clan
6. Alp, cousin of Tambor
7. Zachary, Natasha's son, killed
8. Emin, second squire

The Eagles

Tambor's Team

1. Zargo, first squire
2. Nurzhan, cousin of Tambor

3. Alexei (Cossack), Father John's adpt. son
4. Umar, of Selim's clan
5. Arshana, Persian
6. Metin, got married; replaced by Coskun, Usta's son
7. Tural, Koray's brother, killed
8. Emre, second squire
9. Moussa, tent supervisor
10. Naveed, cadet in charge

Tatar Chieftains

1. **Chief Ibn Haddi**, leader of Muslim tribe in Astrakhan. Dikkatli's father-in-law; Marwa's father.
2. **Lord Shafiq Ibn-Moussa**, trader, lives in Muslim tribe outside Kazan.
3. **Chief Resmi**, leader of the tribe on the east side of the Volga. Daughter Yeter married to Metin, son of Dalgali. Tengrist tribe.
4. **Chief Serhat**, leader of Muslim tribe northwest of Sopasi.
5. **Chief Umut (hope), son of Onur (honor)**, chiefs of one of the Three Yurts.
6. **Chief Ufuk**, leader of Tengrist tribe west of Sopasi, nearest to Sopasi. .
7. **Chief Volkan**, leader of the Three Yurts.
8. **Chief Ubashi**, leader of the East Volga Kalmyks. Great-nephew Ubashi, new chief.

Russian Characters (All names in this list begin with titles when applicable)

(Note virtually all Russians and Greeks are named after a saint or feast day)

Alexei (known as Cossack)
One of Tambor's officers, an original cadet. Adopted son of Father John in Astrakhan; orphaned with his two sisters Lyuba and Nadia. Misha's godfather. Marries Olga, eldest daughter of Dalgali and Havva.

Archimandrite Father Dmitri
Abbot of Holy Dormition Monastery, Chuvashia. Tambor's monastic father to whom he writes his confession.

Captain Alexander (Zander) Stepanovich Tretyakov

Officer in charge of the Garrison at Tsagan Aman on the border of Volga Kalmykia.

Captain Yaakov Varisovich Boutenko

One of the officers in charge at Cherny Yar. Translator for administrator.

Commander Matvei Natanovich Gratianov

Officer in charge of mercenaries on the northern shores of the Caspian. Friend of Tambor. Son, Maxim Matveich.

Father Gleb Florovich Montoyov

Priest at Mikhailov at the time of the siege.

Father Ivan (Batushka John) Makarovsky

Assistant pastor of Holy Nativity Church in Astrakhan, iconographer.

Matushka Meryem (Maria)

Tatar wife of Father John. Parents of: Anton and Feofil. Adopted Alexei, Lyuba and Nadia.

Father Yaroslav

Russian priest in Mtskheta, Georgia. Interred Officer Grigory in Mtskheta.

Grigory Yurevich Ureic, Retired Russian officer

Accompanied the troop on the mission to Trabzon. Died and buried near Mtskheta.

Wife, Verusha. Sons, Sergei and Pavel. Grandfather figure to Kiymetli (Vnouk).

Konstantine Alexandrovich Lapukhin

Assistant administrator at Cherny Yar. Later transferred to Moscow and then Saint Petersburg to be in charge of Tribal Affairs and after to Kazan. Friend of Tambor.

Lazar (God Helped) Leskovich Tatarinov

Free servant of Father John. Born near the Black Sea. Dealer of books, housewares, and jewelry. Brought Alexei and Feofil to Sopasi. Stayed and married Pembesi.

Masha and Ivan Fedorovich Yashkin

Proprietors of the Saint Vladimir's Hostel in Cherny Yar.

Matushka Meryem (Maria),
Tatar wife of Father John and sister to Uyari.

Petya, peasant boy killed by Nissim at Mikhailov.

Sima and Anyusha, proprietors of the Azov in Astrakhan.

Vassili Andreivich Daruvenko
Master of Mikhailov and husband to Katya. Killed by Chabuk at the siege of Mikhailov.

Persian Characters

Arshana (Hero) and Pishana (Predecessors)
Orphaned twins. Nephews of Kuru. Of the first team of Cadets.

Kuru (Cyrus)
Persian nobleman reduced to slavery for refusing conversion to Islam. Camel master bought by Tambor and freed. Accompanied mission to Trabzon.

Mardunya
Second son of Kuru. Speaks some Turkish. Marries Meraz, second daughter of Ruxsar.

Naveed (Good news)
Youngest son of Kuru. Became fine young warrior, Tatar style. Marries Irina, daughter of Dalgali and Havva, both baptized. Cadet in charge.

Vishtaspa (Having ready horses)
Eldest son of Kuru; speaks Turkish. Marries Hanna eldest daughter of Ruxsar; two children.

Ruxsar
Yezidi woman from Azerbaijan purchased for her daughters. Married Hazir and had two more daughters: Pinar (Spring) and Hazan (Autumn). Son, Zargo.

Zargo
Yezidi son of Ruxsar, brought from Azerbaijan. An original cadet and Tambor's squire. Sworn brother to Kiymetli. Squire to Tambor. Married Natalia, daughter of Natasha.

Greek Characters

(Note: virtually all Russians and Greeks are named after a saint or feast day)

Anna Maria Nikolaou

Married to Athanasios. Mother to Nissim, Timov, and Livvy.

Athanasios Nikolaou (Turkish name, Yusuf Nasser)

Husband of Anna Maria and father of Nissim, Timov, and Livvy.

Fathers Theodosius and Michaelangelos

Greek monks who were living at a monastery at Tbilisi and whom Tambor took to the monastery of Saint Davit Gareja, in Kakheti in eastern Georgia.

Father Tryphon

Priest in small village not far from Trabzon (Presvytera Pelaghia). Performed the baptism of Tolga and Kiymetli.

Yanni and Christo Stefannidis

Altar boys during the Trabzon mission.

Xenophon

Proprietor of a gift and hardware shop in Batumi during first mission to Trabzon.

Turkish Characters

Fahesh

Son of Mehmet Pasha. Turkish Cadet in Trabzon who exposed Nissim as Christian. In charge of his father's estate at the time of the Trabzon mission.

Mehmet Pasha

Turkish nobleman. Kept Nissim and Timov as house slaves until he sold them to thieves (wrongly called Kurds). Anna Maria and Livvy, slaves of his Harem.

Moussa

Ethiopian slave of Mehmet Pasha. Freed by Tambor and brought to Sopasi.

Kozan

VOLGA RiveR

Russia

Sopasia & mikhailov   Stupino   Rezmi's yurt   Aktubinsk

Zazypkin

Cherny Yart

Nikolskoye

Velikan Tsagan Aman

Astrakhan

Kalmykia

Grigory's farm   Astrakhan City

Caspian Sea

South to Dagastan

Crimea
Don River
Rostov-on-Don
Sea of Azov
Russia
Krasnodar
The Kuban
Novorossysk
Black Sea
Sopasi
Mikhailov
Chernyi Yar
Tsagan Aman
Volga River
Astrakhan
Kalmykia
Astrakhan
Grigory's House
The Three Yurts
Caspian Sea
Dagestan
Makachkola
Derbent
Georgia
Mtsketa
Tblisi
St David
Guraji
Batumi
Persians
Trabzon
Rize
Warriors
Karaka
Kura River
Armenia
Azerbaijan
Baku
TURKEY
The Ottoman Empire

Prologue
Obedience

It is good to keep the secret of a king,
But it is glorious to preach the works of God
—Tobit 12:11 (tr. The Orthodox Word)

My dear Father Dmitri,

Only holy obedience could require of me this undertaking. It would certainly not be my will to write these "confessions" of mine, as you call them, except that you require it of me. You tell me that many saints have written confessions before, and so you have chosen this sacred genre by which I am presumably to humiliate myself. Being a man of pride, it should be only to my benefit to do so. Yet how shall I compare myself with these saints, dear Father and Abbot, who looks back on a past of such pride and such humiliation? Were it not for me a condition for my tonsure, for my vows, I would never start. Never. This is now January, the week of Theophany, and I have been here under your guiding hand for two years. It has not been easy; you are a sterner man than Father Gleb. But you are Chuvash, and although I am a Tatar, we are both of the same heritage; our languages and traditions are similar. I cannot, therefore, at least with you, hide behind my supposed barbarity. You expect more from me, and I respect you for this, though I still hate to be under command.

As we have discussed, I shall be writing this in Russian; I know not if there is anything written in Tatar save the translations of the services and some scriptures done by Father Gleb and his disciples at Mikhailov. Even my Russian is more the traditional

Slavonic, which I learned from Father Gleb on our travels and for which I am indebted to him. Although I am at ease with native Russian, my own speech is a little clumsy, and I need help expressing myself. I am pleased and grateful for the fine young professor from Nizhny-Novgorod, Chariton Petruvich, whom you have brought here to teach at the monastery. Mercifully, he has taken some time to help me smooth out some of my choppy writing.

The Great Fast is approaching, and you are expecting me to have this finished by The Dormition of the Mother of God in late August, around which time I expect to be made a monk, if the Lord so wills. I sit here by candlelight slightly chilled, the fire reduced to coals. Father Nicolai, my cell mate and prison keeper, sleeps silently in the corner waiting for the matins bell to ring. Pray that I slumber not before I write at least one page. May the Mother of God be always at my side so that I give an honest account of my struggles.

I must apologize, Father, if I cannot provide dates and times as the Russians do. The tribes are not great on keeping records. We think more in terms of generations, in sequences of events, rather than specific days and years. We think poetically, as Father Gleb once remarked, rather than historically, as the Russians do.

YOUTH

Two things I now remember,
Nay three:
The dry and acrid winds blowing over the steppes,
The dire warning of my grandsire,
And the sultry sadness of my mother.

It seems ironical that I, who was raised on the back of a horse, should be sitting now in a monastery writing a confession. You might say that it is somewhat out of character. Believe me, Father, that in recollecting my youth and childhood I can even now smell the horses, feel the pounding of their hoofs beneath my loins, and the slap of hot air against my cheek blowing over the dry plains of Astrakhan. I can still hear the exultant voices of my companions and the laughter as we kneel, out of breath, to drink from the cool streams that flood into the Volga. I miss it, Father. I do miss those days of innocence.

We learned the art of the warrior: the thrust of the spear, the twang of the bow, and the slice of the sword, though we rarely used these weapons. Those were days of peace for our people. That does not mean that the Russians were not around; they were indeed around, but our hostility toward them, and presumably theirs toward us, was not so pronounced as at other times. My own father, Dalgali, traded with them. He was the trader in the tribe, and although I respected him, indeed admired him—he was so very smart—I had to learn the ways of the warrior from the other men of the tribe. It was a warrior I wanted to be. I had a reason.

The earlier days, Holy Father, were not so happy, I am told. I was brought up in Astrakhan, but our tribe was not native to the region. During my great-grandfather's time, we emigrated from the Kuban area in the Caucasus because we were being harassed by the Kalmyks, who were under oath to the Russian tsar to subdue our people. We left the forests and mountains to settle in Astrakhan, a dry and, in some places, even desert land. Here we were called Kubanshyi, though that was not our word. We called ourselves Nogay and were part of the Nogay Horde, which, along with the Astrakhan Tatars, attempted to force the Russians back to Russia. The Tatars of Astrakhan were welcoming. We spoke the same tongue. All Tatars speak the same sort of tongue, as even you Chuvash speak as we do. All of us who kept the nomadic way of life dwelt in yurts, the circular foldable tents made of strong felt and wood. We intermingled with the Astrakhan Tatars. We traded with them; our young people sought wives from among them, and some of us converted to the Islamic religion. The capital of the area, also called Astrakhan, had been subdued by the Russians, but our tribe was still nomadic, raising mainly cattle and horses with some sheep and goats. We learned to settle in the wide plains beside the Volga. We were possessive of the land we claimed, and generally speaking, we were not harassed. No tribute was required of us, and the Russians had long ceased paying tribute to us. Nevertheless, we took and maintained our independence.

We, the Nogay, did not take to cities like the Bulgur Tatars of Kazan in the north, nor did we appreciate farming like you Chuvash, although apparently we were good at it when we lived in the Caucasus. Nevertheless, we felt that farmers and city folk would eventually lose the warrior spirit, although it is true, I must admit, that you Chuvash and your northern neighbors, the Mari, put up a noble fight against the Russians a generation ago. My father traded with the people of the land, but we were forced eventually to fight those villages and Russian settlements that challenged our right to trade and keep our land. The Russians knew better than to thwart us and make dishonest deals with the merchants that sailed down the Volga. We demanded equal rights and even the Astrakhan Tatars often joined us to set things aright. If the Russians thought they could attack us with their army and fancy weapons, we could easily put them to the chase. There were not enough of them in this part of the land to handle our ferocity.

This was where I got my training, and I excelled at it. The Russians thought we were cruel and savage, but that is not fair. It was simply a question of pride. In other words, if anyone treated us poorly, we took vengeance and even spoils. Unlike our forbears, we generally avoided bloodshed, but we left devastation. As a youth, I participated in these raids. I suppose you could call them that. For me it was a question of honor. I became skilled in these battles. After a few skirmishes where blood was shed, the defending militia knew to back off. The khan well knew me, and even before I was twenty years of age, he gave me the responsibility of planning and leading those battles. But attacking these villages and outposts was mere child's play. I had a particular goal in mind.

The khan, Akilli Khan, was a fine man. He was actually a tribal chieftain, but we had such respect for him we called him our khan and believed him to be the son of Tengri, the all-powerful Sky. Even the Astrakhans, who were a true Khanate, allowed him the honor of being called Khan. I believe I loved him, perhaps even more than my own father Dalgali, whom I feared and respected—not that my father was a rough man, for he was rather generous with us and toward many others. It was just that he was so distant, spending so much time away from our tents. The khan, however, was involved personally with the dwellers of our yurts. There was always an invitation to discuss all problems. He knew everybody. He was wise; he could always be relied upon to provide a sensible answer to any dispute, even if it did not work out in one's favor. As I look back, I thought of him somewhat like Solomon.

The khan's father was the chieftain who led us from the western Caucasus to Astrakhan and set up our yurts. But it was the khan who gave our tribe the dignity and status we achieved during our sojourn here. Even the Russians would come to him for advice because of his reputation for being politically astute. The old chief was still alive and in charge when the Cossacks, under the rebel Stenka Razin, began harassing Astrakhan. Those Cossacks were incredible warriors for Slavs. Unlike the Russians whose soldiers were paid, Razin's Cossacks were men of honor bonded to their Ataman, who would fight not necessarily for the tribe but for his cause. But he was a traitor, and we Tatars despise traitors even if he was a traitor to the Russians. The Mongols, who conquered us some hundreds of years ago, seeing our warlike spirit, put us Tatars in the front lines during their campaigns until we eventually took the whole western area and began to govern it ourselves. We were left with their legacy, and we were called the Golden Horde, as you well remember.

When Razin came, I presume the old chief thought he would do the same—that is, that Stenka would leave us to take hold of the territory under our own domination. But this did not happen. We were actually subjugated by him on his way to overtake the capital, Astrakhan, which he did perhaps over thirty years ago. He forced us Tatars to fight for him rather than with him. Rather than allies, we were made to do his dirty work. His attitude toward us was hardly better than the Russians. The old man's son, our present khan, said we should avoid fighting for someone who was a traitor because it could not be favorable.

"Fight if you have to," he always said, "but do not join forces. A traitor is a traitor, and you cannot trust a traitor."

However, the old man, the khan's father, was regrettably seduced by Razin's apparent care for the poor ones, the peasants, and the slaves, and by his hostility toward the boyars, the rich land owners. Stenka, at first, probably feeling that tsar Alexei Michaelovich had been duped by the boyars, had perhaps always considered himself loyal to the tsar though he fought against his army. Yet with all his noble ideals, he was not a wise or disciplined man. As a slave of wild passions, he did some stupid and cruel things—that is, cruel in our sense—meaning, without honor. But that we shall speak of later. I was perhaps fifteen years old when Stenka died or, rather, was executed.

We were shamanists, our tribe; we worshipped Tengri, the sky god (the one you Chuvash call Tura) and Yer-Sub, the earth. The khan did not forbid his people to practice other religions, such as Islam, which was becoming more and more popular, but the tribe in general kept the old ways as do most of your Chuvash. Personally, I was not a very strong believer. Oh I kept the seasonal festivals, indeed. I danced and sang. I even admired the women who, when dressed in their finery and swirling to the rhythms of the drums and pipes and harps, took on a beauty never seen in the plain workday of the tents. The old religion seemed sensible to me, that's all. If you want the weather to be favorable, you appeal to the winds and the sun; if you want to have an increase of flock, you sacrifice to Umai, the wife of Tengri. The wives who wanted to have babies would go to our shaman Lazim and, with a gift of food or woven fabric, would obtain some herbs and ointments and talismans to increase their chances. I did not think it was magic by any means but simply a matter of nature. Sacrifices to Umai never required the slaughter of animals, but gifts of milk and dairy products were offered her. The god Water also ensured human fertility. It all just seemed sensible to me.

Most of us were convinced that the real power was with Uyari, the woman who lived with Lazim. They were not married, but she ran the old man. We could not figure out the old man's age; he seemed to have always been around. They had no children, for Lazim always said that contact with women diminished power, so presumably they had had no relations. Uyari was not old, maybe as young as my mother. She was an Astrakhan Tatar who had been sent away when her tribe accepted Islam. She fled. Either flee or get killed; there is no room for a woman shaman in Islam.

In the Crimea, they were called wise women and were tolerated, so I'm told.

Uyari always seemed to have something against me. She told my mother that the demons of night followed me. That I was born with green eyes, I need not tell you, Father. Most of the tribe was born dark with dark eyes as was true of most of my siblings. Where the green came from, we shall never know. Some of you in the northern Volga can be fair and light eyed, but you have also mixed with the Finns and other peoples which we have not. We may have been mixed with the Cossacks back at the Kuban, but that was many generations ago. We never mixed with the Kalmyks. They are Mongol people and follow the Buddha. They look like the Mongols with reddish skin and narrow, often yellow eyes. They do not mix with anybody. In any case, Uyari took my green eyes as a bad omen and figured I was ill luck for the tribe.

I did not take Uyari's hostility toward me personally. I recognized that she was governed by superstition. She may also have had some sort of intuition about me, some sort of warning, but I did not figure that having green eyes was sufficient enough reason for her to suspect me. I was saddened finally that she started to turn my mother, Yerinde, against me. She told her that I would bring shame to the tribe. But the khan would hear nothing of it. He gave her dire warnings for her evil mouth. Once he whacked her after giving a harangue, and though I tried to placate her, nothing I did could change her feelings.

Still my mother started to believe her, and her affection toward me appeared to wane. I was her second son, but I did have brothers and sisters from my father's concubines and slaves. She was the only wife of my father. She bore several children and was the mistress of our tents. Her command almost exceeded that of my father, who was frequently away. Because of Uyari's hostility, I became aware that I was different. I loved my mother, and it saddened me that she was becoming more and more distant. It was enough that my father was often so far away, but to lose her love hurt me intensely as a youth coming to maturity.

Yerinde, my mother, was talented. Her weaving was unsurpassable, the envy of the camp. The wool she wove was soft as silk and brought a large price on the market. Kazan was the place to go for profit. Even the Russian ladies, in spite of becoming accustomed to the silks and satins of the new styles imported from the West, purchased Mother's fabrics to make warm coats for the harsh winters. My father once bragged that a German merchant in Astrakhan one year bought five bolts. But western things and customs were not as widespread as later when the Great Peter began ruling as tsar.

Father idolized Mother, but God forgive me for saying so, it was probably more for her economic advantages than her beauty, which anyway she did not lack. His affection for her was well known in the camp; none of his concubines stood a chance when he returned from his trips. I was proud that I was a natural son. My brothers and I had a certain amount of status in the yurts, and particularly in hers. That is partly why the waning of her affection toward me troubled me so much.

I spoke to Mother about it once. I was hesitant, for I didn't want to put her on the spot, but it was for me important enough to do so. I was young, probably twenty, a crucial year in my life, and though I was already skilled in battle, I was not skilled in expressing my feelings. I chose a time when Mother was busy and could not escape. She was up to her elbows in dye, with vats of vermillion and indigo hot at her knees. This was a critical time for her; the wool was fresh as the shearing had just been done and the rolling of felt for the yurts was finished. She could not escape me. When I dismissed her servants and the other ladies, she looked startled, not afraid, but startled, as though she had been waiting for the confrontation.

I tried village talk, business, how much she expected to yield that year, the quality of the dye, or was the loom in good shape? Finally she became blunt.

"You didn't come here to interrupt my work to discuss business, my son. What is it that is bothering you?"

"It is you," I stumbled. "We don't talk anymore."

She gave me a long stare.

"You are my favorite son, Tambor, and I will always love you. But you are a mystery to me. Rather, I should say you have become a mystery to me."

She took my hand and squeezed it, perhaps a little too fiercely, and looked intently into my eyes. "Where did you get those eyes? And what secrets do they hold? I do not talk to you, my son, because *they* no longer talk to me. And it is *not* because they are green. Something is going on inside you that I am unable to reach," she paused, "something I fear. You left your father many years ago, and he knows it, and now you have left me."

I tried to reply, but she continued, "Oh, yes, Uyari talks about curses and omens, but it is more than that. The khan says you have a destiny to fulfill, so what can I say? But I love you and will always love you no matter how far away you are. Tambor, your father goes away for months on end, but he is never as far away as you are, whom I see every day."

She took both my hands and looked into my face. She never appeared to me quite as beautiful as at that moment, her face smooth and taut, her hazel eyes trying to penetrate mine, and her black hair flowing down her back and tied with a colored band at her forehead. She was a beauty among our people. I kissed her on her head and brought her face to my breast, and for that moment, all my love flowed into her. When I released her, I saw that tears flowed down her face. As she wiped her face, the dye on her hands stained her skin, and I laughed as I tried to wipe it off. I was a child again but just for a moment.

I said quietly, "You are right. There is something I must do that only I can do, but I am not ready, and I can talk to no one about it at this time. But I will be restless until it is done. I will always love you, Mother, and I am proud of my father, though I cannot follow him."

She seemed to understand.

We never talked about this again. At times, however, I could feel her eyes looking at me, no longer hurt or hostile. It could not be that she was praying because we did not have that kind of relationship with our gods, but it was as though she were placing my being involuntarily into the hands of something she did not quite understand. I would sometimes catch her trying to look into my eyes. I would smile at her, and she would turn softly away.

Holy Father, at this point I cannot even mention my secret though I shall speak of it presently. My youth was dominated by one event and one desire. Not even my father could suspect my secret and my vow. The khan seemed to know, though words never passed between us. This was certainly in keeping with his wisdom and his discretion for which I am ever in his debt.

My father came home about a month after my conversation with my mother. My older brother Dikkatli had accompanied him as was becoming a habitual event. I was glad that he had assumed that role. Even Chabuk, three years younger than I am, accompanied him once a few years before. This was a relief to me; I did not have to feel so guilty for my lack of interest in commerce. Father had done quite well according to Dikkatli. He had also married off my elder sister, Vermek, at last, to the son of a merchant in Kazan and got quite a good bride price, which, as tradition demanded , was placed in my mother's hands.

Having arrived at dusk, Father sent word to the khan requesting a meeting in the morning and went in then to my mother. He often brought a concubine or two on his business trips, but it was easy to see that his desire was for my mother. I thought at first that the meeting with the khan was intended to share the wealth, as Father's chief concern was for the prosperity of the tribe. But Dikkatli said there were other urgent matters and that I was expected to attend the gathering. Kattu, as we used to call him, seemed rather heated but would say no more. I enjoyed my older brother's approval. He had taken a bride from Ibn Haddi's tribe a while back. She was now pregnant and anxiously awaiting him. Marwa was her name. It was a sight to see her run to his embrace, trying at the same time to maintain good behavior. Reared as a Muslim, she was more modest than most of our own maidens.

I could barely sleep that night for excitement. I had never been to my father's councils with the khan, nor had he ever given me such, shall I say, adulation. Somehow, Reverend Father, I felt that this was my coming of age.

That morning I woke early. I washed in the cool water that the servants laid out for me. Lifting up my hands, I did grateful reverence to Tengri and his son Koyash, the life-giving sun. I even blessed Erlick, the god of darkness, for an uneventful journey through the night, bothered as I was occasionally by unpleasant dreams. Then Dikkatli emerged from his yurt, smiled at me, and likewise washed. I learned from the servants that Father had been up for some time and had gone to Lazim to give him his customary gifts, presumably in thanksgiving for his prosperous journey. I knew that Father was an important man, but this morning I was more in awe of him than ever before. I scolded myself for being nervous, having prided myself on being detached and composed.

Kattu and I entered the khan's official yurt, quietly and, folding our legs, we sat close to the entrance. A serving girl brought us tea flavored with rose water and other herbs in a pottery cup. This was to me a reflection of the khan's graceful manner and, above all, the importance of the assembly, which was itself called a Yurt. I believe the khan was aware of my presence, but he left me time to finish the tea. Still quietly talking with my father and a few other elders, he at last let his eyes rest on me.

"Tambor, my dear young warrior (except for my father's presence, he would have called me son), do come closer."

I looked at Kattu, expecting him to join me, but with a gesture of his hand, he urged me forward. I stood up, and going toward the khan, I prostrated before him, my head to the carpeted floor. Touching my shoulder gently, he raised me. I could see in his face a pleasant smile while behind his eyes I perceived an intense seriousness. I glanced next to him to see my father looking proudly, indeed, almost affectionately at me. This confused me, and again I felt disconcerted, though I tried my best to conceal it.

The khan said to the assembly, "Before Saban-Tui, the summer sacrifice tomorrow, let us speak of some urgent matters so that our present concerns will not mar the joy of the feast. Lord Dalgali," he gestured toward my father, "our dear friend and noble elder, has again returned to our Yurt with prosperity and wealth, which out of duty he shares with us. Much appreciation, Lord Dalgali. I shall also thank all of our hard workers in the fields attending the flocks to provide us with the wool and skins, which bring such abundant profit, as well as the herdsmen for their excellent care of our most prized treasures, our horses. We shall also convey our approval to all the women of the yurts, the weavers, the boot makers, the dyers, those who sit at the loom, and those who create those magnificent garments that have made us Kubanshyi famous.

"I must also add that we who follow the old ways and do not farm are dependent upon our flocks, our cattle, and our horses for sustenance. We are not farmers. We grow for grazing. We have no orchards, but Dalgali returns to us with melons, figs and dates in exchange for our wool, our felt, our garments, and spiced meats. We have few wheat and buckwheat fields, but we have bags of flour and kasha in exchange for sheep, goats, cattle, and our excellent horses. We must thank Koyash, the sun; Yer-Sub the earth; Water; and the precious Air that we breathe. Above all we praise Tengri, the mighty sky, for his favor, and continue to offer sacrifice as we shall tomorrow for the continuance of the same."

He paused. "It is a harsh land, Astrakhan. Even with the Volga passing through here, there are many dry months and heavy windstorms. My father used to tell me of the lush forests lining the Kuban river, the hills, and also the winters and warm soft summers. That we are prosperous here in Astrakhan is evidence of the favor of Tengri and our native gods. But we are Tatars, and we are also warriors who are always on the defense, who must still fight to keep our ways and protect our right to live well. The Russians, whose lands we live on, though they ask no tribute, now dominate the territory, which once belonged to us, left to us by the Mongols, the great khan. If we can live in peace with the Russians, so much the better."

He looked straight at me. "But there are times when we cannot. At these times, the warrior spirit arouses in us, and our love for a just revenge emerges. This is one of those times."

He was eloquent, Father. I could not possibly translate into Russian all the nuances of the language he used. He spoke with the poetry and passion of our bards that so roused in us the rhythmic hoofbeats of our cavalry, that the memory of our glorious past flooded the assembly. Then, turning to my father, he said with some fervency. "Dalgali, tell us why."

It was, I am sure, a hard act to follow. However, Father did not hesitate.

"With Akilli, our most honorable and favored khan, brothers, let us bless the gods who have traveled with us and sustained us for these many generations and also bless the memory of his noble father who led us here, as well as our ancestors who died in the hills of the Kuban."

The assembly prostrated in reverence. I was moved.

He continued. "It is true that many, if not most, of our people now give reverence to a single god, either the Muslim god or the Russian God, who is both One and Three. We do not judge them, nor indeed do we look to rouse the disfavor of any god. But I sense that whatever gods we worship, all are displeased. I have traveled from Astrakhan in the south to Kazan in the north, all along the Volga, and have found the same thing. Oh yes, we prosper, but only in the big cities and villages where many of our people dwell and where the caravans pass through. What has happened to the days when all the ports of the Volga were available to us? Over the years, we have let the Russians dominate the shore and inhibit the ships and merchants from trading with us. It is almost as if the Kubanshyi and other tribes like us are being urged to move out or rather to move to pastures nearer the cities, where we can be controlled, as it is in Kazan. Tatars are still, at least officially, forbidden to live within the city gates although our settlements surround the city walls. Of course we are still able to trade freely; the Russians still love money.

"Though I have been aware of this gradual change, I had never voiced it until I visited the camp of Ibn Haddi, my son's father-in-law, near the city of Astrakhan. You know that he lives in the city now, he says, to be closer to the mosque, but over some fine entertainments, he confessed to me that he too had been feeling the pressure to abandon our nomadic way of life. This pressure came not only from the Russians, who would have us absorbed more fully into the empire, but also from the Mullahs, who want more religious control. More control, brothers. I say more interference from both.

"We were already prepared for the heavy trek up from the city to Kazan, many miles up the Volga. We of course do not travel by boat, and the trip through the forests, which we know well, is sometimes treacherous especially during the winter months. But it used to be that we could trade at the ports along the way. But nowadays, we seem to arrive either too early for the ships or too late. This has been the case for many years now.

"I mentioned this to my friend Shafiq Ibn-Moussa who lives just outside Kazan, and he cautioned me as to what was happening. There indeed has been a plot these past years to reduce the nomadic tribes in the area, or at least to reduce our independence. For example, a little over five years ago, a boyar from the north moved down to Astrakhan and bought some land at a place now called Mikhailov, northeast of here along the Volga. It is a pleasant place, temperate and unbothered. The man, whose name is Vassili Andreivich Daruvenko, has built a large dacha there, originally a summer residence. He now resides there with his wife permanently. He has quite a business there not only with new breeds of sheep and cattle, which he has transported from the north, and large well-run farmlands and accessible pastures, but also with the shipping industry. He builds cargo vessels financially supported by the tsar and dominates the commerce on the lower Volga and the Caspian. Right under our noses, brothers and sons! Right under our noses. The peaceful relationship is a deception. We are convinced that this is part of a larger plan to deprive us of access to the Volga and thereby to reduce our power and independence and our wealth. The Russians want us to be absorbed into Russian political life. They want us to disappear!"

He paused to let this settle in our minds. Then all of us began to stir.

"Shafiq," he continued, receiving the response he wanted, "says that we should use legal means to combat this injustice by taking it to the courts in Astrakhan where there are magistrates and spokesmen among the Mullahs capable of curbing some of this activity."

Almost all of us started talking heatedly.

"That is all fine and dandy in Astrakhan, the capital, but not here!"

"We have our own ways of meting out justice!"

"Who pays attention to the Kubanshyi?"

"Right, brothers, only we ourselves!"

The khan raised his hand to quiet the assembly, and when he regained their attention, he looked straight at me.

"And what is going on in that head of yours, my dear Tambor?"

Such a direct and unexpected question threw me completely off guard, and he knew it. All our conversations before were about his observations of our war games or his pleasure at the success of our raids, which as I said before, were mere child's play. Now here, in the midst of an important political assembly, he was asking me what I would do. Out of the corner of my eye, I could see my father staring intensely at me. I felt alone. Yet I also felt energetic as though some surge were passing through my body. The khan had achieved the desired effect.

"Vassili Andreivich Daruvenko must be destroyed."

A hushed whisper passed through the assembly.

"Yes," the khan replied, with an equal hush. "Then you, my son, must do it."

I turned to my father, just slightly, and saw, for the first time in my life, his face flushed with pride. There was no going back for me. I was now a warrior.

FRIENDSHIP

I danced like a warrior,
The blade swinging high.
I loved like a pauper
Who never drew nigh.
But my friendship will last
Till the day that I die.

The rest of the day dazzled me. When the meeting broke up, I expected the elders to say something to me regarding the commission I had just been given, but no words came except their customary greetings, which, I must admit, were somewhat warmer than usual. The khan busied himself in the yurt as the servants cleaned up after the assembly. Even Father and Kattu, who accompanied me, made no effort at all to discuss the proceedings. After the council, I was energized, but now all around me was the bustle of a different kind of life. It took me a while to calm down, and when I did, I began to realize that the whole community was thoroughly busy and excited about the coming feast. Of course, I thought, it was also the summer festival we were preparing for, not just my father's arrival. It then occurred to me that the camp had been preparing for days, but my mind had been somewhere else. I heard Father talking to Kattu as though I were part of the conversation.

He was saying, "As usual I try to return at the right time just before Saban-Tui, the summer festival. The wet spring winds, which occasionally slow down easy travel, were propitious this year, and warm winds welcome the festival. The dark powers retreated below before we left our camp with the blessing of the gods of the sky. May both be merciful to us."

Kattu replied, "Yes, Father, God has indeed been merciful this year. May he protect us till autumn."

I sprang out of my stupor at once. He was using the singular word for God and using it somewhat clumsily. We could talk about a god or the gods, but *God* as a name just did not seem to work, at least not in our tongue. If we referred to a single god, it would have been Tengri, perhaps. He was likely trying to avoid using the word *Allah*. I said nothing. Father didn't seem to notice it, so I surmised he had gotten used to this usage during the course of their journey together. No doubt Marwa had something to do with it.

When we arrived in mother's yurt, I became aware of how hungry I was. Mother, like all of the other women, was busy and fussing. Two servant girls brought us some food. Mother took the liberty to sit down with us though she never ceased to complain and sometimes even to shout commands to the servants. A servant brought us some heated flat bread and some eggs with yogurt. When there was a pause, Father said to Mother, "Tambor was honored at the assembly this morning."

"May our son always be so honored," she replied.

Nothing more was said; no questions were asked. I was aware, however, of a slight smile on her lips followed by a frown, but the flush on her waxen cheeks could not so easily be erased. She then turned to Kattu and asked about Marwa's health. This seemed a little strange to me since she had been with her daughter-in-law daily the six months Kattu had been away. But what did I know about women? It was not our custom for women to make direct references to pregnancy with men. Kattu blushed and, with his handsome smile, gave her the response she wanted. I was beginning to relax. I would enjoy the day.

Chabuk, my younger brother, arrived with Dalgin, who was one of my half brothers, and with them a neighbor's son. With much noise and bustle, the boys told how Bashina, the marksman, had given them the day off. They were elated. These boys were under my direct supervision and were very good warriors in the making. Chabuk had a hot streak, which needed to be tempered, but I was fond of him and admired his energy. He was still a boy, and I reflected that perhaps I had never been fully one myself. He had accompanied Father before and enjoyed it, but he had also gone on our raids and fought enthusiastically. Even at fifteen, he had shown promise, and now at eighteen, he still was very diligent at his training. I thought he could be a good leader but needed more detachment and a little more attention to detail. He also had a slight speech impediment such that when he spoke, his voice was coarse and he always seemed angry, which was not always the case. Dalgin was his closest friend and understood him better than most people.

We had been practicing for the following day's games, and the dozen or so young warriors that Bashina and I had been training were flushed with excitement. They were also awaiting some warriors from some neighboring tribes coming to compete at the games. I secretly hoped Father and the khan would let Chabuk accompany me on my task.

When we had all eaten, Father brought out the gifts. There was jewelry for my sisters and their mothers, his concubines. These were, I suppose, trinkets and baubles and small shiny golden coins. They were to be worn for the festivities. Even the servants received gifts. Of course there were no objections. It was important for Father to show off his wealth. To Marwa, whose head was always covered in Muslim fashion, he gave a beautiful ring, a sapphire, I believe, and a silk head covering of deep violet embroidered with gold, which he said was from India.

To Mother, he gave several bolts of linen and some lace, presumably from Europe, as well as two bolts of silk from China. The other women sighed in envy. Father made it very clear it was for her, and she must not use it for selling. He also gave her a large emerald "as green as my eyes," they jested, which was to dangle from a golden chain on her forehead. To the men, he gave various forms of weaponry, and to me, a silver dagger made by the Russians, in the city of Kazan. The handle was in the form of a serpent holding a moonstone in its mouth. He also gave me a deep red shirt of a shimmering material, which was from Tibet. When I asked him what Tibet was, he described it as a very mountainous country north of India, which had been part of Chinggis Khan's empire. Of course I would wear the shirt tomorrow. To Kattu, it shouldn't have surprised me, he gave some writing materials: ink, paper, and several quills—not unlike the materials I am using now—which delighted him. Obviously Kattu could read and write. I was a little envious.

Then came the sweets: figs from Palestine, dates from Arabia, loukoum from Istanbul, candied fruits of all sorts, and hard cakes from Europe, with sugar on top. Breakfast was topped by a jug of sweet red wine from Greece.

Mother told the girls not to drink. "There will be plenty tomorrow when the work is done. Let's go!"

The men laughed and talked a bit but all in good humor. When I asked Father where all of this came from, he replied that he had met up with several caravans enroute. These were becoming rarer and rarer as the Europeans became more dependent upon sea trade. I did wonder why it was with such opulence and such obvious signs of success that Father should be so adamant about destroying Vassili Andreivich and his enterprises. But then, as I reasoned, it was a question of honor more than economics.

A few of us stopped to note that a young lad from one of the other tents came to Father and spoke in his ear. Father took his arm, thanking him affectionately and offered him some sweets, which he eagerly accepted. Father later leaned over to me and told me that the khan had invited me to sit with him at dawn for the sacrifices; I would spend the night in his yurt. I was honored, flattered, and disappointed all at the same time. I thought it would have been a treat being close to Father now that he was showing me affection. However, to sit with the khan was an honor I would never have expected at my young age, and I would not pass it up. I merely nodded. I admit, spiritual Father, that I would love to have embraced my father at that moment, and it saddened me to think that there might not be such an opportunity again. But then, he did not seem to invite it.

Men were needed to supervise the field outside of the encampment to be used for the feast. It was by a tributary of the Volga near a grove of sacred birch trees, which our tribe had planted many years back for this purpose. There had not been many birch trees in Astrakhan, but when we came, the land seemed to welcome them, and now there was a small woodland near the water. Our community was even called the Birches, or in our tongue, *Falaka Sopasi*, and we called the river the Sopasi River.

The khan was to have his yurt moved for his temporary use, and the field was cleared for the games and the dancers and musicians. A few of the senior elders would have smaller tents and tipis, just big enough to sleep in. The families would gather in groups and bring their own food to share. It was a time for the women to show off their prized dishes. The pits that were used to cook the meat in year by year were cleaned and made ready for the sacrifice, and old Lazim barked orders and fussed over things though he would not have much part in the sacrifice according to our tradition. No one took him too seriously. I decided to help Father get our portion ready.

Later in the evening, we prepared our clothing. The men, in general, wore traditional garb. Silk or woolen shirts were worn from the neck almost to the knee and tied with a leather belt at the waist, showing just a bit of Russian influence. We used to wear them longer, like the Kalmyks. Baggy pants tightened at the ankles accentuated pointed leather shoes, although some men and women wore ornamented leather boots. I, in my new Tibetan shirt, which folded over the breast doubly, would look different. Father was obviously proud. All the men were to be bareheaded during the sacrifice according to custom, however some of the men would be wearing the wide fur or fleece caps so important for our warriors' dances later in the day, the ones we wore into battle. Scimitars, shields, and lances were brought out for these dances. We would dance around the fire performing mock battles. Men, of course, did not dance with women, although at the height of the feast both would be dancing at the same time. I loved these dances almost as much as battling because they spun out the stories of our people and the glories of our victories. Ilhami, our bard and weaver of tales, would sing and recite the glories of our battles and my half brother Dalgin would join him. The women would sing sadly of the long wanderings, of the lovers left behind and never seen again, of the boys taken from their mothers' embrace forced to serve in the great khan's army. These were the same stories as the warriors would be singing, but differently. How I looked forward to it!

Not many Tatars would have kept this feast as we did. Most of the Tatars in the Crimea were Muslim, as were the Tatars who lived in the vicinity of Kazan, and they did not keep the ritual any longer though they do keep Saban-Tui, the celebration. They, like the Russians, do not reverence nature and strongly object to animal sacrifices. Only about a dozen communities in Astrakhan at that time kept the old faith, but I know, even in our day, Father, many of your Chuvash people still keep the feast in the villages, but in early spring. There were perhaps four or five tribes on the other side of the Volga who would be celebrating tonight, another three to the northwest, and four in the south toward the capital on this side. There were probably others. Some of our warriors competed at their games as we also welcomed some of theirs to compete with us. At least *we* would give the gods their due.

When the sun had set, it was time for me to leave the family and set off for the khan's tent in the middle of the village, for the Birches had now become a village of tents. One of the servant boys who normally attended me came along to carry my clothing and some weapons. The street torches were extra bright this evening. Excitement was all around. I exchanged greetings with those sitting in the summer air. Most of the wealthier families lived closer to the outside of the encampment in order to be nearer to the fields where the grazing areas and the stables were. So the walk to the center was a little long but not too unpleasant. Everyone was cheerful.

The sacrifices would begin at the very moment when Koyash appeared over the horizon. Everyone would have to be there including the Muslims, even if they did not bring sacrifice. The khan said that at that moment they were to pray to Allah and ask his blessing; Tengri and Yer-Sub would not be jealous. Some of the families were already on site. The khan would be leading his own procession, and presumably I would accompany him. Father would also join the procession to the sacred ground with the intention of offering two lambs and a ram for sacrifice and three ewes for the feast offering. Chabuk and another brother would be offering for our family as Kattu and I had done the previous year. As you probably know, Holy Father, women took no part in the sacrifices. I was not particularly interested in the ritual sacrifices, but I confess I loved Saban-Tui, the celebration. This one year I remember more than all the rest.

When I entered the khan's yurt, I made the customary prostration, and after a slight gesture, he beckoned me to lie next to the table. He was not relaxing, however. He was fussing over some garments with two menservants. Lacking a mirror, save for a metal shield, he found a second opinion necessary.

"Tell me, lad," he addressed me (obviously the servants would not do), "What would you suggest I wear tomorrow, the green one or the blue?"

The green robe I thought was magnificent: it was dark and trimmed with white fur. The blue one was pale silk with some colored bands in red and violet. It had a border of gray fur with a black fleck.

"Of course, I prefer the red coat your mother made me, but I wore that one last year. Hmm, so what do you think a khan should wear to tomorrow's feast?"

For myself, I thought that the pale blue one would accentuate the long mustache and long black braid.

I said, "To wear blue like the sky would show you to be Tengri's son."

He laughed. "We do not talk much like that anymore, Tambor. It makes our Muslim brothers just a bit uncomfortable. We do not want to challenge their loyalty. But I will wear it just the same." I found his casualness novel but very relaxing.

He added, "I expect Dikkatli will succumb to Islam in time. His father-in-law is very righteous, I am told, and his daughter is virtuous. Well, be that as it may."

He lay down gently on the other side of the low table and called for some food and drink.

"I know that you have probably eaten, but you can share a few sweets with me tonight. They probably do not match your mother's fine eating, but I am satisfied."

This was the second time he mentioned my mother; I was curious, and he caught it. "You know that your mother, Yerinde, and my first wife Kibar were sisters, don't you?" He caught my surprise. "Yes, and my second wife and they were cousins, not that I want to bring her to remembrance, that mule of a woman. I might have taken your mother too had she not been married to your father. But it was fortunate for her that she was. Yes, they were in Astrakhan when the plague struck about twenty-two years ago, so they didn't return on my orders until health was restored here. Those days Yerinde traveled with Dalgali, a little before Stenka Razin's time."

I was taken aback and felt somewhat ashamed that this was the first time I had heard of it.

"Mother told me once that her family was wiped out by that plague," I remarked.

"That is more or less so," the khan answered. "Both her parents and both my wives were taken. Kibar I miss even today with all my heart. She died with our very ill son to her breast weeping until she expired. I have never loved anyone as much as I loved her. The other died cursing the gods and ignoring our daughter who also died soon afterward. I can imagine her stirring up so much trouble in Erlick's world that I'm surprised he hasn't kicked her out of the underworld to come back and harass the Russians." His grimace turned slowly into a chuckle.

"Ah well." He sighed. "Old Derman, her uncle, your grandfather, in fact, who is still around, survived, as did I and your paternal grandfather. Derman is not quite old enough to perform the sacrifices."

The mention of my paternal grandfather caused me to wince somewhat, and the khan studied me somewhat, but I put it aside and put on "the cold face" for the sake of the feast and the khan's wonderful hospitality.

I quickly regained my composure and said, "Then it must be that you are my *uncle!*"

He replied with a wise look, "Why, yes, that is indeed so."

At that point, we were interrupted by the entry of Bashina, the old master and my personal mentor. Bashina prostrated in respect and kissed the hand of the khan who bade him sit.

"Bashina, my dear friend," he said affectionately. "This year you will not be honoring my yurt with your presence."

And turning to me, he explained, "This has been a longtime tradition for us two single men. This year, old friend," he resumed, "you will be attending Dalgali at his yurt. It appears you are needed there to supervise a band of ruffians. Chabuk, that headstrong colt, and his bunch will be tearing down his father's yurt if you do not keep order."

The old teacher was not put off but replied with a pleasant grunt, "I'm sure his mother will put him in his place, but I'll be there to help out anyway. This, my young stallion, is obviously needed here." He said this with a wink and a slap on my thigh. He then touched his head to the floor and was off, while I admired the agility of his body, hoping I would be so vigorous when I reached his age.

A servant girl came in and placed a tray of sweets on the table, while another brought a pitcher of kumis with a couple of silver goblets and then left. The first girl remained and slowly poured the clear fermented milk first into the khan's cup and then into mine. Her eyes met mine just for a moment; she smiled and left. The khan's eyes followed her and then focused on mine.

"My dear son,"—he obviously wanted to talk—"you are a very serious warrior. I can see that you are totally dedicated to your work. In the past two or three years, you have excelled far beyond those your own age. By this, I do not refer simply to your physical skills, which are well performed, but you have an uncanny ability to plan and foresee every one of your military operations. And we have every intention of exploiting these talents. But there is one aspect of life which I fear that you lack. Yes, lack," he emphasized. "You have not yet learned to balance your work with leisure. You must learn to make time to relax and enjoy this wonderful life that the gods have provided for us. Otherwise, a warrior will wear himself out. Leisure coupled with discretion can often provide the fuel for a good warrior's fire." He paused.

What is he getting at? I wondered. He smiled wisely.

"You know, Tambor, I can tell that all that is on your mind at the moment is tomorrow's games and your upcoming mission. You and Bashina have trained and trained these boys these past weeks and of course you want to push them on to greater accomplishments. And we shall all cheer as our sons hit the mark or finish the race. Your body is aching to leap and whirl as you fly over the sword at the dance. I've seen you dance as though your life depended upon it. While the camp enjoys the dance, *you* live the battle. Admirable! Dalgali's son wins the prize. Holla! Admirable!"

I was astounded. I was out of breath. The venerable chieftain saw my confusion and, with a tender smile, poured another cup of kumis. He called out to the servant for more drink and insisted I eat. As the girl came in, she knelt next to me. For the first time, I became aware of the scent of jasmine on her clothes as her sleeve brushed against my face. As I sat up to give her some room, she said very simply:

"Forgive me, my lord."

She continued to pour the kumis, and I became totally aware of her physical appearance. She, like the other girl who did not reappear, was dressed in white and pink. Long pleated full sleeves covered her arms, the pattern repeated in the Persian-style pantaloons she wore. These were a sweet soft pink. Over her blouse, she wore a white embroidered vest which gave her a modest appearance, and around her neck was a string of red beads. The cap was the typical flat topped cap worn by men and women alike, but with a tail of lace down the back of her neck partly covering her thick black braid. She was beautiful.

As she left, she bowed toward the khan and then turned toward me. As she gave me a wide smile, her eyes became like two half moons. All the time, the khan was watching without uttering a word.

He continued to be silent until I gathered myself. His ability to see into me and into others, which I had always thought admirable, at this particular moment, I found annoying. Women had not held much interest for me up until now; I had been too busy. Besides, that was father's affair. As with Kattu and Vermek, our sister, he would provide a good marriage for me. But now I had just been thrown off guard like a horseman who had missed his mark and nearly fallen off the horse's back, but worst of all, it had been in full view of the khan.

Finally, he said, "You know, my young friend, when my wife, your aunt, died my world fell apart. Thanks to the gods, the other one died soon afterward, or misery would have accompanied my great loneliness and sorrow. I escaped into my work training horses and the boys who were to ride them. I resented that I no longer had a son, but I wanted to give attention to these lads, many of whom had lost their fathers in the plague. Dikkatli and you came along a short while later. Bashina, who was older, advised me to take another wife, but he could never really understand me and my sorrow as he had himself never married. I had a few concubines and a number of female slaves, so I thought I would drown my loneliness in pleasure. It didn't work; it was only the blessing of time and my own gradual acceptance of Kibar's absence that brought me back together.

"You can never really tell how the concubines live as we don't put our women into harems. I presume they are faithful even though they are fairly independent, unless they have a mistress like your mother. However, the servants seem to know their way around, and lacking status, they devise their own social lives. My own suspicion is that the girl who served you may even be my daughter, as I spent much time with her mother. She cannot be a true daughter as her mother was a slave I had captured on a raid, but I have a great fondness for her as I still have for her mother. And since I have a special fondness for you, my nephew, I am giving her to you."

I cannot tell you, my dear Father Dmitri, how I felt at that moment. I could have had a slave at any time; I had, after all, two boy servants. My mother could have given me any one of her maidens if I had asked. I was both angry and intrigued at the same time.

"Tambor, I want you to trust my judgment. I want to pull you out of the games tomorrow—ah-ah, I don't want you to say a thing. Trust me!" Then he added more calmly, "I have already spoken to Mehtap, and she has agreed. She was most willing, in fact. And when you tire of her, as in time you will, do not give her to your mother, who would work her too hard, but send her back to me. Tonight I have prepared a small yurt where you can have some privacy, and tomorrow after the feast, she will go home with you. We are to be up early tomorrow. Before Koyash rises, all must be at the sacred ground."

He was firm. I could say nothing. Even with his mouth set and his long mustache twitching, I could still see the twinkle in his eye. I could have laughed.

Mehtap was a virgin. It was not important insofar as she was not a wife; otherwise it would have been; it was rather that since I was totally inexperienced, I would have preferred to discover the rules of this particular art with someone who would not laugh at my blunders. She was a good-natured girl with a good sense of humor. I was pleased that she was not afraid of me as a man and her master. In this case, we could laugh together until we got it right. The khan's boy servant (actually Mehtap's brother) awoke us before dawn, giving us enough time to wash before I should join the khan for the procession to the birch grove. The sacrificial victims were themselves adorned with ribbons. The khan in his sky blue robe looked as though he were Tengri himself. As the stars faded, a honeyed dawn flowed over the horizon until the golden sun turned the gray sky to blue. The sacrifices then began and lasted until noon.

Originally, dear Reverend Father, I had intended to describe the rituals, but I know that you would find them barbaric. I know that you have in mind the conversion of Chuvashia to the holy faith and therefore have a mission to draw your people away from these vain and useless customs, and certainly before the Muslims make headway into your land. I shall say for myself that secretly I found these sacrifices a waste of good livestock. It seemed to me that the gods had little need for this blood and flesh and that, rather than obtaining their favor, we were actually insulting them. Such feelings, which I had never articulated, emerged from deep within my soul year after year and that particular year no less. Yet tradition was so rooted in me that I could not speak to anyone. Yes, and not even to Kattu, who now seemed to be drawing away from the old faith, would I have trusted with these feelings.

Saban-Tui was what I really loved. I had been preparing for weeks with the young warriors, and I would have loved to join them. Sitting with the khan, however, gave me an opportunity to see the competitors as a spectator. Some of the other men, in their twenties and thirties and a few even older were still vigorous and skilled. They returned frequently to the training fields to keep up their practices, but I really wanted to show off the talents of our lads. They competed with the older men who had likewise been the students of Bashina and did exceptionally well. As a tribe, our men were particularly skilled in archery and mastering the art of shooting at a target while riding at top speed. We could even reverse in the saddle and shoot behind us. It was something we learned from the Mongols. I was particularly proud of Chabuk, as was the khan. Our men could also as easily shaft a spear and swing a scimitar, a particular skill of Chabuk's. Father, Mother, and Bashina joined us for a while and shared a pitcher of kumis. The athletes did not drink during the competition.

Mother was beautiful. She wore a white turban of silk and lace, no doubt hastily made though no one could have told it. Her robe was also made of white, embroidered with black. All this, of course, accentuated the beauty of the emerald at her forehead, which in turn accentuated her own beauty. The khan expressed admiration.

I did not see much of Mehtap during the day. She was busy with preparing and serving, but occasionally she would throw me a glance and a smile. She gave a few long looks at Mother. It seemed she knew who she was; however, I could not read the meaning behind those looks. Mother gave no apparent response to this, not even when Mehtap offered her some food. She was being ignored as any servant would be.

She had told me earlier that she would be dancing in the evening, and I hoped the khan would not deprive me of the dance. Although we ate during the day, especially since we fasted until all the sacrifices were done, it was not until after the games that the roasted meat was to be shared throughout the camp. The contestants relaxed in pompous laughter chiding and shoving playfully and bragging about their accomplishments on the field that afternoon. Everyone came to the khan for his blessing before eating and drinking. They remained outside of the yurt because of the limited space inside nevertheless the khan was already outside to greet them. Several bottles of sweet red wine, presumably a gift from Father, were offered to the warriors before the eating began.

"I don't want you men to become sick before you enjoy the food. Feast well, my boys, but a good warrior feasts moderately. Besides, if you drink too much, you will not be able to dance well tonight, and without concentration, a poorly swung saber may slice an unwilling ankle, and you know how much we need all your ankles."

We all laughed as they went to their tents somewhat more calmed. Of course the Muslims politely excused themselves from the wine. Father and Mother went back with my brothers, but Bashina decided to stay.

"My dear Tambor," the khan addressed me, after some order had returned, "I notice you haven't spoken much during the day. In fact, Tambor, you are not a man of many words, but I wonder if you have been observing the talents of our fine athletes and warriors. There are a number of talented warriors whom you were not responsible for training. This is why Bashina is here, for both he and I have trained them. While they are good athletes, we have not had a leader emerge from among them."

There were a few interruptions from loyal families and bondsmen who came to pay their respects to our leader. The khan was gracious and expressed gratitude for their gifts, but I was anxious to get on with the talk.

He smiled at me. "While I feel, my son, that you have great leadership qualities, one cannot perform the role of khan until some patience is learned. We are feasting after all, and my people love me as I love them."

Bashina grunted and slapped me on the thigh, adding, "How often I had to be patient with you who was so impatient with yourself."

All of a sudden, I began to see an image of myself. I realized that all these years, I had given such little thought to anything apart from my training.

"From earliest boyhood, I have watched you work," the khan continued. "There has been nothing in your life apart from soldiering. You are young, perhaps too young, for the great task ahead of you. Our warriors are strong and talented, but apart from your band of ruffians," he quipped, "their skills have not been put to the test. You will have to lead into battle men who are older than you, men who have wives and children. They will have to kill and destroy, sadly even women and perhaps children, and risk being killed themselves, leaving widows and orphans and weeping mothers behind.

"All you see in this venture is glory, and it is true that we must revive that thirst for the glory we once had when we rode with the Nogay Horde or with the great khan. You have this desire. I see it in you. It seems your destiny to seek glory. But this is more than a game, my son. You are going to have to breathe this spirit into your men. Your boys will have to grow up, almost overnight, and become men. The older ones will have to desire glory above their comfortable way of life. They will all need discipline and must learn to take orders, even from a colt like you. Every man will have to envisage the destruction of a vicious enemy, and you will likely do battle with the Russians who now use artillery, for there is a garrison nearby. You will have to do this in such a fashion that we will appear above accusation and reproach." He paused and perked up his ears.

"Hmm, we shall now have to move outside again. Fortunately the evening air is warm and pleasant. Listen to the music my lad. The dancing is about to begin." Then, with his strong hand on the back of my neck, he breathed into my ear, "Dance, Tambor, dance tonight with passion. Dance as you have never danced before!"

I awoke the next morning knowing that it was late. Mehti's back (for this is what I called her) was lying against my side, and although I wanted to caress it, I wanted more urgently to recall the events of the previous night. I lay very still so as not to alert my boys or to waken Mehti, for then my mood would surely be destroyed. I remember wanting not to disappoint the khan who encouraged me to dance passionately. So I remembered letting the music enter into my being. First, the women danced and sang. They danced in a line, which, with the sway of the melancholy melody, turned into a circle and then into a series of circles, back and forth back and forth, and ever on. We do not touch each other as we dance. Mostly the slaves danced, as it was not fitting for a high-ranking lady to dance, or at least not so soon in the evening. Mehti was one of the dancers. She knew I was observing her. Of course she knew I desired her too. Sad though the song was she couldn't help smiling and, when she did, her flushed cheeks forced her dark eyes into two reversed half moons. This was a special quality of her smile. She was enchanting. As the music increased in rhythm the women broke the line and began swirling, some with hands on their hips and others with arms upraised. Mehti wore pale green and her skirts whirled out like a yurt.

She must have danced like this before, I thought to myself and wondered how I could ever have missed her last year and the year before.

I then became aware that the khan was eyeing me intently. He said nothing but offered me a cup of ceremonial kumis.

There were many more songs and dances, and I enjoyed them all, but it was the saber dance that I awaited the most. It required athletic skill. The drums beat slowly with the harps. The pipes were silent. The men of the audience provided more percussion and the dance began. A huge roar came from the spectators and a number of voices called out my name. We danced slowly, lined as in battle. The sabers, which had been placed on the ground were pointed toward the middle of our circle like a single bright star reflecting the fire, but when the time came to grasp them, the crowd roared again with approval and delight. We swung the swords slowly so as not to touch each other. As we swirled, we had to keep from getting dizzy. When the rhythm increased, we lowered our sabers and, in a pattern, began to jump over each other's, making sure they would not strike the ankles. The more skilled dancers could leap above two or three blades, even four, swinging at their feet at the same time. The dance began to slow down as the line of women surrounded the whole dance field until the sabers were placed back into the middle before it ended. I am told that we learned these dances long before the coming of the Mongol. The Russians, at that time, called us Polovtsi or Kipchaks. I have since read some of their stories.

What followed was still a bit vague in my mind. I remember the khan's boy and the elder of my two boys, Nissim, carrying my gear back to my tent, for it seems my own area was made even more private with some extra hangings. Mehti walked with us carrying some food, perhaps as a gift for my mother.

How we got into bed, I could not remember, but I do remember we made love fiercely that night and fell asleep quickly, or at least I did, probably overcome by the kumis.

I decided to let Mehti sleep, so I cautiously slipped out from the covers. I just had time enough to cover her when my servants came in, likely hearing me stir. With the warm water they brought in, I washed before going out to greet the sun, who had probably waited a few hours for my greeting. The boys said nothing but wiped me with fresh cloths and dressed me. The younger of them couldn't wipe the smile from off his face. He needed a clunk on the head. The elder respectfully attempted to be more discreet, but I did notice him trying to catch a cautious glance toward the low bed. I couldn't fault him for that.

Of course, the fuss awakened Mehti. I noticed that she had covered herself though she wasn't naked. I smiled at her and wished her Tengri's blessing. She looked a little disappointed. Perhaps she had wanted to wake up in my arms. I hadn't thought of that. I dismissed the boys, asking that fresh water and some food be brought. Did I see some disapproval on her brow? I wondered if I should ignore it.

She spoke quietly, "I should like to have served you."

I laughed. "Not until you get to know my mother. The kitchens are her territory."

"But she does know me," Mehti said. When I raised my eyebrows, she added, "She often visits my own mother who manages the khan's kitchens. I think she might want me to serve you, as is befitting."

Suddenly my routine life seemed a little complicated. I had to fit her in and give her some job, maybe even some status. I sincerely doubted that Mother would let her get that far, but I certainly did not want her to become one of Mother's staff.

Timov, the younger of my two boys, came in struggling with a pitcher of water, and the metal bowl, which had already been cleaned. He said simply, "Nissim will be back with the food."

"When he comes, he is to stay outside until I invite him in."

I never had to be so watchful before. I used to let the boys come and go freely having thought of my yurt basically as a place to sleep. Mother had always said I was too easy with them.

I walked over to Mehti and raised her by the hand, giving her a kiss on the forehead as I pulled her up. She raised her eyes and seemed content.

"Are you going to watch me wash?" she asked.

I was confused. "Do you want me to leave?"

She turned abruptly and fell on her knees. "Forgive me, lord. I have no right to ask anything. I am your slave."

This was not going well. "Why don't you wash up, and we will discuss things after eating."

I was annoyed, and she saw it.

"Oh, Master, please do not be displeased with me!"

"Please, Mehtap, just wash. I must think about this." I spoke perhaps too abruptly, and added more reassuringly, "We shall work something out."

She turned and began to wash. There was a little bag near the wash table with some things she had brought, from which she extracted a large comb and a bottle of some liquid, likely fragrant oil. I decided not to look at her and walked closer to the door, which was curtained off where the boys usually slept. I saw Nissim coming toward the yurt and called back to her, "Let us know when you are ready. The food is here."

We really did not work things out, but they seemed nevertheless to fall into place. Mehti took charge of organizing the yurt, beautifying it, getting the most attractive hangings and carpets. It was beginning to look like the khan's yurt, and I could see how well her mother took care of the old man. She recruited Nissim to help her, and I was a little surprised not to see him objecting to the changes, for he was extremely devoted to me. I was amused to see the boys work under her as though she were the mistress. She even got the boys to smuggle out some equipment from Mother's kitchens so that she herself could cook outside the tent. I largely ignored the proceedings and left it to the three; I figured any improvement was an improvement, why object?

In truth, Holy Father, I was as usual ignoring everything domestic. I was busy. My young warriors were being trained under Bashina, not only in technical skills, but also in shaping the attitudes of a warrior. Chabuk and some others had been on a few raids with me, and all were eager to do some real work. I was also attempting to recruit the more seasoned men, some who had not really battled seriously for a long time, if ever, and some who had fought before but thought me perhaps an overexcited, though talented boy. These were harder to reach.

The khan accompanied me to the bondsmen and their families and sometimes visited the training fields. This token of approval relieved me of some uncomfortable situations. Their objection was not necessarily the advisability of the project but whether I was best to take charge of the venture. While the khan was well able to deal with these objections, I proved myself quite capable on the training field not only as a warrior but also as a leader. I eventually gathered a group of officers, and we began to make some battle plans and spy out the land. When finally some of the older ones suspended their objections, we began to work together.

Mother and some other women had also become invaluable to our plans. They would visit Mikhailov ostensibly for trade, selling their wares in the settlement. They were planning to visit the garrison to observe the number and equipment of the soldiers. They had already gone to the docks, which were part of the estate, and watched the trading ships and tried to make deals with the merchants. They once observed a fine older man on a horse for whom the others made way as he approached the ships. He was very strangely dressed in fine wool and shoes with buckles. He was not bearded, as Russian men usually were (before Tsar Peter made beards illegal), but had long curly brown hair and a thin mustache like Turkish soldiers. It seemed that he was much older than his costume displayed. He wore a wide hat with a plume in its brim. My father commented that that was how the Germans and the French dressed, claiming that the hair was not real. He had traded with these Europeans frequently up north.

"But he did speak to the ship captain in Russian," said my mother. "Probably asking who we were and what we were doing there with our mules and carts loaded with goods. He took some time to observe us and passed on. No doubt he was the master.

It's a shame we have to destroy the place." She added, "As it was such a good trading place we made lots of money. Our spiced meats and pastries were so popular they asked us to bring back a cartload."

I looked forward to her next adventure in espionage.

These days I hardly ever stayed at home and usually came home very tired by nightfall. Mehti and I shared the bed, but less frequently, and not with the same fervor. Often I just went to sleep. Earlier in our relationship she might pout if she felt ignored, but lately the disappointment waned.

One day I returned early. Mother and her troupe had just come back from one of her expeditions, and I wanted to get a report. Having some equipment to drop off, I made for my tent. When I entered the outer part of the yurt, where my men servants slept, I was shocked to see Nissim curled around Mehti's shoulder, both asleep on his mat. I stood for a moment, trying to gather the multitude of thoughts going on in my mind. I should have been horrified, but I wasn't. I *was* angry! Nissim was the first to awake, and he sat bolt upright. He was silent, but his movement awoke Mehtap, who pulled up into the corner gathering the bedclothes up to her naked breast. Her eyes, full of fear, were now full moons. I grabbed my horsewhip, which was around my shoulder, for I had come back on horseback, and was about to strike the lad when he fell prostrate at my feet clasping my ankles.

"No, Master, I beg you, please do not beat me! Not you too, my master! O my god!" I heard him sob. "P-please f-forgive me!"

In the midst of my wrath, I thought, *It took either raw guts or complete stupidity to ask that.*

But it was not that that deterred me from striking him; it was the sight of his naked back and the vicious scars that lined it, which made me pause. I had never seen him naked. Unlike the Turks, we Tatars rarely buy slaves naked at the market place;

we seize them in war, as I had taken Nissim and Timov, or we breed them.

While still very angry, my rage died down as swift as a desert wind. I turned to Mehtap and, with a gesture, motioned her farther into the yurt. She grabbed her clothes and, wrapping the sheet around her, quickly and silently disappeared. I told Nissim to get up and dress and asked where Timov was. He told me he was out playing with the village boys and asked him if he usually arranged it that way. His silence and look of shame answered the question emphatically. I stepped out of the yurt.

This gave me some time to calm down and think matters through a little more clearly. It was not that I suspected that Mehtap and I wouldn't tire of each other eventually, but rather that she would probably not have tired of me at all if I had not been ignoring her. She lost her virginity to me, and she might have expected more, but I obviously did not give her what she needed. I admit quite honestly that I used her, but maybe I did not use her enough, though I did not expect this to happen. In her loneliness, she found consolation in the arms of another servant and I had to admit, though I had not really noticed it before, that Nissim was a handsome young man, and they had been alone together all the time I was busy gathering an army. Then I remembered the scars on his back and wondered if I shouldn't have added a few more to them after all. I heard him fussing in the tent and knew he would be out any moment; I would have to pursue this another time. I knew Mother would be waiting for me. I gestured for him to come with me; I didn't want him out of my sight.

Mother was already well into the discussion when we arrived at her yurt. I motioned for Nissim to sit at the back near the door. A servant brought me tea and some sweets, which I eagerly took, and tried to catch up with what she was saying. Father was sitting nearby with Chabuk and a few other brothers, and Mother was surrounded by her women.

She was saying, "Then the lady leaned over to me and, in our tongue, but different, complimented us on our goods and hoped we would come back."

My father interrupted, "You mean the big woman—"

"No no no, it was the young one, the beautiful one, maybe her daughter. I guess I must have looked shocked, but she smiled sweetly and told me her family had once had a dacha on the Black Sea where she learned the Tatar tongue playing with the neighborhood children. She seemed somewhat sad. The big one snapped something at her, and she moved away to join the men who were watching the ship being unloaded. She looked back once and gave a few coins to some of our children."

"What sorts of goods were being unloaded?" I asked.

"Oh, lots of lumber and metals—oh yes, and even some cattle. There were also crates filled with hens and geese."

I commented, "So it was a big ship then, rather than one of the small traders usually seen on the Volga."

"A big ship it was indeed, and beautifully carved, with the men dressed all the same!"

"Humph," grunted Father. "These are the ships that little by little are replacing the caravans, but they can't so easily get into the interior parts of China or Tibet. They must be made in Russia since they have no ports to the western seas. Perhaps Vassili gets them made for himself. However, if they can get past the Persian pirates on the Caspian Sea, they can make good trade with the caravans from China and India. I presume this one was on its way to Persia!"

I needed more information. "How about soldiers? Any of them around?"

"Oh, about half a dozen or so. Judging by the way they flirted with our womenfolk, they didn't seem to be working all that hard. Probably they were sent just to prevent any trouble. We shall probably visit the garrison next week."

Small talk followed and I was left with my thoughts. I asked one of the girls to send some food to Nissim and then made my way to Father, giving Mother a big unexpected kiss on the way. I stayed with him a bit, inquired about his health and answered questions about the progress of our venture. Much of the day was left, but being anxious about the job I had to do, I left quietly with Nissim.

We were both silent as we trudged back to the tent. I suppose, dear Father, I do not much care for confrontations. I told Nissim to stay outside and saw raw panic on his face.

"Nissim," I scolded, "I am not going to hurt her, and if I wanted to kill her, I would be within my rights." At the same time, I chided myself for feeling I had to explain myself.

I began to realize suddenly how complex life could be. With a snort, I turned from him and went in.

The yurt was cleaned, and everything was in order. Mehtap was silent and averted her eyes from me. I thought I would get right to the point.

"I give you a choice, my dear. If you want to stay, you can go and serve my mother. You will work hard, but she will treat you fairly." I paused and waited. She was silent. "I didn't think that would appeal to you, and frankly that doesn't appeal to me either. Actually I'd really like to send you back to the khan. There would be no shame in that. I will let him know you are not needed here, and there will be no mention of Nissim. Go back to your mother, my sweet, and do not remember me. Another will love you better than I can."

At this she threw herself in front of me and grasped my ankles. She began sobbing.

"No, no!" I said gently, "Go, and enjoy your life. The khan loves you, and he will care for you. You are probably his daughter. Get Timov to help you with your things and what you can't take the khan's boy will come for."

I thought for a moment I should kiss her but quickly dismissed the thought. I left, taking Nissim with me.

I needed to think, to get away from the bustle around the yurts. I moved to the back of the complex where I had left my horse. I mounted and motioned Nissim to get on with me. I let my arm down to give him balance, and he slipped lightly on to the horse's back. I had never seen Nissim on a horse and was puzzled at how gracefully he mounted.

"Have you ever ridden before?" I asked.

"Yes." His answer was simple.

So I rode out to the stables where I had another horse, a mare, which I had just recently broken in. I told Nissim to get her ready and watched him closely. I was amazed at how adeptly he prepared himself and how good he was with the mare. Of course, he was there with me every day. He then mounted, and we were off.

I often think well when I am riding and needed some time to myself. We took the route northwest beside the river past the sacred birch grove. I needed speed, and Onyx, my steed, gave me that thrill, but I wondered if Nissim could keep up. When I saw him beginning to tire, although he kept up with me, I stopped at a little wooded grove where I had often spent some time alone. I dismounted, and Nissim followed silently as I walked toward the water. We sat, and I asked him where he had learned to ride.

"I am from Macedonia and am Greek by birth and a Christian, but I was brought up as a Turk, and many of the Turkish nobility are still trained as soldiers."

"What are you doing here as a slave?"

His answer was mildly agitated, "Master, you rescued me from the Kurds two years back."

"Rescued?" I answered, "Why do you say rescued?"

"The Kurds were very cruel to me as the Turks were before them," he said quietly with some emotion, "the ones who sold me and my brother to them. You rescued me."

"Your brother? Timov is your brother?"

He nodded. "Master, you have been so kind, and I am so grateful."

I answered somewhat perturbed. "Why should I treat you badly? You work well. You are always obedient. You have never given me any trouble until now, and even now I have not beaten you though I have the right to kill you if I wanted to."

At this a look of ashen terror covered his face.

"Are you afraid of death?" I asked.

He was quick to answer. "No, Master, I have often wished for it, actually. It is just that I do not want to die with sin on my soul. My God is displeased with me. While I have offended you, I have sinned against him. I have lost my virginity, which is very precious to us, Christians, and if I were to die unforgiven, I would not be able to face the Lord before his seat of judgment."

I thought, *A very peculiar God indeed, like a Khan. But I suppose even Kattu might feel this way about Allah.*

"Master, if you forgive me, maybe my God will be merciful to me. I have never loved another man since I was taken from my father, and it grieves me that I have offended you."

"Nissim, how old are you?"

"Seventeen, Master."

I looked at him long and then said, "I am only three years older than you." Then I began to laugh. I began to realize what the khan had been driving at. The world was going by me, and I never noticed it. All around me people were living their lives, and I never noticed them. Nissim had served me for two years, and I knew nothing about him. At the same time, I couldn't see what was happening to Mehtap; I ignored her as I ignored everybody around me. This is why Mother said she no longer knew me. Maybe Father was so distant because I was so distant from him. Chabuk and the boys were companions at training, but I had never really sat with them and laughed and been free as they were with each other. I have had one thing in mind, and that alone interested me.

This had to change. If I was to lead my men into battle, I should know what their needs were, what made them happy, or what caused them pain. Besides the present task, *they* did not have the mission that I had, and they were not driven to fulfill a vow as I was. I was determined to resolve this indifference immediately. And I would begin with Nissim.

"Nissim," I asked, perhaps too bluntly, "would you like to be a warrior?"

He swallowed, and his face flushed and looked confused.

"Forgive me, my friend," I said as I realized what I had done. I laughed at my own insensitivity. "Here you are, expecting me to kill you and leave your body to the vultures, beside my secret grove, and now I am asking if you want to become a warrior!" I paused, "Now let me begin again."

He was relaxing, and I could see the briefest edge of a smile on the right side of his lips. He was handsome, and again I could see how he and Mehtap became intimate. A touch of vanity aroused in my soul, and I excused it by saying to myself that she was attracted to him only by default. I felt silly. He interrupted me.

"Master, please tell me what you are trying to say. I am confused."

"Nissim, I can see that you are an adept rider. I presume you have not been on a horse for a very long time, yet you rode Cereyan as though you both had ridden together for years."

"My father encouraged me to ride. He gave me a pony when I was eight as he also gave Timov. And I had been riding his mare since I was twelve."

"You are strong, I can see that. Have you ever wielded a weapon?"

He reminded me that he had been trained by the Turkish nobility and was being prepared for a military career in the Turkish army.

"Well then, I ask again, do you want to be a warrior? I can train you."

He said, with some concern, "Master, I am your slave. I am not free to answer that question."

"No, I guess not," I replied. "So we will have to do something about that. I'm not sure how we will do it, but I will check it out with my father and the khan. Since I took you as spoils, I think I have some right to change your status, if that is what you want, of course. I'm not forcing you. You have a fairly easy life with me. If you are satisfied with that—"

"Master!" He was almost shouting, "What are you saying to me? I have longed to ride with you. Have you never seen me sitting on the training fence watching you? I used to arrive early just to see you. I have always admired you and have been jealous of your brothers and friends."

I confessed to myself that I had indeed never noticed, and again that sense of shame arose. I calmed him down in his distress. As I began thinking, a plan began to emerge: he could be made my personal companion. Later on, I would learn the word and status of squire or shield bearer, a rank which the Knights of Europe had found essential. In this way, Nissim would at the same time both serve me and learn the art of war until such time as he would become a warrior in his own right. However, the word *companion* was the one that came to mind at that moment.

"We'll work something out, my friend. And if my forgiveness of you might persuade your God to forgive you, so be it. You have my forgiveness. We will let him concern himself about it. Friend, the water here is very refreshing. Let us bathe before eating. I brought some food. We *should* be home before nightfall."

Believe me, Holy Father, I was looking forward to sleeping by myself again, but in fact, I found myself missing Mehti. Virginity and its accompanying innocence are very beautiful, but once the flame has been lit it seems impossible to be ever the same again. I lay on my pallet wondering if I had done right both by her and by Nissim. It even crossed my mind that he might be feeling the same way about her as I did. A touch of jealousy arose in me again, which I rejected immediately. I also had to consider that approaching the khan tomorrow might be too soon. He might suspect something. But if I did not go to see him tomorrow with some explanation of Mehtap's departure from me, she might be compromised. I surely didn't want her to be in trouble with him because of me. Perhaps tomorrow would be wisest after all.

While I was pondering all this, I heard one of the boys get up presumably to relieve himself. But whoever left the yurt went in the opposite direction of the latrine. I could hear clearly because of my wakefulness. My curiosity was aroused when he didn't soon return, so I too got up and went in the same direction, though I could not hear him quite yet. Timov was fast asleep, so it had to be Nissim. Then I heard some shuffling behind one of the storage tents. Of course, Nissim would be familiar with the area. I quietly edged myself along the side of the tent, fearing I'd trip against the empty clay jars outside the storage. Then I saw Nissim in the moonlight. He was prostrating himself to the ground several times, falling on his hands. It was not like the Muslims who prostrated from a kneeling position.

After a while, he stopped, and I heard him say some prayers in what I thought must be the Greek tongue, though I had never heard it before. Then he began praying in Turkish in an accent I was beginning to recognize as only slightly different from Tatar though it is more different from Chuvash. In this way, I understood him to be talking to his God.

He was saying, as I remember, "O blessed Lord of heaven and earth, I pray that thou wouldst have mercy on me, a sinner, unworthy to look upon thy face. Be thou thanked for having found favor of me in thy sight, who am unworthy of even the slightest blessing. Forgive me for abusing my master's benefaction toward me, and forgive me for causing Mehtap disgrace in my master's eyes. Bless my master with all the virtues of the heavens and grant him to see the Light of eternal day. May his family prosper out of the bounty of thy hands. And may our glorious khan be granted health of body and mind."

At this, he fell again in prostration, and on his knees he continued, "And grant, oh Lord, your mercy on Timov, and may our master see how kind and blessed he is and how much he loves him. And do thou take pity on my father, wherever he is, and allow me to see him before his death. In thy mercy, keep my mother and sister safe and grant that no ungodly person abuse them. All this I ask in the name of Jesus our Lord who hath saved us. Amin." The rest he said in that unknown tongue, and made some sort of sign over his body, and stopped.

I stood a little stunned for a while, maybe embarrassed, as though I had walked in on some very personal event which, of course, I had. I was moved that Nissim had such an intimate relationship with his God, for I could never talk to Tengri that way. That he brought me and my family before his God touched me profoundly. But I was equally aware that I had to get back to the yurt before he did so as not to bring my presence to his awareness. It might be very fortuitous to have such a God on our side. I almost tripped over some jars in my haste to depart. Making it back to my pallet, I heard Nissim settle in shortly afterward. I was now able to sleep.

I awoke very early as usual, half expecting Mehtap to be beside me and perhaps a little disappointed that she wasn't. The boys were already up and preparing for me to wash. I went outside and lifted my hands to Koyash and Tengri and asked the boys to bring the water outside to wash in the warm summer sun. I could see bustle around Kattu's tent, but he did not emerge. Once the boys dried my back, I went inside to dress.

"This will not be one of your responsibilities anymore," I said to Nissim. "Timov can take care of me from now on. But we shall bide our time until things are official."

Timov, always alert and quizzical, looked to Nissim to see what I meant. Nissim quietly nodded his head in my direction and prepared to wash himself. I had always insisted that my staff be clean, which was somewhat of a novelty among those of the old faith. I could see the younger boy agitated with curiosity.

"You will have to be patient, my young lad. Now that Mehtap is gone, things are going to be a little different. How old are you, Timov?" I asked, realizing that I had always called him "boy."

"I am fifteen years old, Master," he replied.

"Hmm, you were just a boy when I took you, and now you are becoming a young man. You will need to get more serious if I'm going to do anything profitable for you. It is quite up to you, Timov. You can play in the fields and streets with the other slaves, or you can become serious and learn better ways. Do you want this, Timov?"

"Yes, Master. Yes...yes, Master." I noticed him looking to Nissim for support, which Nissim did not give.

I had to laugh. "Relax, boy. Did you help Mehtap get back home without any trouble? Did you tell the khan what I told you?"

"Yes, Master, and I did it all by myself. Akilli Khan was very kind and told me he was glad she came back and would like to see you, today, if possible."

"Well, Nissim, I guess that is what we shall do. Hmm, I don't want you to wear your tunic. We'll have to see what I've got for you to wear. You are slimmer than I am," I said, "but let's have a look." Timov looked aghast. Again, I laughed and slapped him affectionately on the back of his neck.

I thought, *At least I shall always know what he is thinking although that is not always such a good thing, at least for him.* I looked at the brothers, and almost for the first time, I recognized the resemblance. They were definitely not Tatar; their features were too fine with strong noses; they were certainly too dark to be Russians, nor were they as dark as the Armenians and Georgians I had met. Why I had thought they were Kurds, was only a matter of circumstance, for they also did not resemble Kurds. It was primarily a matter of my own inability to see.

As Nissim and I walked to the center of the camp where the khan dwelt, I began to contemplate what I was doing. Nissim was also lost in his thoughts, and I didn't want to disturb him. I began to wonder whether I had acted wisely. Of course I had been impulsive, a victim of my own confusion. But at that moment, I was reminded also of the many things that the khan himself had told me: how single-minded I was and how unaware of what was going on around me. I had to accept that in spite of all I had hoped to achieve for Nissim, he was still just a slave. Why was I taking a risk for someone who carried on with my mistress behind my back?

Three qualities went for him however. He had always been devoted to me, quite happy to serve me, not wily like some other slaves I knew who couldn't wait to have their masters out of sight. He had served me as though my needs were important to him. His prayers convinced me of that. Also his penitence toward me was sincere and heartfelt, not groveling and pathetic like some unruly slave, but with a sense that he *had* betrayed me and was inconsolably sorry. Lastly, and I couldn't get this quality out of my mind, he was extremely adept with a horse. Could there be anything more convincing? I wanted him to excel. It was also deep in my heart, Father, though I would not have been conscious of it at that time, that we would become friends, for as yet I could never say I had one.

Drawing near to the khan's tent, I took a short look at my companion. He was wearing the same clothing that I had discarded a few years ago because I had outgrown them. Although he was slightly taller than me, I was wider at the shoulders and hips than he was, for he would have more to grow. His shirt was white, though perhaps not as white as it could have been, and he wore my violet pantaloons somewhat short at the ankles. I thought how handsome I must have looked when I was able to get into them. I also wondered how the khan would react on seeing him. The look on Nissim's face showed his anxiety.

I offered, "Don't worry, my friend, the khan is a wise and understanding man, who sometimes knows things we don't know ourselves." I then considered that this comment was perhaps not exactly comforting.

There were two armed bondsmen at the entrance of the yurt who were well acquainted with me. After exchanging a few pleasantries, one of them went in to announce my arrival. I was told to go in, and I took Nissim with me, suggesting he wait in the outer area. The khan was warm and open with me, and I made my customary prostration.

He began, as was fitting, "Tambor, thank you for coming to me. I can always count on your promptness. You disappeared from the field so swiftly yesterday that no one knew where you went." He paused to let me talk, and I took the advantage.

"I had much to think about, uh...not only with regard to training but also things closer to home."

"Go on."

"Forgive me, but I have been unfair to Mehtap." (I guess I am too blunt at times.)

"I see. Perhaps you can explain."

I continued, "As you know, most favored Khan, Mehtap is a very sweet and loving girl. But I have been just too busy to pay attention to her, and I think she was very unhappy. Actually I am sure she thought that *she* was the one who was making *me* unhappy."

"I see," he pondered. "And so you thought she would be better off at home serving me with her mother."

"Yes, exactly!" I responded, maybe a little too fervently, all the while thinking that he could see through me. But it seemed to be going well anyway.

"Well, it is not as though I hadn't warned you this would happen. I am very glad you returned her to me. And yes, she is very happy to be here." He paused and called for tea. "Is there something else you wish to discuss?"

"Yes, Favored One," I replied.

"Go on."

"I am sure you remember the trouble we had with that Kurdish caravan a few years back when we offered them hospitality and grazing ground and they turned around and tried to rob us."

"Indeed I do, my young stallion. You and our boys were magnificent. That was the first time I had ever seen you in action, and I knew that no one could ever fault you for your youth. The elders all agreed, and that is why you are in charge of the present plans."

"Yes," I said, but that was not where I wanted to be heading, so I continued, "I took a few boys as slaves assuming that they were Kurdish slaves. Brothers, they were, and the eldest of the two, Nissim, is devoted to me. I am embarrassed to say that I found out only recently that they were in fact Greeks."

"Greeks? Indeed," he interrupted.

"Yes, Favored One, and Nissim has had some training in soldiering amongst the Turks."

"Is that so?"

"What I would like to do, Favored Khan, is release him from his bonds with your permission."

"With my permission? He is yours for you to do as you please."

"True, Great One, but I do need your permission to train him as a warrior. You should see how well he rides."

The khan was quiet for some time, and I didn't want to say more as yet. The tea came in, and the khan told the slave to bring another cup.

"I take it you have brought the young man here. Well, bring him in." I went to the part of the yurt near the door and motioned for Nissim to enter. He prostrated reverentially and waited to be seated.

The khan gave him a long look and said, "Nissim, please sit down." He studied him further, and tea was served to the three of us. Nissim hesitated to drink.

The khan looked at him again and said, "Lord Tambor says that you are a free man now, so you may drink in my presence." He added gently, "I think freedom will take a little time to get used to. You may talk to me as is necessary because I have some questions to ask you. But first of all, relax and drink."

He called for some food and asked that Mehtap bring it. I held my breath for just a moment and glanced quickly at Nissim, whose eyes were averted. I was glad to see that he could keep the cold face. Mehtap came in with a tray of food, looking as beautiful and cheerful as ever.

The khan asked her, "Do you have something to say to Lord Tambor, my dear?"

I was surprised at the intimacy.

"Good health to you, my Lord Tambor. Greetings to you, Nissim." If she were shocked at Nissim's appearance, she never let on. She was playing her part admirably.

The khan dismissed her, saying, "Keep the samovar hot, we may need some more tea." Then he turned to Nissim. "As you might expect, young man, I need to know some things about you, so you will endure my interrogation. As the property of your owner, this was not necessary, but now you are a free man in my yurts and accountable to me. You are also not Nogay and are therefore a foreigner." (I had not thought of that.) "My dear nephew speaks highly of you and tells me you have been serving him exceptionally well so he wished to reward you."

Nissim, spontaneously prostrated before him, and I could see the khan's approval. He smiled.

"Normally you would be free to go, but Lord Tambor has other plans for you, which I expect you have agreed to. You wish to serve in my army, for I am sure you are aware that we are reforming it, and you need some training. Tambor will be your master, though not in servitude but rather as a pupil. The knights of the west would call you a squire or a shield bearer (*köy ağası* in Turkish). A squire would often come from a noble family and serve a lord as a companion until his training was complete. After this, he would himself become a knight, or in our terms, a warrior. Are you willing to accept this?"

"Yes, noble Khan, God being my helper."

I was amazed and wondered how the khan knew these things.

"We shall call you köy ağası, a Turkish word, but perhaps *companion* would be better. How does that sound to you, Tambor?" he said turning to me.

"Yes, noble Khan, that is exactly the title I had in mind." The truth was that everyone in the camp eventually began to use the word *squire* regularly.

"Now, young man, where exactly do you come from and how did you get here? Be brief but honest. If I need details, I will ask for them. You referred to God being your helper. Are you Muslim?"

"No, Great One, and that is why I am here. I am from the city of Thessalonica and come from a Christian family. Father was Greek, but Mother was a Macedonian Slav from a wealthy borderland family."

"Indeed." This was not a question; Nissim continued.

"As you likely know, Christians have no status in the Turkish empire, and the followers of Christ are very poor, heavily taxed, and ill educated. My father, amongst others, posed as a Muslim in order to maintain status and wealth, for he had a good business going as a perfumer. We observed Christian traditions and spoke Greek at home, although Mother taught us some Slavonic also. However we kept up Muslim appearances. My father was always ashamed of this, for he knew the words of our Lord, 'Who said that if we were ashamed of him before men, he would be ashamed of us before his holy angels.' Nevertheless, when it came time for me to be circumcised at the age of seven, according to the Turkish tradition, he relocated to Nicomedia, which the Turks call Izmit, east of Istanbul, where his business flourished even more. This way, his new neighbors would think me done already. He also viewed our prosperity as a sign that our secrecy was approved of in God's sight. When it came to Timov's time, we moved to Trabzon for the same reason."

"Trabzon! That is on the eastern shore of the Black Sea!" The khan seemed surprised.

Nissim continued. "That is true, noble Khan. There are many Greeks there and not too much persecution. You probably know it is a large trading and commercial center. It is one of the most important ports in eastern Anatolia. As would be expected, Father kept his Turkish ways. He was fearful of exposure, and he did enjoy his comforts. As we were near a military center, my father enrolled me in the small military academy there where I was to learn the art of war. I was a rider at a very early age, and I did learn some weaponry. I enjoyed soldiering.

"Often after practice, we students bathed together, but I always wore my loincloth. On one occasion, however, while swimming, one of the other boys grabbed the loincloth in jest, claiming there was nothing inside it. You know how boys can be. I was twelve or so at the time and well after the proper age. Thus it came to the ears of the administrator who approached the local Mullah. When the authorities came to question Father at our home, they insisted that I receive the rite immediately. When they questioned why he had refused me the rite, he would not answer. They deduced then that we were Christians, and according to Turkish custom, if anyone appeared Turkish or even suggested in haste that he wanted to convert, he must become Muslim. Therefore in the hopes that I could deflect punishment from my father, I cried out that I was a Christian, had always been a Christian, and would always be a Christian. On hearing this, they tried to persuade me through flattery to accept Islam, reminding me of all the benefits I would receive from accepting their faith. But I would not listen to them. They were not really cruel people, noble Khan. They were just trapped by their tradition.

"Seeing the futility then of both their promise of reward and the threat of punishment, they took me and my father. They tied our hands together with rope on opposite sides of a pillar in our house, facing each other, and beat us mercilessly with horsewhips. We could see each other in the throes of pain. My father fainted. I thought he had died, but I tried to keep his body upright for the sake of his dignity. Timov was spared this because he was only ten, but he and my mother witnessed it. No doubt the Turks thought if he could not be persuaded by flattery and riches the threat of pain would change his mind. When they finished, they dragged my father away, and I have not seen him since, though I was told by another Christian that he survived and had been sold into slavery. The last I heard, he had been taken to Thrace. My brother and I were put into servitude with a local Muslim, Mehmet Pasha. My mother and sister were taken somewhere on the Black Sea, apparently not too far away, probably at Mehmet Pasha's country estate.

"Under his charge I was given an alternating diet of cruelty and flattery. One time, the scourging was so fierce that an infection developed and I almost died. After this, the Pasha stopped punishing me this way. I would like to believe he was not a cruel man. He was simply a victim of his own system. Finally we were sold to a band of Kurds who were instructed to treat us cruelly. They were not nearly as vicious as the Turks. They worked us very hard but did not beat us. Unlike others, this particular tribe was made of thieves, as you well know. You Tatars, who are reputed to be a savage and cruel race, actually gave me a home, even though I was in servitude. I am ever grateful to my Lord Tambor who has granted me my manhood."

"Tell me something about your names for they are not Turkish," Nissim continued. "Our names are Greek, and according to our custom, we are named after saints. My saint is Onesimus, which is my real name. It means *useful*."

The khan laughed and slapped him on the knee. "Well, I hope so, yes, indeed I hope so."

"Onesimus," Nissim continued, "was a runaway slave during Roman times, who became devoted to the mighty apostle Saint Paul in Rome and took on the yoke of Christ. But he was sent back to his master Philemon, also a disciple, with the advice that he was to be treated as a brother. Eventually he was freed and went back to Saint Paul. My Muslim name was Ibrahim, which is also used by Christians."

"Interesting. And your brother?"

"His name is Timotheus which means 'honoring God.' His Islamic name is Abdul Melik, 'the servant of the king.' Yeah, most Favored One, may my brother always honor God and ever serve the khan."

At this point, Mehtap refreshed the tea, and the khan bade her wait.

"You know, my young men, this is not without some concerns. Your fellow warriors, Tambor, will not take to this so easily. They will not want to train with a foreigner who was once a slave, and they may not trust him. Chabuk will be very jealous of this relationship; I do not believe he loves you as greatly as you think. Rather, as Bashina says, he is more concerned about status, and thus he reveres you. I shall speak to your parents on their next visit. Neither of you must ever let Nissim's story come to Dikkatli's ears. I suspect he is already a Muslim and such knowledge will bring hostility between you and him. Dikkatli is genuinely fond of you, Tambor, and we do not need a rift between the two of you, especially at this point. My approval of Nissim will close mouths, but only time will open hearts.

"Oh, and Nissim, you must cease calling Tambor 'master.' 'Sir' will be enough. It shows respect to him, but 'sir' is the expression of a free man, not a slave. I will expect much of you, for I feel you have a special destiny to fulfill, and your status as a Nogay warrior will get you places you may not otherwise go. There is another matter here. When you have successfully finished your training and have become a full-fledged warrior, I will release this fine young woman from her servitude to marry you, if that is suitable to both of you. This will then make you part of the family. But until then, you must stay far away from each other.

"Think also, Nissim, if you would be ready to kill a fellow Christian in battle. In the future you may have to. At the present, you will not be ready or permitted to do any fighting. This will give you time to consider the possibility. But now you must go. Mehtap, come and kiss the young men."

She came and knelt and kissed both our cheeks, blushing especially as she held Nissim's hand. All three of us prostrated as the khan rose. He dismissed us with the wave of a hand and a veiled smile. We left the door and saluted the doorkeepers and looked at each other as two free men. I felt for a moment that it was I who had been freed from bondage every bit as much as Nissim. We looked at each other and embraced.

"Well, my friend, it appears that your God has blessed you abundantly," I said. I would never tell him how I had eavesdropped on his prayers, but I was glad to know that he prayed for me.

"Yes, and far more abundantly than I deserve," he responded. It would take me a long while before I could conceive of what he meant by that.

"If you haven't anything better to do now, let's go for a ride. I think Cereyan is waiting for you. You have gotten a fine horse there. It seems I broke her in for you already. I find her a bit jumpy as mares can be, but you handled her superlatively. It is as though she were meant for you. I inherited a few horses from the Kurds, and Cereyan was a foal from our breeding. Father thought these horses should be part of the family herd and bred for profit, but I insisted on a herd of my own."

"Thanks, uh, sir. You are very generous," he said quietly.

"Not at all, Nissim. It is strictly business. How can I possibly train a Nogay warrior who doesn't have a horse?" We both laughed, and this released some tension. "By the way, when we are together, please call me Tambor. *Sir* or *Lord* is too formal, meant for the ears of our warriors, and for my mother's sake. We will have to work quickly, and I will have to ignore you somewhat while I am preparing an army. You will be around, but not for sitting on the fence again. I will speak to Bashina, who will keep an eye on you while I am busy."

"What exactly have you been planning to do?" he asked.

"Why, we are planning to destroy a man and his town, and even a garrison of Russian soldiers."

"Oh!"

That day was very important to both of us, dear Father, for it established a bond which we have never broken. Although he is away from me now and cannot share this life God had chosen for me, Nissim and I have been closer than any brothers. In a very real way, he has been an instrument of my salvation.

It was a particular joy to be able to tell him Cereyan was his. I called it my freedom gift to him. I can tell you that he was awfully confused, shy, and enormously grateful, which was to be expected of him, but not required on my part. This gratitude he rendered to God rather than to me for whom he prayed incessantly; this I know though I never eavesdropped on him again. Later when I was at my lowest, even when I was angry with him, I knew his recourse was to prayer, and this gave him an inner strength, which helped us both through that very tough time. I trust you shall meet him someday in the future, and I would ask you, Father, to pray for him, for he too is on a quest only half fulfilled.

That day we rode and rode across the plains, down hills, and through thickets as though we were boys, laughing and full of freedom and joy. I think it was the first time I ever saw him smile. Father, it was freedom for me as well as for him. My work henceforth became more meaningful. Both he and Mehtap taught me to open my heart to those whom I would be leading. It was not just about arrows and sabers. It was about the people I was working with, and they responded. Now everything was not all work, but work took on a lightness I had not discovered until then. Even the older bondsmen, the skeptical ones, and even those secretly hostile began to warm up to me, or was it my genuine personal interest in them, which began to endear them to me. On one occasion, when the khan came to inspect the warriors' training, he looked at me as I rode to meet him, a long and penetrating look. He said, "Now you are dancing, my dear Tambor. It is almost time to make war."

The following day, after our discussion with the khan, my father called a family assembly. He was planning a fall excursion to Astrakhan as he did every year and wanted his house to be in order. But he said he would wait until our enemy was destroyed and the acrid smell of blood continued to penetrate every Russian nostril. Our plans were taking shape. This was the middle of July; we would be ready to war by the first week of September, and he would leave before the birches turned yellow at the end of the month. He hoped to travel down the Volga trading in all the ports on the way. He also implied that the warriors in our family might consider accompanying him even just for a short vacation and, of course, a show of strength. Perhaps this time I would go along also.

I felt a certain coolness from Chabuk and Dalgin, and I was sure the news was already out. We were not there simply to discuss itinerary, which could have been done at any other time. Father broke the silence.

"My son," he said. This was a good beginning, I reflected wryly. "Your mother and I paid a visit to the Wise One this morning at his request." He paused as though he were choosing the correct words. "He informed us that you have freed your slave, Nissim—I believe that is his name—and that you will be training him as a warrior. You have every right to do so. After all, it was you who captured him and his younger brother." I saw Chabuk's hair almost bristle like a wolf. "Of course you were smart enough to consult the Wise One, and he gave his consent—well, actually, one might say even his approval."

"But he is a foreigner," Chabuk interrupted. "Sorry, Father! How do you expect us to work with a former slave who is not even Kubanshyi?"

Father continued, ignoring the comment. "It is not our custom to free slaves, Tambor, at least not in our family. We do not want to start a precedent causing the servants to resent their servitude. It is not healthy."

I was glad I told Nissim to stay back. I did not want him to hear such unreasonable hostility.

When Mother spoke, I was nervous. "It may be as you say, you, my men folk, that it is not our custom to grant freedom to slaves. My concern is that we have lost a damn good slave." (I suppose I inherited my bluntness from her.) "Never have *I* had such a respectful servant. He would often go beyond his duty to please me, asking if there was anything *more* he could do, and he was Tambor's servant, not mine. This was each day after he had taken care of Tambor. I often saw him paying particular heed to Tambor's horses and making sure of my son's concerns. This was done," she said turning to me, "without your knowledge, my son, and probably without seeking reward, unlike much of the sniveling help we have around here. I will miss him."

Mother, I thought, *you have finally come through, and I don't even know if you intended it*. After that there was silence.

I spoke, "My Father and my beloved brothers, Nissim did not grow up in this household. You should know that I took him from the treacherous Kurds, whom you and I slew a few years back. I thought he was one of them and never had the wit to find out the truth about him. Nor is he a Russian peasant taken in the spoils of war. He comes from a noble family in the Turkish empire. He was made a slave for reasons that no Tatar would ever deem worthy of slavery."

I took a side glance at Kattu to see if he might be figuring out Nissim's situation but saw only concerned interest. "Furthermore," I continued, "as a youth, he studied at the military academy in Trabzon. Brothers, he is more useful to us as a warrior than a mere servant. If he can swing a saber and shaft an arrow, he will be of more service to me than carrying a pitcher of water so that I may clean my armpits. And, brothers, he can ride a horse like the wind across the western plains."

"What about the other one, Tambor?" Kattu asked. "Are you going to free him too?"

"*There's* trouble if I ever saw trouble!" Mother interrupted. "He's *too* smart that one, nosing into family affairs. He comes here and plays with the other slaves and hangs around looking like he's a spy for the Russian garrison. He once sneaked onto one of our carts going to Mikhailov, and you never even missed him, you were so wrapped up in your work. I must confess he was a good salesman, though. Humph, a real talker, and I think he even speaks some Russian."

"In fact, he is Nissim's brother, and I assure you, he is not a Russian spy, Mother." I laughed, and so did she. "But I will keep my eyes open to see how he will be of use to us. By the way, could you spare another servant? Please, send a boy. With two such handsome men as Nissim and me around the tent, a girl would be hopelessly distracted." At least they were all laughing now.

Mother said she was hoping to take a trip to the Russian garrison with some of her ladies to spy out the situation and make a bit of money. I told her that would be invaluable. This time, she could take Timov along with my permission. We had to get that nosey mind to work for us.

Chabuk and Dalgin passed me on their way out. We whacked each other playfully, but I knew that Chabuk would need some time. *It might be good to ask him,* I thought, *to train Nissim in the art of the scimitar since that was his particular skill. That might just break the ice.* Kattu was pleasant, but a little distant. Father was busy, of course, and I had things to do.

It was my responsibility over the following weeks to appoint officers and delegate authority. Chabuk and Usta, an older man recommended by Bashina, were to be my right and left hand. I wanted Chabuk close to me to curb his impetuousness. Usta would swing in from the south, and Chabuk and I were to come on straight from the west and head with our men to the manor house at terrifying speed. Usta would take the south road and attack the harbor front. He would probably encounter soldiers. Dalgin was not to be one of the officers; he was only fifteen, and while an enthusiastic fighter, he tended to be a dreamy lad and hesitant about making quick decisions. He would ride with Chabuk since they were inseparable and familiar with each other's styles. I was concerned about his youth, however.

We needed three troops to attack the garrison, which fortunately was situated by a little woodland perfect for us to lie in wait. The soldiers would come from the north toward Mikhailov a little south where we would intercept them. No doubt they would hear the commotion or see the flares the Russians now use. The whole garrison campaign would be headed by a widowed man by the name of Hazir, whom I came to respect for his excellent attitude. Although he was somewhat older than I was, he showed me the finest respect. We also trained well together with the scimitar and the bow. Hazir would be responsible for destroying the garrison; he and his men would wait in the woods till the dispatch of soldiers, being alerted, was on the road and would attack from the rear. At that point, another group was to hit head on as they were turning to meet the others. We would have to be ruthless and fierce and cunning enough to avoid their guns.

Mother and her troop of spies had come back from the garrison with some important information. They had had some trouble being welcomed into the fortress. The captain was suspicious, but then the ladies that Mother took were handpicked for their beauty and charm, and they did not hesitate to use these skills. Fifty lonely and womanless men were after all in need of some attention and some dainties. A few soldiers even remembered them from their recent trips to Mikhailov. Eventually the commanding officer was persuaded to relax the rules.

As I had asked, Mother had taken Timov with her along with a few other boys so as to evade further suspicion. My boy came through, and I was very proud of him. He had thoroughly investigated the layout of the fortress. Being constructed of wood, it could be easily burned, which, of course, was to our advantage. There were also barracks that would house perhaps forty to fifty men. Timov reported that, in spite of its size, he counted no more than thirty soldiers, unless some had been out on patrol that day. Obviously the officers were anticipating no threat. Timov also noticed a large edifice in the central back near the rear set of stairs, which led to the walls. There was Russian writing all over the building, and in all likelihood, these were warning signs. It was a rough-hewn building and not at all like the officers' residence closer to the center. This building provided easy access to the stairway to the wall, so Timov suspected it contained the garrison's stash of artillery. A couple of well-aimed fire shafts might just set the whole place on fire. Timov had scrupulously drawn all this on a sheet of paper. Hazir and I were overjoyed at this unexpected piece of information.

Mother suggested that we, being an army, should perhaps look like one. The Russian soldiers all dress the same way; why shouldn't we? She made the observation that if we all looked alike, our tribe could not be identified. The Russians, at least those who might escape and report on the battle, would not be able to accuse our tribe of the slaughter. She had spoken to the wives and mothers of some of our officers and fighters, and all had agreed to make specific uniforms. The long knee-length shirts would be made of light-blue wool, the color of the sky; under which we would wear a jacket of boiled leather, which we use as armor. We would wear dark red-brown pantaloons tucked into our leather boots. Since it was summer and still hot, we would wear turbans like the Turkish militia. The lower part of our faces would be covered. This might cause more terror than seeing a band of Tatar ruffians on a raid. We all cheered her insight.

Later, Kattu overtook me on the way back to our tents. He remarked at how surprised he was at Timov's intelligence and how perceptive he seemed to be. He and Kattu had worked on the diagrams together. He also told me that Timov knew how to read and write not only Turkish but even a little Russian, which Timov called Slavonic. Obviously, Timov was clever enough not to mention Greek. So because of Nissim and his brother, I was fortunate to have access to reading and writing since I was too busy to learn to read for myself. Until those past few weeks, I never knew what I had had available to me in my very own yurt.

When I got back to our yurt, I poured out all my plans to Nissim—all my hopes, all my feelings, and all my anxieties. I gave Timov the day off, but he asked if he could stay with Nissim and me. I let Nissim know how proud I was of Timov, and I could see he was visibly pleased and hugged his brother affectionately.

"Well, it seems that everyone is involved in this venture except me." He paused. Timov and I were both silent. "Bashina is pleased with my progress with the bow, but the khan doesn't want me to fight. I don't see what his concern is. After all, my archery is up to par, and Chabuk is pleased with my swordsmanship. You have seen me on the field, Tambor. Yes, perhaps I have trained only a few weeks, it is true, but I am no novice. It's just that I feel left out. Even your mother is involved."

"Yes, and even Mehtap went out to the garrison with us, and you know how she and your mother do not get along." At this Timov snickered, and I gave him a long look as if to remind him of his place.

"My friend," I said, turning to Nissim, "please forgive me. Of course you want to participate, and again I have been insensitive. No," I said slowly and pondered what I could do, "you must accompany me. After all, you are my shield bearer." I paused again. "We will obey the khan. You will not fight, but there will be something at Mikhailov which will be very important for you to do. I don't know exactly what..." I paused and grinned. "But we'll figure that out when we get there. Now, Timov, I want you to get us a jug of mother's freshly brewed kumis before we go to bed. And bring three cups."

A few weeks back, I had offered to extend my yurt for Nissim to use, but he had refused. I knew he wanted to stay by the door with his brother. It also occurred to me that he would want easy access to the outer door for his nightly visits to his God.

Therefore, I asked him, as casually as possible, when Timov had left, "Nissim, would you please pray to God for the success of this venture. I know that it may mean killing some Christians, but surely your God is just. If Christians do what is unjust and dishonorable, surely they must be dealt with. I would expect the same for my own people."

"Yes, Tambor, you can be sure of my prayers. May God's will be done!"

PRINCESS

Out of the eater came forth food, and
out of a strong one came forth something sweet.

—Judges 14:14 (lxx nets)

My dearest and most holy Father, please forgive me if what I recount next is offensive to you, but I feel it necessary to provide details for the following. Censure me after the fact, but I must write the truth. You will not surely be able to fathom the heights of my repentance until you see the depths of my sin. It is not that I was conscious of sin at the time; I believed myself to be an honorable and just person on a necessary and justified mission. Perhaps even now I have not grappled with true repentance until I recount by pen and ink what I have done.

On the Thursday of the second week of September, our band of fifty-seven Nogay Kubanshyi warriors rode for over an hour at top speed just before sunrise to the village of Mikhailov where what we called the Birch River, or Sopasi, flows into the Volga. We were to arrive fiercely with no pause before encounter. Tatar warriors are known to be able to ride into battle after two days of nonstop riding. This would be a short trip. We separated ourselves into four troops, each with a specific job. The venture was timed to exactness. When the troop from the south, led by Usta, was to overwhelm the docks on the Volga side, our troop was to come from the west and veer north to the estate. We were concerned that the rising sun would obscure our sight, but since the estate was built on a turn in the winding river, we would actually come in facing the north. Although we had never been there before, we had a more-or-less accurate map of the area, drawn up by my brother Kattu and Timov, who had surveyed the area, and in the long run was quite accurate.

There was no road going into the compound where our group was attacking, so we had to jump a small stone wall to get in. There were two small sheep gates in the wall, but we ignored them. At the same time, Hazir and his men had gone on ahead and were to conceal themselves in the woods by the Russian garrison to await the exodus of soldiers rushing to defend the estate. The Russians would be met head on by fifteen skilled archers on horseback before they could get their firearms ready. Hazir and his troop of swordsmen would then come out from the woods and attack from the rear. Archers under the command of Hazir's brother were to be camouflaged in the trees near the camp, ready to ignite their arrows aimed toward the garrison where we supposed the artillery unit inside the walls would be. The whole strategy was stealth, surprise, and swiftness. In spite of the speed, we were to be silent in order to startle our adversaries. We had learned this from the Mongols centuries before. We had inherited their legacy and their fighting style.

In the raids that we were used to and skilled at, our main emphasis was loot. We rarely encountered violence on a wide scale; the idea was to take cattle, horses, and perhaps sheep (although sheep and goats were slow animals and not easily rustled). This time, however, death and destruction were the main emphasis; loot was secondary. Everyone was to die, and all buildings were to be burned. There was only one exception, and I spoke to the khan about it. I loathed to destroy the church there. I had nothing against any god or angel, and far be it for me to arouse the wrath of any divinity. It was Nissim's job to guard the temple and anyone who found refuge in it. Although he was armed, he was not expected to fight.

This being the plan, I shall now provide some details. The manor house was on a hill overlooking the wharf. It was surrounded by barns and grazing fields. Some of these pastures were outside the stone walls. It seemed that inside the outer wall, crops, which were not for grazing, were grown although I was sure the animals were taken farther out to pasture through the gates. There were small barns and dwellings on each of the three sides.

Peasants who were working in the fields fled in terror. Any who found escape inside these buildings would not survive as our warriors sent flaming shafts onto their thatched roofs. Those who were outside received an arrow or were struck down by our sabers. Inside the second wall were orchards. Baskets on the ground attested to the present harvest. Another field had a series of wooden boxes spaced carefully. We didn't know what they were so we left them alone.

Within this part of the estate was the church on an unpaved road to the north facing east. Our party took this road as it seemed to be the easiest access toward the house. The main road coming up from the dock and paved with cobble stones was inconvenient for us. Nissim stayed outside the gate to the church. Many of the peasants and servants headed for the church but hesitated on seeing Nissim. I didn't have time to see how he would handle it as we were striving on.

We were dashing toward the manor when all of a sudden, shots were fired from within the house as we approached it, or likely from one of the buildings close by. Apparently the owner had a group of bodyguards housed in a few of these buildings, which was something we hadn't counted on. One or two men fell, but because of our speed, none of the defenders could get an accurate shot at any of us. Again, a volley of arrows, some flaming, forced the men outside where they encountered our weapons. Our training had certainly paid off; our skill at marksmanship while riding at top speed was excellent. No one was to be spared.

Guns were devastating to us. They were fast, and no shield could protect our riders. It was the first time we had encountered firearms firsthand. An arrow would be less fearful because they were visible, but these bullets could not be seen. The noise was louder than our battle cry, and most of us confessed to a little fear later on while sitting around the campfire.

As we approached the house, which was on two levels (unlike the houses of most of the other boyars in Astrakhan which are low and on the ground), we surrounded it quickly. The artillery men who were part of the boyar's bodyguard slowly piled out of the guardhouse in the back, some coughing because of the smoke and one or two rolling on the grass still wet with the dew to put out the fire on their clothing. The appearance of surrender was etched upon their faces, but we would have nothing of it. A swift arrow to the heart or the slice of the scimitar across the neck finished them off. (I am amazed and regretful at this point in my life, Father, how unaware I was of these men as persons and at the same time, how easy it was to kill them.)

As soon as we approached the house Chabuk, Dalgin, and I, and about five other warriors, quickly dismounted and ran to the front door of the house and kicked it in. Another group barged into the back. I could hear crashing. Never having been inside a house before, I was at a loss as to where to go. There was a large staircase to the left side and I motioned some men to go up. This happened so quickly that each room was immediately filled with warriors. I could not imagine how fast all this was happening, and of course, neither could the inhabitants.

A few of the remaining bodyguard (perhaps three) inside the house, disheveled in appearance, ran out into the center with their rifles, but we answered too swiftly for them to put them to use. One of them had a pistol, which killed one of my boys. Another of my lads shoved a sword just under the man's rib. There was screaming and terror all around. I grabbed a servant and demanded, "Where's the master?" This was in Tatar, but the old fellow got the idea and pointed. I killed him.

Vassili was having breakfast. He wasn't wearing his wig, and a bib was tucked around his neck. He sat quite still as the four of us rushed in. He did not look afraid, but I could see wrath welling in his eyes and consternation as to what to do. The table where he was dining provided a small but temporary fortification.

The servants flailed around in confusion, and a few got struck down; the ones that didn't, made it to the back, presumably to the kitchen. Their attempt to survive our attack was in vain. We did not allow a place of safety anywhere. From the upstairs, we could hear crashing and screaming.

Chabuk was behind me, and Dalgin was behind him off to his left. I could hear others climbing the stairs at the spacious hall we had entered. There were more shots fired.

Until then, my eyes were fixed on Vassili, and his on mine. He perceived his imminent death; nevertheless, he seemed to be waiting for a moment of weakness wherein he could do some damage. And he got it just for a moment. Out of the corner of my eye, I saw another warrior behind him who distracted me so that I briefly turned aside to look. What I saw in fact was a large mirror, something I had never seen before, and the warrior I was staring at was myself. The image of what I saw could have been any of us as we were all dressed the same. What caught me off guard, however, were the bright green eyes staring from behind the mask. That moment gave Vassili enough time to reach into a drawer and grab a pistol. It would have been wise to pause and aim, but in the panic of the moment, he shot wildly. This sobered me immediately.

It didn't take a moment before I saw Chabuk leaping over the table to sink his saber into Vassili's neck. That swift blow killed him. At once I heard a shriek from the hall that led to the kitchen, and a tall hefty woman charged toward me with a large kitchen knife in one hand and, what I was told later, was a heavy metal candlestick in the other.

She lunged at my arm with the candlestick but overreached. The wrist hit my shoulder, and the candlestick went flying. She moved back and threatened me with her knife, shouting angrily at me in some wild language, and charged again. I sliced at her arm with my saber and heard it snap and shoved the silver dagger, which I had in my left hand, into her gut. She collapsed.

Dalgin had been hit. Vassili's shot had hit him somewhere in the leg just below the knee. Chabuk was holding him up, trying to encourage him in his rough way. Dalgin was in pain; it showed on his face, but he uttered not a word. Two others came and tried to lift him up gently. Then I heard the church bells deep, heavy, and slow; not the joyous sounds I was later to think of as welcoming. This sound apparently was the warning. It then occurred to me that this was how the estate was supposed to alert the garrison. I wondered why that part of the siege had not yet taken place. The timing was wrong. What were the warriors doing who were to attack from the head? They should have been engaged with the Russians by now. But in that very moment of concern, I stopped in my tracks.

Emerging from behind the heavy velvet curtains in the dining room was the most beautiful sight I had ever seen. There before me in the empty room, as though she had been waiting for me, stood a young woman with red-gold hair, simply but richly dressed, with a blue stone at her neck matching her eyes. Our eyes met. She was not afraid.

She said quietly in the Tatar tongue, "Take me with you, please. Take me away from here. Rescue me from this prison." She held out both of her hands and said, "I have no weapon warrior. I am helpless."

I put my sword into the scabbard and the dagger into its sheath, red with the blood of her mother, and reached out for her hand. Our eyes met again as she took mine. In the midst of the entire furor around us, there was a moment of incredible peace.

But this was not to last long, for in the distance, I could hear the trumpets blaring and knew at once that the soldiers were leaving the garrison. The bells stopped. At the same time, I could smell smoke from the kitchen area and knew that the house would be ablaze within a few minutes. We had to get out, but there was one thing I had to do. Seizing the candlestick from the floor where it had dropped, I picked it up and flung it at the mirror which smashed to bits, and I saw my image disappear. We rushed into the foyer where a few warriors were making their getaway amidst the bodies of the servants on the carpets and stairway.

As we stepped out, we saw Chabuk on his steed with Dalgin tied to his body with a rope. I mounted Onyx and reached down to pull up the woman who perched herself sideways in front of me, as her skirts were too voluminous for her legs to go across. We drew near to Chabuk, and I asked how Dalgin was doing.

"Look at him!" he exclaimed at me angrily. I never knew whether Chabuk was angry or not, but looking at his face, I knew he was grieving.

"Go home, brother. See if Lazim or Uyari can fix him up. You did well, brother. It's you who was the hero." I actually felt he was comforted.

Dalgin was in a swoon and was lying forward on his brother's shoulder. Chabuk looked at the woman I was holding and snorted, "It looks like *you* got the prize."

At this point, I realized that the other warriors had gathered around us. I pointed to two of them and told them to attend to our wounded. Already, smoke was billowing out of the house. "Leave the dead. They will burn honorably in the midst of the defeated enemy."

The rest I told to go north and reinforce the troops fighting the soldiers. I could hardly get the words out of my mouth when we heard a tremendous explosion. None of us had ever heard one before, and the horses balked and neighed in fear. From the north by the river, we could see a huge mountain of flame and black smoke dirtying the sky. We had never seen such a fire!

"You'd better go immediately!" I commanded. "Come back by way of the church. Kill everyone! If we have wounded, bring the ones that will most likely survive. We'll gather the dead tomorrow."

The horses were so jumpy I found it hard to keep the young woman from falling off my steed. When the horses calmed down, I made my way to Nissim by way of the dirt road to the church.

Chabuk left me and rode quickly, saluting Nissim as he went past. We looked behind and saw Vassili's beautiful house in flames. Smoke was also wafting into the air from down the hill where the docks were, and I was confident Usta had done his job.

A few moments later, a small dispatch came after us to report the proceedings from the dock. A young warrior, a nephew of Usta, described the scene. "Our troop," he said, "swung around the outer walls of the estate according to plan and connected with the road that followed the southern shoreline from the east. There was some private militia stationed there in a few buildings with small holes used for rifle fire. They must have heard the shots and our war cries from up the hill because they were ready. We were the ones taken by surprise. These buildings turned out to be guardhouses at the most southerly point in the complex. (It seems that Timov and Kattu had incorrectly identified these as storage units.) The guns took down a few of our men. But we were quick to respond. Obviously these men were unaware of how accurate our bows can be even when we are mounted on horses. We had flame, which we fired into the buildings, driving them out. Usta commanded half the troop to finish the job while he proceeded with the rest toward the ship which also had guns. We lost some warriors, Lord Tambor, but when Usta sent us to you, things seemed to be under control. We met your men on the way."

The woman turned to me and in a low voice said, "This was well planned, wasn't it?"

"We are skilled, my dear," I replied. "We learned the art of war a thousand years ago."

Nissim was at the church gate, and as we approached, we saluted each other. All was quiet.

I said to the woman, "This is Nissim, my companion. I don't know your name."

"Katya" was all she said.

"Well, Nissim, this is Katya."

"And what shall I call you, sir?" she asked.

"I am Tambor, Lord of the Nogay warriors and son of Dalgali."

"Dalgali? Isn't he the merchant everyone talks about?" she replied.

I replied, "My father is a trader."

Then she noticed a body beside Nissim's horse.

"Oh my dear god, that's Petya!"

"Well?"

With the slightest hesitation, he answered me, "Well, sir, here I was guarding the gates and letting the refugees in, mostly children and a few women, once they realized what I was here for."

"There was a small school here for the laborers' children," Katya interrupted. "Petya is…was a farmer in that farm over there." She pointed to a small thatched farmhouse burning. "These were serfs."

"Well, sir, Petya attacked me on a mule with a pitchfork and a scythe. I thought he was coming for refuge, but he was actually coming to attack. I tried to dodge him, but he kept on barreling in on his mule. I knocked him off, but that was even worse because he then attacked me on foot. I feared for Cereyan who reared a few times. The priest kept calling out: 'No, Petya! No, Petya!' but the boy wouldn't stop. Honestly, Tambor—er…Sir Tambor, it was either he or I who would be killed. So I knocked him with the flat of my sword hoping to render him unconscious, however the blow killed him. He can't be more than Timov's age."

"He was fifteen." Katya said, making a strange sign over his body. "His mother was a widow and was always sick. I often nursed her. Matushka, that is the priest's wife, and I were often there." She paused, "Sir Tambor, may I talk with the priest?"

"Speak to him, but mention no names."

"*Batushka*, are you all right? Where is *Matushka*?"

He replied in Russian, "She was with Petya's mother. I presume both are dead. There are about fourteen children in here including my three. The warrior did his best not to harm Petya.

It was Petya's foolishness that got him killed." She translated the words for us.

Nissim replied in Macedonian Slavonic, "Say a special panahida for him, Batushka. He was a brave warrior and died a warrior's death."

I told Katya, "Ask him to forgive me for his wife's death." She did.

The priest called to her, "Take my horse, Princess. I'll make do with Petya's mule. Chenko is around the back."

"Princess?" I mused as it was being translated.

I let her down and asked Nissim to fetch the horse. "Batushka, I know it is a hard time for you, but may I have your blessing? I am going with these men," she said and turned to me translating.

The priest replied, "Let me give you something. Wait for a moment."

As Nissim was coming around from the back, he remarked that this was the first time he had seen the doorway empty all morning. I presumed it was because there were no more refugees. But the priest quickly returned with two pieces of painted wood upon which two portraits were depicted. They could be opened since they were joined with hinges. It showed two women, one on each of the wooden pieces, face-to-face, one holding a baby and the other holding a cross. I later learned that these portraits were icons, and that this format was called a diptych. Katya folded her hands as the priest handed them to her, and she kissed his hand. He said something quietly to her and made that sign over her.

Later on, Nissim told me that, although he could only barely hear him and was not sure of his Russian dialect, the priest told her to go with God's blessing into the new life she had been praying for and warned her not to fall deeply into sin, but that God's forgiveness was abundant.

"He also said that he felt you were an honorable man and that he would pray for you."

"Hmm," I thought, perhaps a little wryly. "Now I have a priest praying for me, presumably to the same God as Nissim's, I can't go wrong now." I mused later with some amazement that he would pray for me, who was responsible for his wife's death.

The warriors were coming back. Little by little, the rest of my men were gathering and wending their way toward me. We were to have come together a little farther up the road before the church, but there we were and there we might as well stay until we were altogether. I asked Nissim to have Katya mount the horse and retreat into the grounds of the church until we were altogether and asked him then to join me. The priest, with the help of a peasant woman, was already dragging Petya's body toward the church, but Katya remained mounted, staying somewhat apart from the gathering troops, watching.

These were the men who rode with me: the captain, an older and respected man, and a young officer. The captain began his report. He said that all the houses and dwellings, barns, and sheds had been destroyed. I looked back to see the manor house. It was still burning but was essentially destroyed. Only the stone fire places, and chimneys, and the iron stove stood. The younger officer reported that all of Daruvenko's militia had been killed. However, three of our men had been killed by gunfire. One was a young man with a family, and two were from our boys, one a relative of mine. I told him that Dalgin was wounded and that Chabuk had raced home with him.

Usta and his men joined us. They were a bit jaunty and perhaps a little cocky with success. They confirmed the report Usta's nephew had previously given. There had been a large shipping boat in the harbor which they destroyed. Apparently another small group of militia had been stationed at the docks that no one had counted on. We lost a few men, but all the Russians were killed by our arrows, and all the buildings had been destroyed except for the ones made out of stone.

It took a little longer for Hazir's division to return. When they did, they were a little less festive than Usta's troop. They were, in fact, a little solemn.

"What happened, Hazir?" I asked. "Weren't the plans successful?"

"Sir," he replied, "they were more or less successful, but perhaps we were somewhat off on the timing. Our troop was gathered in the woods surrounding the garrison, waiting for the signal. We expected a flare or a trumpet to warn the soldiers that Mikhailov had been attacked, but no signal came, and the ones preparing to do the frontal attack were a bit too early. They actually had to stop and hide in the trees although the woods were sparse along the road. We had hoped that they would not be seen when the soldiers made their exit. We waited, and then finally we heard the bells. There was an awful fuss inside the garrison, but finally the Russians came out in an orderly rush. But we had lost the fear advantage and had to attack from the side. Fortunately this was almost as effective. The Russian soldiers were a bit confused especially when our flank hit them from the rear. Five of our fifteen front riders were shot, but the rear flank killed all the Russians."

"So the church bell was the signal." I commented. "I noticed it when I was at the house, and yes, it seemed somewhat late to me."

Nissim spoke up, "Maybe I can respond to that. Remember I told you that the priest would not leave the doorway for the longest time. But that peasant woman you see over there came out to him, and they had a real squabble just before Petya came along. Finally, in apparent frustration, she turned away from him and barged toward the back and started to ring the bells. She actually pulled the cable for the big one as heavy as it was. It was probably the loudest."

"That sounds right," Hazir continued. "When the soldiers were all out of the fort, the archers who were up in the surrounding trees lit their arrows, and at a signal from my older brother, they were to shoot in the supposed direction of the artillery cabin.

They aimed right. Of course we wanted the soldiers out in case we were not able to ignite the artillery room, but that proved to be no problem. Still we had no idea what an explosion would be like. Tsar Ivan had used explosives against the Bulgur Tatars of Kazan a couple of generations ago and destroyed the city, but we have never had that kind of experience. Not only did the fort blow up, but many of the trees were immediately either blown over or set immediately on fire. All the archers were killed including my brother." Silence. Then quietly as if to compose himself, he added, "His body was torn to pieces by the explosives. He and the other archers were surrounded by scraps of metal and human flesh, some of it burning." More silence.

One of the younger officers finished the report, allowing Hazir to take hold of his grief. "When the Russian soldiers on the road realized that the fort had been destroyed, there was general panic. There was no place close by for them to retreat to. Mikhailov was out of the question, and the closest friendly location was two days' journey. For us, *that* is not a problem, but for a Russian, that is impossible to do without food. The only choice they had was to fight and to die. I must say, Lord Tambor, they fought bravely. It is an honor itself to kill brave and honorable men.

Then, turning to Hazir, I heard myself saying, "I'm so sorry, my friend, for your loss. Know this, it is also our great loss. We all took a chance today. Those results could never have been foreseen. He and the rest of our dead are heroes, and they shall be remembered as such with honor. The khan will commemorate them before Tengri, I assure you." I paused. "Are there any wounded survivors?"

A few voices shouted out: "Aye, sir, they are strapped to our backs!"

"Then you'd better head back to the Birches to have them attended to." I called out to the troops: "We shall send servants back here for the dead tomorrow to usher these brave ones properly to Erlick in the underworld." (As you know, Father,

Nogay nobles do not touch the dead.) "The rest of you round up all the horses now and gather enough sheep to give us a meal at camp. We'll take what is left of the surviving livestock tomorrow. The rest of us will meet at the camp set up half an hour from here as we have planned." I was quite sure we would not be interfered with, and I was right. We were told by my father's sources that a Russian troop came to inspect the damages a few weeks later, but nothing came of it.

As we approached the camp, we could hear drums in the distance. Katya stayed close to me on the left, saying very little. Nissim was dutifully to my right, and beside him, Hazir. My men had gone ahead with Usta's troop, and I suppose they had all begun the festivities.

I motioned to Hazir to draw closer, and Nissim fell back. "Do you want to be excused, my friend? You will have sad news to take to your brother's family."

He paused as if to think. "My lord, I came here for victory, and we have been victorious. My brother came also for victory, and because of him and many others, we have achieved it. He was glad to die as a Nogay warrior, and he is a pride to the Kubanshyi. I shall drink kumis this day in his honor."

I reached over and held his hand. "Captain Hazir," I believe I smiled, "it fills me with pride to hear these words. The warrior spirit still thrives among us, and we carry the blood of our fathers in our veins. I am honored to war with you."

With these words, we entered the camp.

A cheer greeted us loud and joyful. Usta, who was still mounted, approached us with a goblet of kumis, which as he handed it to me, the warriors roared again. Another horseman handed a cup to Hazir and one also to Nissim. Nissim drank and raised my free hand and another roar ensued. Another soldier on foot, one of my men, came between Katya and me questioning with his eyes if he should help her down. I nodded. He reached out his hand, and she dismounted gracefully.

He said to her quite respectfully, to my surprise, "There are other women in the camp, basically servants. You need not be afraid, my lady." She smiled sweetly at him. I couldn't for a moment ever see her afraid.

Hazir and Nissim dismounted along with Usta's men, and I alone was mounted. Drinking the last drop of kumis, I lifted up my cup, and the crowd roared again. I decided at this point that a few words were needed.

"My fellow warriors." All became quiet. "My fellow warriors, you cheer me as though I have done some great thing, and indeed I am tempted to enjoy your praise. But I will not. What I will do is ask you, my men, to reflect upon what we have done over the past few months of training. Oh yes, we have trained our steeds and perfected our bowmanship. Our spears were sharp, and our steel was swift. We have planned stratagems, and even our women have participated in our war effort. And we were good! Yes, we were good!" Another roar. "But what is more important, my fellow Kubanshyi, is that we have revived the warrior spirit." They were all quiet now. "We are all heroes in this because we all fought as one. And behind all this was the inspiration and wisdom of our great leader Akilli Khan." A great roar erupted. I lifted both my hands. "Praise be to Tengri, the immortal Sky, who has shone upon us and destroyed our enemies. He is just and has brought us this sign of his favor. Never again shall we languish and take second best. For we are Nogay warriors, and we are proud of it!" *Enough talk*, I thought.

"We feast here because we need to refresh our bodies and relax our minds. But the real feast is tomorrow when we bring our victory home to the Birches and to Akilli Khan."

I dismounted and was met with embraces of affectionate respect and was led to the officer's tent accompanied by Nissim, Hazir, and Usta. For a moment, I lost sight of Katya, but I saw Nissim and the other soldier go after her. I deeply wished Chabuk and Dalgin were with me. The drums and the pipes began again. You know, Father, I actually felt alone.

We sat on some plain carpets, Nissim and Katya slightly behind us. A servant woman brought some food to Katya and asked her if she wanted to help them serve after eating.

Katya responded not unpleasantly, "If that is what my Lord Tambor wishes, then I shall do so, but not until he gives me leave."

I turned to the slave and said, "The princess is my guest. She stays here." The woman blushed and withdrew, but I noticed her paying special attention to Katya from then on and even chitchatting. I must say that I was somewhat surprised at Katya's ability to speak the Tatar tongue, but I also recognized her Kirym—that is, her Crimean accent and her need to pause every once in a while for the right words. *That will change.* I thought to myself.

Then it hit me as though I had been struck. *What have I done bringing her here? I was supposed to have killed everybody. Is she a spy? How did I let her get away with it?* Again I remembered how impulsively I had acted toward Nissim, whom I also should have killed. And then I thought more. *What is in it for her? We just killed her father and mother, and she is now eating in our tent. And what was this blessing that the priest had given her, saying she had been praying for a new life. Was it because I was attracted by her beauty and her helplessness? Did I do this from the same sentiment as I was moved by Nissim's stripes? I was happy for Nissim, but what will happen to her?*

Then I noticed her drawing close to me. The kumis had had its effect on the others, and everyone except Katya and I was engaged in conversation. I noticed that she had let down her golden red hair and a strand was covering her cheek. When I reached to push it over her ear as I would have with Mehti, she drew back sharply.

"I was not going to hurt you. I just noticed you have let down your hair. It is very beautiful. I have never seen red hair."

"I'm sorry, I was startled. I took the pins and clips off and threw them away on our way here. Now that you have your turban and face mask off, I'll have to say that I've never seen such green eyes. They were even more stunning when that was all of your face I could see." She smiled.

Nissim was talking to Hazir, perhaps comforting him, so I felt free to talk to Katya. She seemed to be concerned about something, so I remained quiet to let her open up.

She said, "Was it your brother who was wounded?"

I nodded. I was curious.

"He seemed to have been shot in the leg." She looked at me for confirmation and continued. "I'm concerned. I have some knowledge of the healing arts and have dealt with gunshot wounds before. What I am worried about is that if he doesn't get some attention immediately, he may lose his leg to infection and perhaps even his life."

I looked at her amazed.

"Oh, don't be so startled," she continued. "I used to make rounds with a wise woman when I lived among the Tatars in the Crimea. Does your settlement have a wise woman?"

"Oh yes!" I grimaced. "And she hates me."

"Well, she and I will have to get along if we are to help your brother. I am sure she has collected much of what we need. Perhaps we can save his leg and perhaps his life. But it is urgent. We need to get to him as soon as possible. Could we leave earlier than your army under the pretext that you need to prepare the khan for the news?"

"I suppose it is possible. Do you consider it *that* serious?"

"I do, my Lord Tambor."

We left early. In spite of the celebrations of the night before, many were up and working already when we left. Usta's men were to come with Hazir later on, but he was to stay behind and supervise the removal of the dead.

Already, long carts were being attached to the work horses that we had brought along to gather our dead. The slaves we brought were to do the work. Our warriors were to be burned in their armor with their weapons at a designated location near the camp. Nissim and Katya begged me not to cremate the Christians who, as she told me, reverence the body, as they await the General Resurrection on the last day.

"How can you expect me to have all those bodies buried? It would take days. Besides, they don't need their bodies anymore."

Katya thought for a bit. "Ask Usta, the captain, if he remembers seeing a quarry just as he was approaching the wharf. There is already a pile of stones near it. We used it for building the wharf. The soldiers could be thrown in there, and the stones and gravel thrown on top of them. No doubt the estate will be abandoned."

Usta agreed to try.

Then we were off. We could have ridden faster except Katya had to ride sidesaddle because of her billowy skirts. She did surprisingly well. When I insisted we stop for a few breaks, she seemed to want to ride on. So we did. As we neared the Birches, she noticed the vastness of our community of yurts and seemed for a moment somewhat unnerved. We slowed down.

"Perhaps you expected the Birches to be a bit smaller?" I asked. "We are one of the largest Tatar yurt villages in Astrakhan and have been here for three generations. We are not Islamic as you likely thought, as your friends were in the Crimea. The old faith serves us well enough here although some of us are Muslim. You, Nissim, and Timov are the only Christians, I think."

She turned swiftly toward Nissim, who gave his strange smile and made that sign over his body (as I thought at that time) which of course, Father, was the venerable sign of the Cross.

"That makes some sense," she said. "That explains why you respected Fr. Gleb and why you supported the burial of the soldiers. Who is Timov?"

"He's my younger brother," Nissim responded simply.

"And you, Princess," I challenged, "why did you desire to come so badly with us? Are you a spy for the Russians?" She paused to think.

"Well, Lord Tambor, I suppose you could get that impression. I never thought of that." She laughed. "I am not a spy. Do you know that all the while I stood behind the curtain, I was expecting to die and was desperately saying my prayers. Yet I was thinking and hoping that, God being merciful, this might be my chance of escape, that in fact you would rescue me. May God forgive me that moment of joy when Chabuk killed my husband and the even greater joy when you killed his mistress?"

"Your husband? His mistress? I…I thought they were your father and mother!"

Katya gave a long, low, almost bitter laugh, which startled me, for there was no humor in what I heard. She quickly composed herself and said, "My parents, who were elderly, died when we fled the Crimea during the scuffle between the Turks and the Russians a few years back. I was sent to Voronezh to my uncle, who wanted to marry me off as quickly as possible for gain. I was sixteen, two years ago, and attractive enough to make a socially acceptable marriage. Vassili Daruvenko was just the right man for their purposes. It was a profitable transaction for both parties. They told me I would never want for anything. But they were wrong. I wanted love and I wanted freedom. I tell you, Lord Tambor, even if you were to make me a scullery slave, I would be freer than I was with Vassili and Heitrun (that was her name), his German housekeeper and mistress. But I will probably be of more value to you free, than as a slave, Lord Tambor. First of all, however, let's attend to your brother."

I had not thought what would happen when we entered the village. I could hear scattered shouts of recognition. The fact that I was not with my army must have caused some concern. But it was the children who made the first noise.

"It's Lord Tambor! Lord Tambor is back! Come and see, hurry come and see Lord Tambor! Victory! Victory!" they cried, until the women and the villagers assembled, crying, "Victory! Victory to Lord Tambor and the Kubanshyi warriors!"

"Victory to the Kubanshyi Nogay!" I shouted back, and they responded. Crowds were gathering.

I leaned over to Nissim and Katya, trying to talk over the roar. "We must greet the khan before anything or anyone else."

Nissim nodded, but Katya looked anxious. "You need not fear him, my princess. He is a very noble prince himself." I attempted to reassure her.

"It is just that I am concerned about Dalgin." She almost had to shout over the roar. I nodded to her to let her know I understood, but this was the time for protocol.

It took an effort to get to the center of the town, to the large square in front of the khan's tents. The crowd was pressing hard, and people were reaching out to touch me and even Nissim, trying to clasp our hands. They looked with amazement upon Katya. Onyx and Cereyan could handle the crowds, but Katya's mare was very fidgety.

I had wished I could have had my faithful and heroic army with me, for I wanted to present them to our victorious khan. Maybe that was more important than Dalgin's leg. Katya and perhaps Nissim would not have seen it that way. Christians, I would become more aware, see many things differently. However, Nissim confided with me, later in our yurt, his regret that the army had not been with us at that important moment. Nissim was thinking like a warrior.

The general hubbub must have drawn the khan out of his yurt, for he was standing between two of his bondsmen when we arrived. He looked pleased, but a little surprised and, when he saw Katya, perhaps a bit stunned. Nissim and I raised our arms in the customary salute and waited for his signal to dismount and approach. The crowd was now silent and waiting.

He raised his right arm and commanded us to approach. Nissim turned to Katya and told her to prostrate before the khan and kiss his right hand. When she gave a strange look, he added with that almost smile of his: "Like for a bishop!" She gulped.

I thought, *You're going to have to learn a few things around here, my beautiful young princess.*

We dismounted, and the crowd buzzed. To actually roar without the khan's favor was the utmost disrespect. The three of us prostrated immediately. I waited. In my mind, I thought in my usual fashion that the best way to deal with a difficult situation was to be perfectly direct. I anticipated his reaction.

"The blessings of Tengri be upon you, Sir Tambor. Welcome back to your home. The news has preceded you. Your father, Lord Dalgali, and your brothers, Dikkatli and the mighty warrior Chabuk, have been to me already, and Captain Hazir has come home mourning. His heroic brother's soul abides with his warrior ancestors in the realms of Erlick." He paused. I hoped it was to consider. He called out to the crowd, "A cheer for our noble victor, Lord Tambor, son of Dalgali, only once until our army returns and is joined with him."

They cheered, perhaps more than he wanted. He smiled, and as he turned to me, I accepted the rebuke.

"My son"—(*Praised be Tengri*, I thought)—"what is the reason for such an abrupt return and without our warriors?"

"Noble Akilli Khan, fortune smile on you forever, may I present to you Princess Katya, who requests of you a favor," I began.

"Princess Katya? Well, Princess Katya, I take it you are Russian." She nodded respectfully.

"How is it, Princess Katya, that you do not give me your patronymic?"

"Yesterday, noble Khan, I was Princess Ekaterina Milanova Daruvenko. Now that I am widowed, I am simply Katya, a willing subject of Akilli Khan, liberated by Lord Tambor, Nogay warrior, who is your devoted servant."

The khan smiled and dismissed the crowds who were still bubbling with mirth.

"That is a good start, Katya, subject of Akilli Khan. Do not be surprised if you still get called Princess. We have few around here. I should normally invite you to tea, but you seem to have some urgency. What is your request, Katya?"

"With all due respect, noble Khan, one of your warriors has been wounded, and I believe I may have the skills to help him save his leg and perhaps even save his life."

"I have many wounded warriors, Katya. But I presume you are referring to Dalgin, son of Lord Dalgali, am I correct?" The khan was challenging her, perhaps to test her nobility.

"You are exactly correct, noble Khan," Katya took a deep breath. "Time is of the essence. If we can deal with the wound before infection sets in, we can save the leg. It is already somewhat late."

"Go to it, Katya. You will work with Uyari and anyone else you need. Tambor and Nissim, make sure everyone cooperates. The recovery of the wounded is rare, my dear. If you can do something, we would appreciate it. Oh yes, just answer two questions. How is it you speak our tongue, and how did you learn the art of healing?"

"I spent a lot of time with a wise woman, a Kirym, when I lived in the Crimea with my parents some years ago."

"Ah, that accounts for your Kirym accent." He paused. "You are expected for tea after your mission, my dear. If you are too tired, send word, and I shall see you tomorrow after you rest. You will probably need new clothes. Tambor, please see to it. And Tambor, we are expecting the warriors at about the ninth hour. You will need to welcome them at the crossroads to the Birches. It is imperative you be there."

"Yes, noble Khan, so be it."

As we approached our colony, we were met with general confusion around the boys' yurt, as we called it, where the younger brothers slept. Only Kattu and I had our own dwellings, although the one I had, he and I used to share before he got married. I could see that with all the fuss and hubbub, Katya was a bit nervous.

She said to me, "Here I want to help, and I don't even have any instruments. I'm going to need a sharp knife and perhaps some instruments I can use for probing."

"Well, here's my dagger," I said, and as I took it out of its sheath, I added, "Once I clean off the blood, that is. Probably Uyari will have the things you can use."

"The khan has sent us a healer." I must have bellowed this because everybody shrank back.

Katya whispered, "Please get rid of all these people. I suppose they've come to watch the poor lad die."

"All right, everybody, clear out! Right away! Chabuk, stay here. Where's Uyari? You, boy, go to my yurt and fetch Timov." I was in command.

One of the serving maids told me that Uyari had gone for some herbs, and I sent her to get Uyari right away. Hopefully we would not have a confrontation. Katya was already on her knees talking to Dalgin. His mother, one of my father's concubines, was in a corner wailing and carrying on.

I addressed her, "Madam, I know how serious this is and how badly you must feel at this time, but your son needs quiet now. Help has come. This is Princess Katya, who is skillful in the healing arts. She has been sent here by the khan. Go to your tents now, and we will inform you of Dalgin's progress."

Credentials were needed at this time. Dalgin's mother, got up, supported by her maids. As she passed Katya, she knelt and kissed her hand thanking her with tears and then kissed me on the cheek as she passed by. She was a sweet woman and had always favored me.

Dalgin was awake, but the signs of pain were written on his brow.

"We did it, Lord Tambor, my brother," he rasped. "I brought down two of those men." He wanted me to be proud of him, and I was.

Chabuk was quiet. Nissim moved over closer to him, and I thought I saw a slight look of disdain from Chabuk, which he covered up quickly. Nissim ignored it if he even saw it and said, "Good work, Chabuk. You got the checkmate."

"Tambor got the queen!" he snarled.

I didn't know whether he meant Heitrun or Katya. Better to leave it unspoken. At that point, Uyari entered.

"Hail, Lord Tambor, and felicitations on your victory."

"*Our* victory!" I corrected. "Uyari, this is Katya, who has some healing knowledge. The khan has sent her to help."

"Thanks be to Umai! I can deal with births and conception and some minor wounds, but I have never seen a bullet wound, let alone healed one," she said this, looking Katya up and down. "Are you Russian?" she asked bluntly.

Katya answered, "Yes. Whatever you have done so far, Uyari, is exceptional. Whatever you put on this wound has interrupted the infection somewhat. I smell camphor and myrrh and something bitter, which I remember collecting in the Crimea."

The two began exchanging the names of all these herbs and how to prepare them. I couldn't follow it all. I took a deep sigh of relief that they were getting along. Then it was down to business. As we were all focused on Dalgin, Timov entered and gently pulled on my sleeve.

He was with my new boy, and I motioned to them to step out with me for a moment. I asked the boy if he could ride, and he told me, "Of course." He was Tatar. I was glad for the answer even if it had been a little flippant. I instructed him to take a horse and go out to the south east crossroads; at the first sight of the army, he was to fly back to me with the news. Timov was to get me a fresh shirt and a leather jacket.

"Right away!" I ordered. "I want you to witness the healing and help out if necessary." He looked startled. "Go! Rush!"

"Yes, Master!"

As I was reentering the tent, I noticed Mother approaching. I waited for her.

She came slowly and quietly said, "Congratulations to you, my son, on the victory of your army. Tengri has blessed you. Dalgin has been wounded as you know. I am told you have brought back a healer who is no less than a princess. Let us go in."

Katya looked at me as though I had abandoned her. I must have grinned. She turned back to Dalgin and pointed to his wound. She was anxious to inform me what the situation was.

"Look at this wound," she said, surprisingly calmly. "You can see where the bullet has penetrated. But look at this!"

She slowly turned Dalgin's leg toward the back, saying to him as he winced, "Sorry, my friend. I'm sure a warrior like you will be quite brave. Notice, Sir Tambor, that the shot, having been delivered at close range, went almost right through the calf of the leg. The wound is deep. The bone doesn't seem to be snapped, but it is probably cracked. That would be very painful. But while the bone may not be snapped, the knee cap may be slightly dislodged, see. We may have to put it back, slowly and gently, yet with some strength, so as not to break the bone if it is cracked. Uyari has kept this marvelous poultice on the wound which, for the time being has halted the infection. But, Sir Tambor, there is an added complication." She paused and continued, "When the bullet hit, it pulled some of the leather from the trousers into the wound. Let me show you."

She washed her hands in a bowl of water that had been provided; she gently placed her hand on the wound and told

Dalgin to be calm. Opening the wound with her hand, she pointed to a bloody clump inside the wound.

I had seen dead and wounded bodies on the battlefield. I had seen arms chopped off. I could imagine Hazir's brother blown to bits. Yet I felt queasy and a little sick looking into my brother's wound. I think she noticed it too but had the grace to pretend she did not. Chabuk was standing leaning against a barrier, looking but not looking. Nissim had moved behind Dalgin on the mat and held his arms when he writhed in pain. Timov had returned and was watching intently.

I asked, "Can't you just reach in there and pull it out?"

"Actually if you did that, you would cause great pain and possibly snap the bone and damage the muscles near the dislodged knee." She looked around and tried to catch Uyari's eye. "I will need some sharp instruments and…"—She looked around for the word— "…pinchers. And if someone can provide some fine gut thread, I would really appreciate those necessities."

Mother said, "I have those things, which I use for sewing."

"Excellent!" Katya said. "Try to bring them to me as quickly as possible. Oh, and yes, make sure they have been cleaned in very hot water. That's important. Can you do that?"

Mother hesitated. It was obvious she was not used to being ordered. But then, she nodded and left abruptly.

As soon as she left, Katya asked, "Who is that woman, Lord Tambor? She seems familiar to me."

"That woman," I paused, "is Lady Yerinde, the sister-in-law of Akilli Khan, and my own mother, the wife of Dalgali. She is the leader of a group of spies, which entered Mikhailov to assay the land, effectively enabling us to plan the entire estate's destruction. You have indeed met her before and tasted of her goods."

Katya said nothing.

After the silence, we noticed Dalgin trying to straighten up. He was fairly conscious all the way through, but he was obviously exhausted. Nissim tried to move him into a more comfortable position and held onto his arm as Katya wiped his brow. So far, there was no sign of fever.

"Quiet, my young friend. When I get my equipment, we'll fix things up. You will have to be brave. We shall need a good strong man with steady nerves." She looked up at Chabuk, who seemed somewhat surly.

"Nissim, you are in the very best place behind him. Pull him up gently onto your lap. You may have to hold his arms down so he will not strike my hands. Someone will have to hold his legs." Again she looked up at Chabuk. "Does anyone have a piece of leather to put between his teeth so that he will not damage them?"

Chabuk bent down and cut a piece of leather from the mat that Dalgin was lying on and, after forming it into a wad, handed it to her and immediately left the tent. I followed and saw him lean against one of the barriers in the yurt.

"My brother, don't despair," I said to him as I took him by the elbow. "You know that there are many wounded in the camp now who will not survive their wounds. Dalgin has a good chance. Katya seems to know what she is doing. Be patient. Let's go back inside."

He didn't snap at me as I anticipated. "So be it. I feel so useless. I should be helping, and Katya wants me to help. But I just can't stand to see him suffer. I know he's afraid he will never ride a horse again, and I guess I'm afraid of that too. What are your slaves doing here? Isn't there any other help?"

I decided not to notice his disdain. "I want them here because I can trust them to do the job, and I don't know anyone better than they are. Here comes Mother. Let's go back inside. Try to be positive in front of Dalgin. You know how he idolizes you."

Mother went in first with her basket and a girl slave carrying a basin for water on her head and pitcher of water under her arm. We followed. She laid her sewing instruments out on a clean towel and laid them beside Katya. Uyari came over with a fresh mixture of ointment. All three women knelt beside Dalgin, who insisted he could take the pain. Katya assured him that he would and that after the operation, he would be able to sleep. They then began washing and applying the myrrh and aloes. Mother poured a large cup of kumis down Dalgin's throat.

I gestured Timov to draw near. "Katya," I said, "this is Timov, Nissim's brother," She looked up and smiled at him. "He has a good head on his shoulders," I said. "He will help you."

"Thank you, Timov. I'll show you what to do when the time comes."

When I saw panic in his eyes, I said firmly, "Timov, I know you can do it. I am relying on you. Listen to Katya's every word and instruction."

Then Katya motioned to me and Chabuk to hold down Dalgin's legs. Now we were about to begin. She gestured to Nissim to be ready as she put the wad of leather between Dalgin's teeth. Chabuk and I each took an ankle. Katya told me not to hold so tight. She took a small knife and slowly entered the wound. Dalgin gasped and arched but did not cry out. She cut away some of the flesh near the embedded leather to make sure it would be loose and not clotted.

I could see that Dalgin wanted to reach down with his arm, but Nissim held him firmly and Chabuk kept him from kicking. Because the lower leg was immobile, I was told to grasp him by the thigh. Eventually he calmed down and took deep breaths.

"Ah, here it comes, my sweet one. It will be just a few seconds," Katya said very calmly as her pinchers probed into the wound. "Lord Tambor, hold the wound open so I can use both hands. Thank you. All right I've got it. There we go…now…that's it. I've got it. Here it is!"

She flung the leather into the tray, relaxed her shoulders, and wiped her brow with her sleeve. "Now we have to go in and get the bullet. It is a lot deeper. I hope to God the pinchers can reach that far." The two other women began wiping blood. Katya leaned over to Timov and spoke quietly in his ear. He nodded agreement.

She said to everyone, "All right, relax a few minutes. The biggest work is yet to come."

She asked the women to move back a bit and bade Timov to come close.

"Lord Tambor," she commanded, "you must hold the thigh very tight. I may have to cut. Chabuk, pull the left leg somewhat over, but not so much as to cause discomfort. That's it, perfect. My lady, please prepare the bandages you brought, and, Uyari, get ready to apply the myrrh and aloes before the bandages go on. Now, are we ready?"

Katya took a fine knife and probed the wound until she felt metal against metal. "Timov, I will have to cut into the wound. When I say, you will have to hold open the flesh wide enough to let me go in. Are your hands clean?" she asked, as she washed her own. Timov did the same. Dalgin gasped as she widened the wound. Because of the leather wad in his mouth, it sounded like a long low growl. Timov held the flesh apart.

"There it is. Dalgin, don't move! Ready, Timov?" She slid in the pinchers and probed. Dalgin's shoulders arched, and Nissim held him by the elbows. Again Dalgin let out that growl. "We've got it, Timov. I mustn't let it slip!" A fountain of blood spewed out, and Yerinde wiped it quickly. With some effort, Katya lifted the little ball of metal and dropped it into the tray.

"Now, Timov," she ordered, "reach down and feel your own knee cap. Do it!" Because he was wearing a tunic, his knee was bare. "Now feel Dalgin's. I need you to move his so that it feels like yours. Be very gentle because the bone may be damaged. The wound is bleeding, so be quick!"

Timov felt his own right knee and then Dalgin's left knee, and then holding Dalgin's right knee, with his right hand slowly pushed the knob into place with a click, or perhaps more like a thud. Dalgin nearly shrieked but didn't. I admired his strength. I was proud of both of them.

Katya felt it and said it was a good job. "Only time will tell." She added almost as though she were thinking out loud. "Now we'll need the ointment and the bandages."

The women got to work quickly. Mother had already needled the thread, and Katya expressed her appreciation. Timov squeezed the wound closed while the ladies did their work. Nissim reached over and brought a mug of kumis to Dalgin's lips and said, "Now you'll be able to sleep, my friend."

When the time came, Chabuk helped turn him over. I had never before seen him so gentle with anything. The ladies needed a pillow to separate the two thighs and when I lifted the right calf, even though Dalgin hissed with pain, the knee was able to bend. We were all a bit giddy. Chabuk went to the back of the yurt and brought back a bunch of cushions, which he placed under his brother's calf to elevate it. Nissim moved out from under Dalgin's head, and Chabuk tossed him a pillow for Dalgin's head.

Dalgin, who was drowsing off, turned to Nissim and said, "Thanks, friend." He then turned to Chabuk, reached out his hand to grasp his, and said, "Thanks, brother," as he fell asleep.

Chabuk, Nissim, and I quietly left the yurt, leaving the women and Timov inside to clean up everything. The timing was perfect for just as we came out into the fresh air, my servant came rushing up on his horse.

"Quick, Master, they're here. You have time to ride to the crossroads."

I had almost forgotten. Noticing blood on my shirt, I remembered that Timov had brought me a change. I shouted to Timov, who had already the bag in his hands. I stripped to my waste and put on the silk shirt and the dark red leather jacket. I told Chabuk and Nissim to get their jackets on and rushed to where we had left our horses and quickly rode off to the crossroads.

We were there in a few minutes, the three of us. We waited as the cloud of dust in the distance turned into a large army. It seemed large to us who had never seen the armies of two hundred thousand, which had preceded the great Chinggis Khan or even the eighty thousands of the Golden Horde. But they were my army, and I was proud of them as I lifted up both of my arms. I called out to them, and they returned my cheer. Usta led them, surrounded by his lieutenants, and as we came together we grasped each other's strong forearms. We turned and led the army into the Birches.

The crowds came out to meet us and accompanied us into the city of yurts with great shouting and festivity. Those who were smart had preceded us into the center where they would see the khan, standing proudly, surrounded by his bondsmen, with Hazir at his side. But all was silent at this point according to custom.

We warriors all lifted both our arms as was customary, and I roared, "Hail Akilli Khan and hail to the ancestors of the Kubanshyi Nogay!"

The crowd remained silent until the khan raised his hand and shouted for all to hear: "Blessed be Tengri and all the gods of the Kubanshyi people who have brought our noble Nogay army back to us victorious. And blessed be Lord Tambor and the officers of our army."

The other hand was raised and lowered as a welcome to cheer. It was a roar. Soldiers dismounted and embraced their kin. A few others embraced with sadness, and I made a mental note to see their families within the next few days. Then I became aware of my own family, mounted and led by my father. Katya was among them mounted on Chenko. Chabuk, Nissim, and I gingerly pressed our steeds through the crowds toward them and we all dismounted before the khan who embraced us warmly and led us toward the council yurt.

Nevertheless although our families entered the council yurt, the largest in the community, we officers were urged outside toward the rear. There a team of bustling servants, including my boys, were waiting with basins of fragrant water and a change into appropriate clothes according to our station.

It was that kind of thought that was so typical of the khan who walked among us congratulating us and expressing proud affection. When we seemed ready, he attempted to hush us and get our attention. It was hard though, for this moment of release was more important than the previous night.

"My men and officers, I wanted to talk to you personally as a leader toward his men before the formalities of the evening. Brothers, this has been a tremendous victory, not only in battle, and I sympathize deeply with all those who suffered loss, but this was also a victory for warriorhood. As you know, Lord Tambor's leadership has been an inspiration to all of us Kubanshyi, for he truly has the warrior spirit. My boys, for I think of all of you as my sons, at times in the recent past, I have sometimes felt that we of the Birches have become so complacent in our way of life here on the plains of Astrakhan that the warrior spirit I remember during my honorable father's day seemed to have, shall we say 'fallen asleep,' since I would never admit that it had actually died. You, my dear friends, relatives, and noble Nogay have made me very proud today. I exult in this victory of spirit, more than the victory of arms. Let us not slip back into ease. Let us be wise. Let us continue to strive for the future as we strove with energy and purpose to destroy the present enemy. Brothers and warriors, keep this spirit alive, and we shall continue to bask under the light and favor of Tengri, the all-powerful sky.

"Let us realize that the Russians who claim this land will not let us rest until we are either absorbed into the Russian system or we are destroyed. But we did not destroy a Russian at Mikhailov. What we did was destroy a pit of greed, avarice, and lust for power. These are vices that the ones we think of as enemies, also despise as much as we ourselves do. But we are the ones who dealt out divine justice, and so long as we are here and retain the warrior spirit, we shall be instruments to hold back or stave off the westernization of this land."

This could have brought on cheers, but it did not. We felt solemn. Some in fact had little understanding of what the khan was saying, but we felt in the grip of something more powerful than our individual feelings. It was that tribal oneness that all of us had in a way forgotten but which nevertheless like an unsown seed gave us our reason for living. Now this oneness had once again been aroused. The seed had been planted and was flourishing. We were Nogay, and we had pleased our ancestors again. Our khan was proud of us, and we were proud of ourselves. The khan had gathered us as a hen had gathered her chicks, a phrase which I learned later belonged to someone else. Now we were ready to be honored.

The khan preceded us into the assembly hall, which was in a large circular yurt made of bent wooden poles with walls of lattice work, draped in a wall of felt, like the old Mongol tents, which we could easily and quickly disassemble if ever we needed to relocate, something we had never had to do for two generations. We call them yurts, however the Mongols call them gers. Many of you Chuvash still use them. We could stand comfortably in this yurt, which of course was necessary at this time. We entered accompanied by cheers and greetings. I could see my father's pleasure as I tried to push by the people greeting me, in order to get to him. He, of course, was standing waiting for the khan to reach the low dais, for no one could sit or recline till then, although the food was already being passed around.

The three of us pressed toward the family, which, being a subclan, were expected to stand together. In Tatar and Mongol society, women have an equal share in festal celebrations with the exception of ritual requirements and sacrifices. This however was a victory celebration, and they were expected to be present. Mother was at her finest, although it amazed me how she could have adorned herself so quickly after the surgery. The emerald that Father had given her at Saban-Tui, was now at her heart rather than on her forehead. Dalgin's mother, Natasha, was also present clinging to Katya in wondrous gratitude. Concubines were honored women whose children were considered legitimate heirs. Another was present, but two other concubines were not present as their sons were still too young to fight.

I approached Father first, embraced him, and kissed him on both cheeks. I saw the pride in his eyes as I had seen in this very place on that day when I had been given this commission. Kattu was next to him and saw the same flushed delight in our embrace. Chabuk had already kissed Father, and I saw Nissim approach him gingerly to take and kiss his hand, but Father would have none of it and took him and kissed him as he had us. I noticed Chabuk looking at this gesture somewhat warily. Obviously Nissim was to be considered part of the family.

Mother's embrace was warm; there was no hesitation. I complimented her beauty, and she flushed warmly. I whispered in her ear that she had had no small part in this campaign and that I was grateful. However someone was missing.

"Where is Timov?" I asked her.

"Well, we sent him to attend to the horses."

I reached out and touched a servant girl who was passing by, armed with a tray of food, which I deftly removed.

"Please have someone go out to the stalls and fetch my servant Timov. Can you remember that?" she nodded. Mother looked strangely at me. "I want him to serve me, Mother. There is no reason for him not to be here."

She nodded her head as if to say that although this was not customary, there was some sort of common sense to it. But then it was Chabuk's turn to greet her, and I never saw how she received Nissim, for the khan was approaching the dais with both arms raised and when lowered, we all prostrated before him. Then he called for kumis and wine and vodka, and so the festivities began.

Dalgin's mother reached out to me and exuded warmth and gratitude, kissing me affectionately. "Bless you, Lord Tambor.

Because of Princess Katya and you, my son will live and walk again."

"Think nothing of it, my good woman. The princess was the one who saved the day. Many of us were involved." At this, I managed to pull Katya away from her grip and take her to where I could thank her myself.

"You have no idea how grateful I am at your skill and knowledge. There would be no end of trouble if Dalgin had taken sick and died. Chabuk and he are inseparable. I will confess to you that I had grave doubts that he was old enough to accompany us. That is why I kept him with me."

"Then I will have to confess to you that what I did this afternoon was only partly skill. It was mostly prayer, guesswork, and a good deal of common sense. I was as terrified as all of you seemed to be. But we won't tell anybody, will we?" At this, she laughed, and I smiled although I had to admit some amazement. But at that point, we were approaching Father.

"Well! Well! My dear son. You have delighted me, and I am very, *very* proud of you, and my boys. Sadly Dalgin is not able to be here with the rest of you. But he is alive and has survived his wound, thanks to the skills of this fine young lady. Your mother Yerinde has already introduced her to me. You boys will run along and seek your honor elsewhere. There will be plenty of time to talk. Princess Katya is from a prominent boyar family and will be the guest of me and my women folk this evening." Turning to Katya he said, "Your father and I had occasionally crossed paths."

"Thank you, Lord Dalgali. That was my husband," she said simply.

The women sighed in shock and rattled on in an embarrassed way.

Katya looked at me, and I caught a glimmer in her eyes as I moved away. Chabuk looked aghast as did Timov, who by then had joined us.

"Do you mean I killed her husband?" Chabuk whispered to me, having the good taste not to question me in her hearing.

"Don't worry, my dear brother. There was no love lost. I killed the old man's long-time mistress." We tried not to burst into laughter, which had she caught it, would have humiliated her. By that time, we were reclining below the dais and drinking a bit of kumis. Kattu had joined us, and I was very glad. Marwa was not able to join us so soon after having just recently given birth to a splendid young girl.

Nissim asked, "What actually did happen at the house?" And all were eager ears as Chabuk and I recounted everything and after much talk and laughter. Kattu asked Nissim what experiences he had had knowing that he had not come with us. So Nissim recounted his story at the churchyard. I suppose that is when I noticed that Timov was standing slightly off from us .

"Timov," I asked, perhaps more bluntly than I'd intended, "why are you standing? Sit down." I handed him my pottery cup of kumis and bade one of the serving girls get another cup.

"Master, you didn't give me leave to sit," he answered as he sat down slowly. I think I was annoyed, and maybe it was too obvious. He made a slight look in Chabuk's direction and then back to me. What I saw in Chabuk's eyes was startling. It was a mixture of awe, amazement, and downright anger. He had always seemed surly and ill tempered, but that we attributed to his speech defect; however, what I now saw was scorn, and it was directed toward me.

"What is this? Are you going to throw a party for every slave who has ever sponged your back? Or is this just a day off because of the feast?" I was just slightly embarrassed at his obvious insensitivity, especially when I saw Nissim stiffen and Timov blush with shame.

It was Kattu who rescued me. "Perhaps our brother is not aware of how important Timov was for our campaign. It was because of his keen observations, both at Mikhailov and while working with me in my yurt, that helped us plot out the plan of attack. Had it not been for Timov actually, the siege of the town would not have been so swift and successful. He and I and your brother needed his amazing recollection of Mikhailov and the garrison, and based on these very exact details, we wrote the map. None of this was done because he was ordered to do so like a slave. It was entirely on his own initiative."

"And remember, my dear brother," I said, stroking Chabuk's knee affectionately, "that if Dalgin walks again, it is because Timov put his leg back in place. Neither you nor the rest of us had the courage to do that."

"I am grateful for that. Too bad he isn't here to thank him himself."

"I'm sure Dalgin will want to do that tomorrow. And, Timov, as of now I would prefer that you call me 'sir' rather than master, and I shall remember not to call you 'boy.' For the time being, your status will be the same, but I'll expect you to attend me personally. The other boy will take care of the housekeeping, and if he needs more help, Mother will provide that."

At that point, I looked up at the dais and noticed that the khan was deep in conversation with my parents. Katya was silent but listening attentively. I wished I could hear what they were saying because she seemed a bit bothered. I saw Mother take her hand as though to support her. And at another point, I caught the khan's eye, but I couldn't read behind the look. I was sure I would find out soon enough. Nevertheless, I was agitated, thinking that decisions regarding the family were being made without my consultation.

Now that we had eaten our fill of the finest of dishes prepared in all of Astrakhan, kumis and wine began flowing, and the guests, now thoroughly relaxed, began circulating. Bashina was making his way toward us, accosted on the way by appreciative wives and mothers and congratulated by the men for the great efforts he made training the warriors. But he was heading our way with all the excitement of a boy, and when he did make it, we all stood and embraced him warmly.

"Tambor, Prince Tambor, and you, Lord Chabuk! How proud I am of you, my fine young stallions! And you too squire Nissim. You all trained very well. How all of you worked together so hard, and this is something of even greater importance." He leaned discreetly toward Nissim. "Young friend, it is a shame you were not permitted to fight. As far as I was concerned, you were ready and your skills were well developed. Even Chabuk was well aware of that."

"It was not that way, revered Bashina," we all piped in. "Nissim had his first contact with battle there when he killed a young farmer coming at him with a pitch fork and a scythe. Nissim struck him on the head with the flat of his blade, dealing the death blow."

"Please, men, tell me, tell me all about it, all of it—from your lips, not some silly marketplace gossip."

We carried on with vivid details, which delighted the old man who listened to every word.

"Sad about Hazir's brother," Bashina said after we concluded our narrative. "He's taking it hard. I told him to go home and rest. I would suggest that you and Chabuk visit him tomorrow or the next day to comfort the family. Don't leave it too long.

"We have had very little experience with artillery. I was informed that the army brought back a cartload of guns taken from the Russian soldiers at Mikhailov. Perhaps we could get some practice training. Tambor, you check it out. We must adapt to a new way of fighting even though it seems to lack sense to us.

"Oh, and yes, I stopped in on Dalgin this afternoon just before the warriors returned. He was sleeping peacefully, and I didn't wake him. To be sleeping is a blessing from the gods especially after being wounded as it was described. Others are not so favored. Take some time to visit the others, Tambor. Perhaps your young princess could accompany you and be of some service."

At that moment, I noticed that the khan had moved back to his seat on the dais and was already receiving a stream of devotees, which would flow all night. I turned toward my father, who met my look. As he stood up, I noticed, as if I had not noticed for a long time, how handsome he was, tall and lithe, his black hair flowing down his shoulders and tied with a colored band at the forehead. In his forties, he still maintained a supple vigor, an almost feline grace. I could see why Mother strove to keep him to herself. He was walking toward me. I sensed something afoot.

"Well, lads, I hope you are enjoying your victory," he started. "Drink up. This is your time. I'm proud of all of you: Tambor, Chabuk, and Nissim, for your cunning and bravery, and Dalgin for his strength and stamina, and, of course, Kattu and Timov for your cleverness in planning the siege. Bashina will agree that this is just a beginning. You must continue with your training since there may be more battling ahead." We all stood and drank.

"As you know, I shall be making my annual trip to Astrakhan in a few short weeks. It is still warm, but the birches are showing some yellow according to Lazim. We shall leave perhaps within a month. We are big on meat this year, for our flocks have well increased. We can also boast the new sheep from Mikhailov, which I am told are exceptionally fine animals. The horses that survived the battle may have to be retrained for our style of horsemanship. Bashina will have to get our warriors to retrain them. It would not be wise this year to bring them to trade so soon after the destruction of the garrison.

"I am expecting Chabuk, Tambor, and Nissim to accompany me, and I shall take a few other sons. Some neighbors have offered to send their sons also. Everyone will enjoy it. We shall take a few of our prize hawks and enjoy a little game on the way. But is most important to show a strong front and be ready to defend ourselves lest it be winded that we were the destroyers of Mikhailov."

I had not gone with Father for such a long time that even I felt it was due. But it did surprise me to see Nissim so very alert and somewhat excited as though he had gotten a prayer answered.

"Kattu," Dalgali continued, "although you have always been my right arm, you must stay home to take care of your wife and newborn daughter. Chabuk, I know that you would like to stay back with Dalgin, but I need you with me. Timov, you are to help Katya with Dalgin's recuperation. Don't be in the way, but always be available. Oh yes, and when Dalgin is better, the two of you are to examine the artillery we amassed together, but don't shoot yourselves." We laughed, except perhaps Chabuk. "Now I would like to take your captain away from you for a few moments." He took me affectionately by the elbow and urged me to walk with him.

The night air was cool outside the tent. Although it was still summer, the breeze told of autumn coming. There were still many people in the village square who tried to hail me down and congratulate me. Father politely excused me and pulled me to the back, behind the yurt where there was more privacy.

Still walking arm in arm, he said quietly to me, "My son, I will be frank with you. Do you remember how you have often said that Chabuk is too impulsive? Well, Tambor, how do you explain bringing a Russian boyar princess into our midst? Ah-ah, before you answer, I will tell you something. I believe Katya is a fine woman, very lovely and very talented, and she wants to stay, but she is an enemy. She was due to be killed like all the rest. And you left alive an Orthodox priest and a bunch of children and old folks. They should have been killed also. We were not discriminating. I know you told me that you would allow the temple to be a refuge since you did not wish to offend any god. I can accept that, but it is different with Katya. She was the mistress of Mikhailov. And now she is here celebrating our victory over her husband's destruction. *What were you thinking?*"

I was speechless. That had never occurred to me quite so vividly.

"But why you did this is not really the crucial question," he continued before I could gather my thoughts. "The question is: what do we do with her?" His pause still did not give me time to respond. "This was a pressing issue for the khan, who by the way, wants to see you tomorrow morning. However, he and the family have come to a conclusion to which we hope that you will agree is the best all round solution. In order to avoid scandal among our troops, some of whom already see this as a breach of orders, Katya must be thought of as a prize, a gift which you have brought home to offer to me."

"What?" I exclaimed.

"Hear me out!" he commanded. "This is for her safety, Tambor, you must understand. The khan of course cannot take a concubine, and a Russian wife for him is out of the question. Many have already questioned the khan about her presence here, and with disapproval I might add. Myself, I have and will have only one wife, your mother, whom I love with all my heart. Therefore the only reasonable thing is for me to take her as another concubine." He paused and scrutinized me. "I hope you did not consider her for yourself, did you?"

"No—well, that is, I had never really thought about it," I said.

"Good, good, my son, I thought you would be reasonable."

I found myself rather meek and a little sad, though I couldn't say why. "Does Katya have anything to say about this? I presume you discussed all this in front of her."

"Actually she had never really thought about it also, and she said as much. We explained that concubinage would be preferable to slavery as it would give her status among the yurts and curb gossip and prattle. Any offspring of hers would be considered legitimate. She informed us that concubinage is not practiced among Orthodox Christians, but that the Church rules that if a woman is taken in battle and becomes a concubine or even a slave, she is not guilty of sin, so I think her conscience is clear. Yerinde, your mother, is genuinely fond of her, which is a remarkable thing." He smiled at me as he said this. "And Dalgin's mother, Natasha, dotes on her and is exuberant about adding her to the family. Katya of course will be expected to give me a child."

"Well then, I guess it is all taken care of," I said trying not to sound as glum as I felt.

"Tambor, I know you are fond of her. I am your father, and I do understand. My son, I encourage your friendship with her. I tell you frankly, I will not be able to give her the attention she needs, so I will rely upon you to visit her often." He put his arm affectionately around my waist. I could never remember being so close to him. "Now I can hear the music. Let's go back inside. But I'm sure you are tired. Stay for a while and go to bed early. Remember, you are to see the khan tomorrow morning. I do not think he will be discussing this matter."

LONGING

Why are you deeply grieved O my
soul, and why are you throwing me into confusion?

—Psalm 42:5 (lxx nets)

*How I loved it up there! My wings were outstretched, and I soared
with the currents of the sultry winds of Astrakhan. My feathers
caught the flow, and I merely lay in the billows as on a bed of air. My
falcon eyes surveyed the land below and observed the business of men.
Soldiers, herdsmen, flocks filed below me in furious affairs, and from
these heights, I looked down with disdain upon them. I was safe.*

*But what was this? A lone traveler was riding across the grassy
plain. Everything was moving aside to let him pass. I watched him
intently, and a current of air enticed me to follow him. But coming to
a little hill he stopped. Even at my great height, I, the hunter, could
see his eyes as he stared up at me. What was this? Without warning,
he took his bow, shafted the arrow, and let it fly toward me. Although
I tried to avoid it, the arrow struck me just below the wing, and I
lost my sight! I panicked! I was out of control, and I swiftly spiralled
toward the ground flitting with my wings and shrieking with my
falcon's voice!*

"Tambor! Tambor! Wake up, Tambor!" It was Nissim. He was
leaning over me and shaking my shoulder. I tried to get my
bearings. For a moment, I had no idea where I was. I looked up at
a star-filled sky with the quarter moon close to the horizon. "Yes!
Yes! I'm all right, dammit!" I snapped. I was ashamed. I was
ashamed, first of all, by having that dream again. I was ashamed
too that Nissim had caught me in it again. Most of all I was
ashamed that I snapped at him.

We had come out to my secret place by the stream to spend the night under the sky. We brought our mats and some food, and we intended to relax and just get away from everything. And we were having fun. We rode all afternoon, ate the food we stole from my mother's kitchen, swam in the cool waters, and rehashed the siege of Mikhailov, just the two of us, boys. Then the dream!

"You haven't had a nightmare like that for over a year now," Nissim remarked. "Was it the same one you used to have?"

"One of them," I replied. "They used to be more frequent. You always used to wake me up, didn't you?"

"Well, you were so noisy. I didn't think you wanted your father's camp to hear you."

"Yes, yes, of course." I was calming down. "You were always thoughtful. I appreciate it. It wasn't the other dream though." Suddenly, I realized I was beginning to share with him an intimacy, which I could never have done when he was a slave. Even then, I didn't know if I wanted to go further. "Do you have dreams?" I countered.

He thought for a moment and slowly replied, "I suppose I have the occasional nightmare, mostly with regard to my slavery in Trabzon, but they are not recurring dreams as yours seem to be." He lay back on his mat and put his left hand under his head. I could see his face in the light of the approaching dawn. "Have you ever talked to anyone about them?"

He is being saucy, I thought. *Does he dare try to penetrate my dark crystalline surface?* I turned toward him and pondered. "Dreams are private things, Nissim, aren't they? I would really have to trust you as my dearest friend, wouldn't I, before sharing this intimacy?"

"Yes, I guess so." He wasn't going to let this drop. It was amazing how much Nissim could say using such few words. I lay back. I wasn't going to rush into this.

I thought about other things in the silence: my audience with the khan two days ago and Nissim's own talk with the khan. I thought about my visit with Hazir and his family and the others

I needed to see. I let my mind think of Katya and her care for the sick, and I remembered Dalgin and his painful recovery.

But Nissim was waiting. I knew it. Again I turned over to face him. Our eyes met. He was testing my friendship. In the silence, he was asking, *Do you really love me as a free man, Tambor, my lord? Are you willing to trust me with your pain?*

"Of course, you won't speak of this to anyone, right?" I probed. This was, I thought, harder than being queried by the khan.

"Who would I tell? You are my only friend. Your brothers merely tolerate me. And my own brother is still a kid."

"A very bright kid!" I interrupted.

"Even so, I would never reveal your story. I love and respect you too much."

So I told him my dream, Father Dmitri, but he was not satisfied. He wanted the other one too, the more painful one.

You remember, Father, my reference to Stenka Razin earlier on in this narrative; well, my grandfather, my father's sire, was one of the key leaders of the first attempt to destroy the city of Cherny Yar. It ended as a dismal failure. The Kubanshyi leaders under my grandfather were executed as traitors and cowards and were all impaled on lances in the sight of all Astrakhan. Stenka could be needlessly cruel. He would not believe what the warriors reported to him.

They claimed that as they were about to storm the city, there upon the city walls, appeared a single solitary boy dressed in black from head to foot. He cried out to the warriors that he had been entrusted by the Lord Jesus Christ to guard and protect the city and that the Kubanshyi were to withdraw and retreat.

Of course, we would never retreat and scoffed and cursed the child at which point the whole army became totally blind and were scattered. When their eyesight returned, they made their way back to Stenka like dogs with their tails between their legs. He mocked them and impaled the officers on spears.

I was about fifteen years old at the time, and I remember sneaking away from my parents and went into the field where the dying officers were. I remember looking up at my grandfather whom I loved. When he saw me, he spoke to me gasping for breath. "Avenge me, boy. You will not rest until you have avenged me." In my innocence, I asked him, "How can I avenge you against Stenka Razin?"

"No!" he tried to shout. "Not Stenka, child. The boy from Cherny Yar!" At this point, he made a final gasp and died.

In my dream, Father, as I told Nissim, I am the one impaled on the spear with my grandfather, and the whole village staring up at me way up in the sky. My grandfather is shouting at me: "Avenge me, boy, avenge me!" Then I fall forward upon the crowd.

I recall that day, as a fifteen-year-old, seeing Akilli, not yet khan, standing not too far from me watching. He never spoke to me about the incident, but I am sure he remembers it too.

I said to Nissim, "The khan is the only other soul who knows about this. But you are the only one who has heard this from my own lips. You know, Nissim, I have not yet avenged my grandfather. I have no peace, and Cherny Yar still stands." After a pause, I further informed him, "About a year later, a less-experienced group of Kubanshyi were sent out again, and the same thing happened, only this time Stenka himself was on the run. He was caught and brought to Moscow where he was quartered in the sight of the people. At home, the khan's father ordered that the officers who failed the mission be stripped of rank and banished from the Birches. The others were to be enslaved."

"You are left with a mighty burden, Tambor, my lord. Do you have any idea when you will be able to fulfill your promise?"

"I need more experience, Nissim. Cherny Yar is a large city, not a village like Mikhailov. I need fighting experience. In the whole of the siege of Mikhailov, I killed only one person—a woman, and a slave. No, I need a real war." I paused a little to think.

Nissim quietly responded almost as though talking to himself, "Then you and I are sort of in the same situation. Petya was only a peasant. The khan said that he was proud of how I handled the situation, and he made some remark about exercising wisdom. But I don't claim it, Tambor. It was strictly self-defense. Maybe in the long run that is what war is all about, having to make choices and hoping the one you make is the best."

It was now morning. Koyash had risen over the horizon. Both of us stood up. I raised my hands and blessed the light and Tengri, the all-powerful sky. Nissim made the sign of the cross and bowed to the ground and touched it with his right hand and stood erect. He said his prayers in Greek. (These prayers I know now in Slavonic.)

After this, we plunged into the cool waters, ate what was left from the day before, rolled up our mats, and rode home.

That day was busy. I had about four families I needed to visit. Comforting them was somewhat of a chore. Women look differently upon the death of a warrior. To a mother, a dead warrior is primarily a dead son, someone who would never come home again. I needed to remind the fathers of valor and courage. I needed to remind them that they were also warriors at an earlier time. The men were easier to comfort than the women. What could I say to the young wives and children? Death, I thought, was final. In a culture where the dead went back to the earth and would be seen no more, despair was inevitable. The girls who had lost their lovers were the saddest. One said to me with tears that the fount of her virginity was dried up. (As pathetically as she mourned, a year later, I saw her betrothed to another young warrior.) But they were all gracious and appreciative; courtesy is part of my job. The khan apparently visited only Hazir's family. I managed the rest. Nissim was very supportive to me in all this; his insights were profound.

Katya had been to see many of the wounded. She was accompanied by Timov for the most part and occasionally by

Mother, who was always busy and Uyari sometimes when she was not delivering babies. A few of the wounded had died, but a good number survived, and a few others would be able to continue training. Katya and I did not cross paths, but Timov filled us in with what he could. At least he was keeping himself occupied.

Preparations were being finalized for our trip to the capital. Father would not be traveling to Kazan this year. Father thought it would be a good experience to explore the trade routes along the north shore of the Caspian and perhaps go west to winter in the pleasant climate of Azov just inside the Turkish empire. Father represented the more nomadic aspect of Tatar life and tradition, whereas I tended to cling to the warrior life. Father, however, wanted warriors with him this year. He wanted to show that the Nogay were still around. To get to Azov, we would have to travel through Kalmykia and the Caucasus, and perhaps visit the Kuban. But nothing was decided as yet. Trade was always the main reason for the trips. Father was a rich man, and he wanted to be known as such. None of this was to happen, of course. Other things were to occur.

I was actually anxious to go. It would be a break from my heavy training. Nissim would be with me; he seemed excited. Chabuk was expected to go as he had had some experience working with father, but he showed some reticence to go as this would mean leaving Dalgin behind still recovering from his wound. Apparently Dalgin had some trouble mounting his horse as his leg had not gained its former flexibility. This made Chabuk grumpy and constantly irritable. What was worse was that Dalgin and Timov were becoming friendlier than he would have wanted. He was always very sarcastic in Timov's presence, and his speech impediment did not help.

The khan felt that Hazir would benefit from the trip so as to provide a distraction for him. However he had not yet approached him with it. The siege of Mikhailov was a catalyst in bringing many relationships together.

I once asked Nissim why he was so excited about the trip. He was somewhat secretive about the reason. I spoke frankly, "Listen, my friend. I let you into my private life a little while ago. You shouldn't have the advantage over me. Come on. Tell me."

He laughed. "I suppose you are right. Well, your father says we shall be in Astrakhan in November, which is when I celebrated my name's day. We don't emphasize birthdays in our faith. In fact, I don't even remember the day I was born. But I will consider myself eighteen on November 2, the feast of Saint Onesimus. Besides that, there is a cathedral there where I hope to make my confession."

"Your what?"

"My confession. There will be a priest there to whom I can bare my soul and tell him all my sins. He will pray to the Lord for me and pronounce God's forgiveness upon me."

"He can forgive your sins?" I was astounded.

"No...no. The ancient apostles were told by Jesus that whatever sins they loose on earth will be loosed in heaven, and whatever sins they retain will be retained. So this commission was given in turn to the bishops and their priests until Jesus comes again."

"How convenient! And what if the priest decides to retain your sins? What then?"

Nissim smiled and flushed a little. "I suppose I will have to be humble and come back when I am ready. I think in that case, the priest would have sensed that I am not truly repentant yet. I'd have to take the chance. The priest will also give me instruction as to how to avoid temptation in the future and if necessary give me a penance."

I said almost seriously, "Perhaps I shall make my confession some day. How about that?"

"The trouble with you, Tambor, is you don't think you have any sins."

I thought about it. "I do have some regrets, Nissim. Maybe, in the future, I'll be sorry for everything I've done."

He put his arm around my shoulder. "That is something we will all have to do, hopefully before it's too late."

Timov approached us. "I suppose you want to accompany us to Astrakhan and make your confession too."

"God knows I need it!" He grinned. "But your father and the khan wish me to stay behind. I think it was mentioned that Dalgin and I are to examine the artillery. Princess Katya has also asked me for help. She, your mother, and Uyari think I have potential." At this, he burst into hilarious laughter. Nissim turned away biting his lip.

"All right, you two, what's so funny?"

"Can you imagine? I could become the first Christian shaman in the world and take over Lazim's job."

"Now don't be disrespectful, brother," Nissim scolded. "Lazim is a noble man and well respected, with all his rattles and smoke. Besides, the Princess is Christian and is as much a wise woman as Uyari and she still honors God."

"If you can learn from them, so much the better, young pup. Besides," I added, "I'm not going to release you until you can show me how profitable you can be."

"Forgive me, sir. I forgot myself."

I saw Katya and Mother in the distance entering one of the yurts. It amused me to see her in Tatar clothing, a dress which I thought I had once seen on Mother. I asked Timov. "Do they need you now?" I asked, motioning toward the two women.

"No, sir."

"Well, do you have any business with me?"

"Actually, I do, sir, if you will permit me."

"Go ahead, by all means." I was amused; I felt like the khan when he questioned *me.*

"Well, you know sir, that you have your own herd of horses, which you took when you destroyed the Kurds. Chabuk gave his share to your father, but you kept your own. Well, this herd has been breeding, and you have increased—much. You also took a fair share of the horses from Mikhailov, which again were added to your herd."

I was fascinated. "Go on."

"Yes. Well, I took the liberty to count your herd and separate them even further, even though I was becoming a nuisance to the stable master and herdsmen. I…uh…told them it was my job and that I worked for you. You may not know, but the horses that you took after the siege are not branded, not even the soldier's horses. Neither are the cattle that you received. You have also a small flock of sheep, although your father took most of the sheep from the Kurds and some from Chabuk's share last week. A couple of dozen were added to yours this month from the Mikhailov flock—to be exact, twenty-five. They are of a northern breed and are quite vigorous. I took the liberty of keeping the Mikhailov herd separated from the rest."

"What are you driving at, my young hawk?"

"Well, sir. You are a very rich man!"

"Indeed!"

"Yes. I have taken the liberty to write down an account of all your livestock and have instructed your herdsmen to keep your flocks, herds, and cattle separate from the rest." He read the figures to me.

For a moment, I was speechless. When I recovered, I put my hands on his shoulders and looked him straight in his eyes. "Why you crafty little dragon! While I am away, instead of playing with the slaves in the streets, you are out counting horses! What can I say but that I am exceedingly grateful?"

"Oh thank you, sir." He went on nonplussed. "If you want to bring some livestock with you to Astrakhan, maybe your father could spare some herdsmen so that you could market your own animals like the other nobles. *You* would have the added advantage of accompanying them, unlike most of the others who leave it to your father and their own stewards." He smiled.

I realized that I liked his smile because it was completely without guile. I turned to Nissim, who was looking dumbfounded. "Your brother is no kid, my friend. Never think that." And then to his brother, I said, "Well, Timov, it's getting late now. You will have to show us everything tomorrow. Let's visit your friend Dalgin and see how he is doing. I am told he is up and walking."

Dalgin was indeed walking but with the use of a cane. As we approached the boy's yurt, we noticed him outside apparently practicing and exercising. He smiled, sweetly and perhaps, I may add, sadly. He always seemed quiet to me, a dreamy sort of lad always somewhere else. I could never see why he had such an attachment to Chabuk who obviously was his hero.

"Welcome brother," he said warmly. "So you have come to visit the invalid." He winked playfully at Timov and nodded to Nissim.

I said, "I came to visit a brave man—a survivor! I am proud of you, Dalgin, and I shall yet be proud of you."

He gave his cane to Timov and started walking. "The pain has more or less gone, Tambor but I have little flexibility in my knee. At least I can walk, but I fear I shall never be able to mount a horse again."

"Nonsense!" I heard a voice from behind. "Greetings, Lord Tambor. This young warrior is talking nonsense again." I turned to see Katya and my mother sauntering toward us. I confess, Holy Father, my heart started pumping. I had been avoiding her somewhat especially with my father in camp. I was startled again by her beauty. Still I could have laughed at her dressed in her Tatar costume and hearing her Crimean accent. She pulled me aside. I motioned to Timov to distract Dalgin while I talked to her.

"You know, Chabuk is the real problem," Katya said. "I had to insist he go out to the training fields today just to leave the poor boy alone. His whole attitude is one of despair and gloom. I am so glad he is going to Astrakhan with you."

"What do you mean?" I asked.

"Tambor, you will be a good influence on Chabuk. He should be glad his brother is alive, but instead he makes him feel like an invalid, like someone who has no longer any life. The person Dalgin needs most is Timov. He gets him laughing and joking, and Dalgin treats him like a friend rather than a slave. Although Chabuk regularly insults Timov, he reacts in a lighthearted way and reverses the insult to get even Chabuk laughing. You know the khan has commissioned the two of them to inspect the artillery we took from the Russians."

"Well, yes." I replied thinking with some amusement of her use of the expression "*we.*"

"Think about it, Tambor." She was serious. "Some of the horses that you warriors took were soldiers' horses with Russian saddles. Even if Dalgin cannot use the short Mongol saddles which enable your legs to fold back, he would be able to use the long Russian saddles which would encourage him to stretch both legs straight."

"Where are these saddles?"

"They are all piled up in the back, on the other side of the stables. Timov knows where they are. This was partly his idea. But we have to get Dalgin away from Chabuk, so he can develop different ways of dealing with things."

"Yes, you are right, Katya." At the use of her name, she raised her eyes to mine. I continued, trying to seem businesslike. "You and Timov can work with Dalgin, and Nissim and I will work on Chabuk." She smiled. I needed some air even though we were outside. In a moment of folly, I asked her. "Are you happy here?"

She blushed, and looking up, she met my eyes again. "It's taking a bit of getting used to. I am given a lot of freedom and much affection, which is a pleasant novelty. Your mother is wonderful, and Natasha is warm and sisterly. You know she is a Cossack and a Christian, don't you?"

"Actually, I don't." I thought again wryly of how little I did know.

"You should speak to her and hear her story. Natasha's father owed Dalgali a large sum, which he couldn't pay either in money or goods, so he offered his daughter (obviously not the eldest) as a concubine, perhaps fearing the Tatar vendetta. Besides Dalgin, she gave Dalgali another son, Zachary and two daughters, Natalia and Lyuba as of course, you know. He often takes her on his trips since Yerinde has stopped accompanying him. She came back pregnant three times.

"Your father is kind and gentle, Tambor. He may not love me, but he treats me with affection and appreciation."

When we returned to the boys, we found them chatting and joking, and even Mother was laughing. Dalgin was walking better, and Timov had rested his cane against a wall.

"See what I mean?" Katya remarked.

"Yes."

The mood was charged with good will, which did not let up even when Chabuk returned with his servants. Yerinde said we would all eat outside and instructed the servants quickly to prepare the evening meal. Father joined us and Natasha too, as well as the other concubines. We laughed and sang all night, and even got Dalgin singing and dancing until the pain set in. Dalgin never used his cane again, but he was never able to flex his knee as he used to.

A week later, we were ready to leave. Father did, in fact, give me a few herdsmen. When I first asked him, he was a little taken aback, I could tell. However, when Timov presented him with the figures on my livestock and herd, he looked at me with amazement. "Well, my son, it looks like you are independently wealthy. What can I say? Too bad Timov cannot accompany you as a steward." He paused, smiling approvingly at Timov. "I have not thought of you as a businessman, Tambor, I shall confess." He thought for a bit and then spoke, "I shall give you four herdsmen and one of my best stewards to make sure that no one cheats you." He laughed. "Yes, Tutumlu will do fine. He is a stubborn and testy person, but he is very honest and not self-seeking. I gave him and his family his freedom a few years ago because the Russians have trouble doing trade with slaves. You may know his son who was part of Usta's troop at Mikhailov."

I remembered. "Tetik, I believe. He was wounded, wasn't he?" I asked.

"Wounded in the left arm just above the wrist. Katya says it became infected and had to be amputated. Timov, you had to help, didn't you?"

"Yes, my lord. I had to cut the bone. The infection fortunately had not got into the marrow. Katya said we caught it in time, and so we removed the hand just above the wrist. Tetik was given a jug of kumis to kill the pain." He sighed. "It was my first amputation. It was hard at first, but I have become used to it. Katya and Lady Yerinde said they needed a man's strength. So I'm the one!"

"Katya has asked me to obtain some opium from the Asian caravans or some hashish from the Turks," Father said. "Apparently they are better pain killers than kumis. I must admit, Tambor, very few of our wounded actually died from their wounds. Many are not able to function fully, as is true with your brother, but they *are* alive."

"How is Tutumlu taking it?" I inquired.

"Of course, he regrets the impediment, but both he and Tetik's wife are grateful to Katya's team to have him alive. I will speak to him tomorrow. It might be good for him to get away. The herdsmen are my own. Oh yes, just to let you know, both Tutumlu and Tetik are expert hawkers. Perhaps we could enjoy some hawking on the way down." (I thought of my dream.)

"We should be ready to leave in two days hence," Dalgali said, and we were, although we were two weeks behind schedule. The birches in the sacred grove had already turned yellow. Of course we had not counted on the delay caused by the aftermath of the siege. This trip would be different, and since I had never been on one, it would be very different for me. Father confessed that he already felt my older brother Kattu's absence. He had followed Father for four years or more and was well aware of the route and the routine. Chabuk and Dalgin had accompanied him before, but they were young at the time and, I assumed, played more than traded. Tutumlu was an expert in these trading treks, but he was assigned to me this time. Tetik had decided to come along in spite of his injury. He would stay with our herd under the close watch of his father. This meant Chabuk would be with our father.

The day before our departure was one of celebration. The khan brought us together in the large tent where family and friends could express their well-wishes for our journey. There would be no tears because that would bring bad luck and provoke the gods to jealousy.

Katya was there with the family and looked radiant in a new dress obviously made by my mother. The dark blue silk and fine white linen brought out the intense beauty of her eyes and contrasted the gilded red of her hair, which, unlike Tatar women, she let flow down her back. There was a glow about her that I had never seen before. I had also begun seeing how lovely Natasha was; now I saw her as a woman and not just as Dalgin's mother. She always gave me the kind of affection that Mother had not afforded me for years.

Dikkatli and Marwa also attended, her days having been accomplished. They were both excited for me and also for Nissim. I had always seen my brother as the epitome of elegance and good manners. Marwa was certainly equal to him. I thought I envied his intelligence and education, though he had no formal education. However, I had neither resentment for nor regrets about him. He was warm and excited for us.

"Listen, you two," he said, which included Nissim, "I shall take Dalgin and Timov, your brothers, underhand and make sure they don't get offtrack. I offered to have Timov stay with me, but it seems he and Dalgin have decided to use your yurt. Don't worry, Nissim, I will keep my eye on him."

I also met Tutumlu that evening and renewed my acquaintance with Tetik, whom I had known from the training grounds. They were with Bashina at the time, and I did not really get a chance to make any plans. Bashina said he would try to reassemble my boys in the absence of Chabuk and me. "They've had too much of a holiday!" he insisted.

I then noticed that Father and the khan were together and that they were beckoning me to the dais. I excused myself and joined them.

The khan, who was in excellent spirits, immediately launched into conversation: "I am of two minds about this venture, young Tambor. I know you first as a warrior, not as a trader. Your father says that he has wanted to take you along and learn the business for a long time. But I am sending you off as a warrior. It is your responsibility to protect the caravan if that is what we can call it. You will have a dozen or so warriors at your disposal. It is not likely you will encounter any hostility on the way as the Russians are a little nervous about Tatars since Mikhailov, but we must put on a good show of strength. At the same time, I want you to be sensitive of the fact that we Nogay are by nature nomads and we have always lived by wandering and trade. My father uprooted our tribe when I was not much younger than you. You need to get the sense of space and distance to cause you to be better-rounded. Observe and be sensitive to your surroundings and the people that you meet. Do not see everyone as an enemy, but at the same time be cautious and wary when you sense hostility. You shall be a nomad for a few months, but you are first of all, a warrior." He kissed me on the cheeks and bade me farewell.

The following day, we left just after Koyash made his appearance. Lazim and Uyari accompanied us on horseback uttering blessings or curses, I could never tell which. Even at his age, he could still dance and shake his rattles. And then we were on our own.

Tutumlu and Tetik had brought some prize hawks along and Tetik's prize falcon. They had been breeding hawks and eagles for years, and some well-trained hawks were being transported in wooden cages. Tetik already had one of his falcons on what was left of his left arm. When I expressed surprise, actually concern, he admitted that he was feeling some pain. Katya had put some new dressings on and strictly urged him not to overexert his arm.

"I'm really just showing off, Lord Tambor. It seems I do not need a hand for this kind of work, but my balance is not quite the same, and the birds know it. See how nervous she is. We'll both get used to it though, won't we, Bayan? Right now, I am feeling a lot of pain, sir, and will put Bayan away shortly." I admired his courage and his refusal to give in to his infirmity, and I told him so. He was about two years older than I was, and I knew we would get along.

Nissim took charge of our horses and our personal equipment. He saw to it that our weapons were clean and sharp and that our quivers were full, with a good reserve of arrows on our cart. Mother had also given him some provisions, which, along with those Tetik's wife provided, gave us a few weeks of pleasant meals. Three slaves made sure all was clean and well ordered. Actually, Nissim assumed charge of them, which left me almost free of responsibilities.

Father and Chabuk were at the lead with a few other traders following him. Of course Father was unquestionably in charge. Our herds stayed in the rear. There were also about fifteen or so warriors to guard the convoy and that gave Chabuk something to do. It was my idea. I didn't want him to spend his time worrying. Of course, he was to report to me daily, though that was a mere formality.

I also learned that Hazir decided to accompany our warriors. He had not reported to me as yet, and I had no idea with whom he was tenting. Since his brother's death at Mikhailov, he had assumed responsibility for his family, so it shouldn't have been a surprise to hear that his brother's only son came along with him. Nissim and Tetik reminded me that it only made sense. A diversion was necessary. The boy was only thirteen, but a fine pleasant lad. Chabuk made the comment, when we came together, that he was the same age as he had been on his first trip. They would be staying with Father and Chabuk.

A few of the herdsmen had brought along dogs. These fascinated me as I watched for the first time how the dogs kept the sheep and even the cattle in order. The herdsmen had their own horses and slept in their own tents. Nissim and I shared our tent with Tutumlu and Tetik, a traveling tent, made of felt but not quite a yurt. I was also aware that Nissim would still get up before the dawn to pray to God, and this comforted me in some strange way.

Dalgali had also brought Natasha with him and two female slaves to serve her. A few of our women cousins came along also with servants. I assumed that this too was a comfort and a diversion for her. Dalgin would do much better without her constant whining and worrying. I was sure Mother and Katya were behind all this. I had not yet told Nissim that she too was a Christian. It would all come out in time; we had months ahead. I wondered if she too wanted to "make her confession."

Spiritual Father, this was a year of awakening; that is why I am making so much of this particular year in my confession. I had thought before that being a Nogay warrior was the ultimate goal of my life and that my main mission was to avenge my grandfather's disgrace, but I discovered that there were other things in life that were also important. There were strange longings in my soul, which gave me both fear and at the same time strange delight. One of those cool nights under the stars beside, but not too near, the campfire, I pondered whether I was happy or not. Pleasant voices could be heard chatting and laughing gently by the warmth of the fire. I was content or at least I thought I was. A little while later, Nissim came beside me and asked if he were intruding, and I shook my head.

After a moment, I asked, "Nissim, my friend, what have you been thinking about lately?"

He laughed, a low quiet laugh, which startled me. "Now *you* are intruding." He paused. "But if you really want to know, all I think about is Mehtap and how much I miss her." He turned over as if to probe my reaction. He was no longer smiling. In all these months, neither of us had mentioned her.

I turned over on my side. There was silence for a moment.

"You love her, don't you? What happened in my yurt was not just a simple romp in the sheets, was it?" I thought he looked a little offended by that. "I don't mean that in a vulgar way, my brother." I reached over and grasped his hand. "I am glad you care. (*Damn it!* I thought. *Akilli Khan knows everything!*) I am glad for you, Nissim. I really am."

He lay back and put his arms under his head. I realized how much I loved him as a friend. He seemed to bring things to the surface. I knew, at that moment, the true source of my discontent, something that, if I had given it much thought, would have plunged me into loneliness for the first time in my life. "May I confess something to you, Nissim?" He nodded and looked at me. "I...I think I too am in love." I slowly drew my breath. "I'm in love with Katya."

"Even your father knows that, friend Tambor," he said.

And so does the khan, I thought wryly. Was it so obvious? Until now, it wasn't obvious to me, and I was angry. I was hurt. I felt I had been cheated, betrayed by the people who loved me most.

Nissim broke the silence. "Don't be hurt, my friend. I can see the anger on your face. If you truly love her, be sure that this was best for her—and for you too. Don't you know that your warriors would have lost respect for you? The tribe loves her not only for her natural talents but because you have honored your father with spoils." I could have struck him. "No no no, my brother! You could never disgrace yourself by marrying the wife of your enemy when everyone was to be killed. Neither could you disgrace Katya by making her a slave with even less status than Mehtap. She knows it. You were not due any preferential treatment. Believe me, Tambor. Your father did the best thing. Trust him. Perhaps, once she has provided offspring, she might be free. Who knows?"

"You're right, Nissim, but it's the thought of her sharing my father's bed that bothers me most. I know he doesn't love her, and he has told me so. I am ashamed to say it, but I think I'm jealous…of my father!" I laughed and Nissim smiled. "Frankly, I'm glad Father is away from her and that he has brought Natasha along on the trip."

"Don't you know how jealous I was of you, Tambor? Frankly, I was glad to see you lose interest in Mehtap. She was really fond of you though, and she always felt she was betraying you, her rightful owner. That is how a slave feels. She could never truly love you, her owner. You would not want to wish that on Katya either, would you?"

"Always wise, Nissim! Always common sense! Wise beyond your years, what could I do without you? Thanks, my brother. Dream of Mehti tonight and tomorrow, for the next day, whenever that comes, she is yours."

"Let's go back to the fire and have a jug of kumis. Leave the stargazing to your brother, Dalgin."

Chabuk and Hazir had joined us, bringing along Hazir's nephew. Father was obviously occupied. Few of us brought women as Father always did. I thought, *How many conceptions were made on business journeys. Maybe even me.*

I was glad to see Hazir. Back at the Birches, I found it a little difficult dealing with other people's grief, especially someone whom I knew well. I was glad that the khan paid him a lot of attention. It turned out that the khan had advised the trip after all and permitted the boy to come along. The boy's name was

Kiymetli, which we shortened to Kym or Kymmy. Even as a thirteen year old, he was bright and alert and anxious to learn. I expressed my sadness about his father and praised his heroism. He answered that he knew his father was a brave warrior.

"My uncle Hazir is also a great warrior, and he loves me too. Since he doesn't yet have a son, he has made me his son." He glowed with pride for both fathers.

Hazir was looking better. He was always a very austere man, tall and gaunt, with brown hair, which was untied flowing down his back. It accentuated his stern appearance. He rarely smiled. Fresh air and good food and plenty of kumis were doing him well. He was probably twice my age but never made the age difference obvious when it came to command. Kym took to Tetik right away and within a few days had become an expert hawker, or so he thought. He had become a veritable library of hawk and falcon information. Tetik said he would train him soon and maybe even spare one of the commercial hawks for Kymmy. Perhaps someday he would even have a falcon of his own. Occasionally he would tent with us and would barrage Tetik with questions into the night until I threatened to take him back to his father.

Chabuk was looking well also. The responsibility of coordinating the warriors gave him a sense of value. The Birches, our village, was in the north of Astrakhan, about two hours' swift ride to the Volga. But of course we were not traveling swiftly; we were leading herds. We took the road that bypassed what was left of Mikhailov and headed south. Tomorrow we would be approaching the town of Stupino. It was our first stop. We had some good trading there, and it was good to see the barges docking. There was a large barge there also that was used to transport horsemen across the river. Stupino was on a narrow twist on the river, and we asked permission to travel downstream to Zasypkin, a small village, but fortunately equipped with a barge which seemed its primary asset. A Tatar village was situated on the other side of the river about an hour's ride from the town, and

Father gave us leave to pay a visit to the chief and his nobles. We managed to get five of us on the barge with horses and took the trip. It was my first trip on water.

Resmi, the chieftain of the village, was pleasant, if a little formal. We asked for rites of hospitality, and he welcomed us. He asked if we had heard about the destruction of Mikhailov. We told him we had but asked him to fill in the details. He praised the well-managed siege and the unknown group of Tatars who murdered the master and everyone there, as well an entire garrison of soldiers. There was apparently a priest who escaped with a group of children, but these were unable or perhaps unwilling to provide any information. All they said was that the warriors were masked. Of course, all of us feigned amazement at the account. I asked if the Russians had intended to restore the village.

"You must be joking," Resmi said. "There is no one to resettle the place. But besides that," he said very quietly, "The Russians believe that the old man's spirit haunts the place. Obviously Erlick doesn't want him." His bondsmen snickered but not too loudly in order not to distract the chief. We kept silent.

As the evening drew on, we were fed and given some ground to spread our mats on and some wood for a fire. The visit was pleasant enough, but it lacked the khan's gracious hospitality. Akilli was in the habit of billeting any guest to our community. But then, that's why he was Khan. The barge would leave Zasypkin only in the morning when the waters were low. We had left Stupino around noon when the waters swelled and would take the barge swiftly downstream. We made the return in ample time. The Russians at Zasypkin seemed somewhat unnerved at our presence. Father rarely traded on the east side of the river and only when he was traveling north from the city of Astrakhan to Kazan as he had done the previous year. It was dryer on the east side of the river and not so forested.

The Stupino traders were very welcoming. We had a good stock of smoked meats, which could be preserved for a long time.

Stupino was a very Russian community although there was a vast array of different peoples in the marketplace. The administrator and his staff were Russian, however, but certainly not like Vassili Daruvenko. Father said that Vassili was very influenced by European culture whereas most of the rulers and boyars opposed the Europeans and their customs in general. Daruvenko was somewhat of a visionary, dear Father, and would have been very welcome in the court of Great Tsar Peter who now rules us and has in these days forced westernization upon the Russian aristocracy.

Although Stupino was a small town, they had a beautiful Orthodox Church there. Zubovka was next. These were on main routes and were somewhat inland from the Volga. Apparently these villages and towns were built in such a way as to avoid the yearly flooding. Daruvenko had been smart enough to build his estate on a large hill and use the stones from the quarry to reinforce the dykes. This now made sense to me. From Zubovka, which was further west from the Volga we veered off from the main track, letting the animals graze in the fields. I wondered about the delay and the reason for moving inland and approached Father about it. Chabuk was with him when I asked and saw him stiffen at my question.

"Father, I've noticed that the roads we have been taking are leading toward the Volga. Why is it we are going inland over ground that seems to be rarely used?"

"Well, my son, we avoid the next stop, perhaps as somewhat of a superstition, you might say."

"Why, sir, what's the mystery?

"We avoid that road, Tambor, as most Tatars do, for that is the road that leads to Cherny Yar. That city is where my father disgraced himself. Many of us do not believe that the Tatars, which Stenka Razin sent to destroy the city, were cowards fleeing for their lives as Stenka insisted. I believe that your grandfather and the Tatar army were bewitched. They were struck blind by a black-robed sorcerer, who claimed to govern the city. That is why we do not go there. That city has not seen a Tatar in almost ten years."

"Forgive me, Father, but what you say implies that we Tatars were intimidated by a Russian sorcerer who is probably in his grave by now. I know that it happened a second time, but unless I am mistaken, those two incidents happened within a year of each other, the second attempt was right when Stenka Razin was fleeing for his life. That was almost ten years ago."

"I must say as a Christian," Nissim added, "that this person, whoever he was, was not a sorcerer since sorcery is a punishable offence in the Orthodox legal system. Shamanism is tolerated only among the Tatars, and the Altai who hold on to the religion of Tengrism, such as our tribe does. The Chuvash who are turning to Orthodoxy have a campaign to rid themselves of sorcerers and wizards. Even the Muslim Tatars, I have heard, have cast out their shamans. Is it not true that that is why we have Uyari amongst us?"

"That is so, Nissim, but we traders and none of our tribe's people who travel the Volga are too willing to tempt fate simply on a matter of principle."

"I wonder, Father, if Nissim and I could take a short jaunt to see the city. I have a personal interest in it and a curiosity to observe it. Our herdsmen and Tutumlu can take care of things while we are away. We can catch up with you in no time."

Chabuk was the first to respond, and it sounded as though he would protest. "No, brother, I am going with you. I have passed it many times and had a great curiosity each time. I do not want to miss out while you are here."

Father pondered the situation for a few minutes and then gave his assent. "I do not see that there would be any real harm, just as long as only the three go. After all, we do not want to alarm the inhabitants. Be wary about entering the city as an arrow could bring you down; nevertheless, indulge your curiosity with caution! Why don't you leave tomorrow morning?"

We set out the following morning at daybreak. Nissim accompanied me as usual as my companion. I think, after the conversation of the previous night and the story of my grandfather, there was more than just curiosity in his mind. Why Chabuk insisted on coming along, I didn't quite know. In spite of the fact that we both had the same grandfather, I very much doubted he had any personal sense of vengeance in his mind. After all he was three years younger than me. I suspected that he just didn't like the idea of Nissim and me having a private adventure. I didn't mind; I wanted to have the two of them get to enjoy each other.

My own feelings in the matter were confused. I could barely sleep that night; I feared my dreams. I did fall asleep when Nissim paid his nightly visit to his God, and in fact, I didn't remember his return. In the morning, my appetite was unusually low, and even when Chabuk joined us for one of Tutumlu's wonderful breakfasts, I just moved around my food. Nissim poured me a strong tea, which I drank with some yoghurt cheese, which we called *Labneya* (actually an Arabic word), which is spread on flat bread with a knife and sprinkled with dried mint. We make it from mare's milk rather than goat or camel milk. It seemed to settle my stomach.

This would not be an easy trip for me. Chabuk was in high spirits, and I had not seen him so well for weeks. His voice did not sound quite so surly, and his attitude toward Nissim not quite so condescending. But I was anxious. Oh I tried to make a good show of being cheerful, but Nissim could see through me. He decided to keep a jaunty profile and managed to joke around with Chabuk to camouflage my tension. As usual, I was grateful to Nissim; I admired his sensitivity. After saddling their horses, they fought over saddling mine in a playful way. Of course, I lightened up, but after riding an hour or so, as we neared the road leading to the city from the north, I became anxious again.

Then we came in full view of the city. I had never seen a city quite so big. I knew Astrakhan was bigger, but I was only a boy the last time I was there (the year my grandfather died), and I had never been to Kazan. Looking at the city from the west, the morning sun in the east was blinding. All I could see was walls. Nissim pointed out pale green cupolas topped with gilt crosses in the distance presumably close to the Volga, which idled by. This city was not like the village of Mikhailov, which was wide open to anyone, and most of the towns along our trade route. I wondered how we would be able to scale these walls. As for today, I wasn't even sure whether we needed a passport to enter, as Russian travelers usually do. So we paused and let our eyes get used to the light.

The city was surrounded with fields and little groups of houses where the farms were situated. A small but pretty church about the same size as Mikhailov's was in one of those groups. A copper dome attested to the wealth of the community.

"It's pretty," Nissim remarked.

"Pretty, yes," Chabuk added. "But Astrakhan is larger and much more beautiful. You'll see it in a week or so."

I thought about how many cities, some of grandeur, Nissim must have seen in his travels. But I did not hear any such response.

"That's true, Chabuk," Nissim said. "I had forgotten."

"You've been there before?" He sounded surprise.

"Yes. I was there with the Kurdish traders whom you and Lord Tambor rescued us from."

"Rescued? Well…I guess so. That's one way of looking at it." Chabuk looked genuinely confused.

You dragon, Nissim! I thought to myself, holding back a smile.

You know, Reverend Father, the only geographical interests I had at that time were battle plans. This would not be a raid or a siege; this would be a full-scale war. We didn't have enough warriors at the Birches to launch such an attack on the city. We would have to get reinforcements from some of the other tribes and communities. How to do that, I didn't quite know. After what my father said last night, no one seemed to be very interested in igniting the old fire. The other two were unaware of what was going on in my mind—well, Nissim, perhaps.

"I wonder how many warriors Grandfather went into battle with against this city. Do you know, Chabuk?" Silence. I had interrupted their banter.

"I don't know." He paused and looked steadily at me and then at the city as did Nissim. "We would need at least three or four hundred men. Inside Cherny Yar, there is actually a Russian garrison. They probably use artillery."

"Yes, that is why Stenka Razin sent us there originally, to prevent that from happening. Three or four hundred…hmm, we don't have enough warriors."

"We were not the only ones involved. The other tribes were coerced also. We provided the officers, and that is why there was such fierce punishment of our men." He leaned over toward Nissim. "By impaling!" He hissed. Chabuk looked wise and knowledgeable. Of course I had been there and seen the death field but he didn't know that. Nor was I about to tell him. Nissim would of course say nothing—I could count on that.

At one moment bells started to chime, from the little church in the fields to the grand one in the city. Nissim pointed and remarked that the gates were opening, and farmers and cattle were moving in. We could see soldiers near the gateway but not really questioning the people. "It doesn't look like they are asking for passports, but they may ask us who we are being strangers."

"We'll take our chances," I said.

"Let's go!" Chabuk said.

It was somewhat comforting to be on a busy road. But the merchants did stare and make comments. "Some of them think we are Turks, but most know us to be Tatars. Our garb identifies us." I had forgotten Nissim understood the Slavic tongue. "I don't hear any real hostility," he declared.

The Boy from Cherny Yar

As we neared the gate, an official craned his neck to see us. He jabbed one of the soldiers who motioned us to move his way.

"Who are you, and what's your business?" the official said. He was curious and perhaps a little suspicious, but not hostile.

"We are Nogay from Akilli Khan's tribe. We are accompanying Dalgali, the trader, on our way to Astrakhan.

"Dalgali, the trader, does not trade here, nor has he ever." He observed.

Nissim answered him in Old Slavonic. "That is true, Officer, but we have come here merely for supplies. We shall be gone before the sun sets."

He paused and looked us up and down. "Where did you learn to speak Slavic? You talk like a priest."

"My mother was a Macedonian by birth. We spoke Old Slavonic at home."

"They are probably runaways and thieves coming here to escape," the soldier said.

Nissim reached for his saber as a gesture of acknowledging an insult but instead said, "Gentlemen, this is Tambor, Prince of the Kubanshyi Nogay. We are not thieves! Nor do we wish trouble."

"All right! All right!" the official said. "You can go in and gather supplies. We don't want trouble either. Welcome to Cherny Yar!" The next, he said with a smile. "But be out before sundown!" And so we entered the city in peace.

I could not recall ever being in a city and felt immediately out of place. Everything crowded in on me. Crowds of people were setting up tents and booths. Chabuk reminded me this was morning, and we were nearing the marketplace. Sheep and goats were being herded into the center of town. Crates of poultry were being unloaded off wooden carts with thick wheels not unlike ours. Coals were being heated to cook meat and other foods. Pastries lined the windows of the bakers' shops. The appetite I had lost this morning was replaced by intense hunger. We were progressing slowly, pressed by the crowds on either side. Chabuk

151

seemed to be relaxed and confident and motioned toward the eating places. I responded enthusiastically. Nissim, however, seemed to be looking for something else; I couldn't imagine what. Then I heard bells tolling again brightly and cheerfully and saw Nissim's face lighten up. A few paces ahead slightly around a corner stood a large wooden church topped by three copper domes, green with age. From the situation and the sound of water, we presumed the temple was near the banks of the Volga just as we had thought. This meant we had come through the city.

"Chabuk and I would like to have something to eat. Are you hungry?" I asked.

"I'm famished, my lords, but if you would give me leave, I would like to visit the temple and light a candle. I won't be long. The service has just started, you can tell by the bells." He nodded for my approval, which of course, I gave him, in spite of the lump of anxiety I felt in my gut. I attributed it to hunger, but I knew it was not.

"We'll meet over there by the red pillars." I looked to Chabuk for confirmation. He looked stunned but pulled himself together.

"Uh…yes. It looks like a good-enough place."

Nissim dismounted and handed me Cereyan's reins. We moved slowly toward the place we indicated and Nissim got lost in the crowd. A wooden bar had been set up near the entrance ostensibly for horses so we tied up our mounts. A bosomy Russian woman with a kerchief slightly askew and blotched with flour, told us in a Tatar dialect that the horses would be safe. She was a jolly sort and made us at home. Her Tatar was not particularly good, and my Russian almost nonexistent. I became aware that Chabuk however could manage a bit in Russian. His speech impediment didn't hinder his ability to joke heartedly with the hostess.

"She's flirting with me, old boy. Let's make the best of it. Relax, brother, you look like you are about to be attacked."

"I've never been surrounded by so many Russians."

The woman returned with some freshly brewed tea, some cheese, and some pastries, which she called piroshki, stuffed with meat and cabbage.

"Start off with these, my boys. Meat will come later. D'ya eat pork?" she asked. We nodded yes. "Some o' you Tatars don't eat pork flesh, ya know." I thought of my brother Kattu.

"We'll need another place. Someone else is joining us later."

Chabuk looked at me seriously. "Listen, Tambor, what is going on with you and Nissim? He walked off just like that: 'If you would give me leave,'" he said sarcastically. "Uh! What's that all about, Tambor? And *then* he goes to a Russian Church no less… to light a candle!"

"My dear brother," I said trying not to sound patronizing, "Nissim and Timov are Christians, Orthodox—I think that means 'true worshippers.' He was badly persecuted by the Turks as a young man because he persisted in keeping his faith. Timov was too young to be beaten. Nissim got it all. He had been brought up in a family that was every bit as noble as ours and rich too. When the authorities found out they were not Muslim, they dragged his father away and enslaved his mother and sister, sending them away. He has suffered enough, but his God takes care of him, and I don't want to offend his God." I paused. "Listen Chabuk. Don't breathe a word of this to Kattu. The khan thinks Kattu is already Muslim, and we do not need any hostility around the family."

He nodded ascent and commented, "Listen, Tambor, you can't go around freeing slaves just because you feel sorry for them or even because you fear their gods. Slavery is a way of life. We don't question it. Even the Russians have forced their itinerant farmers back to the farms as serfs. But you can do what you want, Tambor, what can I say? Nissim has the skills to make a good warrior, and Timov is very smart."

"I haven't freed *him*."

"You might as well have freed him. He does anything he wants. He even runs the stable hands and the herdsmen. All in your name of course."

I had to laugh. "That is why I love these boys. They are completely loyal to me *and to us* as a tribe."

"Maybe so. Well, here comes the food!"

"And here comes Nissim."

"Well, well, another good looker!" said Masha, for that's what she wished us to call her. Nissim blinked wonderingly. "Where are you boys from? If you plan to stay for a while, you are welcome to stay here. We got rooms."

"We are traveling south with Dalgali, the trader, whose herds are grazing a few hours east. But we can't stay after sundown, or we'll be in trouble with the gate master. We are here to pick up supplies."

"Mighty fine to meet you, lads. We don't get to meet warriors in this region. The tribesmen generally avoid us." She was being pulled away by other concerns. Perhaps her husband behind the counter thought she was being just a bit too friendly. We finished our food with much enjoyment and paid the owner in silver, for which he was happy.

"If you want to continue on foot, you're welcome to leave your horses out back in the stable for the day. Just offer a token to the stable master." He was being friendly. We were grateful.

Getting supplies, of course, was simply a ruse to get us into the city, but it was a ruse we felt necessary to apply exactly. Certainly we needed no meat and yoghurt, but fresh fruit from the harvest was welcome. Russian pastries are different from ours, so we bought bags and boxes of the various types. I was delighted to find out that piroshki can be made with many different ingredients, so I was delighted to buy several dozens to share at camp. I had to remind the boys that we were not trading in Cherny Yar so as not to get tempted to spend money rather than trade. Chabuk said that there would be other places on our journey to buy trinkets and cloth.

Then came the soldiers. They were on horseback and slowly but confidently rode up to the milliner whose display was fascinating us at the time. They were not dressed like the Mikhailov garrison soldiers but wore loose fitting garments over their well-fed bodies. Their heads were topped with a fur caps with what looked like a church dome in the middle.

"Good morning, young men, I wonder if you would mind accompanying us," the captain said.

I was a little indignant. "Have we done anything to merit this intrusion?"

"None whatsoever, gentlemen," he said casually. "We certainly hope to keep it that way. Just some routine questioning. Come this way."

"We have left our horses in a local stable. Will we need them?" It took a moment to realize that he was speaking in a Tatar dialect.

Nissim nudged me. "That is Turkish he is speaking."

"And where are they, these horses?" the captain asked, growing slightly impatient.

Nissim said, "At a hostel run by Masha and her husband, Ivan."

He turned to one of his soldiers, "Oleg, go fetch the horses at Saint Vladimir's Hostel, would you, and be prompt." Oleg saluted and left.

"I see you have made some purchases. Can you carry them until the officer returns with your steeds? The crowd has died down so you should be able to walk comfortably. Come along now."

Chabuk looked insolent and sullen. I held his elbow and said very quietly to him, "Just mind your manners, brother. There has been no aggression yet. I suspect we are being brought to the garrison."

I was right.

The garrison was farther down the main street and was actually a short distance to the south of the church. Oleg brought the horses before we arrived. The garrison was a large building with ornate pillars. We dismounted and walked up about ten steps. There were guards at the entrance of the building who saluted our officer. It was a busy place with soldiers going to and fro. Russian ladies with their headdresses and long skirts stopped and chatted with each other. Officials scuttled here and there, and it was somewhat unnerving especially when we were taken into a room lined with books.

"This building is a military garrison designed to protect the area. The soldiers live and train out in the large fields out back just above the trading docks. But it is also the courthouse and the administrative offices for the area. We are also proud of our small library where you are now. There is also a jail below." He was very informative.

The other soldiers had left, and Oleg, a friendly soldier, only a few years older than we were, was sent to fetch someone. When he returned, he was accompanied by a thickset man about my father's age, though not nearly so healthy looking. He had a thick black beard and thick hair slightly graying. This man did not resemble Vassili Daruvenko in the least. His brocaded robe edged in black fur hung to the floor. He looked at us curiously but not in a hostile manner.

He announced himself with a slightly pompous air. "I am Konstantin Alexandrovich Lapukhin, assistant to the administrator of the city of Cherny Yar." This was in Russian, and was repeated by our officer in Turkish. "Captain Yaakov Varisovich has brought you here at my request, after I had learned of your presence here. Please sit." This was the second time today I had sat on a chair. It was a new experience. Our yurts have beds and stools but not chairs. "We presumed you were Tatars by your manner and clothing. Please tell me where you are from and where you are going."

After Captain Yaakov translated, Nissim replied. "We are Nogay Kubanshyi from the Birches a little west of Stupino, and we are on our way to Astrakhan accompanying Dalgali, the father of these two warriors. These men are Lord Tambor and Lord Chabuk, sons of Prince Dalgali, and I am Nissim, Lord Tambor's squire."

When this had been translated, Captain Yaakov asked Nissim how it was he spoke Turkish. Nissim informed him that he was originally from the Turkish empire and was born in Macedonia.

The administrator said, "Well then, I presume you are Muslims."

Chabuk broke in and said in his rough manner, "We worship Tengri, but Nissim worships Christos."

"Ah, so you were the one, the young man, who frightened the ladies at Church this morning? I hardly call this an invasion, however." He laughed as he nodded to Nissim. "Captain, would you call for tea and some vodka."

This looked as though we were having a party, but I was keenly aware that Konstantin was plumbing for information. We would have to appear casual and businesslike and at the same time be very cautious. He wanted information.

An elderly Russian lady with a pleasant manner served us, and Konstantin himself poured some vodka into small glass goblets and served us. "Drink up, boys. Enjoy yourselves. You are my guests." He continued, "If you are from the Birches, you must be part of Akilli Khan's tribe."

It was coming; I could feel it. But we could not lie since that would make it too obvious. I replied, "Akilli Khan was married to my mother's late sister." The look on Chabuk's face convinced me that he had not known that fact either.

"Dreadful, that business at Mikhailov, the whole community slaughtered in a few hours in your neighborhood too. Dreadful! Dreadful! And no one knows who was responsible for it."

"Yes," I said slowly. "We heard about it from Chief Resmi of the Zasypkin community whom we visited several days ago. It seems the siege was well planned. Obviously the work of some well-trained warriors. Are there any plans to restore the place?"

"Heavens, no! You wouldn't get a peasant near the place. They say the old fellow's ghost roams around the estate and the dead soldiers sing at night from under their rocky grave. You know the soldiers were buried under rocks, which is entirely against the Tatar practice of cremating the dead. I'm surprised they buried them at all."

"Are you sure they were Tatars, your lordship? Anyone can mask as Tatars, and we Tatars ourselves are well practiced in the art of deception. The Mongols, our mentors, built an empire with the skill of deceiving their enemies. Perhaps they were other folk made to appear as Tatars. Do you have any eye witnesses?"

"Actually, yes, we do. But they are not really reliable. Apparently (and this is another situation that is rather untypical) the parish church was used as a place of refuge for anyone who could make it there. Our authorities have been questioning the local priest and some peasant women who witnessed all of this. It seems, from what they say, 'a rather fierce Tatar, a giant of a man,' according to one of the women, ordered peasants and children into the church, while all around was devastation. (This became a source of much teasing for the next few days and whenever appropriate.) The priest, at first suspected that the warriors would burn the church and everyone in it, but that was not so. The warriors must also have had some artillery for they blew up the fortress nearby. All the soldiers and the local militia were slaughtered. The priest is useless; he won't tell us more than that all the warriors were masked and seemed to be *wearing a kind of uniform.* Can you imagine? The peasant women are far more descriptive, but I'm certain they were exaggerating." He paused and threw another shot of vodka down his throat. We did likewise. "Drink up and eat, my brothers. You have a long ride back in the dark tonight."

I knew he was trying to lure us into a trap either of self-admission or the possible exposure of another tribe. I parried, "You are very candid with us, your honor. Do you want something from us?"

Yaakov, our translator, was himself relaxing. His words may not have been as precise as they had been earlier in the day. Both Chabuk and Nissim had to help him out at times.

Konstantin thought about something for a while and then resumed his conversation. "You see, our investigators examined the ruins very carefully. We found the body of Prince Vassili and his housekeeper who apparently had both been killed before the fire. Since they were on the floor, the fire did not actually destroy them. But we did not find the Princess Ekaterina Milanova, either amongst the ruins or among the charred remains. The peasant women insist she was abducted by one of the leaders, a very cruel man. The horde stole a horse and forced her to ride away on it while she tearfully begged the priest to bless her, poor woman. Awful business!"

"It's true," I said, barely able to stifle my laughter. "Our people can often be very cruel." I tried to say this quite solemnly. I could hear similar sounds of sympathy from my companions, though I wouldn't dare look at them.

"Her family is devastated and scandalized. I'm sure you can understand why. I'm sure your people would stoop to murder if something similar should happen to one of your women."

"That's true for sure," Chabuk croaked.

"She has folk in Voronezh and Astrakhan, who are awaiting word from us, and we have nothing to tell them. We have been asking anyone from all quarters. Perhaps it is presumptuous on my part, young men, to ask you to advise this office if you ever hear of a Russian noble woman in captivity. We would definitely use diplomatic means to make an exchange, of course. We want your people to feel they have an honorable share in this vast and God-anointed kingdom."

He was eloquent and gracious in his manner and perhaps sincere, and if it had not been for the absurdity of the situation, I could almost have been taken in.

Nissim had the good sense to be equally graceful and actually truthful. "We would be most cooperative, your honor, in complying with your request. I am sure Lord Tambor and Lord Chabuk would agree that if we should at any time encounter a Russian noble lady burdened under the cruel yoke of captivity, we would surely get word to you immediately. Brothers, I trust you will agree."

"Yes, indeed, most assuredly." We both agreed.

"Well, now, I am very grateful. You know, my friends, very few of your people have ever visited this city for many years now, ever since the days of Stenka Razin. I was a very young man in Moscow when the traitor was dragged before us. I am of a sensitive nature, I'm sure you have observed, and was forced to view his demise. I can take bloodshed in battle perhaps, and by no means will I object to Stenka's verdict. However, I thought that the violence of Stenka's death, traitor though he was, partook of a vehemence I could not endure.

"I know that by no means were you people happy to serve him, noble ideals or not, bah! You were little more than his lackeys. Your tribes had most of the land at that time, and you still do. Nevertheless, you were forced to do his dirty work. I am sure your people would have been quite content to continue your lives as ever you did. The attempted siege of Cherny Yar was obviously not fortuitous for you. Your people bore their disgrace well."

I was beginning to get a little agitated at this talk. I had to confess he had deep insights into the situation, but it was not a topic for discussion. I didn't let on, however. Even Chabuk was behaving himself.

He continued, "You see this portrait over my left shoulder. That is Ivan Bogdanovich Milaslavsky. Because the Tatar troops could not secure this city for Stenka, Ivan was able to set up a garrison right here and establish this court and library. I was enormously fond of him and was one of his staff when he came down from Moscow. Thanks to your blessed failure and the prayers of our most esteemed Saint Bogolep, we have firmly established ourselves in Astrakhan."

He talked with us as though we ourselves couldn't be happier about this business. I was astounded. Now I realized why Dalgali and the chieftains were so concerned about the recent trends. Mikhailov was a small incident; now I perceived the bigger picture. These Russians wanted to assimilate us into their system, and by this, we would play a part in making the Russian nation vast and powerful, the very ones who had subdued us. It was not much different from Stenka's use for us. I begged whatever gods were around to hold back Chabuk's temper and Nissim's tongue.

I found myself saying, "That is most informative, and it certainly provides us with a more complete picture of your needs from your point of view."

Nissim smiled. Chabuk looked confused and a bit put off but said nothing. I wanted to cut out my own tongue. I guess I was learning diplomacy. But inside I was screaming, *I am going to destroy your city and everyone in it. Just you wait!*

Nissim was asking Konstantin something as I got control of myself. "Who is this saint you were mentioning, your honor?"

"Ah, yes, you are a Christian, Nissim, and Pravoslav (Orthodox), I had forgotten." I was listening. "Saint Bogolep has been around us for many years."

"So he must be an older man by now, somewhat older than us," I posited.

"Oh no!" he said excitedly. "He died many years ago. In fact his relics are in the Church of the Resurrection, which Nissim visited this morning. Bogolep was no more than a boy when he left this world to be with the Lord Jesus. But he was a full schema monk at that time." Nissim would know what that meant.

Good, I thought. *If he's the one Grandfather referred to, it is not likely we'll get much interference from him.*

As we left Cherny Yar, it was very hard to entertain my negative thoughts and bitterness. Konstantin Alexandrovich was gracious to the end. Not only did he send Captain Yaakov and Officer Oleg to help gather more supplies, he also sent my father a gift as well, a beautiful silver broach with a gray stone to attach his cloak. He even managed to find something for my mother, though I cannot remember what it was.

"This is just a trinket for your folks, lads, with my regards and an invitation for Dalgali to trade with us. However, when you do come, it would be best to send word ahead so that we can make provision for your people down by the docks. Your father is an important man in this region, and his presence among us would be an honor…and very profitable to us no doubt. This is the best time of year for him to visit, during the dry spell. The spring is terrible for flooding."

Konstantin also gave Nissim an icon of Jesus Christ. Nissim kissed him on the cheeks and held the icon to his breast.

"This icon of our Savior was painted by a priest in Astrakhan by the name of Father John, who is one of the foremost iconographers of this area. If you are planning to confess while in Astrakhan, I recommend him. He is an excellent confessor. I advise you to make contact with him. He will make you all welcome. Furthermore give him my regards."

Many years later, when I learned the story of the Patriarch Abraham bargaining with God over the city of Sodom, wherein he pleaded with God that if there were forty just men in Sodom he would not destroy the city and whittled God down (I speak crudely) to ten just men. Well, I determined that since I had met four just men and one just woman in Cherny Yar, as long as they were there I would not destroy the city. I kept that resolve.

Of course, father didn't see it that way.

"Hospitable, yes. Gracious, obviously. Welcoming, doubtful. Oh yes, he certainly welcomed you, but his welcome was driven by fear rather than genuine interest, my son, and that's why I brought a troop of warriors with me. I appreciate his gift, and I will wear it (it is an Indian agate, not so rare in India but unusual here), and I shall perhaps allow myself to be entertained by his generous words. However, Tambor, I shall not be taken in by them. As you yourself said, he represents a movement that is attempting to assimilate all the various different peoples of this vast territory into what is called Russia. It has got to the point where neither rebellion nor submission will prevail to keep our independence. Both Akilli Khan and I suspect we shall be working hand in hand with them in a generation."

"Then what was the siege of Mikhailov all about? Why did we put so much effort into it?" I felt grieved and perhaps a little betrayed.

"Tambor, the destruction of Mikhailov was to a certain extent a setup. Don't misunderstand me, my son, for us it was a question of honor, a reaction to an insult, the exact opposite of the attitude in Cherny Yar. Konstantin Alexandrovich, in spite of his horror over the savagery at Mikhailov, was probably secretly overjoyed to get rid of the old man Daruvenko, who was not popular amongst the boyars: in fact they despised him. He was much richer than they were, and he had foreign business, money, and the pull of the tsar. The Russian nobility of Astrakhan and even as far north as Kazan despises the westernization of Russia. This is quite unlike the Muscovite boyars who play politics with the Swedes, the Poles, and the various German kingdoms, generally against the tsar. But mark my words, my son, and Akilli Khan agrees, within a generation or two, certainly with another tsar, Russia will become a great force in the European world and will begin a course in history we will never be able to reverse."

Of course, Father Dmitri, in retrospect, we both know how true this has become. We both remember how Tsar Peter crushed the rebellion in Astrakhan in 1705 because they rejected the westernization of their land. We Kubanshyi fought alongside the Russians as was true of many other tribesmen, but to no avail. Peter's forces were too powerful. All we can say is that Daruvenko was ahead of his time, that's all. We destroyed him long before Peter took the throne.

I knew to a certain extent that Father was right, but I couldn't help wanting to defend Konstantin. After rehashing this with Nissim, later on, I realized that he also endeared himself to the administrator. However Chabuk's reaction that night as we talked by the fire was swift and brutal.

"I knew I should have killed Konstantin yesterday when I had the chance!"

"You never *had* the chance, Chabuk!" Father retorted. "That is simply nonsense talk, and I do not want to hear any more of it. Killing the administrator would have made your mother a widow and destroyed our caravan. You were wise to keep your temper in. Leave the diplomacy to Tambor, who is more level-headed."

I had never heard my father rebuke Chabuk; neither had I heard him ever compliment me that way. I saw Chabuk lower his eyes. He was hurt, and I felt for him. However, I would never have considered countering my father, especially in front of the nonfamily members who had gathered around the campfire to hear our story.

But I did say, "It is true. That would have been a disaster. But I have to confess that, at a certain point, I would have wanted to react—"

"But you didn't!" Father interrupted.

I was about to add, *Neither did Chabuk*. However I decided to hold my peace. I began to realize that there was something Father held against Chabuk that I knew nothing about and might never.

This whole event was somewhat of a turning point in my life, Father. I was avowed to destroy the city and avenge myself on the boy but instead found the encounter enjoyable. It was a little unnerving. One problem was solved however; the boy was dead.

ANTICIPATION

I am growing up;
Vistas of scintillating sands are stretched before my vision,
Wide green grassy hills pass beneath my horse's hooves,
Tantalizing towns and cities seduce me
with their women and their wares,
And the forever flowing Volga sings to me
Move on, move on, move on.

—Dalgin

That night, my sleep was fitful. I kept sinking into my nightmares and pulling myself out before Nissim would have to wake me. Cherny Yar was no longer a dream word or a city of myths. I had been there and lived some of my personal existence there even for but a day. This was not like Mikhailov where there was an actual person who needed killing. Who needed killing at Cherny Yar? We had been treated graciously notwithstanding the perceptions of my father, whom I suspected would make contact next year in the fall. The one person whom Grandfather kept warning me about was a boy who was already dead and buried in the cathedral there. He would pose no problem ever again. Yet my grandfather kept appearing and reappearing in my dreams all night. There was a new variation on the theme: Katya would appear at the foot of the stake, telling me to come down and rebuking Grandfather for pressing me. Then there was the lone rider in black shooting me down. I suspected he was the boy upon whom I was to requite my grandfather's death. But I didn't wake up as usual. There I would lie on the ground with Katya and her box of medicines pouring fragrant oils into my wounds. At that point in the dream, I would wake up, longing to hold Katya in my arms.

Nissim was not around. We were in the habit of sleeping beneath the open sky. The air was splendidly warm by day as we traveled south, and the slight coolness of October nights made for a pleasant sleep. Besides, my years of solitude in my own yurt at home made the pitched tent a little crowded for my comfort. Sometimes Kiymetli would join us after a particularly talkative spree, but we didn't mind. However, on this occasion, I looked around and felt alone.

We did not have the shelter of trees like our private retreat away from the Birches, so as my eyes cleared, I saw the full moon shining on Nissim afar off. He was praying. He had, I supposed, propped his icon against a cleft in a tall rock and was praying to it. At least that is how it appeared to me at that time. I watched him for a while from my mat, and when he came back, he noticed that I was awake.

"Forgive me, Nissim. I have been awake for a while. I didn't mean to eavesdrop, but I noticed you praying to your icon."

He laughed in a welcoming way, or at least a manner that didn't patronize me.

"Well, I suppose, Sir Tambor," he said, "that it might *look* that way, but it is not exactly how it is. I do not pray to the icon. I pray *before* the icon to the person who is represented upon it. To pray *to* the icon would mean that I considered it to be my god, and that would be idolatry, a very grave sin, besides being totally absurd. The icon is, shall I say, a point of reference, a help to focus my concentration, which, like all men, can easily wander. In the case of this icon, I am worshipping the Lord Jesus Christ, who created heaven and earth." (Having no other Tatar words, he used *Tengri* and *Yer-Sub* for heaven and earth.) I was startled.

"This same Jesus came to earth," he continued, "and was born without a human father in the womb of the Virgin Mary. That is why we can depict him in human form. We cannot depict his Father who is in the heavens, whom no man has ever seen. Of course, I can pray without using an icon, as I have been, but I am grateful to have one because the Church recommends using them. As you know, Katya was given an icon by the priest in Mikhailov." This astounded me, and I wondered about its significance, especially about Tengri and Yer-Sub. I would have to talk to him about this at another time.

"By the way, why are you awake? It is at least two hours before dawn." He paused. "Troubled by dreams?"

"You could have guessed. But they are different—the same ones, somewhat modified or interfered with, as though there are now two powers opposing each other, and my part in them is not so easily defined." I told him about the intrusion of Katya in my dreams: how she pours healing balm into my deathly wounds and how she dares to rebuke the vengefulness of my grandfather.

"It sounds like a delightful intrusion. After all, now the one you love assuages your deepest fears. Perhaps, Tambor, this marks a deep change in your life. Maybe she has been appointed as your guardian angel—that is, until you get an official one."

"An official one? It sounds like Russian bureaucracy. I would be satisfied with a very beautiful human one."

"My dear friend, companion, and teacher, I truly believe you have many friends in the other world, who are deeply concerned about you. You are indeed a hawk soaring above other men, and you would desire to fly into the heavens. But somewhere there is a weakness that will bring you down. Thanks be to the Almighty (he used a Greek word, *Pantocrator*, for this, being unable just then to find a Tatar equivalent) that he has prepared a healing balm for your arising."

I couldn't help but burst out laughing. "You sound just like a Kubanshyi bard beginning an epic. I assure you, I am just a plain Nogay warrior who happens to take his job perhaps a little too seriously. You are the saint, my brother. With all your stories of trials and woes, I have never once heard from you a word of bitterness or a curse of vengeance. In fact, all I have ever heard from you has been gratitude toward your God and a kind of joy I have seen in no one else."

He was sitting on his blanket with his knees tucked under his chin. In the silver moonlight, I thought I saw a tear lightly slide down the side of his nose. I knew he was thinking about his family. I regretted again my insensitivity.

"I promise you, my friend, we shall search for your folks and bring them with us to safety. I swear this to this God of Tengri and Yer-Sub upon my honor as a Nogay warrior."

"It is not a hawk you are, Lord Tambor. You are an eagle!"

We slept a little before dawn, and both of us needed to be aroused. Tetik came around and chided us awake.

"I wonder if Lord Dalgali warned you we were moving on. We hope to reach Nikol'skoye in a few days and Prishib the following day unless the market is profitable in Nikol'skoye as he suspects it will be. Apparently, there is a sizable population of Cossacks there who are always in need of fine horses. My father suggests that you will do well there. I have prepared the horsemen to attend to the grooming of your herd. Of course we will not travel too fast so as not to tire them."

"What can we expect at Prishib?" I asked.

"Farmers, apparently. They will require sheep and goats and perhaps some cattle. Lord Dalgali has considerably more sheep and cattle than you have. My father suggests that your somewhat smaller flock be kept until your father has sold most of his. He apportions his livestock according to the communities he visits and the clientele he already has." Tetik leaned over and whispered, "My father says it is best not to interfere with Prince Dalgali's business prospects. You can pick up where he leaves off."

All that Nissim and I had to do was gather our few things from the place where we slept. I was grateful that the servants were there to do the rest. I had one boy, Berker, to attend both of us. Hazir and Chabuk were approaching our area of the camp and seemed a little pushy and officious. When I greeted them, I tried to be somewhat lighter in tone and assured them we would be ready in time. The servants asked if we needed to eat because we, of course, had not breakfasted. We told them we had plenty of food from our trip to Cherny Yar. Reaching into a sack, I threw a piroshki to Nissim and another one to Chabuk. I let Hazir choose one of his own. He was older, and I felt respect for him. We would become more familiar as the journey moved on, such that I could joke around with him. We were given each a mug of strong tea, and we were ready and satisfied.

As I mounted Onyx, I moved closer to Chabuk and quietly said to him, "I hope there was nothing I said to cause Father to rebuke you yesterday, my brother."

He looked at me long and pensively as though he really did not want to talk about it. As I was about to turn away, he said as quietly as he could, "Tambor, I shall be nineteen in the new year, and I suppose I have a lot to learn yet. Father was justified in reminding me how I humiliated him two years ago when Dalgin and I traveled with him. I think and I hope he has forgiven me for my indiscretion, but as we shall be traveling through Kalmykia next week, he was reminding me not to get hotheaded again. I suppose my comments about Cherny Yar warranted the rebuke. That's also why Dalgin and I were forbidden to travel with him last year. Our absence was not just for training purposes."

"I don't mean to pry but what actually happened, Chabuk?"

"Of course, as you know, the lower Volga is mostly dominated by Astrakhan, but there is that narrow piece of Kalmykia that juts into the Volga and gives the Kalmyks free access to the river. Of course that was granted by the Russians who are allied to them. That part of the Volga is relatively narrow, and the Kalmyks have built two bridges on each side of their territory. We don't use the bridges because our numbers are too great, so we pass through their territory alongside the river using the same route we use now."

I found Chabuk unusually talkative. Although I would have expected him to be less wordy, I was delighted with his openness.

"As you know, the Kalmyks and the Kubanshyi have been hostile toward each other for a few hundred years. It was because they harassed us so badly that we left the Kuban under the khan's father. So for us to cross their territory is almost a declaration of war. But Father, like you, has a way with enemies and has managed to avoid trouble with them. Between you and me, I think he bribes the leaders. What's a little bribe between enemies? Father always was able to play innocent when he was insulted, just as you did with Konstantin. Well, I didn't feel that way two years ago.

"I suppose they insulted us. I remember feeling that way. It was probably something trivial, but I wanted revenge. That night, Dalgin and I sneaked into their camp as they were sleeping and slit the throats of the offenders. It was a stupid thing to do because they attacked us the following morning and killed three of us before we could even defend ourselves. Two others died in the skirmish that followed.

"Now all of Father's diplomacy has been wasted. That is part of the reason we warriors are here. Last year, he had some trouble at the border, but he talked his way out of it or paid his way out of it. Of course, Dalgin and I were absent. This year, they are possibly somewhat afraid of us and are more likely prepared. Many suspect we were responsible for the destruction of Mikhailov, even though we covered our tracks. So who knows what will happen?"

I drew Onyx close to his silver gray mount and reached my hand around his elbow just for a moment. "Thanks for telling me, Chabuk. I love you, my brother."

Tetik was right. I sold many horses at Nikol'skoye. The trading was so good because Tutumlu was an incredible auctioneer. All we had to do was ride the horses, and Tutumlu would do the rest.

Even Father was impressed. I would like to have saved more for Astrakhan so I could show off down there, but Tutumlu said it wouldn't be as profitable.

The livestock sold well. I noticed that Father had not brought any of the Mikhailov animals. He told me he wanted to use them for breeding. "Maybe next year will be safer," he said. "I noticed you brought a couple of dozen. Guard your tongue, my son. These sheep are a very healthy breed, but not everyone around here is familiar with them."

One greasy-looking Russian actually got pushy. He spoke Tatar. "A very interesting breed you have, young man. Where did you get them? I haven't seen them locally."

I said, "They come from up north, a northern breed."

"Indeed, and I suppose you have been traveling in the northern areas?"

"Not at all. They were sent down by ship, and I happen to be the proud owner of them."

"Well, I was under the impression that only one person had this kind of sheep. Ah! But alas he is dead!" He made the sign of the cross.

"Perhaps his death reopened the market. In which case, we might all see his death as a blessing."

"That is one way of looking at it," he said pursing his lips. If his remarks seemed caustic, mine must have sounded offensive. Nevertheless, the rancher bought a dozen of them, three rams and nine ewes. We parted amicably with him saying that it was good to see new blood on the market (I think he meant mine) and said he hoped to see me again next year.

Father said, "I warned you about the sheep, my son. But I must say you handled that situation very well."

Tutumlu flattered me. "You really did well with the horses. We make a good team, you and I. However, the sale of the sheep was entirely yours, and you got a good price for them."

Nissim said, "I hope you bring along Timov next year. This is just what he is capable of doing. He can train well with Tutumlu. After all, Tetik is more interested in breeding hawks than in selling them. Timov would be a good apprentice."

Chabuk said, "So look who's the businessman now. All you ever wanted was to be a big, bad warrior, brother dear. Next thing, you will be competing with Father. I should have taken your advice and kept my share of the Kurdish horses."

And I said, "The Mikhailov horses have just been divided at home. You can still have your share. Perhaps if I give Timov his freedom, he could give you a hand divvying up your herd. He serves me now, but for a good wage. I'm sure he would have no trouble harassing the stable masters and herdsmen on your behalf." He snorted his objection. "Besides, who knows whether I'll be coming back next year?"

We were going to make a final stop at a small port on the Volga called Vetlyanka for some supplies and perhaps some sales of our spiced and smoked meats. Father suspected that with Daruvenko out of the way, the ports along the river would reopen to us, and he was right. But what really excited me was encountering a rather large caravan of camels. Apparently they were from Persia and were on their yearly trip to Istanbul with many treasures. I do not know what got into my head, but I wanted some camels. I had seen camels used by the caravans who respectfully crossed our territory. I always found them clumsy and not much use for battle although I had heard that the Arabs used them for conquest all the time. But that was not my interest today. I had a pocketful of Russian rubles, and I wanted to put them to good use.

I took Nissim and Tutumlu with me. Tutumlu apparently knew some Russian. I got the attention of the caravan master and called out, "Does anyone speak Tatar or Turkish or Russian?"

"Turkish!" was the response.

"Are you selling any of your camels?" I said this in Tatar, but he understood me.

The master grinned as though he were playing a joke, and I wondered if I could trust him. "I have six good camels and a nursing colt; that one will go for free. Each camel has a well-trained slave going along with it. I'll give you a good price to get them off my hands."

Tutumlu addressed him in Turkish, which I understood more or less, and we made a good settlement. Besides the money, they wanted a few horses. I asked Tutumlu. "Is this a good deal? I have no idea the price of camels."

"Yes, it is an unusually good price."

I asked, "Why are you selling them at such a good price?" By this time, the caravan master had dismounted. He was about my father's age.

"I will tell you the truth. The slaves who drive them are Zarthosht. This is the ancient religion of our land, and they will not convert to our holy Islamic faith. There have been no end of arguments all the way, and I regret buying them. We don't beat them as the Turks would, so I would rather sell them for profit. I'm not making much on them, but I need some peace. I hope you get some."

I responded, "We are Nogay, and we still follow the old Tatar religion. This should not be a problem for us. Shall we make the deal?"

"Indeed!"

So I now had six (and a half) camels and six new slaves to feed. I wondered how wise I was. But a plan was growing in my mind.

Needless to say, the camp was in a whirl when we entered with our new acquisitions. The first person I saw was Chabuk, whose expression was as if to say: *What in the name of Erlick are you doing now?* The next was Father's. He was haggling over some fabric we were selling with a merchant from one of the trading boats.

Father was insistent, I overheard, "My own wife makes most of the cloth we sell and supervises what the other women do. You won't get a softer or silkier piece of wool in all Astrakhan or even in Kazan. I don't need your business, Evgeny. There is a Persian caravan just arrived here going to Constantinople (The Russians preferred to use the Greek name) who I am sure—what on earth is my son doing? He has just brought some camels, probably from *them*—if you want to do business with me this year, Evgeny you will have to do it now. Sorry, that is my final price." Getting a positive although gloomy response, he left the details to his steward.

He came toward me in haste with knitted brow, but I was determined to get in the first and only word. "Father, I know what I am doing. You will see it unfold in time. My function here, with all due respect, is more than that of guard and part-time salesman. I have something in mind, and you will be proud of me for it. Besides, camels carry more merchandise, and they are better than these clumsy carts we have. Please, Father, trust me."

"Who are these people riding them? What are their loyalties? Tambor, I'm giving you the benefit of the doubt. This breaks all my traditions."

"Father, having *me* along also breaks all your traditions."

"Yes! Yes!" He broke into a smile. "Well, let's go check them out, my strange and unpredictable son. I thought Chabuk was a problem. Come, Nissim. Perhaps you are the most sensible of the three. Tutumlu, check in with Chabuk and Hazir. I suspect we shall have trouble when we enter Kalmykia tomorrow. We want to leave very early. Trading was good here." Tutumlu bowed and left.

The drivers were still perched on their camels when we approached them. We beckoned them to dismount and led them to Father's fire, which was still ablaze after the noon meal. They were bidden to sit near the fire, and the women servants brought some victuals. They were only too happy to eat. They were different. They wore long white robes, pulled in at the sleeves and tied at the waist with leather belts. The only thing colorful they wore were their vests, which were heavily brocaded. Their hair was wrapped in white linen turbans. They were different.

I began. "Are there any of you who speaks Turkish or Tatar? Ah, two of you. Turkish, well that's to be expected. Which one of you is the leader?"

A younger man pointed to the older man and said, "This is my father, Kuru, who rides the dromedary. He speaks very little Turkish. I am his eldest son, Vishtaspa. My Turkish is not perfect, but we can talk. My two brothers are Mardunya, who speaks Turkish, and Naveed, who speaks some. The other two are Pishana and Arshana who are brothers and our cousins. We all speak some Turkish. Our language is Farsi, and we come from Persia. Some of us speak a little Arabic. Our families were sold into slavery, even though we successfully raised camels, because we could not pay taxes to the Islamic government. We follow the religion of Zarthosht, which the Greeks call Zoroaster, and we refused to convert to Islam. We worship one god, Ahura Mazda."

"Vishtaspa, it is a good thing to honor your father." I nodded respectfully to him. "However, you will be answering directly to me from now on. Please inform your family that you are now their leader and spokesman, but please give my respects to your father. I mean him no dishonor."

This he did in his own tongue, and it seemed agreed upon.

"I am Tambor, a prince of the Nogay warriors. We are known as Kubanshyi. This is my most honorable father, Dalgali, chief trader for our tribe and master of this caravan. Our leader is the noble Akilli Khan, and we live at the Birches, which in our language is Falaka Sopasi. We speak Tatar, which, as you can hear, is similar to Turkish. We can understand each other. This is my companion Nissim, who also speaks Turkish. My father has some questions to ask."

My father asked them in Turkish. "In a few days, we shall be entering the small portion of Kalmykia that juts into the Volga. You likely came from that direction. If you have ever met some

Kalmyks, they were probably gracious and hospitable. Not so with us. We are mortal enemies, and we expect trouble this year. Are you men fighters?"

"Yes, yes, we are. Like you, we have learned to use the bow while mounted, on camels, of course. It was necessary for us who are in danger from robbers and pirates on a daily basis. The Afghan deserts are very dangerous. We will of course fight for young Tambor, who is now our master. We are also pleased to fight for the noble Dalgali, who frequently traded with our previous master."

"That is fine," he said quietly. "We shall be closing our trading in about fifteen minutes. After the evening meal, we shall be having a small conference. Tambor, you and Nissim are expected and also Chabuk and Hazir. Vishtaspa and Mardunya, you will accompany Lord Tambor also."

Since the camel drivers were now part of my responsibility, they would be traveling at the rear with us. I introduced them to my men, who although somewhat cool at first, found that they could communicate with each other in a cooperative fashion. Their former owners had taken away with them all but one sleeping tent, which provided shelter for Kuru, the elder man, and the twins. I was please to see our herdsmen willing to help. Kuru took his nephews, who were young, about Kymmy's age. I offered my place in our tent to Vishtaspa, and Nissim gave his place to Mardunya, since we continued to sleep outdoors. Naveed found a place in one of the herdsmen's tent. I noticed that night that Mardunya decided to sleep outside where the camels were tied up. I expressed my pleasure at this arrangement with all of them when we were having our evening meal.

As we were finishing eating, Chabuk drew up to our fire. I introduced him to the new men. He was friendly enough, and I felt some of that snide exterior softening.

"I heard you men fight. Where are your weapons?"

"They are in a holster on each of the camels," Vishtaspa said. He brought Chabuk over to demonstrate. "As we told your father, we also shoot from the saddle as you do. I presume the Kalmyks also fight this way. We also have the slight advantage of height as it is easier to shoot down from the camel onto the enemy. They have to shoot upwards. We also use the javelin." Chabuk was impressed.

He drank a bowl of tea with us and then motioned us to join Lord Dalgali toward the front of the caravan. We spoke together on the way. "They seem like very intelligent men. I hear you paid a fairly good price. I suppose that once you have trained them into your retinue, you will free them and they will feel obliged to serve you even as free people."

I laughed. "Perhaps, my brother, I am just a good businessman. Think of them as an investment if you must, but what I want is for each of my men to develop himself to his maximum ability and this they cannot do under slavery." I turned to Nissim and asked him if he felt like an investment.

He did not answer my question but turned to Chabuk. "When Tambor offered me my freedom, I had already proved myself totally unworthy of it. But Tambor offered me something even more valuable. He offered me his friendship. It may not be important to you at this time, Chabuk, but you too have my friendship if you want it." I saw that Chabuk couldn't meet his eye and drew his horse ahead.

"Well, Father is itching to get together, so let's get a move on it."

It wasn't at all what I expected. We sat around the fire patiently and silently awaiting a word from my father which would call the meeting to order. We were offered some kumis, which implied some sort of celebration. Father was quiet; it was annoying. Finally when we were somewhat relaxed and talking, Father brought the meeting to order. First of all, he thanked us for our cooperation and hard work and expressed his desire that this venture should be relaxing, more like a vacation.

"So far, everything has been going well—that is, going well on the surface. I very much appreciate the fact that my two sons, Tambor and Chabuk, have accompanied us this year and also Nissim, whom I consider one of the family. I tell you that I very much miss Dalgin, who has so often accompanied us even as a young boy. He is a good singer and poet who has often entertained us at campfire. Besides, his mother constantly reminds me how very much I miss him." We laughed. "But you will all agree that he needs to recover." He turned to Tutumlu and nodded. "I am proud to see your son Tetik with us, and I praise the gods that he has recovered well. His hawks are selling well, apparently. Is that so?" He got the desired response from Tutumlu, and everyone present expressed approval. Father continued, nodding to Hazir: "I am also pleased to have your new son, Kiymetli, with us. I am sure that in doing this you have rendered your brother honor and comfort. Kymmy's enthusiasm for learning and working *and talking* is inspiring if not a bit vigorous.

"As you know, my son Tambor has acquired a small group of camels and their drivers. They have been traveling as camel drivers for some time, and we have traded with their former masters. They are now part of Lord Tambor's team. We have here—I'm sorry, I have forgotten your names. Ah yes, Vishtaspa and your younger brother Mardunya. Welcome to you." The Persians nodded respectfully. "Their father, Kuru, is with them and another brother and two cousins. Is this correct? And we also have a camel colt." That caused some laughter. "Vishtaspa and Mardunya have informed us that they are trained fighters because of having to travel through deserts filled with thieves near the Afghan border. This is the reason they have been invited here tonight, acting as spokesmen for the family. With the impending trouble approaching, we must have all the fighters we can get. We must be sensitive to the possibility of attack. We must also be prepared to deal with it correctly when and if it comes. Have you any questions so far?"

Hazir responded, "Lord Dalgali, you speak in terms of possibilities rather than probabilities, and you have gathered us here to make battle plans. In my mind, I am not exactly sure what we are to do individually. Could you be more precise? What should I expect for myself?"

"There has been growing unrest amongst the Kalmyks, many of whom do not want us to pass through our territory. The history of our mutual hostility goes back several hundred years to the time of Kublai Khan, the magnificent, one of the descendants of Chinggis. Our leader, the Tatar king Nogay, was likewise a grandson of the great conqueror and was involved in a conspiracy to replace a young heir to the western throne. Nogay did not assume rule immediately but left the western Tatars to the rule of Tuda-Mongu, a Mongol.

"After the assassination of Tuda-Mongu, his two sons gathered an army and submitted their fealty to an eastern ruler, Toktai, who heard their case and decided to champion their cause. No doubt Toktai saw some political and economic advantage to supporting them and demanded that Nogay appear before him. Under no circumstances would Nogay submit to the demands of a foreigner. No doubt he thought the next thing he would do would be to put these men in charge and extract tribute.

"Both Toktai and Nogay knew war was inevitable, and each began to amass an army. Toktai led 200,000 Mongol warriors and Nogay had 150,000 native warriors. Nevertheless, Nogay, who suffered great loss, sent them back to where they came from farther east to their yurt. Although it was not exactly a victory, as he lost territory, he nevertheless achieved independence. Many of the enemy's soldiers were from China and Tibet and followed the teachings of the Buddha. These retaliated and at the next battle Nogay was killed. We became known as the Nogay Horde and we governed our land a generation.

"But this time, we were defeated and retreated west, some of us to the Crimea, where the Tatars gave us hospitality. Our refugees, our own ancestors among them, retreated into the hills of the Kuban River in the Caucasus Mountains where the Cossacks dwelt. Some of the Nogay went even to Europe and set up centers in Bulgaria and Macedonia. We managed a hasty and not always an honored alliance there. However, some of the great khan's forces did not return to the east. These claimed the lands we had abandoned. Of course there was a great mixing among the peoples. The Kalmyks, however, have maintained their own traditions. They follow the Buddha, even to this day.

"The trouble came when the Russians descended upon us a few generations back when we were weak and lacked unity. The Cossacks in the Ukraine, the Borderlanders, allied themselves with the Russians, becoming free of the Eastern yoke, which had badly weakened. We of the Nogay Horde were hostile toward the new rulers and would neither pay tribute nor recognize the tsar. This was the normal Tatar response no matter which tribe we belonged to."

(I will interrupt my father's eloquent, though perhaps exaggerated speech, to remind you, Reverend Father, that the northern members of the Golden Horde as well as you Chuvash and the Mari were also united in this.)

"However, to our surprise, the Kalmyks willfully submitted to the Russian tsar. As a result, they were given access to the Volga at exactly the location over which we will be passing. They were also given the commission to keep us in check. We were forbidden nomadic rights and trading excursions in their areas. We were prisoners in our own territory. They habitually harassed us and often attacked our villages. All we could do eventually was pack up and go and even this was not without harassment. That is what Akilli Khan's grandfather did. Even as a young man, not much older than Tambor, he persuaded our fathers to take everything we had and leave. Other tribes went south to the Turkish lands.

We chose Astrakhan, even if it meant traveling through enemy territory and relocating in Russian territory. These were the days before Stenka Razin came along. When he passed as a wave over Astrakhan, the khan's father was deceived into submission. But, my friends, that is a story for another time.

"These days, we more or less cooperate with the Russians. They get no tribute from us, but our caravans make them enough money that they are not so inclined to press us. Our venture at Mikhailov was a not-so-subtle reminder that our traffic is very valuable to them and to lay off. My sons' venture into Cherny Yar convinces me that cooperation pays off. However, I do not believe that the Kalmyks feel exactly this way. We go through their territory, but we do not trade with them. They will have nothing to do with us."

Vishtaspa interrupted. "The Persian and Turkish caravans trade with them regularly, Lord Dalgali."

"Precisely, Vishtaspa! Their hatred for us still smolders. All these many years, I have been bribing their leaders, especially the chief of the eastern shoreline. We got along moderately well until that unfortunate incident two years ago when two of our boys attempted to rough them up at the cost of some lives on both sides. Last year I was lucky. This year we may not be so lucky."

Father then turned to me and said, "I am pleased that you have wisely invested in camels. It seems that we now can include another group of fighters to go along with them. When the three of you were in Cherny Yar, I took the liberty to call for reinforcements. My instructions were that they were to be sent only if they were not needed there, but as yet, I have had no word from Sopasi. If they fail to arrive in time or arrive at all, we still have the advantage of your men. I am not sure I wish to linger. So let us move on. I need your advice as to the defensive battle plan. We will not be thought of as the aggressors."

After such a speech, I think we were all struck with silence. I have come to admire my father's eloquence. As far as I am concerned, the only one that could match the excellence of his speech would be the khan. He looked at us intently, one by one, as a gradual smile lit up his face.

"Come, come now, are you all shrinking in fear? I can't believe it!"

I could see Chabuk stiffen at that. I suppose I did too. "Father," he said, "we may be uncertain as to what to do, but we are certainly not cowards. In fact, I am looking forward to a confrontation. I want to restore my honor."

"Don't look forward to it too much, my son. Besides risking our lives, we do not want to endanger our flocks and herds. Much of our defense requires the protection of our livestock, which is our livelihood. We do not want to return to our people empty-handed. My experience in these matters is one of protection rather than glory-seeking. Let us plan wisely. Battling on the move is very different from leading a raid. We *could use* the double- or triple-arrow formation. If we are on the move or sitting at camp, we must keep this formation even at leisure. Until we get past Kalmykia, we will be at war."

This was a formation for a caravan on the move. It consisted of three triangles or arrows pointing forward. There could be more or fewer arrows depending on the size of the livestock within the arrowheads. There would be one lead at the tip of the arrow and two warriors at the back one on each side. The livestock would be in the middle. An equal number of warriors would be stationed from the tip to the ends of both sides. This protected the livestock within the triangles. No warriors would guard the space between the two back guards, which was the reason it was called an arrowhead rather than a triangle. Chabuk would lead the first arrow, and two warriors would flank the both sides. Two other warriors would protect the center from between the tip and the rear. The herdsmen who were not trained warriors could still shoot an arrow and also swing a saber. However, their main duty was to keep a tight rein on the herds so that they not panic but stay together. Our herdsmen were well trained, in spite of the fact that these skills had rarely been put to use.

Hazir was to lead the second arrow backed up by four other fighters in the same formation as the first arrow. The center bore the tent of the women. This was one of the transportable already assembled yurts, which would be drawn by oxen or sometimes heavy work horses. These traveling tents are the kind of yurts we inherited from the Mongols. The women were safe within the yurt. That was Natasha's domain; some of the warriors brought concubines. The slower animals would stay within this arrow. However, there would be two campfires within this arrow to provide food and tea, one near the lead serving the first arrow and one in the back serving the rear. Eating time was staggered, and all the men would be sleeping out at these times, with one eye open.

I was to lead the rear formation with Nissim and another warrior at the back. All my own livestock was with me. Normally, there should be two or three warriors backing the rear arrow, but we hadn't the men. However, Mardunya broke in, advising us as to how the camels could be employed. He had once had to use the arrow formation while on a trip through the Afghan mountains when the caravan he was on was threatened by outlaw tribesmen. He suggested that one camel should accompany the lead horse within the arrow but not far behind. Two camels were to guard the women's tent and the final three would close the back arrow. He reasoned that the camels, being rather more massive and less maneuverable, would provide greater protection from within, it being easier to shoot down from the greater height.

Now we were providing some activity. The discussion was noisy and vigorous, and Father spent much time trying to keep us in order. But I think he was actually delighted to see our enthusiasm. As he had never seen the trader in me, so I also had never, until that moment, seen the warrior in him. I was proud of him. Occasionally, his eye met mine, and he would let out just the slightest grin. We would be battling together. I was excited. Chabuk was unusually quiet though. I could only make out that he was still sensitive about being the possible or partial cause of this trouble. Nissim was also pensive, this being his first real battle. However, I did not sense hesitance. He, like Hazir, was interested in details and was paying obvious attention to father's every word. The women had joined us and were serving tea and fermented yoghurt with sweet bread.

I leaned back and observed everything. Natasha made a point of coming over to me. She was, as usual, warm and generous, but I did, of course, sense a bit of anxiety from her. She poured me some tea and gave me some yogurt in a wide bowl along with some flat bread. If she wanted to talk, she could do so when she felt comfortable.

"How are you enjoying the trip so far, Tashi?" I used to call her this when I was just a boy. I think it made her feel a little more at ease.

"I have always enjoyed these trips." She giggled. "It's the only time I can have your father to myself. Yerinde is fine with it. I usually come home carrying a child. I suspect, by the way she is so close to Uyari, that she takes some herbs to prevent conception. She once told me that she has done her duty by him. Your father is such a lusty man." She whispered this. "But more than that, he is a kind and gentle man, and I love him."

Nissim joined us at that moment and she gave him the same attention she gave me. I was surprised to see her ruffle his hair affectionately.

"I wish the two of you would visit me more often at home. I do enjoy the company of men. Timov has been a real comfort to me and an encouragement to my boy. I wish he had come with us. Look at Tetik, how able he has become even without a wrist."

"But, Tashi, Dalgin was not able to mount a horse before we left."

"Oh, I know, I'm just complaining. Tell me, young warriors, what is going on? Dalgali has told me that there may be some fighting. I suppose I am a little afraid." She paused. "It's not that I am afraid of dying…I am. It is just that every year when I go to Astrakhan, I go to make my confession, and I do not want to die unconfessed. I am not much of a sinner, but I am far from being much of a saint. It is very important for us Christians to enter God's kingdom with cleansed hearts. I don't know if you can understand."

Nissim took her hand and said. "Pray for me, sister. I will have to shed blood, and I too do not want to die unconfessed. I have not confessed since I was enslaved in Nicomedia five years ago."

"You and Timov are Christians? I had no idea."

"Please do not noise it abroad, Tashi," I said firmly. "Timov works with Kattu, who is pro-Muslim. The boys did not leave the empire on good terms with the authorities. It is best to be quiet about it."

"Indeed, my Lord Tambor. I am also quiet about Dalgin, who was baptized many years ago. I usually insist he accompany me to confession and communion. That's why I wish he were here." She turned to Nissim. "You know I have tried to teach my children the faith. Every Voskresenie (Sunday), my children gather for prayers and religious instruction. We have permission from Dalgali, who encourages it, but we must be quiet about it. You men are welcome to join us. We have a small service of prayer. Dalgali insists Dalgin be present, but I confess my son is not very attentive. I think Chabuk tries to keep him from taking it too seriously. Timov has been with us a few times with Dalgin, but I didn't know he was Christian. Perhaps there will be a change."

"What is Dalgin's baptized name, Lady Natasha?" Nissim asked.

"Why, he is named Daniel. Dalgali insisted he be named Dalgin to give him a native identity. But I like to call him Daniel, my dreamer. And what is your name, Nissim?"

"I am named after Onesimus, the runaway slave. And Timov celebrates Saint Timotheus, the friend of Saint Paul. How did you happen to come amongst the Kubanshyi?"

"Well, let me tell you, my boys. I am actually a Cossack by birth and a loyal Orthodox Christian by faith. I am a third daughter to my family and was not necessarily marriageable. We were struggling financially, and my father was in debt. He had done some trading with your father and owed him a considerable sum of money. My father begged Dalgali to release him from his debt by taking me as the payment, no dowry being necessary. Dalgali pondered this for a few days and then asked to meet me. I loved him at first sight. Although the Church forbade Christian women from becoming second wives or concubines to non-Christians, it was contracted legally since the Russians tolerate the Tatars, who are considered notorious polygamists. Of course I was anxious and fearful to enter life in the yurts since I was little more than a girl, but I knew your father would treat me well, and he still does. I was permitted to keep my religion, and after a few years of penance, the Church restored me to communion. That's why I like to go to Astrakhan, where my confessor lives, and sometimes to Kazan as we did last spring. There is a precious icon of the Virgin there which is miraculous."

Miraculous indeed, I thought. It seems even Christian women have their superstitions. But I loved Natasha and indulged her in her fantasies.

Nissim said to her, "Perhaps I shall go and venerate her at some time, and you can show me around."

I was growing steadily more impatient with this women's talk and was even irritated that Nissim was involved with it. I was able to tolerate this one God business, but talking about miracles and penances and polygamists was just too much. Nissim noticed my chagrin. I tried to hide it from Natasha but made no effort to conceal it from him. As usual, he was able effortlessly to shift the conversation back to current affairs.

"Anyhow," Natasha continued, "I admit to being afraid of this confrontation, Tambor. In all my life in the tents, I have never experienced violence or danger. Dalgali says everything is taken care of, but he doesn't feel my fears. Women are so helpless sometimes, and I now wish that I had learned the bow like your mother."

"My mother? Yerinde can use the bow?" I was shocked.

"Oh yes! She occasionally rides out with a few of your sisters to hunt for small animals. You know, ducks, geese, and rabbits. She makes these dishes especially for us women. How she can cook! I sometimes ride out with her too. Some think she is bossy and tight. I think she is a lot of fun."

"I am so glad to hear you say that, Tashi. As for being afraid, don't concern yourself. You will be well protected. Two of my camel drivers will guard the tent." I reluctantly added, "Here, Tashi, until the trouble is over, use the knife, which Father gave me at Saban-Tui this year."

"Bless you, bless you, my son," she responded, kissing my cheek. "I was serving your father when he bought it for you from the Russian silversmith who visits him whenever we are in Kazan. He actually asked *me* what I thought you would like, and I chose this. I don't know whether I would have the courage to use it though."

"Tashi, when your life is at stake or there is a threat that you will be taken away, believe me, your God will give you the courage. But I don't think it will get that far. Go serve Dalgali, Tashi. He is looking over here."

"Imagine that, Nissim," I said as she left us. "My mother, using a bow? Can you believe it?"

"She is actually quite good. I used to help saddle the horses for her little hunting party and once, or twice, I saddled up and sneaked out after her…for reasons of safety and protection, of course!"

"Of course!" We both snickered. Again I thought how blind I had been to these little but very important things. At moments like this, I doubted my maturity. I still felt like a boy rather than the man I was becoming. I guess my friendship with Nissim helped me feel I was not alone and that there was one person with whom I could truly be myself. And then I thought of Katya.

Next morning, Chabuk and Father rode out and gathered us all together. "We are moving out this morning. Be ready in an hour. Gather all the food and gear, and have your weapons ready. We are to look like warriors on the move. All herdsmen are to be armed and ready for battle. I don't expect trouble today, but we are to look ready for it. Get the dogs to work and assemble the flocks. You know what to do. Captain Hazir will instruct you in battle formation."

I could see him coming up the east side appointing the warriors and putting them in position. Kiymetli was with him, looking very important. In spite of the boy's youthful stature, he was wearing a suit of leather armor just like the rest of us. I had to smile as I waved a greeting to them. Our arrow was almost already in place. The camels were a little slower getting in position, which was something I would have to get used to, but when they were in order, the whole caravan looked like a war party or even an army. I was proud and excited.

"I have already briefed Hazir this morning as to what will happen," Father said to me. "We should reach Tsagan Aman inside the Kalmyk border by nightfall. If we fail to do so, we will camp and stay within formation until the morning; then we will move on. There is a Russian garrison at Tsagan Aman, and the captain is an acquaintance of mine. Hopefully if we arrive tonight, we shall see him early in the morning. You and Nissim and Chabuk will accompany me. Hazir will stay behind and keep order in the camp. Any questions?"

"Actually, Father, I am curious about something. When did you get word that there may be trouble ahead. Is this just an intuition you had?" I asked this quite seriously.

"By Tengri, certainly not! I had my suspicions after last year's coolness by the old chief, of course. But didn't I tell you? When you were in Cherny Yar, your friend Konstantin sent three soldiers to our camp to warn us that there would likely be trouble. I had to spare two warriors to send for reinforcements from the khan as secretly as possible. They have not arrived yet, but we cannot wait. Didn't Konstantin tell you what he was doing?" He paused for an answer that didn't come. "Hmm. How very discrete. You certainly pick your friends well."

He then turned. "Come, Chabuk. Tambor, keep peaceful and level-headed. You are absolutely essential at the rear. In fact, you are absolutely essential. We shall meet up later on." He slowly moved up front encouraging all the men on the way. He commanded and got respect. In a short time, we moved on.

This part of the journey was very quiet. This was partly due to the fact that, being in position, we were not close enough to each other to chat. Mainly, of course, we were thoughtful and anxious. This turn of events we had not expected. Yet I could see from my position how well we were working together. Being quiet, I could see the steady and deliberate pace of the camels and admired their dignity and strength. I could also see that the camel drivers had as much bonding with their animals as we had with our horses. If I could have known how to thank you, Lord, for this rash decision on my part, I would have done so, for I was indeed grateful, though I didn't know at that time, to the one who governs the hearts and minds of men. Nissim was at the end of the arrow on the right side. Other travelers on the roads seemed aware of our formation.

I had also the opportunity to observe the activities of the hounds and their herdsmen. I realized that, if Father would grant me these herdsmen permanently, I would also be the possessor of these very smart and well-disciplined animals, lithe and lusty, who were also well bonded with their breeders. I could observe only the ones ahead of me, but they had the herd in close command, almost as though they figured out the formation themselves. Of course the herders kept on barking orders, which they obeyed.

Because of the silence, we moved somewhat more swiftly than usual, though at a speed that would not tire us out. Father's experience and wisdom paid, off for we arrived just outside Tsagan Aman just before nightfall, just in time to assemble the tents and prepare our second meal for the day. Father did not call another meeting because he didn't want to break formation, but he came up the east side, the Volga side, personally encouraging the men. Hazir came up the west till he got to Nissim and said something to him. At the same time, Father approached me and reminded me that we three brothers were to accompany him to the garrison tomorrow. We each, warriors and herdsmen, alike took turns to eat from the two fires. Since one was immediately in front of me, I was able to talk to the men and discern their mood. Anxious as we were, we all anticipated any attack, should there actually be one. We were Nogay warriors, and the herdsmen were noble and loyal Kubanshyi. Although the Persians were strangers, they were mine.

One time, Kuru, the elder, tried to do reverence to me, but I would not let him. I had one of his boys tell him that since he was a noble father whose sons and nephews respected him, I would respect him too. He was grateful but still bowed before me. I smiled at Vishtaspa, who accompanied him; he explained that his father was grateful to serve me, and he knew his place. I let it go; that's the way things were.

I slept quietly that night.

Father was up before all of us. No doubt he had wakened Chabuk, who was with him. We didn't have time to bathe in the Volga as we had become accustomed to. Nissim came around as I was washing, and Father and my brother came around again. Father seemed somewhat impatient though he was in high spirits. I was amazed at how he seemed always to have contacts he could rely upon even if his contact might be a Russian. In this case, it was the Russian army he would speak to.

Captain Zander Stepanovich Tretyakov may not have been as warm a man as Konstantin Alexandrovich Lapukhin, but he was certainly as hospitable, if a bit formal. Obviously vodka served as a drink for proper occasions as kumis served for us. In fact Father offered a jug of very fine kumis to the captain as apparently was his custom.

"Thank you once again, Lord Dalgali, for your ever-thoughtful gift. Presumably this was likewise brewed by your wife. How mare's milk can be made so tasty and sweet is amazing to me. Our vodka may fall short in flavor, but I'm sure you will agree it makes up for it in punch. I've met Chabuk before," he nodded, "but who are these other two gentlemen? It seems that Dikkatli is not accompanying you this year."

"This is my second son, Tambor, one of our finest knights, and his squire Nissim, who is part of the family."

"Ah, so this is the trio who met Vice Governor Konstantin at Cherny Yar. He was very impressed with your lads. Apparently they were very diplomatic and cooperative, obviously well trained by their father." He nodded to us. His air of formal propriety annoyed me somewhat.

"I am afraid I have been somewhat neglectful as regards to Tambor," Dalgali said. "I am a man of business and have not been home much. Tambor's talents, to be quite honest, must have been developed by himself." I was feeling uncomfortable. A smile on his part might have been welcome.

He was a handsome man, mustachioed, and well maintained. I could see that he was well built under his tight uniform; he was not wearing his coat. The gold ring on his right hand told me he was married. A slight look of sadness softened his countenance for a moment.

"I know what you mean. I've seen my wife and son only three times over the past few years. I wonder if I will ever get to know my son. I left Tonya with her family in Vladimir. Although I tried to get her relocated here, everyone advised against it. It is such an outpost here. Semyon would hardly get a good education. Antonya's family objected to her marrying a soldier, and this is their way of rubbing salt into the wound. Fortunately I am up for relocation and will be given some time off. After that, my rank will increase, and I will have greater flexibility relocating."

Father said, "I know that I shall surely miss these visits with you. But your wife needs you more than Kalmykia does. You also have good relations with the local Kalmyk chieftain Ubashi whose tribe governs this area. Last year Chief Ubashi almost refused my customary gift. Thanks for your intervention. How ridiculous to express such hostility against a small caravan peacefully crossing a piece of uninhabited land."

"Chief Ubashi was here recently. He was expecting his regular payoff, which I proffered on your behalf, but you know, Lord Dalgali, he also said that although he would not cause trouble, some of the younger men may go against his orders. He was kind enough to stress this as a warning. He had also been informed that he knew you were arriving in battle formation. Of course he does not want a slaughter."

Father took out another little bag of coins and handed them to the captain, obviously next year's payment. "My informants have also warned me of this possibility. We will not attack, but we are prepared to defend ourselves."

"You understand that I am assigned to Astrakhan. Tsagan Aman, while on the border, is within Kalmyk territory. I can neither defend you nor oppose you once you have crossed the border. But I will help in whatever way possible." He turned to Nissim. "Young man, I am told you are *Pravoslav*. This is very unusual for the people of the yurt." He looked at Father for confirmation and continued. "I trust that you are in constant prayer for your lord Dalgali and your friend Tambor. There is a priest in Astrakhan by the name of Father John. Look him up when you get there and give him my regards."

Nissim replied, "Others have also advised this. He must be an important man. By the way, Captain, is there any place in the garrison where I can buy some weapons?"

"Yes, see the officer on the way out. They are *Russian* weapons, you understand."

"Yes, thank you."

After the captain was out of earshot, I pressed him. "What do you need with other weapons? You have a good bow, a spear, and a sword. What more do you need?"

"Trust me," he replied. "Come and indulge your squire." He laughed.

I had given him some money from time to time, but I had never seen him spend it. He needed just a few more rubles, and I gave it to him. With it he bought a strong silver ax with an oak handle, which was called a *topor*. He also chose a heavy hand hammer and a simple but sharp knife. There was also a belt that he swung around his shoulder to hold them. He looked at me with his deep-brown eyes and that almost-embarrassed grin, which twisted up at one side of his mouth.

"I didn't go to a military academy for nothing. You have taught me to fight Tatar style, but I have a few other tricks under my belt."

Father was waiting for us mounted, but not as impatient as I had expected. He tossed me a warm piroshki and slapped me on the shoulder as I mounted. "I'm told you like these." He bit into one and said, "Hmm, they're good. Let's relax a bit tonight. Tomorrow we shall be well within enemy territory. It will take us two days to reach the other side." He said this as we rode off. "I presume we will be watched. No bathing in the Volga until we have cleared the route. I am presuming that the attack will come tomorrow morning. We shall be surrounded before they let out a hoot. They fight like us. They may surprise us though. We have got to be alert and sleepless. We have heard no word about reinforcements." He shrugged.

CONFRONTATION

In surrounding they surrounded me, and in the name of the Lord I
fended them off! They surrounded me like bees a honeycomb, and
they blazed like a fire among thorns and in the name of the Lord I
fended them off!

—Psalm 117: 11–12 (lxx nets)

Some of the blessed Psalms of Holy David, dear Holy Father,
spark my mind with some of the most scintillating memories…
memories that are so clear the clash of battle still sears my nostrils.
It happened just as my Father had said, early in the morning. I had
dozed off late in the evening. It was Nissim who had awakened
me after finishing his morning prayers. He sneaked over to me
and shook me on the shoulder quietly so as not to startle me
unduly. The sun had not quite risen.

He said, "I have to get back quickly, but I know they are here.
I can feel it. They are just observing and waiting for the advantage
that dawn brings. I have been praying in the name of the Lord. I
know you have courage," he whispered, "but what we all need is
faith." He silently disappeared.

I felt it too. I could see that we were all ahead and in our
proper places stirring ever so slightly. The horses were restless but
remained silent. The Persians on their mountainous camels were
tense and alert. I mounted Onyx, my bow in my left hand, and my
right hand as ready to grasp my sword as ready to pull an arrow.
I tried to see but in vain; the darkness still consumed us. But it
was from the trees lining the Volga that I felt the greatest danger.
The west side was a flat grassy plain. I would be able to see the
shadow of a rider or a rabbit. Of course there was a thicket to the
north behind us where anyone could be hiding. The waiting was
excruciating. This was different from Mikhailov, I mused. There,

we were the aggressors; here, we were the ones on the defense. Faith! I had never thought of faith as a needed aspect of war. I suppose I was not exactly afraid, but I felt myself praying, not to Tengri, but to Nissim's God. Even though I felt the enemy near, I felt a strange peace in the presence of this Divinity.

"Keep us safe in your care…God. Don't let any of us act foolishly. Thank you…uh…God." I said this just as the sun sauntered over the east side of the Volga.

I could see it through the trees, just as the shadows swiftly emerged from the trees and the first war whoop was sounded from the woods. My arrow hit one of those shadows with a thud; it tottered and fell. A dozen arrows flew toward the shadows, which were backed by the brilliant sunshine. I realized that with the sun shining directly in our eyes, they had the advantage.

The dogs attacked. There were about ten of them. Our dogs were not short ones like the northern ones. They were long lithe hounds. They could leap, straight at the thighs, quick enough to pull a man down and smart enough not to be struck. We could see the enemy now. Fortunately the trees shielded us to a small degree from the blinding sun. The dogs provided a distraction and allowed our archers a momentary advantage.

So focused were we on the eastern attack, we didn't count on an attack from the west. All of a sudden we heard the thunder of a score of horses' hooves. Nissim at the rear west responded to the attack first and his group sent a volley of arrows. Two riders came down. I could see, way at the front, Chabuk turning on his steed and sending a few newcomers flying off their horses. So far the riders had not attacked the front but rather the middle arrow. There was no attack from the back as yet, and I saw two of the camels move ahead. They actually dived toward the newcomers throwing their horses into confusion. Some of the horses reared and threw their riders down. I could see what the Persians meant about being high off the ground. I could see the ease with which they could spear their victims below. The camels seemed massive and the dromedary towering.

I felt the whiz of an arrow pass my ear and realized I was under attack. The one who shot the first arrow shot another and dived toward me with his bow drawn. I dived toward him with my sword drawn and my shield in my left hand, but in his speed, he passed me and had to turn rearing his horse. I saw that his face was filled with fury. He came toward me again, and this time we slashed swords until, with one swoop, my scimitar came down on his neck. As he tumbled off his horse, a wild cry came from behind me. I twisted and lifted my sword to block the downward thrust of another warrior, which was so heavy it nearly pulled back my arm.

At that very moment, I saw Nissim coming from behind the warrior on Cereyan. In an instant, Nissim was off his horse and, with a few steps and a swing, sliced my opponent with his silver ax and severed his thigh. With a cry, my opponent turned, looked straight at Nissim and received Nissim's ax into his throat. I wanted to say "Good work!" but didn't have the time because Nissim had mounted Cereyan again and started off toward another rider. I wanted to watch him work, but that would have put me in danger. I wanted to see his style. Again I saw him slide down the back of his mare and approach a Kalmyk from the back. This time the ax struck the waist. As the rider began to fall, Nissim grabbed the hammer from his belt and in an instant bashed the back of his skull with it. In a flash, he was on Cereyan's back again. I couldn't believe the swiftness. Of course his mare had been interbred with one of the steppe horses, shorter and easier to mount, unlike the northern steeds now popular. The Kurds and Kalmyks still trade in steppe horses. Onyx was however a tall steed, one of the horses we got from the thieves.

But now I was under attack. I sheathed my sword and took my bow and drew an arrow. I was quick enough with the arrow to bring my opponent down, but a second came from behind him.

This time, one of the camels attacked the rider. Old Kuru sent an arrow straight into the rider's eye. I was greeted with a wide smile of white and gold teeth. An enemy archer tried to shoot up at the old man and missed; my returning arrow didn't. In the distance near the front formation, I could see Chabuk engaged with the scimitar, his favorite weapon. our father was not far from him. They were on the outside, and I saw now that they were being overwhelmed.

Seeing the situation, Nissim moved in swiftly, and as he drew near, he caught sight of two Kalmyks coming down on Father. Nissim shouted a warning, which could hardly be heard in the noise of the battle, but Dalgali turned around almost helplessly and swerved. At that moment, an arrow struck one of the attackers from behind; I think it was Mardunya on one of the big camels. At that very moment, Nissim flew off Cereyan's back and, taking the other warrior by surprise, knocked him off his horse with his hammer.

The warrior was quick to recover and stood up looking straight at Nissim, who faced him with his topor in his right hand and his hammer in his left. Anger and confusion was all over the Kalmyk's face, but he was brave and skilled. I saw all this as I drew near. Father's horse had reared and had almost thrown him as the camel charged. As slim as he was, Nissim seemed like a giant of a man, his nostrils flaring and his chest heaving. A touch of fear brushed over his opponent's face, and Nissim took the advantage. The Kalmyk had but a sword in his hand and was obviously not trained in fighting with anything else. Nissim let the topor slide down his arm to give the ax full length. The warrior waited to see what Nissim would do. I didn't see it all as I had to fight off a few opponents myself. But I did see the warrior move in which was what Nissim apparently intended. Nissim swung the ax and hit his opponent below the rib cage with the blunt of the ax causing the warrior to double over. He was young however and recovered swiftly enough to swing at Nissim from below. Nissim hit the sword with the handle of the topor. The Kalmyk held on and swung back, getting too close, giving the advantage to Nissim whose hammer hit the boy just under the right armpit, causing him to fall. Nissim struck the top of his shoulder slicing off the neck with the ax as though it were a tree branch, killing him.

Father had already recovered and steadied his white horse, but I lost sight of the two of them in my own encounters. Two of our warriors were brought down and a few herdsmen hit. These herdsmen were marvelous in spite of it all. With all the violence going on around them, they still managed to keep the herds in order. The dogs had returned to the sheep and cattle, and the horses, all tied together, were kept from panic. Then I saw ahead of me three or four Kalmyks heading for the women's yurt. Father saw it too, and both of us attacked from our different directions. The camels attempted to block the attackers, but being overwhelmed by the sheep and goats at their feet, they could send off only a few ineffective shots. Two of the enemy riders had dismounted and were heading for the yurt. One went in and never came out again, but the second one didn't get too far; he fell out of the tent and landed on his back, blood oozing from his bowels. "Good girl!" I cried. Tashi must have killed the other. A spear from one of the camel herds hit the third in the back. Father was engaged with the fourth attacker but more were coming in. How long we could keep this up, I didn't know. The attackers were so numerous that they had moved in from the outside toward the inside of the arrow formations. They were converging upon the yurt. Who knows what they wanted?

Then came Nissim. Again he was on the ground. We are horsemen, Father, just like the Kalmyks. We prefer not to fight on the ground. Nissim's style took them by surprise. His method was to break their legs with his hammer or chop his opponent with his ax. It seems he wanted to get them on the ground and then take advantage of them on their feet, if they could actually stand. Sword, hammer, ax, whatever, if he could get them on the ground, they were done for. He was virtually a one-man infantry. The arrows buzzed around him but not a single one hit. When he saw me, he turned around and cried out: "Have faith, brother!"

At that very moment, it couldn't have been better timed, we heard a loud war cry, and thirty blue-masked raiders swooped down upon our enemy from the north and overwhelmed them. Both Nissim and I were exhausted. This part of the battle took much longer, Holy Father, but I shall leave that to your imagination or perhaps to your discretion. Finally the battle was over.

My father and I looked at each other and raised our swords. Nissim mounted Cereyan and shouted again, "Have faith, my lords!" Chabuk and Hazir closed in with us and let the masked army clear the field. Bodies were strewn over the ground, and we could see about a dozen Kalmyk riders fleeing toward the west.

When things seemed to have quieted down, the leader of the Blue Raiders came over to Prince Dalgali. He never loosened his turban, but we all recognized his voice "Greetings, Lord Dalgali. I am impressed. You battled close to two hours before we engaged, and only a few of your men fell. We held off until things became critical. Your reputation as a warrior must never be in question. Word will be out. This will never happen again."

"Where did you come from? How long have you been here?" Dalgali asked.

"We have been tracking you for days and spent the night in the copse back there. We nearly persuaded the khan to accompany us, but alas he declined. He gave us strict instructions that we would join the battle only when it looked like you were about to be overcome. Soon, I am sure you will receive visitors from the garrison, and I have no doubt that the old chieftain will have a look at the carnage. Akilli Khan is convinced that he was behind it. No more tribute or bribery will be permitted. But we must go. Lord Tambor, Lord Chabuk, greetings to you. Respects to you, Sir Hazir, and to you, Sir Nissim. You are of the original Blue Raiders. Hail, Lord Dalgali!"

Everyone shouted "Hail, Lord Dalgali!"

"We'll see you all at Saban-Tui, when all of the Blue Raiders will be honored."

The Blue Raiders left slowly. Usta was the only one to have identified himself even then without showing his face. I knew right away that I was one of them. A few cuffed me playfully as they silently passed me. The same affection was shown to all four of us and to the other warriors. Not a word was said. We did not know who they were. We were not to know who they were. Usta may have been in charge, but I was their first leader.

It was so silent we could hear the rush of the Volga to the east like a nearby stream. From where Koyash was in the sky, we could see that it soon would be noon. Gradually we became aware of our surroundings, but we were still unwilling to say anything. Even the livestock had ceased their sounds. Except for the birds in the trees, nature stood still. Onyx nudged up to me and grunted, and I slapped his moist cheek affectionately. Neither he nor I had ever experienced such violence, not even at Mikhailov. Tashi was standing on the ground just below the cart near the opening to the yurt. She too was silent, holding my bloodied knife in her hand. I looked at her, and she at me, giving just a slight smile as though to smile more would break the spell. What broke the silence was the body of the Kalmyk warrior whom she had thrust out of the yurt. He was writhing in pain at my feet. I did what I thought was an act of mercy by thrusting my sword into his neck. At that point, Tashi began to sob, and Father moved toward her to support her.

Little by little, the rest of the women came out of the tent and looked around at the carnage. One of them began to chant a dirge, a folk song about dead warriors; the others joined her, and one by one, they kissed Dalgali's hand and embraced Natasha who had saved them. I could see that in their eyes *she* had become a warrior. Now she could smile even with tears in her eyes. Father had taken the knife out of her hand and motioned to me to come and get it. As I approached him, I felt a swell of pride and love for him and fell on my face to kiss his feet. He lifted me up and embraced me. We were both warriors, and we were both traders. We were father and son.

Chabuk looked at me with not a trace of envy in his eyes and likewise embraced our father.

"Now, Chabuk, your honor has been restored and your shame is washed away in my eyes." He took Chabuk by the neck and kissed him on the lips.

Blood was streaming down Chabuk's face, and it was now evident that an arrow had grazed his cheek and had torn off part of his ear. A finger closer and it would have killed him. The scar would be permanent.

His only comment was "It seems I paid for my shame in my own blood."

"Come, Nissim." Father commanded. "If Sir Tambor will permit it, I will release you from your squirehood." He turned to me, and I nodded. "In such a short time, you have proved to be a courageous and capable warrior. In fact, you and Mardunya saved my life. In my camp, you shall be known as Sir Nissim, and I am certain this will be ratified formally at Saban-Tui by Akilli Khan. From here on, you shall be my adopted son." The warriors cheered.

He paused as though stunned but managed to say, "I am honored to be your son, Lord Dalgali, and will serve you faithfully." Another cheer. Only Chabuk was silent.

"Sir Hazir, let me once again ask the blessing of Tengri upon you. You fought wisely and craftily. We have fought together before, and you were wise and brave at Mikhailov. I thank you, a true Nogay warrior. Ah, but where is the lad?"

"Here I am! Here I am!" A smiling face peeked out from behind Hazir on his mount. "I have been here *all* along!" He was tied to Hazir's waist.

"Yes, and I have been terrified that he would be hit from the back, although he was hidden behind a shield. But he has been spared and I have thereby been spared a greater grief."

Father continued, "Let us all cheer the rest of you, warriors. Two warriors have been sent to the halls of Erlick, there to be honored among the other Nogay heroes." Two of the Blue Raiders had also been hit and another was dead. It was crucial that the blue uniforms be removed and hidden. our leader raised his hands, and all cheered. The women ululated loudly.

Again he raised his hands and blessed the herdsmen and horse masters. Tetik rode up and reported that the cart that had supported the hawk cages had been overthrown. Nevertheless Tutumlu had verified that all the hawks had survived. One of the herdsmen had been killed, and one of my own horse masters was lying wounded and at the point of death. I wanted to see him before he departed this life. One of the Persian boys had been hit by an arrow in the shoulder and was being attended to by his cousin Mardunya and Natasha. He would survive. Natasha said she and some women would attend to the wounded.

She said, "Uyari and Katya have given me some healing medicines and have shown me what to do. I will try my best. Lord Tambor, thank you for the knife and for the courage to use it." The servants were dragging the other dead Kalmyk out of the yurt.

Since Nogay noblemen do not touch the dead, there were only a few slaves who would be able to gather ours. Nissim commented that since he was Christian, he could help out. Prince Dalgali gave him doubtful permission.

"Leave the Kalmyks to attend to their own dead. They follow the Buddha and have their own customs. We shall burn our dead a little farther on, and our wounded should be put into the utility carts till they either die or recover. Leave them to Natasha. We shall move a considerable distance further south to avoid the scent of corruption."

Nissim and I left to visit the horse master who had been struck down. Hopefully we would make it in time. A servant ran after us with a basin full of water so that we could wash the grime and sweat from our faces and the blood from our hands. We were grateful.

"You wash first, my brother. We are both free sons of Prince Dalgali," I said.

"I have another father who is not free," Nissim said sadly.

"I told you, my brother, we would do something about that." After washing, I took my knife, which had just been cleansed, and cut the fleshy portion on the palm of my hand, just below the thumb. I did the same to Nissim and clasped our hands together. "This is a sign of my vow to you, and I will keep my promise." We embraced.

My horseman was dying. "You have served me well, my friend," I said to him. "It is your time to go now as it must come to all of us." His name was Ender. The three arrows that had struck him down had been removed or broken off and lay next to him. I handed them to him. "Take these with you to the house of Erlick and present them to your fathers. There you may abide in honor. Tutumlu and I will visit your wife. Do you have kin to take care of your family?"

"Yes," he hissed in his agony, "and two sons"

"Nevertheless, I will take your sons into my service."

As he smiled, if that is what it could be called, a trickle of blood slid out of side of his mouth. He lifted his eyes to mine until there was no life left in them.

At once, we heard a commotion. There were people approaching from the rear. My father had already seen them. He, Chabuk, and Hazir were already riding out swiftly to meet them. Nissim and I hastily mounted and raced after them. It turned out to be a small Russian guard led by Captain Tretyakov and half a dozen Kalmyks. We could tell even at a distance that these were noblemen by their flat-topped fur hats. Behind them were some hooded figures, which I presumed were priests. One of them was more ceremonially dressed than the others. I was told he was the local lama, for the Kalmyk priesthood followed Tibetan tradition. They carried red candles and large sticks of burning incense. They were already chanting.

Prince Dalgali stopped before their approach, and we lined up in a row behind him.

Father lifted his hand and pointed at the khan. "Shame! Shame! Shame! Let the blood of your warriors cry out from the earth your disgrace! Never again shall my gold, the token of my good will, enter the palm of your hand. If I have to destroy as many villages as I have fingers on my left hand, you shall never again show such disrespect to me or to our revered Akilli Khan.

"Will this hostility never end? Will we two tribes still fight wars that finished four hundred years ago? Will we still ferment the foul stench of our ignorance and coldheartedness? Will we continue to stain the earth uselessly with the blood of our sons?

"I have always offered peace and gratitude, and you have betrayed me. From now on, the only thing I shall offer you will be horse and camel droppings as I peacefully cross your land, or else *be it known*, the cries of your widows will be heard from Astrakhan to Kazan!"

By the solemn look on his face, we knew that Khan Ubashi and his nobles understood every word my father said. Captain Zander Stepanovich Tretyakov then solemnly approached us.

"I am speaking on behalf of the tribal nobility. They wish to pray for their dead, Lord Dalgali. They have brought their priests from their monastery. I see you are already preparing to leave. They request that you move far enough away that the smoke from your funeral pyres will not mix with their incense. Khan Ubashi is grieving. I believe two of his sons lie dead here. I understand some of their customs. The nobles will gather the bodies of their kin and take them to a sacred hill near the monastery where they will be dismembered and fed to the vultures, which they believe are divine beings. Look up. The others, the common fighters, will be left here to be devoured by the vultures overhead. It used to be that the locals threw the corpses into the Volga, but the Russian authorities have forbidden it.

"But your sons are alive, Dalgali. Thanks be to God! As for me, all I can say is, God's will be done! For he will have mercy on whom he will have mercy."

He leaned over on his steed and questioned Father very quietly in our hearing: "Do you have any idea who these Blue Raiders were? That's what they are now called. Obviously they rescued your party."

"In fact, my dear Captain, only the leader spoke to us. He said he was sworn to secrecy. All were masked. Of course, in gratitude we will honor their vow." Zander had the good taste not to mention Mikhailov.

"Oh yes," he said, reaching into his pocket, "I am returning next year's tribute to you at the chief's request."

"Thank you, my dear Russian friend. Keep it for yourself, for Semyon's education. I shall miss you." Prince Dalgali was gracious. My father was always gracious.

That night we bathed in the Volga.

The rest of the trip to the city of Astrakhan was somewhat uneventful for me. We stopped at many of the cities and villages on the way and sold more horses and all my sheep. The farther south we got, the less we heard about the siege of Mikhailov. Some of the Tatar tribesmen we met casually mentioned it to Father, but none of the Russians made reference to the source of my little flock of sheep. All they were interested in was obtaining them.

They *did* hear about the slaughter of the Kalmyks, however. The Tatars spoke of it with indignation: "It's about time someone put the Kalmyks in their place." The Russians expressed some concern and wonder about the event: "Hopefully, this will not repeat itself. The last thing we need is a full-scale war to break the peace." Some from both quarters asked about the Blue Raiders with not a little anxiety: "They attacked the Russians at Mikhailov and then the Kalmyks who are Russian allies. Who's next?" Our response was this: "Who knows? All we can say is that we are grateful to them."

We generally ignored this gossip, not wanting to feed this talk. Father kept busy buying. He purchased a lot of grain products and dried fruits such as figs, dates, and apricots as well as nuts of all sorts. He made contact with other caravans both local and foreign. He too was running out of herds and flocks. Tutumlu advised that I should keep some horses for the market at Astrakhan so as to build up a reputation, even though I could have made more silver in other places.

I became aware that this was the actual purpose of these trading trips. It was indeed trade, and it was purposeful for the tribe. Unlike me, my father traded cattle for grains such as barley, wheat, buckwheat, which was called kasha, and also millet for our use. These grains were of finer quality than the ones we cultivated crudely at home for the herds. There were other grains like oats and kamut, which were imports and very expensive; these he didn't buy. There was another grain that came from the foreign merchants, I believe from India, called rice, which was plentiful and relatively inexpensive. He had been aware of it before and had questioned Natasha about the advisability of buying some for our use. She gave her approval and, with her maidens, questioned the merchants about its use and asked them for cooking instructions.

Natasha often accompanied Father when he was buying because her opinion reflected the needs of the people who cook, namely, the women. I also began to realize that Natasha was not necessarily the sweet but ineffectual woman I had thought but rather she proved to be an astute and perceptive businesswoman. Neither had I realized how close she was to my mother to whom she often referred with affection and some humor.

Natasha would often make a few comments about Yerinde at which she and Father would chuckle. At first, I took it as irreverence and was a little piqued but slowly I came to realize that Mother was not exactly perfect, and with chagrin, I too joined in the banter, which was by no means hostile or offensive. I regretted, with some melancholy, the distance between my mother and me both physically and emotionally. Tashi noticed my reserve and sadness and tenderly comforted me. I think she had also realized for some time how attached to Katya I was but had the good sense not to mention it. I was glad Tashi was around, and so obviously was Father. He also inquired if Nissim and I were interested in some feminine companionship, but we both respectfully declined.

This was also a time for us to relax and recapture our friendship. Because we were no longer in battle formation, we could ride together, hunt a bit, or do some falconry with Tetik and Kym. Father was pleased with us, I could tell, and would sometimes join us on our rides when he wasn't buying or selling. Chabuk was getting used to Nissim's presence although I would often see him cast sidelong looks at him as he rode. While I was well used to calling Nissim brother, Chabuk kept his reserve, calling him only by his name. However there was never any further mention of Nissim's former slave status. That Nissim was a warrior, no one could deny.

Nevertheless, both Chabuk and I were intensely curious about Nissim's style of fighting. I must confess I had never seen a warrior fighting on foot like that, nor could I imagine any sort of fighting on foot for that matter. Nissim, as usual, made no comment about it until we finally broke down and demanded an explanation. He had killed at least half a dozen Kalmyks; there was no doubt of the effectiveness of his style.

"Brothers, I am a Greek and was brought up amongst Turks. The Turks are very smart people and can recognize a good quality when they see it. Like all the people of the steppe, they entered

Constantinople on horseback but for a great many decades, fought the Greek infantry and admired what they could do. The Imperial Army was actually Roman, and after the Turkish conquest of the Imperial City of Constantinople, the Turks made haste to adopt many Roman and Greek ways. As a boy in the military academy at Trabzon, I learned all the military arts. I excelled in weaponry and learned not only the bow but also the ax and the broadsword. The ax I use, I am told, is called a topor. It is thick at the hand but fine at the tip and covered by metal. It is used mostly by Russians and only for battle. I consider it superior to the Roman ax. At Trabzon, we were not ignorant of Greek and Roman ways. But I think I was perfectly Tatar in throwing the enemy into complete surprise."

"There was no doubt about that!" We all laughed.

"Tell me, brothers, did you never see me practicing on the field? I thought for sure you would see me dismounting and remounting as quickly as I could. It was as much a training for Cereyan as it was for me. She had to learn to stay with me even when I was on the ground. A foot soldier can't have his horse run off. She learned so willingly. Haven't you seen her? I am very proud of her." These horses of the steppe are smaller than the Turkish and Russian war horses. The Kalmyks use only steppe horses.

"You know, brother, you could teach our Blue Raiders some of those techniques," I said.

Chabuk added in a surprising moment of lightheartedness, "For sure! Yes, Bashina could be the leader of the first Nogay Military Academy in Astrakhan." That produced a round of laughter.

"Why not, Chabuk?" Nissim commented. "We also have a large store of artillery. Let's put all our resources to use." Nissim gave a wide smile, which curled up at the right side of his mouth. I thought for a moment that he was happy. I knew, at least for the moment, that I was.

We arrived in Astrakhan toward the middle of November and assembled our yurts on the outskirts of the city but not so far away as to make the city inaccessible. It was much larger than Cherny Yar. Very soon after, Natasha visited our tents, ostensibly for companionship. Dalgali was in town making contact with his friends and acquaintances in the city. It was cooler now, and we needed to sleep in our tents, but we still warmed ourselves around the fire in the evenings.

"If my Daniel were here, he would be singing songs and reciting the heroic deeds of the Nogay. We have a harpist and someone who plays the reed, but without the voice of my son, it is not the same." For myself, I still could not get used to calling him Daniel. He would always be Dalgin to me. Even now this is so.

She turned to Nissim, first of all apologizing to me. "The Christmas fast began a little over a week ago. Do you want to keep it with me, Nissim? I'll cook the food."

Nissim became thoughtful. My own curiosity got hold of me, and I blurted out: "Fast? What fast? Is it Ramadan?" Kattu kept Ramadan.

"It is similar, Lord Tambor. For six weeks before the feast of the Nativity of Jesus, we keep a fast in preparation for the feast. It is a time for prayer and meditation...oh yes, and almsgiving. In this way we honor the feast. There is even a greater fast in the spring."

"Do you keep it the same way as Dikkatli does?"

"Not exactly," she replied. "Those who keep the full fast, like monks and nuns and some of our clergy, do not eat or drink until after the prayers of the ninth hour (the third hour of the afternoon). They eat once and not again till the next day. Most of us however keep a lesser fast. If we have to eat during the day we have only vegetables and fruit with grain or bread. We do not eat meat, milk or eggs. Fermented drink, fish, and oil are restricted to the Sabbath and the Resurrection Day (Saturday and Sunday). Shell fish and caviar are permitted at all times."

"No meat? Is it possible? We Tatars live on meat and milk. Have you always done this Tashi?" I asked.

"Yes, and even Daniel keeps it, although I don't know what he does when he is out of my sight." I actually couldn't recall it myself.

Nissim finally came out of his thoughts and said, "I think I'll try it. I haven't fasted since I was at home with my father." Turning to me he added, "Always secretly, of course. We also did Ramadan."

"But you need your strength, brother! I just don't think you can carry on your work without the strength of meat."

"Let me give it a try, Tambor. I will do it for my parent's sake. But if I can't, I'll discuss it with a priest and get a blessing to eat according to my need."

"That's sensible, brother. Maybe you both can pray for me while you are fasting."

Nissim grasped my hand. "Agreed!"

Tashi looked ecstatic.

Tutumlu looked bewildered.

Chabuk looked at us wide-eyed and open-mouthed. We had obviously all gone out of our minds.

I knew Nissim could do it.

Reconciliation

Restore to me the joy of your deliverance,
and with a leading spirit support me.
I will teach lawless ones your ways and
impious ones will return to you.
Rescue me from bloodshed, O God, O God of my
deliverance; my tongue will rejoice at your righteousness.

—Psalm 50: 14–16 (lxx nets)

Even at this point in my youth, dear Holy Father, I was aware that every time Nissim drew near to his God, somehow or other I was invariably drawn in also. It is not that I resisted, Father; it's that I was only partially conscious of what I was experiencing. I thought myself cynical of religion in general and indulged my friend in a half-amused way. But it was more than that, dear Father; it was that it seemed as though someone were actually watching over me. Ever since that night when I eavesdropped on Nissim's prayer, I became conscious of a presence. *Not like Tengri*, I used to say to myself. Tengri watches over everything; the sky sees, but not in such a personal way. When Nissim began his fast, I became part of it. I could have my mouth stuffed with a sausage and would still feel the force of the fast. Sometimes it seemed like an intrusion into my privacy although, back then, I would never have described it that way. Whatever my brother Nissim was doing, I was part of it. I did not recognize it as love at that time, and it was surely not like loving a woman, but it was an intense sense of oneness with him.

It was with this sense that I accompanied my friend, my brother, to the Church of the Nativity of the Mother of God. It was just the two of us. Chabuk and the others remained back at the camp. We had never given up war games, especially now that we were resting in leisure. Chabuk was drilling the men in the use of the saber this morning. He was cheerful enough. Natasha also did not accompany us as her spiritual father, an elderly man whom she had known for years, was priest of another temple toward the center of the city, an archimandrite named Pavel. He was the one who had informed us where Father John served and how to get there.

When we arrived, Nissim pointed to a teahouse down the street, thinking that I might have wanted to wait there, but I told him, "There is no way I want to miss this. You will be confessing my sins too."

He smirked. "Then you will likely have to stand at the back of the temple. Besides, there are probably benches along the wall."

"Where will you be?"

"At the front with the priest. I hope he will be there."

"You mean you will be off alone talking to him? Can't I listen in?"

"Of course not, you dupa!" I feigned offence, and he laughed.

"You looked so nervous, brother. You needed a little cheering up. Hey, just think realistically. You are actually going to dump a basket load of sins, why are you so glum? Cheer up! Look at it this way. You will be as free as a hawk, and I, I don't even know what sins I'd need to confess. So you are way ahead of me."

"Not so far away, Tambor," he said quietly as we entered the temple.

I know you were born into the faith , Holy Father Dmitri, and likely cannot relate to that first experience as I did. Nissim had already explained that *temple* generally referred to the place of worship and that *church* referred to the community of worshippers, even though these words were sometimes used interchangeably. There was no service going on, so I could appreciate the solitude and my thoughts. Obviously he knew the protocol of the temple, yet he never gave me the sense I should imitate him.

He whispered in my ear. "Just relax and don't feel you have
to do anything. There is hardly anyone here, so you won't be
disturbing anybody, but be reverent." He motioned to a bench
against the right wall. "Men stand on the right side and women
on the left. We don't stand together."

We were dressed in clothing that we hoped would not identify
us as Tatars. Nissim wore the shirt and trousers I had given him
when he first met the khan, and I, something similar. I suppose
we didn't look Russian either as the chilly weather required us to
wear our leather jackets. By the look of his clothes, it was obvious
he was still growing. We needed to get him some new clothes.
I had stopped growing. Like my people, I was thickly built but
lean with wide shoulders. Nissim turned out tall and slender like
his people.

There was an elderly couple at the back of the church
removing candles from a canvas bag and laying them on a table,
ostensibly to sell. The women smiled politely, and the man nodded
suspiciously. The fragrance of beeswax was heady and, combined
with the lingering scent of incense from the morning service, was
somewhat dizzying for someone like me who was used to the
ever-present open air and the smells of our animals. I needed to
sit. Nissim went over to the couple presumably to ask if he could
see Father John. The old fellow said something and slowly moved
to the front and entered a small door to the right side.

While we were waiting, I took a closer look at my surroundings.
Everything was color, mostly blue and red with a smattering of
gold everywhere. There were icons all over the place, and eventually
I made out that there was a kind of order in their placement,
though at that time I couldn't really identify it. The church seemed
huge to me, taller and grander than our council yurt. The dome
in the ceiling was awesome in its magnificence with the icon of
Christ looking down over the whole assembly of icons. There was
a sense of power I had never identified with Tengri who observed
everything but had no relationship with anything he was looking

at. I remembered Nissim calling God the creator of Tengri and Yer-Sub. Such power seemed overwhelming.

However these ponderings were interrupted when the door in the front opened, and the elderly man came out followed by a black-robed priest with a short fair beard. His youth surprised me. Around his neck, he wore a gold scarf that came to the ground. The old fellow went back to his work. Nissim waited. The priest looked toward us and gently motioned Nissim to approach. Nissim drew near and bowed toward the priest touching the floor with his right hand. The priest blessed him, and Nissim kissed his hand. Then they went over to the woman's side where there was a stand with a golden book on it, which Nissim kissed reverently, and a stand for candles. I was told later that it was the book of the Gospels. Then they began to talk.

At first, from my range of view from the back of the church, it seemed like an ordinary conversation. Nissim did most of the talking. The priest then started questioning him quietly. This continued for a while until I noticed that Nissim was beginning to be somewhat disturbed. He was not being berated as the priest kept a calm and serious manner, but it did seem as though he were probing into my friend's mind and heart. Nissim, whom I had always relied upon to be cool and levelheaded, was upset or even perhaps in pain. I felt a wave of resentment go through my body, and believe me, Father, it took all my will power to resist putting this confession to an end.

It was all quiet. I couldn't hear them talking, but I was sure Nissim was weeping. Tatar men usually don't express emotion by tears, but we can be very emotional at times and not be thought unmanly or irrational; however, usually we kept what we called "a cool face." As for myself, I couldn't remember ever having cried. Therefore I interpreted my friend's distress as pain, and I did not want to see my brother in pain. After all he had been tortured enough in his lifetime.

But lo! Just at that moment of great distress, Father John leaned over and kissed him on the head, holding his elbow until Nissim pulled himself together. Then Nissim knelt down, and the priest draped the golden scarf (the Greek word for it I can still not pronounce) over his head and said a lengthy prayer. I knew in my heart that at that moment, Nissim's sins were being washed away like a broken off tree limb swirling down the Volga. After all these years, Nissim was free. And somewhere deep within me, I was free too.

Nissim stood up and kissed Father John's hand, and both started walking toward me. Nissim's large brown eyes were swollen, but he gave me that strange smirk, which turned up the right side of his mouth. He was at peace. I wanted to tease him but knew it was neither the time nor the place.

"Lord Tambor!" the priest said. "It would do me a great honor if you and Nissim would spend the day with me. It is not often I have the pleasure of meeting a Nogay prince and his warrior friend. I have often heard of your father Dalgali, but I have never personally met him. Please accept my invitation."

I was a bit thrown off but nodded my acceptance.

"Let me get into my walking clothes. I'll be back soon." He left quickly.

"How do you feel?" I asked.

"Just as you said, brother. As free as a bird." He grinned. "But more like a dove than a falcon. My soul is so quiet. I had to tell him *everything*, Tambor, since my last confession, which was during the great fast when I was in Trabzon, the year we were all separated. I had to mention my father and our deception, and I told him about the Kurds. I confessed my sin with Mehtap and my betrayal of you and of your forgiveness. I told him about the death of Petya, though I didn't mention Mikhailov (I called it a raid). He said I was not responsible for the death of the Kalmyks as it was defensive, but he said I was to hold a prayer service for the soul of Petya, called a *Panahida*, once a year for five years and however often I wished thereafter. The first one is tomorrow after Liturgy (Mass). He said also that when I marry Mehtap, he wanted to perform the baptism and the wedding ceremony. Natasha will instruct her and will probably be her godmother."

"All that?"

"And more." But Father John had come back. He had taken off his stole and was now wearing a small velour hat called a skoufia. He didn't look all that different from the priest at Mikhailov, except that that other priest was darker, older, and more bearded than Father John.

"Well, shall we go?" he said. "I shall send a message to Matushka, my wife that is, that we shall be around later. I have two children and take care of three orphans, so we shall have no quiet there. And I need to talk to you both. Would you mind if we went to the Azov, just across the street. They have a private nook reserved for me. I've not had a chance to eat after the service so we will have a bite. Agree?"

"Sure!" we said. I was beginning to like him. The teahouse, which he called the Azov was the one we saw before we entered the temple.

"Batushka! It has been so long since you have come," the owner said. "Sure, it *is* the fast, we understand. I'll have a plate of dumplings, no cheese but with onions and cabbage." He called them pirogies. The place was full of smells. We were famished.

"Thank you, Sima. That sounds good. And a couple of plates for my friends. Is my nook free?

"Yes, yes! Anyusha, three plates for Batushka. We have company!"

"Sima," he said in Russian, with Nissim translating, "these are my friends from upriver. We need to talk." Sima was a stocky man, not old, but also not young. It was then I noticed that Father John had been speaking to us in Tatar. "Do you speak Tatar my friend?" Father asked Sima.

"Yes, yes! I speak everything." Turning to us, he said, with a strong accent, "In my business, I have to speak many tongues, and I learn them from my customers." He paused and turned to the priest. "Dalgali is in town again. You want a really good horse for your carriage. You should go and see him." Turning to us he asked, "Do you know Dalgali, young men?"

"He's our father," I answered as modestly as I could.

I could see he was dying to ask, and rather than give up the ghost on the spot, he blurted out, "Then you must have fought the Kalmyks! Yes, yes?"

"Yes, yes!" I answered back playfully, in Russian (Da, da!). "But please let it be our secret. Agreed?

"Da, da!" he answered with a twinkle in his eye.

Anyusha came in with a serving girl, both laden with two trays cluttered with plates and steaming bowls. There was already a samovar on a small table near the mantle, and the maid poured tea into small glasses and stoked the fire in the fireplace.

"Go on, you buffoon," she said. "You know when Father comes he wants some peace and quiet!" She pushed him affectionately on his shoulder and turned to us. "Anything more you want, Batushka, you just call!"

"Thank you, Anny," he said quietly, and to Sima who was leaving, he said loudly, "Bless you, Sima."

Anyusha cupped her hands in front of her for a blessing, and she kissed his hand, as did the serving girl. Both disappeared.

"We are alone now. Hopefully we will not be interrupted by other guests. The samovar is hot, and we can take advantage of it." Father filled up what was lacking in our glasses, smiled sweetly, and sat down. After a few moments of silence, likely prayerful silence, he began to talk. "Sir Tambor, this afternoon, your friend Nissim shared with me some powerful information. According to the rules of our Holy Orthodox faith, once a sheep has entrusted his sins to a shepherd, the shepherd surrenders them into the hands of God. I must never speak of them to anyone—that is, without the permission of the sheep. I would ask you, Sir Nissim, if I may refer to events within your confession, not your sins mind you, but situations I need to clarify. As your spiritual father, is this agreeable to you, my son? I believe that neither of you consciously holds back anything from each other."

Nissim turned to me, and I shrugged my shoulders in agreement. *This would be a challenge*, I thought.

"Good," the priest said. "Forgive me if I address you by name. It is not disrespect but rather the need for familiarity. After all, Nissim is now my spiritual son."

I turned to Nissim, trying to hold back a smile. "I can see, my brother, that you are accumulating fathers. But don't mind me. I'm just a little jealous."

"You will have a spiritual father in the future, dear Tambor, but it will not be me. You will save the soul of your first spiritual father. Your second one will lead you to your own salvation. But your most reliable spiritual brother at this time, or better, your soul mate, will be Nissim." I knew he was right, but I was bothered that he could see it so clearly. Had the khan said this, I would have accepted it more gracefully. I wanted to dismiss what he said, and he knew it. "How is it that you two have searched me out, my lads? How is it that I have the honor of your pursuit?"

I laughed. "Actually you were recommended by two friends of yours, the co-administrator Konstantin Alexandrovich Lapukhin of Cherny Yar and Captain Zander Tretyakov, commandant of the garrison at Tsagan-Aman. These noble gentlemen both send their greetings and led Nissim toward you. My father's concubine Natasha is Christian, and her confessor, Archimandrite Father Pavel, told us how we could find you."

"Well, well! I do come recommended. Father Pavel is actually my spiritual father, and these fine and pious men you refer to are two of my spiritual children, as sinful and unworthy as I am. Let me tell you, my friends, you who are not much younger than I am, I bear the title of Father by no merit of my own. The Lord himself said to call no man father, for you have but one Father in heaven. I am but an ambassador of the Lord, and my title only represents, very poorly, his wisdom, his holiness, and his magnificence."

I stopped eating at this. I didn't understand him. What he just said made no sense to me at all. I thought, *If he is so unworthy, how does he come so highly recommended?* And even as this thought was trotting through my mind, Father John answered it.

"But you know, Tambor and Nissim, as unworthy as I am, the merciful Lord, who is no respecter of persons, oft time leads me to reveal hints of his divine plan to those whom he loves. But later, later. Let us eat, my friends. We have time to talk ahead of us."

It was Nissim who broke the silence. "Are you from around here, Batushka?"

"Actually I was born not far from here. My father owns a small estate on the northeast shore of the Caspian. He had hoped to get rich on the land which is very fertile around there, but that didn't work out. Half the year, it floods from one of the rivers flowing out of the Volga into the Caspian, and the rest of the year, it is dry and hot. The property needs proper damming and irrigation. Some crops can stand that weather. The vineyards produce a pleasant local wine, but it is not of much value commercially. He made it big with caviar though, but even there, he has had to struggle. Persian pirates often raid the area. My brother and I were raised here, but when we got older we went to Moscow for our education at Saint George's Seminary. Fillip stayed in Moscow and married a cousin of a cousin, if you know what I mean.

"I came back home, unsettled and idle. I was attracted to the priesthood, but my father wouldn't hear of it. Besides I had to be married before ordination could take place. Behold here I am a priest, but not without a few years of disgrace."

When we had finished eating, Anyusha brought some sweets and refreshed the samovar. We were a bit more relaxed by then.

Father John slowly turned to me and asked, "Now what about you, Tambor, are you happy with your life?" I was caught off guard. It was a question I had never asked myself.

"Er…I suppose so. I don't think I am happy or unhappy, Father. I…I don't think I am unhappy. I am a warrior. It is all I have ever wanted to be. I love and am loved by my family. I am rich. And I have a good friend. Sure, I guess I am happy."

"You have a good heart, my friend. You genuinely want others to be happy. You don't even know that that's what you do. People around you thrive on your openness."

This is different, I thought. *Especially after the khan's concern about my social relations.*

"Just look," Father John was saying, "at how you have given Nissim the honor and dignity he could never have expected. And the only reason you haven't given Timov his freedom is for his own good. He's not ready for it as yet, but you will do so when it is just the right time. Yes, and you treat your Zarthosht people as though they were already free. Nissim told me. They are devoted to you even at such a short time. Your father Dalgali doesn't know what to do with you. He cannot make you out and neither can Chabuk. Not even the khan, who treats you like a son and knows you as much as you think he does. No, no! Don't be upset at me for telling you this!"

Oh, he was smooth. It seemed he was stripping away layers, and I then knew exactly how Nissim felt during his confession.

"Listen, my friend." He let his hand rest on mine, and I wouldn't dare pull it away. "The hand of the Lord is upon your head, Tambor. You will not rest until you accept it. It will be a heavy hand, my son, and you will know the throes of sorrow and pain. You will wrestle with him until you fall. You will have no rest until then, but after that, you will attain peace. Trust Nissim, my friend. Even in the midst of your anguish, trust him." He paused. Neither of us could say a word.

He turned my hand over in his hand and saw the scar I had forged, which was still somewhat fresh. He looked straight at Nissim and said not a word. Nissim placed his hand on the table and turned it over.

"You have made a vow."

I answered, "I made a promise that I would help him find his family and especially his father."

"Yes, do so. But first of all, rescue his mother and sister. I think you have already got a plan in mind. They are languishing, Tambor, and Nissim's sister is fearful for her virginity. God will guide you. I believe your father will not object at the apparent delay. You are a warrior. That is a warrior's mission."

He turned to Nissim. "As for your father, my son, he is not ready for rescue. I am sure he is still alive, but at the moment he is saving his soul. God will keep him. Tambor will know exactly the right time to act. Trust him, my son."

"How do you know this, Batushka?" Nissim asked. I was alert.

"It is not magic, my lads. There are no incantations and rattles or throwing of herbs on charcoal. Tambor, you know how it is. You must have a shaman in your camp. But it is not like that. I cannot even say that an angel tells me these things although it may be so. And I also take the chance that I am entirely wrong. You must understand that.

"But, my friends, if I can trust your discretion, let me tell you how it happens." He paused to gather his thoughts. "There is a voice within that tells me, not what I should say but rather that I should speak; that's all. Then I speak. I could hold back. I am free to do so, and I used to do so. However when I did, everything inside would say something is very wrong. It was often painful, this sense of wrong. But then I read a passage from the Holy Prophet Jeremias, who said, and I have copied this passage onto my heart, 'And I said, I will not name the name of the Lord and will no longer speak in his name. And it became like a fire flaming in my bones, and I became limp everywhere and I cannot bear up (Jeremiah 20:9, lxx nets).' So I have decided to speak. The voice didn't come when Nissim was confessing. From his confession I heard your stories or some of them anyway. I was guided to take your time this afternoon because I knew I would speak and I could already sense that God's love was upon you. It is as simple as that."

"I think I can relate to that, Father," I said. "We have a shamaness at home who has had something against me since she came to us from these parts, three or four years ago. She has swayed my mother against me and tried to provoke the khan. He hasn't taken her seriously, fortunately, for me. She said my green eyes would divide the tribe in time, and she said I would destroy it."

"Tambor, she was groping around in darkness. The voice within her was clouded by unclean spirits, and any truth she may have felt was distorted. But she *did* perceive something. You do have a destiny, and you will fulfill it. Your very strong will cannot prevent it. In fact, the destiny of many others depends upon your calling. I can say no more except it has nothing to do with your green eyes."

I was trembling. Was it a kind of fear? But there was no enemy; nothing and no one as yet to fear. Father John again held my hand.

"Fear nothing, my friend. Trust Nissim's prayers, and I tell you there is another who prays for you intensely, and perhaps others. But let us go. Matushka is waiting for us. Relax and enjoy the rest of the day. I presume you have found out that we Russians are not as bad as you thought we were." He laughed, paid the bill, blessed Sima and his family, and promised to come back soon.

The rest of the day was equally blessed. The gloom I had experienced at Father John's nook quickly passed. Father John walked home, so we took our horses and walked with him. I saw how he was loved. Everyone greeted him, many asked his blessing, and others bowed and stepped aside. What impressed me mostly was the attention given to him by the children. These would run toward him, pulling on his robe, even pulling on his knee. The older ones were more respectful and would kiss his hand. He would ask some of them how mother was, if Yuri was feeling better, if Nana got the position at the manor, when papa was coming back.

"These are my jewels, lads," he said. "It is my desire to present them to the Lord for his crown. Some of them won't make it to adulthood. Poverty and disease are their greatest enemies. I hope someday to open a hospital or an orphanage, but I just don't have the money to do so."

Wherever he went, he exuded hope. Behind his peaceful smile by which I myself had been seduced, was sadness, a grief, heartache, and I glimpsed the glimmer of a tear in his eye as he fondled his gemstones. I was profoundly moved. I realized how blessed I had been to grow up at the Birches. I had taken for granted the wealth of my father, the majesty of the khan, the devoted nurture of my mother. We had no poverty, the shepherds and herdsmen were well fed, and even the slaves lacked nothing but freedom. Yet here was this humble man walking the streets of Astrakhan, loving and being loved by all.

It is true as I have said before, our tribe went through many hardships in the early days fleeing from the Kuban and there was plague and sorrow, but only our old folks remembered that. Our generation had been spared. A gratitude rose in me from whence and to whom I wasn't sure, but I offered it to Father John's God. I reached in my pouch to give to the children, but Father held my hand.

"You don't have enough for all, and if one person is missed, he will grieve. I try to help them when I make my rounds. But the Lord sees your compassion and your gratitude." It seemed he was always a step ahead of me.

Finally the crowd of children dissipated, and by the time we arrived at his home, we were alone again.

A servant met us at the entrance of the house and took our horses. We entered to another shower of children. Father John picked them up, kissed them, cajoled them, scolded them, and loved them. If the other children were jewels, these were diamonds and pearls. Eventually a maidservant came and scuttled them off. It was an old house; we were told it was part of the church property. Unlike the manse at Mikhailov, with its stairways and mirrors and chandeliers, this house was low and flat. One had to bow down to enter a room to avoid bumping one's head. It was simple and warm. The evenings were beginning to be chilled, and we were grateful for the fireplace. A samovar stood on a table near the fire, probably to keep it doubly warm.

"I would offer you some vodka or even kumis were it not for the Nativity fast. Tomorrow is the Sabbath, and the Church relaxes its rules for the Sabbath and for Sunday (Voskresenie), the day of Resurrection. I hope you will stay the night. Nissim will take communion tomorrow, and I want him there early. My servant will inform your father, whom I intend to meet perhaps on Monday. Frankly I need a new horse for my carriage."

Nissim chided, "Perhaps my brother will make you a deal. He's got his own horses, you know. What about it, Tambor? Shall we stay?"

I nodded. "I'll make a good deal, Father (I almost said Batushka), but I want you to meet my father, Dalgali, anyway. I presume you have found out that we Kubanshyi are not as bad as you thought we were."

Father John laughed. "I'd be honored, my friends." He called for the manservant and gave instructions and directions. The man actually looked startled and seemed to protest.

Nissim leaned over and grinned. "I couldn't understand it all, but the last thing Batushka said was 'They won't eat you!'"

A few minutes later, the maidservant returned with a tray of glasses for tea and some bread. She was followed by a very beautiful woman with dark eyes. Even though she dressed in

Russian fashion with a loose white embroidered blouse tucked into a long indigo skirt with an apron at her waist, she did not appear Russian to me. Father John stood and greeted her with a kiss and introduced her as Matushka.

"Welcome, my lords, to our humble home. Please be comfortable in our dwelling." Nissim noticed at once that she was speaking our tongue in an Astrakhan accent. I was a little slower to recognize it.

"You speak our tongue, Matushka," he said.

"That's because I'm Tatar," she said simply.

"My dear," Father John began, "this is Sir Nissim and Lord Tambor, from the north country. Nissim has made his confession and will receive communion tomorrow. Lord Tambor is the son of the well-known merchant Dalgali from Sopasi." Something flashed in her eyes for a brief moment and disappeared.

She said sweetly, "we're glad you are here. Sir Nissim, forgive me, and I mean no offence, but are *you* Tatar?"

"I'm Greek by birth, Matushka, but I am now a Nogay warrior."

"And what a brave and clever warrior he is, this my brother!" I added proudly.

"Bravery and cleverness are a marvelous combination. Add piety to those, and you have a very special friend, Lord Tambor."

I thought, *What a combination you and Father John are!*

"You have just had breakfast, I'm told, so we shall eat later, but the children are dying to meet you. Batushka, shall we let the children in?"

A hoard of Kalmyks couldn't have attacked us with more exuberance than those children. Apart from the blond boy, they were all over us. There was no shyness in this family. Our weapons, which had been deposited at the doorway, now became common property. Before we had set out this morning, we thought that we should come armed, but not armored, since we were strangers in the city. The two dark-haired boys, Father John's children, decided to practice swordsmanship in the middle of the spacious room. Father put a quick end to that, and I promised a controlled practice outside, which satisfied them. The two girls claimed territory on our knees. I apologized for sitting on the floor, being used to stools rather than chairs. Lyuba, the four-year-old, had found my knife, which I kept in a scabbard at my side. She was more interested in the decorative handle than the blade and asked me why the serpent had a stone in its mouth. I had to think quickly, so I told her that the dragon thought it was a fruit. This seemed to satisfy her, but it left me wanting to know what the real answer was.

Nadia, who was three years old, was fascinated with Nissim. She kept stroking his newly grown but haphazard beard. I could only claim a few strands on my upper lip. She also played on his slave ring, which, I noticed for the first time, he had not removed from his ear. (When I questioned him later on that night, he told me that he felt he couldn't take it off until he knew his father was free.) Anton was twelve, the child of the first year of marriage, and Feofil was eleven, and both were dark and strong featured like their mother.

After a while, Matushka came over to me with the Russian boy, who had been clinging to her skirts.

"This is Alexei, Sir Tambor."

"Greetings to you, Alexei," I said, not knowing quite how properly to address the lad.

"Aren't you going to greet our guest, Alexei, like a proper boy?" Matushka asked. He took my hand and kissed me on my cheeks.

"This is indeed a pleasant greeting, Alexei," I commented. "Why don't you also greet Sir Nissim." He lifted his eyes to Matushka, who nodded to do so.

When he was out of hearing, Matushka said, "Alexei's father was a soldier in the Russian army, who lost his life defending the farmers, along the Caspian. They have been much troubled by the invading Persian pirates. His mother died soon afterward. We have sort of adopted them. He is eleven years old like Feofil, but he remembers his father. The girls remember only vaguely. I think he may have suspected that you were an enemy. But see, he is getting along with Nissim now. Pay a little attention to him, Sir Tambor. He needs to learn to trust you men folk."

"Thank you for confiding in me, Matushka. And please call us by our names."

The boy was now coming back in our direction. Lyuba had lost interest in me and was now trying to take Nissim away from her sister.

"I have sisters and brothers about their age. I think it is about time I paid attention to them." Soon I sat a very uncertain young lad on my lap until he eventually warmed up to me and started asking questions, only a few of which I understood.

The following afternoon, I instructed the boys in swordplay. They were really too young to handle the weight of the swords, so I held their hands to strengthen their grasp. This time, Alexei joined in. The other two had each other and the comfort of their father's care and, although Father John sincerely loved the orphan, Alexei was nevertheless an outsider. For this reason, he seemed to latch on to me, although we had some trouble communicating. It was easier for him to learn Tatar, which Matushka spoke than for me to attempt Russian. The minds of children seem to be more flexible.

The next morning, after he had been to church with Batushka (as I now started calling him, rather than the Tatar word for *Father*, papaz, as before), Nissim seemed to want to be quiet, so I had all the children to myself. Even the girls wanted to join in. Nissim sat near an outdoor oven, which Matushka used for baking bread in the summer when the weather was hot. But the days were getting chilly and even now there were hot coals in the oven. Occasionally Matushka would bring him a glass of tea or some pastries, which were permitted on the weekends when oil was allowed. Nissim was grateful but ate sparingly. Eventually Nadia, his darling, went over to him, and very soon he was telling stories to all the children.

I found a grassy place where I sat down, and Batushka came over and pulled up a stool. He looked at the children gathered around Nissim's knee and said quietly, "It looks like the children have really benefited from your visit. I can think of two sayings of our Lord when I see the two of you: 'Let the little children come unto me and do not forbid them for of such is made the Kingdom of heaven.' And the other is 'Whoever does not receive the kingdom of God as a little child will by no means enter it (Luke 18:16–17, nkjv).'"

"He said that, did he?" I remarked, not needing a response. "Batushka, I left in the middle of the service this morning. I went over to the Azov and had some food and tea and some chitchat with Sima and his wife. It is not that I didn't like the service, don't misunderstand. The music was very beautiful and stirring although I didn't understand the words. It is just that I didn't feel that it was my place to be there. I hope you were not offended."

"Not at all, my friend. This particular service is really for the Orthodox. If you were planning to be baptized, you would be called a catechumen, and there is a part of the service where catechumens are asked to leave. Perhaps you instinctively left at the right time, only God knows."

"I did happen to return for the small service, which you chanted at the side of the church, afterward near the Cross. I presume those prayers were for the soul of Petya. Nissim was always bothered about having killed him. You know he didn't intend to." I paused. "I suppose that will ease Nissim's conscience." Then I laughed wryly. "It didn't seem to bother him to kill a half dozen Kalmyks."

"As you know, my son, I cannot comment on that." He looked toward the house and said, "Ah, look! Matushka is calling. She has prepared a feast! Actually a *fasting feast.*" He smiled warmly and got up.

It was a splendid feast and altogether a wonderful day. I was beginning to realize that Russian hospitality could indeed compete with ours.

Later on in the day, Father John took us to a little building next to the main house. I might have thought it to be a storage place except that it was very well kept. As he pulled out the keys, he told us that this was a very special place for him and that very few ever visit the little house.

"This is my place of refuge where I am most myself," he said shyly.

To my mind, I entered another world. The walls were covered in icons, and there was a prayer corner at the front of the one room with hanging lamps.

Nissim gasped and said, "Where did all these icons come from, Batushka?"

Father chuckled and said, "These are some of my vain attempts at iconography."

"Vain?" I asked. "These are wondrously beautiful." I looked over toward a large window (unusual for Russian houses before Tsar Peter) and saw a table that was on a slant with many brushes and pots, which were in many colors. "This is where you paint them, Batushka?"

He nodded, humbly. I perceived that he was almost embarrassed to admit it. "Do people buy these icons?"

"Some do, my friends. Those who cannot afford them I sometimes give away. But I am only practicing. I have a friend in Georgia, a Father Abo, who paints churches. He trained me for about a year or so not too long before I was married. I feel I must make these icons because the only well-known iconographers are too far away, and we need icons desperately for the many churches that are springing up all over Astrakhan. Sadly, these churches have to put up with an amateur like me. Nevertheless as I work at them, they become easier to produce."

Nissim added with some emotion, "Batushka, anyone would be blest to have one of these!"

"Nissim, my son, take one now, and I will do one of Saint Onesimus and one of Saint Timotheus. They may be a long time in coming, but I promise you them. And, Tambor, I'll give you yours the day you are baptized."

"I'll have to wait that long?"

"Yes, dear one, even if it takes that long."

Nissim took an icon of the Holy Virgin.

We came back to camp early the next morning. As I had expected, my father did put on a good show when we arrived Sunday afternoon after the service at church. Batushka's servant had let Father know we would be there, and my father was prepared and was obviously delighted to have our hosts as *his* guests. I began to realize how gregarious he was and how much he enjoyed entertaining. Both my father and Batushka were warm with each other after the formalities were offered. Natasha could hardly contain herself for delight. Tears filled her eyes as she asked Batushka's blessing. Matushka was calm but friendly, and while she responded to Natasha's questions in Russian, she addressed herself to Father in Tatar. He raised his eyebrows.

Natasha then noticed us boys. She threw herself at Nissim, kissed him affectionately, and ruffled his wavy black hair and tugged on his new beard.

"There you are, my sweet dove, all shriven and clean!" Nissim gave his little crooked grin and looked immensely shy. I was put out, and she noticed it. "Now don't get your water in a boil, Tambor. You know that next to Danny, you are your Tashi's best love." She threw her arms around me and kissed me on my beardless cheeks. I could feel her feminine warmth, and it disconcerted me somewhat.

"Come on now!" Prince Dalgali commanded. "These are Nogay warriors, Natasha, not little boys playing in the fields."

"Oh, I know, my dear, but they are such beautiful warriors, like Saint George and Saint Dmitri, aren't they, Matushka?" She looked to the priest's wife for support.

"Indeed they are," she responded.

"Let's go in, milady. I've prepared a feast of fasting food," Natasha said as they entered the cooking area. "You Tatars are going to be fasting today, and you are going to enjoy it!" She ordered a servant to get a jug of kumis. "You will taste Lady Yerinde's best brew. Nothing surpasses it."

The feast went well. Natasha excelled in her preparations. But what she really excelled in was building a friendship. It is amazing how much a friendship can develop over the sharing of recipes or the weave of a fabric, but I saw the two women getting along fabulously. On the other hand, I, father, and Batushka hit it off on horses. Tutumlu was invited to the festivities and made minor comments on the lack of meat offered in the meal. He then leaned over at one point and pointed out that my horses were not suitable for Father John's needs. My horses were meant for riding,he informed me but Prince Dalgali had bred some very fine horses, which could be used for carriages. These were not the heavy horses used for hauling things or dragging carts, but ones for pulling a buggy or even a troika in the winter, not that there was much snowfall this far south. Father John had decided upon one well-trained horse and two nanny goats for the yard.

Chabuk joined us for the eating as did Hazir and Kiymetli. Tetik of course joined his father. Generally, according to our tradition, the women ate separately from the men until the eating was over; however Russians do not keep this custom as all eat together; Matushka, being Tatar, accepted this as a matter of course. However, when the eating was done, the two women served tea and wine and sat with us. Batushka tried to chat with Chabuk, apparently trying to draw him out of his normal gloomy self and to some extent was fairly successful.

Matushka asked if Chabuk was a son of Natasha. Before Natasha could say a thing, Chabuk told her that he was a son of Yerinde and was a full brother to me. He seemed proud of that fact. Natasha was not a bit put off but bounded on not missing any opportunity to talk about Dalgin and his younger sisters and brothers.

"He was baptized Daniel, Matushka, but Dalgali calls him Dalgin. He is a sweet boy and a beautiful singer. Unfortunately he could not come with us as he is recovering from a wound he received during a…uh…skirmish recently."

Her eyes darted back and forth; I assumed she thought she was talking too much. She tried to change the subject. "We have both a wise woman and a healer at the Birches. The wise woman supports the elderly shaman. Another woman, the healing woman, saved his leg without amputation, thanks be to God."

Tetik piped up and showed what was left of his forearm. "They make quite a team. Very few of us have survived these kinds of wounds. Timov, Nissim's brother, was the one who severed my broken arm, which had become severely infected."

"Well, glory to God. I suppose not too many tribes have such a medical staff."

"That is very true," Dalgali cut in. I think he was concerned that someone would say too much. "The healer is one of my concubines, and the wise woman who is a skilled midwife came from this part of Astrakhan." I noticed the priest and his wife exchange a quick glance. "Tell me, Matushka, how is it you speak Tatar so well?"

She hesitated but slowly, perhaps cautiously, continued.

"I'm Tatar, my Lord Dalgali. We were part of Ibn Haddi's tribe. You may know that maybe ten years ago Ibn Haddi encouraged us all to embrace the Muslim faith. He was generous about it and gave us a few years to study and eventually convert. We were worshippers of the earth and sky, and all the free Tatars were asked to leave. As for myself, I had already met Batushka, who of course was not yet a priest. He was working with the poor of the city, squandering his father's money on the sick and especially the children." She smiled modestly at her husband. "He was very compassionate toward those of us who were displaced, and I fell in love with him and was baptized, taking the name Maria a year before we were married. My younger brother, Evgeny, also became a Christian, but my older sister had been training with the shaman, who died during the free years, and my sister took over the work. But she rejected both Islam and Orthodoxy. It was hard for her. No one wanted her and she grieved. Finally, Evgeny decided to take her north, perhaps to Kazan. Yev managed to get a boat ride, at Father's expense, since he thought they could get work up north. In fact, Yev got a job on one of those fancy vessels owned by that Daruvenko man who was recently murdered. We feared that he was on the ship that was destroyed there, but thank God, he was on another of which he is now a captain."

What a relief! Hopefully they didn't catch our few sharp intakes of breath. She continued, not seeming to notice. "The last time he saw her was on the dock at Stupino. She has apparently never tried to contact us. Unfortunately, Uyari doesn't read or write."

The silence inside the yurt was deafening. All eyes were fixed on her including those of the servants. Matushka looked startled.

"Forgive me, honored guests," Dalgali said. "This has just taken us all by surprise. Your sister Uyari is safe among us. She is our wise woman and midwife. She lives with and cares for Lazim, our shaman, who is growing old."

It was now her turn for silence. Since she was across the raised eating table, her husband could not even take her hand. At first, she began to tremble, and she brought her hands up to her face.

Natasha held her in case she should faint. She wiped away her tears and reached for her husband who had just come around.

"Thank you, my dear Lord God!" She choked on her tears. "Your mercy endures forever. Uyari is my sister." She put her head on Father John's chest and wept.

After she calmed down and let all those years of anxiety flow out through her tears, Batushka said, "Thank you, my dear friends. You have no idea how this has weighed on our hearts these many years. Tell me, how did Uyari link up with you?"

My father answered, "Our caravan was in Stupino at the time. We were not really trading since it was our last stop before going home to the Sopasi, the Birches. Yerinde, my wife, was traveling with us at that time, and when Uyari heard her talking in the marketplace hearing our tongue, she approached my wife. After Uyari told her story, Yerinde brought her to me. We needed a good midwife. Lazim's assistant had recently died of old age, and Uyari came at a perfect time. Furthermore, I knew Ibn Haddi very well, being old trade partners, and I felt he would not object to our taking her in. We are Tengrists, and so there would be no conflict along religious lines. Ibn Haddi's expulsion of the non-Islamic tribespeople was not a frivolous affair. He told me himself how deeply pained he was to have lost some good and dear friends and workers. He had to weigh the various factors involved in such a decision. Islamic life cannot abide 'infidels' amongst them."

Batushka interrupted politely. "We Orthodox are not so. We believe ourselves to be the vessels of the true faith. That is why we are called Orthodox. In Greek, as Nissim can tell you, this means 'true worshippers' as does the Slavonic word *Pravoslav*. But we can live and move amongst the non-Orthodox as a matter of course. We try to be as hospitable as possible, although militarily and politically we have not treated the tribespeople very well, may God forgive us. Dalgali, your reputation amongst the Russians is exemplary. The opening of Cherny Yar to your sons is virtually a miracle. It is God's providence that we met up with you and that

Nissim chose me as his confessor. I would be honored to serve you in any way possible."

Prince Dalgali replied, "We are very touched by your fine words, Father John, and we shall convey them to our glorious Akilli Khan, who will much appreciate them. We are also delighted to form a bond between your family and our tribe. I'm not sure how Uyari will respond. She is somewhat bitter about her past, but we will work on that. As for me, my friend, I am a businessman. You flatter me by calling me—what did you say, *exemplary*? I forge relationships between our people and others because it gives me the freedom I need to sell the finest horses, sheep, and cattle from Astrakhan here in the south and"—he said pointing a finger—"even to Kazan in the north."

I had often seen my father's generosity and his care for others—just look at Uyari—and I knew he was lying. It took me a few years to realize what a deeply humble man my father was. It was a time for me to increase my own love and respect for him. If money were a particular goal of his, it was only out of a sense of duty toward the tribe that compelled him. But his generosity, *that* came from the heart! That day opened my own eyes, and I knew then that I loved him.

While I was musing on this, somewhat absently, the kumis working its wonders, the subject had shifted to Nissim and me. My spinning head snapped with a whiplash when I heard my father speak to me with a little edge.

"What is this, my son? Father John tells me that you have a mission you should be talking to me about."

"Sorry, boys!" (The priest had been addressing us in a familiar way for a few days.) "I suppose I have to stress the urgency of the situation. Will you forgive me for bringing it up?"

At that point, I was fully alert. I looked toward Nissim, whose body I saw stiffen and his dark-brown eyes grow very large.

"Well, what is it you want to ask? Go on, speak up."

I was, I confess, a bit intimidated at his authoritative voice. It was probably meant to impress Father John, but I was put off, and I couldn't answer immediately. Nissim saw my dismay and spoke up respectfully but with some confidence.

"My dear father Dalgali, you have blessed me by calling me your son. Your son Tambor and Father John both know how grateful I am. I wish always to make you proud of me. I do have a very special request, most honored Father. As you likely know, for I have revealed it to our glorious khan, that Timov and I were not born into slavery. Nor were we taken in war." He paused.

Dalgali nodded. "Yes, the khan has told me. I know the situation." There was a buzz around the table.

"I and my family were enslaved, after being exposed as Christians, after years of masking as Muslims. I was sold to the Kurds after many years of brutality. I honestly do not believe that my master, Mehmet Pasha, was a genuinely cruel man. He was simply obeying his traditions and the local law. He had the right to turn me over to the authorities for execution since all his efforts at converting us had failed. But he didn't! My father in the flesh was deported apparently to the far ends of the empire, and my mother and sister, I have reason to believe, live today as slaves on Mehmet Pasha's estate near Trabzon, the city where all this took place. Tambor has made a vow to me that he will help me relocate and bring back my family. Father John believes my sister's virtue is in jeopardy." Again he paused and turned to me, hoping that I had regained the use of my tongue.

"Father," I said taking a deep breath, "for many weeks now, I have been working on a plan to rescue Nissim's mother and sister and bring them back with us. Of course, at first we shall try to buy them. We'll make up a story of some sort why we have to buy these two and see if that works." I could see the trace of a smile on my father's lips and knew I was getting through. "Of course, if that doesn't work, I have a backup plan, but for that, I shall probably need another warrior."

"Not Chabuk, Tambor. I want him with me. If you have not returned by spring, I need Chabuk to introduce me to Konstantin Lapukhin should I want to visit Cherny Yar on our way home."

I had never seen Chabuk so disappointed, and I was curious as to why he wanted anything to do with Nissim. I guess I was wrong about him. Or was it because he dreaded to have to be polite to the administrator against his will? This year, it would be only a social visit as most of our produce would have been sold by then.

Father was thinking. "Perhaps Hazir could go with you." Turning to him, he said, "You could leave Kym with Natasha if you think it is not safe for him."

"Please, Lord Dalgali, please let me go." Kym's voice, which was changing, almost shrieked. "Father, you would not leave me behind, you would *never* leave me behind. I will be no trouble. I promise. I am not lazy, Lord Dalgali. I will work hard. I helped Father fight the Kalmyks. I was brave, and I want to be a warrior like both my fathers and your sons."

"All right, my boy, all right! I hear you. But you must show more respect to me." Kym prostrated, and Dalgali forgave him. "It's up to you, Hazir. I don't think we shall have any more trouble on the way back. I would rather send you along with a few of the younger warriors. Think about it."

I had to chuckle inside watching my father making plans even before he gave his official approval.

"I need to take my camels and my Persian warriors also. As I say, I have been working out some ideas in my head, and I have a plan. Not even Nissim knows what I have in mind. But we will talk about it tonight." I turned to my father. "You still haven't granted Nissim his request, my father. Do we have your approval?"

"You have my official approval."

Everyone rejoiced. I thought Nissim would pass out. Tashi put her arms around him and kissed him.

"Well, my young warrior," Hazir said to Kiymetli, "I guess we're going too. Sir Tambor needs our help."

"Yay!"

"If I might make a suggestion—" Batushka said.

"You have another one, Father John?" My father interrupted.

"Well, yes, I do," he said shyly. "Next week is Nissim's name's day. Although he doesn't know his exact birth date, we shall celebrate the name of his saint, Onesimus, who is in heaven praying for him. Saint Onesimus has another feast day in the winter, so we shall combine the two I guess and make him eighteen years old at the same time. You are all invited to our humble home to feast him."

Turning to me, he said, "But it is important that you and Nissim leave Astrakhan shortly afterward in order to reach Tbilisi, the capital of Georgia by Christmas. We shall miss you here, and you will miss Natasha's name's day, but Christmas, the birthday of the Lord Jesus, will be glorious in Tbilisi. I shall send word ahead and make arrangements for you to visit my friend, Father Abo, who should put you up at the monastery where he lives. He speaks Turkish and Russian as well as his native, Georgian. Georgia is a mountainous land, and you will feel the winter snows. I shall also obtain certification from the administrator of Astrakhan, who will provide you with passports, which will allow you to pass freely through the southern part of Kalmykia unharassed. The camels, of course, will slow you down, so you need to get underway as soon as you can. Isn't that correct, Lord Dalgali?"

"That's the way I see it too."

There were days of preparation ahead. Much had to be discussed, much had to be gathered. We had to decide on food and what monies we had to bring. Should we bring extra horses and appear as a caravan, or would that slow us down? Talk, talk, talk. Everyone had his opinion. Finally Nissim and I made the final decision with my father backing me. I had revealed my rescue mission plan to Nissim, and he grew very excited as I knew he would. Hazir was a little more conservative about the idea but wisely and humbly offered a few suggestions. The fact is I did not reveal the entire plan yet.

The Persians were ecstatic. I realized how much they loved to travel, and it delighted them to think that they were a part of a major operation. But even more importantly, they knew the route through the steppes of Kalmykia and then into the Caucasian mountains. Father said he remembered the area of the Kuban River when he had traveled with our tribe as a boy to the plains of Astrakhan. However we were going south. Even then it would be somewhat cold.

"I wish I were going with you, my boys. Had it not been for the troubles in Kalmykia, we might have swung northwest to the Sea of Azov. There we would have traveled across our homeland and traded amongst the Turks. Nevertheless, it has been an exceptionally good season. We still have horses to sell and cattle. Our flocks are almost all gone and what we have left we shall likely eat. Our pockets are heavy though, and we have not yet completed buying supplies for the tribe, and a few gifts."

"So you think you will be soon moving on?" I asked.

"Yes, I want to visit your friend Konstantin before the Volga floods in the spring. Cherny Yar apparently gets hit badly. I owe him a debt of gratitude. If he hadn't warned us, we wouldn't've been prepared. Yes, and it would be nice to spend the spring at home to see the greening of the birches. Perhaps we could take the western route next year. After all, we should be able to cross Kalmyk territory without harassment."

Eventually we decided to take a few extra horses with us. Tutumlu was in charge of selling the rest. Tetik asked to come with us. In spite of his infirmity, he was becoming more adept with the hawks, and hawking would provide a good source of meat since taking sheep and goats along would slow us down. I think Tutumlu was a bit worried, but Tetik swore he could handle the trip. We thought we should take only the small sleeping tents rather than the portable yurts, but Father said that something more comfortable should be provided for the women whom we were to bring home. So we decided to purchase a yurt from a Tatar tentmaker since we didn't have an extra one. We also decided upon larger tents (tipis, also made from felt) that would hold four or five persons and would provide a draft that would allow a small fire to warm us. Forest trained, the Persians said there were no carts necessary as the camels were well able to handle the load. We actually decided to take the carts; they were needed for the birds and the slaves.

I felt my father's eyes on me, with some admiration. Finally he confided in me. "You have grown up a lot this year, my son. I can see your independence and your ability to plan in advance with a certain amount of astuteness. I am proud of you. You seem to have been taking a different path from me all along, but like me, you have set your own direction. Our people do not treasure such independence. I encountered a lot of criticism when I decided to become a trader and not a warrior like my father. Still I weathered it, and now I am almost indispensable to the tribe. So do what you have to do whatever it is and be assured that you have your mother and me behind you, and the blessing of our noble khan. Without your even knowing it, you have the power to inspire people and make them feel valued."

Nissim had told me what a name's day was, but I still didn't understand. I suppose I was looking for simplicity like a birthday, but it obviously was not the same. Yet even with us, a birthday, as a public event, was restricted to the aristocracy. Not even I was due one as yet. My father, yes, and of course the khan, but even though I was often called Lord Tambor, I was still but a warrior, a knight, I suppose you would say, a bondsman to Akilli Khan. Yes, we had some family events, but we didn't have a birthday celebration. None of this applied to slaves. The way name's days looked to me was that some saint in heaven had a yearly celebration or feast. The family would go to church to give him honor and anyone who had the same name cashed in on it. Obviously he would get the saint's prayers; then there would be a party. Friends and relatives would come for it, if the family had money, and there would be lots of food. Nissim always would laugh at this explanation and tell me I had missed the point.

"No way, my brother! No disrespect, but if you look at this name's day thing straight in the face, that's what is left." This is what *I* said.

"What you need is a saint to pray for you. Then you'd understand," he said this with a grin.

"No no no, my brother. I've got you and Father John to pray for me and someone else, maybe Natasha. Why do I need to get prayers from some dead person?"

"In any case, you're coming for the food," he replied, shaking his head.

"I think we are still in the fast. But I've got to confess the food's good. But," I was thinking out loud, "it seems a shame that your feast always falls when you are fasting."

"I suppose," he said solemnly with a shrug.

It was quite a gathering. We decided to come in style. It was a marvelous procession with Prince Dalgali mounted and dressed in the finest Tatar ceremonial clothing. It felt almost as important as Saban-Tui. I rode with him. We were to pick up Batushka, Nissim, and Natasha at church. Chabuk followed with Hazir. He had decided to bring two other young warriors with him, who were near relatives. He had been gathering a following on the training field, and this pleased me because his attitude was changing somewhat. I suspected he missed Dalgin a lot, and I suppose Nissim and I were a little too intense for him. The three of them had also been taking advantage of the female slaves that Father routinely brought with him on these trips. Chabuk was not so lonely. However we certainly couldn't discuss plans with these ones around.

I decided to have Hazir with us, although he was not related to us, even though it may have seemed to break the rules of protocol at this time. In any case, he was happy enough to leave his boy with Tutumlu. Kym and Tetik had become good friends. In fact, Tetik was more or less the lad's mentor. The young hawk that he had given Kym was in training, and Kym was ready to train with it. Two of Natasha's companions followed, accompanied by some servants who were expected to help Matushka with the feast. Father wasn't sure whether this would be offensive or not, but Natasha believed it would be welcomed. Nissim had told them it would be a big honor for them.

The closer we drew to the temple, the thicker became the crowds. Apparently in their minds, a major event was happening. Everyone loves a celebration. When I think of the scene, I have to admit how impressive it must have seemed. After all, it was not every day a procession of mounted Tatars marched through the city in full ceremonial array. We carried swords but not our bows and quivers. The ladies dripped with gold and silver bangles around their heads and jewels in their noses and ears. Our women covered their heads but not their faces. I would love to have had my camels and my Persians with me, but Father had thought it unwise.

Most Tatars in Astrakhan stood their yurts in the rolling plains surrounding the city; it was essential for the cattle and horses. There was a mosque in the city, and some of the elders of some of the permanent tribes lived in houses near the mosque. But what was happening today was exceptional.

We could hear, "Tatars…barbarians…pagans…infidels…" But we could also hear, "Dalgali…Prince (*Knyaz*)…warriors… women…horses…rich!" I tried not to burst out especially when I caught my father's stern eye. These were simple words I knew.

The bells were ringing as we neared the church. Worshippers were coming out, but Batushka had not appeared. We stopped. Every eye was on us. What *were* we going to do? Presumably not burn the temple down.

Father turned to me and said, "Dismount and come with me." He turned back and motioned Chabuk to come. "All stay mounted!" he said to the rest. "Unbuckle your swords," he commanded us quietly, giving them to the other two warriors. "Now come and follow me."

He slowly went up the walkway and mounted the short flight of stairs. "Quickly!" he whispered. When he got to the top, he stopped; I was on his right and Chabuk on the left. "Now prostrate with me." This was another quiet command. We did, and a sharp intake of breath was heard in the crowd followed by silence. We stood up and waited. Again he said to us quietly, "Tengri and Yer-Sub will not be jealous of an innocent little boy and his pure mother." I thought to myself, *I can't deny that.*

When Batushka came out, the crowd cheered although he didn't have any idea why.

He smiled at Dalgali and said, "Well, this is some reception, my Lord Dalgali. They'll talk about it for weeks. My carriage will be in front in a moment, and Nissim and Natasha's mounts will come also."

"Why don't you lead the way, Father? We need directions."

We were introduced to an older priest, Father Varnava, who climbed into the carriage and accompanied us to the feast. He was the pastor of the congregation. Matushka had stayed home in preparation for the feast and was sad she couldn't come to church. Nissim fell in behind , the Prince and I fell back with him to make room for Natasha.

Of course as we approached Father John's house, everyone came out to meet us and our wonderful procession. The children, all dressed for the celebration, came out screaming with Matushka and the nanny, who was trying to put a hold on them but not too seriously. Father John was the first to get out of the carriage, helping Father Varnava, who seemed to need no help. He came over to Prince Dalgali and took his hand.

"Welcome to my humble home, most honorable guest, Lord Dalgali. In the Name of our blessed Lord, may you and your family be always welcome here."

Matushka approached as Lord Dalgali dismounted and kissed his hand and embraced Natasha warmly.

As Nissim and I dismounted, the children ran noisily toward us. I gave them a stern eye and said, "Shh, shh, children, you must greet my father first."

"And your mother too?" asked one of the boys.

"Uh...well one of them." What could I say? Anyway, that explanation seemed to suffice.

Matushka was already gathering her chicks and, once establishing order, brought them over to kiss Dalgali's hand. The girls were shy and perhaps a little afraid. The little one insisted upon being in Matushka's arms.

The formalities being done, Dalgali said to them with some humor. "Now you can go and greet Sir Tambor and Sir Nissim."

"Yay!" they all yelled and started talking all at once. I sought out Alexei with my eye and gave him a discrete wink, which he caught, his pale skin flushing.

By that time Chabuk and his boys had dismounted, so I asked the children, "Do you know who these men are?"

"They look like warriors," Anton offered proudly.

"They certainly are," I replied, bringing them over to Chabuk. "This is my younger brother Chabuk, and my even younger brother Tolga. His mother is over there. Koray is our cousin." They fussed and tugged on them and demanded answers for multitudes of questions.

Chabuk amazed me. He was so natural with the children. Even the rough harshness of his voice seemed to soften when he talked to them. The other two were part of my youthful team and both had served at Mikhailov. Koray lost his older brother there but seemed to have come through the mourning period. Now they were the center of attention.

Nissim saw me observing all this, and his sharp eyes inquired of me what I was thinking. "It looks like Chabuk has taken over my job, holding together my troop," I said.

"That's because he will have to assume temporarily the leadership of the Blue Raiders," he commented.

"Perceptive." I truly wondered if Chabuk would be ready.

As we started in, I felt someone taking hold of my hand. I looked down and saw that Alexei had grasped my hand. He looked up at me and made an attempt to wink as I had before. He looked up at Nissim, who gently squeezed his shoulder.

The celebration was perfect. I suppose it was a little more subdued than our feasts; we can be somewhat noisy and even rowdy. Father John produced a jug or two of vodka, apparently stilled on his father's estate. Natasha had advised me earlier that we were running out of kumis but nevertheless brought two jugs along to be served with the meal. . Apparently the bishop of the city had given Batushka an *ekonomia*—a dispensation—permitting us wine and oil on this feast. Matushka had prepared a platter of piroshki stuffed with onion, mushroom, and cabbage.

The children were performing mock battles with Chabuk and the young warriors. I was glad to see that Alexei had joined in with them. The girls were enthralled with the beautiful princesses in their pretty dresses. They understood enough Tatar to have some conversation. Natasha doted on them and told them how she missed her own little girls and asked if they would be her little girls just for today. They agreed. Matushka mentioned that they were orphans, and I saw that Natasha's tender heart was moved to compassion. She had also noticed Alexei's attachment to me.

Even the servants enjoyed themselves. They ushered themselves into the kitchen area offering help. However, the Russian servants couldn't communicate with them, so they gave up trying. A large table was brought into a room next to the kitchen where the servants normally ate. The Russians brought them a jug of vodka, a loaf of fresh warm bread, and some piroshki. Our servants brought in our food to share. Eventually there was singing from these quarters in both languages.

When the time came to sit for the meal, the company became serious. While the table was fairly large, not all of us could be seated there. Rugs had been placed on the floor for those who felt more comfortable reclining. Father John sat at the end of the table with Dalgali sitting on his right and Nissim on his left. Father Varnava sat beside Nissim, and I was seated opposite the priest beside my father so that Nissim and I were able to make eye contact. A few other members of the congregation had also come. Matushka sat opposite Father at the end of the table, and Natasha sat to her right. Chabuk and the warriors along with the princesses reclined on the rugs, and the children begged to be allowed to join them. What a treat to eat on the floor! The fire blazed warmly to ward off the December chill. It was also a treat for the women to eat with the men, which would have been unheard of at the camp.

After the meal sweets were served along with rich red wine. This was followed by tea and a thick, dark, and bitter drink served in small cups with honey and a pod of cardamom. Father John said that the beans, which are finely ground, are imported from Arabia, some say, but others say Africa. Nissim said it was a common drink among the Turks and Greeks. The Arabs call it *ah'weh*; the Russians, *cofé*; and the Turks *kava*. Just before the end of the meal, when we were full and well drunk, Father John stood up and raised a glass of wine.

"It is a particular joy for my family to welcome our guests from the north to our humble table. This is especially true of Lord Dalgali, who is well known in these parts but whom I have never met until recently. Blessings to you and your noble and fine family. We pray that you will feel welcome to visit us whenever you come to the city of Astrakhan. It is also a joy to be able to celebrate the name day of your newly adopted son, Nissim, who has now been reconciled to the Church. He is named after the Blessed Saint Onesimus, the companion to the Holy Apostle Paul. Onesimus, which means *useful*, was found in Rome after escaping from his master Saint Philemon in Greece. Onesimus was baptized in Rome, and a little later, when Paul discovered that he had been his friend Philemon's runaway slave, he sent him back to Philemon, reminding them both that they were now brothers and that Onesimus should be treated as such. Eventually Philemon freed Onesimus, and today both are recognized as saints in the Church. This story has some similarities with our brother Nissim, who has recently been adopted by Lord Dalgali and made a Nogay warrior. My spiritual son, Nissim, I bid you, in the name of our Lord Jesus to execute this noble office in all honesty and seriousness, obedient to your new father and devoted to the noble Akilli Khan. May God grant you many years."

Nissim stood and bowing, received a blessing from Father John. The priest then bowed toward Lord Dalgali saying, "Prince Dalgali, it would be most fitting if you could grace this table with a few words."

Father stood up and surveyed his audience. He was quiet. All looked at him, and when he had everyone's attention, he spoke.

"Father John and Matushka, and with respects to Father Varnava, on behalf of our glorious Khan Akilli, the members of my family and our tribe, the Kubanshyi Nogay of Sopasi Falaka, I offer you the profoundest gratitude for your excellent hospitality." A polite murmur of agreement went around the room. "This happy occasion has certainly been the highlight of our trip this year to Astrakhan. Of course we had some trouble before coming to your city, but you have provided ample compensation for our labors." My father's words were simply music. The whole rhythm of the Tatar tongue was in his voice. It was no wonder Dalgin could sing; he had his father's gift for poetry. "You know that I am a businessman. We travel this route almost every year. We grow wealthy, thanks to whoever favors us, but we are not greedy. We are here to provide for our tribe. Our prosperity is your prosperity and the prosperity of the many others whom we have had the good fortune to meet and trade with.

"But you, Father, have blessed our family with your graciousness and your spiritual guidance. We hope that you will grace Sopasi with your presence since you now have a special reason for coming to us. But we are here for another reason. We want to honor a young man who has just become part of our family and in another way has presumably become part of yours.

"A year ago, I did not know Nissim. He was one of the many servants who crowd our yurts carrying this here and that there. We always hope that these servants are working to their maximum because they are being fed, taken care of, and sheltered by their masters. This is a mutual responsibility. Unknown to myself, my dearest wife Yerinde had had her eye on him for a long time. 'This boy is no slacker,' she used to say. 'He is wasted on Tambor who doesn't appreciate him.'

"But Tambor did appreciate him. I have never found out why—Tambor has his own unique reasons for doing things—but just after the summer feast, he announced that he had granted Nissim his freedom. Nissim was Tambor's servant, so he could do whatever he wanted, but he actually sought out the khan's favor to allow him to be trained as a warrior. What could I say? They seemed to have a good effect on each other, so I invited Nissim to accompany us here. And it was well we did, because Nissim proved his loyalty and bravery to our tribe. Behind that shy smile and those sad eyes is a very fierce warrior. Many live today, including myself, because he wielded his ax with determination, fearing no danger. I wanted him to be my son.

"After the battle with the Kalmyks, I sent word to Akilli Khan advising him of my intentions toward Nissim." (Actually he sent word by Usta but he was wise enough not to identify himself with the Blue Raiders.) "Just a few days ago, I received a letter from Khan Akilli, which I would ask Batushka to read. I do not believe that our people have ever had their own alphabet, so the khan sent the letter in Russian." (I wondered who provided the Russian text.)

He read, and he himself translated. "My dear Lord Dalgali, greetings to you." (Father John apparently edited out all the Tengri passages.) "I am grateful for your discretion and your desire to make the correct decision in a situation such as you mentioned, namely the knighthood of your son Tambor's squire, Nissim. You said that you would be adopting him as a son, and so by the time this reaches you, that part shall already have been done. He is a fine young man, honest of character, with dignity and respect. That he loves your son Tambor and that he is loyal to the tribe, I have no doubt. That he should be elevated to the rank of a warrior or a knight of the Kubanshyi is, as you rightly said, for my official decision. My research shows me that the young man has exhibited extraordinary courage, cleverness in battle, and devoted obedience. These three qualities alone should grant him his knighthood, but I would also point out another virtue to his favor. What endears me to him is his humility and, close to that, his piety. Would that all warriors added these virtues to their knightly qualities! It would get them out of a lot of trouble. In this case, recognizing the distance between us, I shall rely upon you to perform the necessary formalities. I would be glad to have him as my bondsman. When he returns to the Birches in the spring, he shall be introduced to the Yurt as Sir Nissim. Please remind the young man of the promise I once made to him. Again, I pronounce my blessings to you and your troop, Lord Dalgali. Akilli, your leader."

A murmur of approval passed through the listeners. I took my eyes off of Father John and looked straight at Nissim. His head was bowed for just a moment, and when he raised it, I saw that his cheeks were flushed. I recognized my brother's proneness to tears and somewhat envied his ability to be easily moved, I who could never remember having cried in my life. I wondered how he would deal with the situation. Finally he caught my eye upon him. Then he stood up, and every eye turned toward him. We were all waiting; he wanted to talk.

Nissim was quiet. I knew he was struggling with tears. Yerinde had often said I was born silent and never cried as a child. But *he*, in fact, was the silent one, usually. I thought, at that moment how little he had ever talked to me. A shrug of the shoulder, a curl at the lips, a widening of his already large brown eyes were all I needed to know what he was thinking, and I didn't doubt it for a moment. That is how close we were. Yes, I knew at that moment he did not want to let those tears out. While we Tatars never abjure tears, although we were taught to keep a cold face when in trouble, I'm sure he felt the need for dignity and composure. I nodded my head as if to say, *Go on, my friend, you can do it.* I added a smile, and he returned it.

"My dear Father and Lord Dalgali and my confessor, Father John, with respects to Father Varnava, I must tell you how overwhelmed I am today. A year ago, my brother, Timov, and I were the personal servants of the young prince Sir Tambor, son of Dalgali. Most of you will know that I was unique among slaves. Most of my fellow servants, at least those of my own age, were born into the Birches. I however was won in battle when Sir Tambor destroyed a clan of treacherous Kurds who had abused our most honored Akilli Khan's hospitality. That I and Timov escaped was for me a miracle. We were the only ones who survived the general slaughter. Of course it is not customary, indeed disgraceful, for Nogay warriors to destroy children. My gratitude to Sir Tambor for rescuing me is undying. Although he barely noticed me, I turned all my efforts into pleasing him. After doing my duties every morning, I would race out to the stables in the hopes that I would saddle his horse before anyone else did. I even tried to get out of felting so I could watch him on the field. As often as I could, I would sit on the fence around our training grounds and watch him train with the young warriors every day. He never saw me sitting there, and when his day was done, I would unsaddle his horse, Onyx, and I myself would clean him down refusing the help of the stable hands. How I envied his brothers Chabuk and Dalgin who were always with him seeking his favor.

"I had had some military training in Trabzon on the Black Sea as a youth, having come from a wealthy family. How I longed to ride again, how I prayed for my circumstances to change! Yet even if they didn't, I was satisfied with serving my master. However, they did change. I cannot provide details, but they *did* change. Tambor all of a sudden, because of a certain circumstance, noticed me and wanted to make me a warrior. He approached the khan who gave his approval, making me a companion, a squire, to Sir Tambor until I proved myself. I am unbelievably grateful to you, Lord Dalgali, for blessing me with your graciousness. I am deeply humbled to be looked upon with favor when I know myself to be so unworthy, but at the same time, I am very proud to be the adopted son of such a fine and noble prince. I cannot express the depth of gratitude to our glorious Khan Akilli, may he ever be blest, who has acknowledged your request to make me a warrior of the Kubanshyi Nogay and has acknowledged me as his bondsman.

"My gratitude also extends to Father John, who has shown me and my brother Tambor such friendship and hospitality. We were determined to seek you out, Batushka, having been recommended by two of your other spiritual children, officials upriver who pushed us in the right direction. By Batushka's prayers and the mystery of confession, my sins have been forgiven, and I am now reconciled to the Church.

"I have been carrying a heavy burden for many years. I have been blaming myself for the calamities my family in the flesh endures. Because of an indiscretion on my part, my parents have been separated and sent into slavery. Batushka tells me that I am not to blame. He says, and I believe him, that the Lord himself has been working out something we will understand only in the fulfillment of time. Timov, my brother, and I have managed to stay together, which has been a comfort. However, unless things have changed, my mother and younger sister are, I suspect, domestic slaves at an estate near where we were parted. I do not know where to find my father. My brother Tambor and I, and a few others of our camp, will be going on a trip to seek out my mother and sister so that we may, God willing, bring them back to Astrakhan. Again my father Dalgali has shown his generosity by making it possible for us to leave in two days. With God's help, we shall find them and increase my joy. I sincerely ask your prayers and well-wishes in our venture. And may there be many blessings upon all of you too."

Everything was silent. Every eye was fixed on him, even those who did not understand. Father John beamed, my father stared in amazement, Chabuk scowled, Natasha gleamed, and Matushka discretely wiped her eyes. I had never heard Nissim speak at such lengths. For the first time, I realized how thick his Turkish accent was. More than that, I could see how much this speech alone took out of him.

He was just about to sit down when my father came to himself and said quietly, "Come over here, my son." And turning to Father John, he said, "Father John, while I am authorized to pronounce Akilli Khan's blessing and acknowledge Nissim as a warrior of the Kubanshyi Nogay, you are authorized to ratify this blessing before Jesus his God. I would therefore ask you to stand with me and share with me this noble task."

Father John bowed and moved closer to Father. Nissim prostrated and knelt on his right knee.

Dalgali began.

Ride swiftly with the breeze at your back
But fear not the wind that strikes your face.

Be one with your horse
And feel the very beat of her hooves upon the land
As though they were your own.
Drink the waters of delight
And breathe in the waft of destiny.
Choose well your companions,
Seek those who are brave and wise
And honest.
Incline your heart to virtue
And raise your thoughts to seek the truth.
May your enemies fear your swift judgment,
But scorn not the pauper or the slave.
Be an honor to your family
And bring no shame to their name.
Serve your khan with gratitude and devotion
And be a blessing to his honor.
Serve all generously
And always tell the truth.

This my father said, and when the blessing finished, he kissed him on the head and gave him a new and exquisite sword, which he put to his forehead. I remembered my own blessing less than a year ago just before the siege of Mikhailov. Akilli Khan pronounced almost the same words over me, but the impact of them didn't strike me until now. It left me breathless hardly able to "breathe in the waft of destiny."

Then Batushka approached him and made the sign of the cross over his head. Nissim kissed his hand and knelt on both knees.

Father John began, "In the name of the Father and of the Son and of the Holy Spirit. Amin. My beloved spiritual child, Nissim, brethren in Christ, most noble Lord Dalgali, and honored guests, a wonderful thing has happened just now. A young man from an honorable family, who, by certain circumstances, was reduced to slavery, has been granted freedom and has proven himself a loyal and brave warrior.

"I have no doubt that the hand of God has wrought this miracle, for a miracle it is. Sir Tambor, when you freed Nissim from his bonds and took him as your companion, the Lord was speaking to your heart and you responded to his voice. Your life was in the palm of his hands. Lord Dalgali, when you were moved to adopt Nissim as your son, you too were responding to the gentle voice of the mother of our Lord and perhaps the sweet urging of Lady Natasha, his adopted mother. Your noble khan also listened to the voice of the Lord when he honored your letter and advice, and as a result, gave his approval. And I too must, in profound humility, recognize that the voice of God drew me to this young man who has been touched by the Divine Hand.

"There are many warriors who have become saints in God's Church. Just look over to the icons on the far wall, and you will see Saint George, who is slaying the dragon, and Saint Demetrios, who is killing a corrupt gladiator. I shall tell you about them sometime. There is also Saint Theodore the General and Saint Menas of Egypt, Saint Mercurios and of course the Emperor Constantine, who established the reign of the Cross in Roman lands. These were blessed saints and glorious warriors many of whom gave up their lives for their Lord." He lifted his hands in prayer.

> We therefore beseech the mighty majesty of our Lord Jesus Christ, through the prayers of these valorous saints, that our brother, Nissim, strive to keep the commandments of God, that he obey his rulers, and that he honor his father and mother in both families. We pray that he serves his master as unto God. We pray 'that his light so shine before men that they may see his good works and glorify the Father who dwells in the heavens.' May our brother Sir Nissim 'fight the good fight of faith' that he may lay hold of eternal life, looking unto Jesus, the author and perfecter of his faith. (Refer to Matt 5:16 and 1 Tim 6:12)

The rest, Holy Father, he said in Slavonic, and I didn't understand it. I presume he was calling upon the Lord, his Mother, and the blessed warrior saints. I do not want to say much more about the celebration. There was a great sense of joy and good will; I was amused to see Tatars and Russians enjoying each other although we all stumbled with our words. Father Varnava gleamed and blessed everyone, even Chabuk. There was no music, save in the servant's quarters, because we were still within the fast. But we celebrated nevertheless.

I didn't realize to what extent people were drawn to Nissim. They seemed to be drawn to his deep sensitivity. But I didn't go to him. It was his day, not mine. What I really wanted to do was examine the warrior saints on the icons. I thought I was not being too obvious trying to slip over to the far side of the room where they were. The icons were fairly sizable, so I could easily make out what was happening. One of the warriors rode a white horse. He had just stabbed a foul-looking animal down its throat with a very fine spear. I thought it might be a dragon. Mother had some silk cloth that Father said was from China. It had dragons all over it.

The warrior was not even looking at the dragon. His eyes were quiet as though he were thinking something. I couldn't tell whether he was happy or sad; he was just thinking. An angel seemed to be dropping a crown on to his head. But it was never actually put on his head. *Strange!* I thought.

The warrior in the other icon was not much different from the other. The warrior in the first one was facing the second one, as though they knew each other. He was on a red horse, and he was stabbing an armored person with the same kind of spear. But he too had that same inner look, which unnerved me. I think I had seen this look in Nissim's eyes before.

All of a sudden, in the midst of my reverie, a moist hand slipped into my left. It was Alexei with a pastry in his other hand, which he was offering me. He pointed up to the white-horsed warrior and said, "Sviati Yuri." Turning to the other, he informed me, that the warrior on the red horse was called Sviati Mitri.

"These are Alexei's favorite saints, Tambor," Father John, who seemed to have sneaked up on me, said. "Forgive me for startling you, my friend. You seemed so absorbed in these icons. Would you like an explanation?"

"Well, yes, yes...of course. I am puzzled by them." I didn't want to have seemed too startled.

"Perhaps I can give you a detailed account of the lives of both these saints when you return from Trabzon. Actually I'll let my little lambs tell you with great fervor, especially Alexei. Icons are not always what they seem at first. You can look at them in three levels. There is the obvious one. Saint George is on a white horse killing a dragon, and Saint Demetrios is on a red horse killing a warrior. Already you have seen this. The second level is based on the stories of the persons themselves who are imaged on the icon." He used the word *imaged* as he didn't have the Tatar equivalent in his vocabulary. His Tatar was not perfect, and sometimes he stumbled for words. However I loved the word he used and still use it, Holy Father, to this day.

"However there is a deeper level, and that is the one I can address in a short time. The dragon in Saint George's icon represents not only the dragon he killed on the shores of Lebanon but, more importantly, the dragon inside, the violent beastly passions that lie within a man's breast. Saint George, by giving up his life in martyrdom, destroyed these passions and entered a vastly more beautiful life, a more divine life.

"Saint Demetrios was actually not a warrior but an administrator of the city of Thessalonica. The warrior he is killing is a man called Laieos, a foul, arrogant, selfish, and mercenary man whose sole job was to provide the bloodthirsty citizens of Thessalonica with the entertainment of killing Christians in the arena. This man had no honor, just brute force and the love of gold and hero worship." It was hard for me to understand these words. But I was fascinated nevertheless. He went on. "It was his friend Nestor who actually killed Laieos after Demetrios told him God would give him victory."

"However, when the Roman emperor Maximus, who hated Christians, found out about this, he had the two of them killed, or martyred, as we prefer to say. Laieos represents not so much the passions of the flesh but rather the cruelty, greed, and wickedness found in this world. By Laieos' death and their own martyrdoms, Demetrios and Nestor destroyed a great injustice and made way for some peace in the Christian community.

"Tambor, I see in you two young warriors the same spirit in these two men. I believe Nissim is at war within himself and battling his very own desires and faults and sense of guilt. You... you are at war with injustice and dishonor. Even though you are not yet a Christian, you have displayed strong moral leadership. You, like Saint Demetrios, have great compassion and great courage especially when you are confronted by injustice. Your noble khan sees this in you and desires you to excel. Saint George and Saint Demetrios never knew each other, but you and Nissim both know and love each other. The two of you together are a formidable pair."

At that point, our party was about ready to return to our camp. Amidst expressions of friendship and peace, we departed as magnificently as we came.

MOUNTAINS AND VALLEYS, RIVERS AND LAKES

Who is that staring at me through all the stars in heaven
and all the creatures on earth?
What is there for you to see?

—from the poems of Saint Nicolai of Ochrid

Snow had fallen. It was not cold, at least not the cold that often sweeps over the northland as I remember it. Father had been prepared for the winter and had brought fleece skins, fur coats, and woolen blankets. Some of these were draped over our horses, and others would be left for us to sleep in. *Gone are the days when we could sleep in the open air*, I thought wryly. We wore leather coats lined with fur or fleece and a layer of soft woolen under garments. As I said, Father was always prepared and ready for any change in plans. Last year, he took up and decided to travel north to Kazan in the middle of winter. The Volga was always somewhat temperate in spite of the snows that fall closer to Kazan and few other traders would risk such a journey, but Father was always prepared.

I was not. A gloom had settled over me, and the excitement of the oncoming mission had been replaced by a kind of loneliness and homesickness. Familiarity had fled from me; I was entering another world and leaving my father. He had left me for such long periods of time when I was at home that I had gotten used to it. But there was always the tribe. There was always Mother. There was always the khan. I suppose however that I had come to love my father deeply these past few months.

He and Chabuk and a few others were accompanying us out of the camp. Natasha had stayed behind after some tearful well-wishes. Father was talking and talking, but my gloom kept me from appreciating all these tidbits of advice and information. I began to see that he too was reacting to our departure although he was compensating for his loss by talking.

"You should have little trouble going south along the west shore of the Caspian. You have never seen the sea. I'm sorry, son, I should have taken more time with you. But I did not expect such a change of events on your first trip south. The shoreline will be more beautiful, in fact, balmy, in the springtime when you return. I wish I could share it with you." I smiled at him. I knew he was a little anxious watching me leave the protection of the tribe and the watchful eye of either him or the khan. I too was anxious.

Nissim had fallen back and was talking to Chabuk and Hazir. In spite of the cold and dampness, the sky was beautifully blue and bright. If saying good-bye to Tashi was hard, it would be more so with my now well-beloved father and Chabuk. It was an important moment for both of us. I could imagine how heartwrenching it must have been for Nissim to have seen his father dragged off.

Father was still talking.

"...and then Vishtaspa and Mardunya have made this trip before and know the way. Buying those camels was a great investment. The Persians are your boys, Tambor. I think you can rely on their loyalty."

I agreed and told him how much I appreciated them; indeed they were essential to our mission.

"And you need not concern yourselves about traveling through Caspian Kalmykia," he continued. "The Kalmyks here don't know you, and as far as they are concerned, you will be just another small trading party. They'll leave you alone, and if they don't, you have a passport sealed and signed by the administrator of Astrakhan. Be tactful, or more than that, be gracious to them. They will be better friends than enemies. The Nogay in Kazakhstan have experienced no end of trouble with the Kalmyks on the east side of the river.

They are called the Jungar or Zungar there, and the Nogay are unable to dwell with them peaceably. If the Nogay there were more united, it would be different. But that should not trouble you here in the west, my son. Remember, be gracious."

"I appreciate your advice, Father."

"Now the reason you are going west before going south is that there are marshlands to the south…too much water. The land around here descends to the sea. It is low at this time of year but when the Volga swells and other rivers flow into her she raises a fathom (I did not know the word) but that won't happen till spring."

We had moved somewhat beyond human habitation and I looked upon a vista of snow with a few leaf-bare trees sticking out of it. It looked somewhat like home except we had rolling hills and little thickets of trees and brush next to the Sopasi River. River? It was really a big stream, shallow and easy to cross; only in the deepest winter did it freeze over. Mind you, it did widen as it flowed into the Volga at Mikhailov. I was homesick. I did not want to leave my father. I wanted to go home.

We stopped, and all of us drew up and surveyed the scene. The time of departure had come. It seemed that even the camels sensed the immensity of the journey. They knew the route. Our horses would have to slow down to their pace. But our trip from The Birches had been slow and leisurely so what would be so different?

"Well, Tambor and Nissim, my sons, your adventure is about to begin. Do not think that I am not concerned. There is always danger. Mehmet Pasha may not be willing to part with some valuable slaves. You may have to fight. Yes, yes, I know you have a plan and a fight may occur. We can never know the outcome of any event." What he was saying was that we might never see each other again. "However, I know in my heart that you will act honorably as sons of Dalgali and clansmen of our noble Akilli Khan." At this, my gloom snapped!

"Father, I am bound by a vow to my best friend and brother. Whatever happens, I shall fulfill what I have vowed. I do not fear death if that is my fate, but I will surrender to my destiny doing my duty. If Nissim's God requires it, then whatever happens, I am in his hands. Whether I live or die, my father, you shall be proud of me."

At this, Father drew ahead and faced us all. He was mounted on his white horse with the yellow mane, Kizh Mevsimi, snorting and blending into snowy landscape, except for the crimson woven blanket my father sat on. Father was handsome, tall, and slender, unlike most Tatars who are thick and muscular, like me. He took off his fur-lined leather hat and let his thick braid slide down the back of his crimson leather coat, which had been dyed and embroidered by Yerinde, my mother. He pulled himself up to his full stature and raised his hands. Softly in the stillness of the winter air, as though all creation could hear his voice, he blessed us:

> My sons and warriors
> Heed not the chill of winter
> But may the fervor of your resolve
> And the firmness of your resolution
> Fan the flame of your desire.
> Be filled with the warmth and love of honor.
> Fear not what comes against you.
> May heaven provide you
> With welcome winds
> And may the earth be firm at your feet.
> May the Almighty, the Creator of heaven and earth,
> Guide you with his beneficent hand.

I was still out of breath when Father came toward us; I was always astounded at his beautiful speech. He drew Kizh Mevsimi over between Onyx and Cereyan. He reached over and kissed me and then turned to Nissim and kissed him. He moved over and grasped Hazir's arm and took Kym's hat off to pull his pigtail.

He shook Tetik's hand and waved to the Persians. Only after this did we say farewell to the others. Then we moved on, never looking back.

My depression had lifted. I was myself again. Nissim drew nigh, and I grinned. He said to me, "I haven't seen you in such a gloom before, my friend. I wasn't sure you wanted to talk."

"Nah! I finally experienced a bout of homesickness, and I now know what it feels like." I giggled perhaps out of embarrassment. "I realized how much I would miss my father, Nissim. Maybe it is not a good time to say it, but I thought how painful it must have been to see your father dragged away."

"You had better believe it. There were times when I had to bite my lips and bury my face in my blanket, if I had one, to keep from bursting into tears. I feared they would torture him to death. And I was fearful of what they would do to Mother and Eleftheria and, after what Father John said, I am even more fearful. You see, I felt responsible. Even now I blame myself for our misfortune. Livvy, as we called her, would be fifteen years old now, maybe even sixteen, and ripe for the plucking. She is a slave after all and has no rights. What a pretty sister she was, and she is probably now a beautiful maiden." He looked worried. His eyebrows frowned over his black eyes, which were shining below his pointed Tatar cap like two heated coals.

"Do you think Mehmet Pasha would have her?"

"Oh no!" he laughed wryly. "No, he is actually a very righteous, a very moral man. He has only one wife, at least when I was with him, and he loves her. But I don't know if they are even alive now. It's his son, Fahesh, I am worried about. He's my age. We went to academy together. In fact, brother, he's the one who exposed me. He was a rake of a boy then and not much of a warrior." He shrugged. "Who knows how he is now?" He changed the subject. "Listen, Tambor, where did your father's blessing come from? 'The Almighty, the Creator.' Where did all this come from?"

"Yes, I know. It surprised me too." I replied. "Well…I suppose this year he was surrounded by Christians. Last year he was surrounded by Muslims in Kazan. He married off my sister Vermek to a merchant's son, a Christian, in Kazan, and Kattu is married to Ibn Haddi's daughter, Marwa. Both traditions are in our family. (We had dined with Ibn Haddi a couple of times not long after arriving in Astrakhan.) The khan believes that Kattu is a Muslim already. Obviously, the lure of a single God has some attraction to my father." I wanted to steer away from that direction so I wouldn't have to commit myself. "You know, brother, we haven't had a chance to talk together for a long time. We've been so busy with our plans that we haven't had a breather for weeks. Too bad the ground is so icy or I would race you."

"We could take a trot, you know, and check the surface of the land. I'm glad there is a cloud cover now. The sun on the snow was blinding this morning."

"I suppose we could. Did you ever see such flat land? I miss those rolling hills."

"It is probably prettier in the summer months," Nissim observed. "Vishtaspa and Mardunya say that we shall be in Kalmykia in four and a half or five days. The land is layered down to the sea. We won't see the Caspian before then. Maybe just less than a week."

"Well, let's go and trot then." I shouted out to the others. "We're going to check out the land. Catch up to us, we'll wait for you.'

"Be careful, Master!" Mardunya cried. "Underneath the snow there may be ice. Not good for the horses!"

"Thanks, good man. We'll heed your warning."

Vishtaspa added, "There is probably a road ahead about an hour from here. If you wait there, Master, we shall catch up with you and break camp before dark."

"Good idea! Hazir, you're in charge!"

He saluted.

We trotted for a short while. The snow was moist and not too crisp. That was because the weather was mild and underneath, the snow had not frozen. So we decided to increase speed. We were exhilarated. My energy and sense of well-being had returned. I was amazed how well Cereyan kept up. She was a half-breed steppe horse, whereas Onyx was a bigger horse, an Arab stallion. I would have thought Onyx could overrun Cereyan, but that is not so. Later Nissim reminded me that Chinggis Khan had conquered the world on steppe horses. They were built for speed and agility, and they were native to the land.

All of a sudden and not too far away, we heard a shot, which brought us to a halt. Immediately I was on guard; my bow in my hand, and the arrow ready. As we turned, we noticed a man standing in the doorway to the small snow-covered house we had just skirted by. He called out in Russian, "That is just a warning, boys. Don't trample over my lands." I looked around in vain to see a fence and thought, *What lands?*

Nissim drew nigh to speak to him, his topor ready to slice, and the man let the rifle drop down. He showed a bit of fear when he saw our weapons and stood ready for a response. "Our apologies, *gospodin*," Nissim said respectfully. "We need to find the eastbound road before it gets dark. Can you help us?"

"Are you both traveling alone?"

"No, good man, we have some camels who are meeting us shortly."

"You won't make it," he said abruptly. "Where ya ofta?"

Nissim seemed to understand him.

In broken Russian, he asked if the old fellow spoke Tatar. He laughed. "I speak as much Tatar as you speak Russian. Where ya ofta?" he asked again.

As always, Nissim was calm and polite. "We're on our way to Tbilisi."

"Why ya doin' that fer, boys? Got a big caravan?" It seemed his hostility had completely abated.

Nissim countered with a question. "How is it a farmer has firearms?"

"Ha-ha!" He laughed. "I got it fight'n for the Russians many years back. We got to keep our guns. Scared ya, I guess! Ha-ha!"

I'd already put my bow down, but I was still wary. Nissim turned to me and explained what the old man was saying.

"Wher'ya come from, lads? Why ya goin' t'Blisi? Lotsa snow down there 'cause o' the mountains. Dry around here. Don't 'spect to get much more for a while in the flatlands. D'ya cross the Volga? No ice on the big river."

"Yes, we crossed it this morning. We were told the best way to travel is past the marshes and straight into Kalmykia."

"That's some real good figuring there, but it would save some time going through the northern lakes close by here. You could skirt some of the villages there and pick up supplies in the towns. Y'can save 'bout two days going past the lakes. They're fine for travel during the snow season. It's the route the Kurds take on their way back to the empire. The bigger for'n caravans skirt the south a' the sea. Whatcha selling?" We realized he really didn't want any answers, so we skirted the questions.

Nissim of course related all this to me, confessing that he had trouble understanding everything he said. While we were talking, the old man went inside and brought out a glass jug of vodka and some clay cups. "Figured you guys are a bit cold f'm ridin'. Ya need to get warmed up. The old lady's makin' some tea. Rest yer horses in the shed out back. Come 'n' sit. We don't see too many strangers 'round here. We'll keep our eyes out fer yer boys 'n y'all can camp here till the morning." We dismounted.

"God bless you, friend. I'll pass on the vodka. Give it to my friend here. Tea sounds just fine for me." He looked quizzically at Nissim and then to me. He was obviously assessing us.

He said to Nissim. "Yer Pravoslav, are ya?" Nissim nodded. "It's good to do things right, lad. But out here where yer caught in the cold and the wind, we bless the good Lord fer a good shot of vodka especially during the fast. What about you, sir? Y'll have some?"

I nodded gratefully. I didn't know what he said, but I did know what he meant. I took a shot and felt the warmth rising through me. I asked Nissim if the old man, whose name was Grigory Yurevich Ureic, stilled the vodka himself. He answered with a proud smile on his face.

"Most around here brew their own." I wondered who *they* were. "Mine's pretty good, they say. Some of the others brew donkey piss." He broke into an infectious laughter. We were having some fun. I was glad to be with Nissim again.

His house was warm and clean even if somewhat worn. The old lady was silent and kept her eyes lowered. Mercifully, the sun had still not set when the others passed this way. They were a little farther off, so I rode out to meet them while Nissim practiced his Russian on old Grigory. Hazir was visibly relieved and grateful for the hospitality.

We set up camp in a hurry so as to be ready before the darkness came. Besides the three warriors, all cousins or maybe one was a half brother, we had five servants, not to mention the Persians. Tetik brought his birds, and at the last moment, Tutumlu had decided to come after all. Hazir's three tribesmen completed the company. Grigory managed to find some shelter for the horses. The shed out back was adequate for three extra horses, and the others were taken farther on to a barn to share the night with Grigory's cattle and goats. The camels stayed outside. Three of the camels and the colt were dromedaries, which had been purchased in Egypt before the family had been enslaved and the other three were smaller hairy camels with two humps, which had been bought by their Persian master at the same time as the family. Mardunya, it turned out, was more talkative than Vishtaspa. He informed me that the camels with one hump much preferred the heat of the desert to this damp climate near the sea. They would be a bit cranky until they were warm, but the others were used to snow and cold weather.

All of us worked together quickly and efficiently. Hazir seemed to command the whole operation and even risked ordering me around. I am not good at setting up tents. For the first night out, we made it admirably, and of course we invited Grigory to join us in our meal and campfire. We viewed a golden red sunset, which shed a river of color over the bleak snow-covered plains. I thought how much I would have enjoyed one of Dalgin's songs but resisted the temptation to sink into another bout of homesickness.

It turns out that Grigory Yurevich had been a soldier for twenty-five years and spent much of his career serving a Russian outpost in Turkmenistan across the Caspian where the Russians had joined with the Turkmen to repulse the invading Persians.

He dismissed his wife with a kiss on the forehead and pulled up a low fleece-covered stool to sit by the fire. After feeding ourselves, I sent the servants to their tents after making sure they were warm, and then we got to talking. However, as usual, I insisted that the Persians stay by the fire.

Vishtaspa and Mardunya were always with me nearby. Tonight Kuru wanted to stay along with Naveed, the fifteen-year-old. The lure of the fire must have broken down their usual shyness. Pishana, who had been wounded by the Kalmyks, and his twin Arshana, both, of course, fourteen, stayed behind in Astrakhan with the caravan. Natasha felt that the lad needed more time for recovery, and amid protests, Pishana eventually accepted the fact that it would not be possible to lead a camel across the wilderness of the western steppe into the Caucasian mountains with a wounded arm. Of course what fourteen-year-old orphan could resist Tashi's mothering? The boys would probably be speaking Tatar by the time we got back.

Old Grigory, well enjoying his vodka, began to speak about the many times he as a soldier sat with his buddies around a campfire talking about victory and the men they had killed and the fellow soldiers who left widows behind. After a few soldier stories from the old man, we heard a little disturbance around the Persians.

"These boys Persians?" the old man asked. I nodded. "Well, Lord knows. Hey, boys," he said in Persian, and he moved over and barged into the conversation. He looked back at Nissim and shouted, "Ain't talked to a Persian since I left the army ten years ago."

There seemed to be an argument among them, and Grigory joined in. After a short while, Mardunya motioned to me to come over.

"Lord Tambor and Sir Nissim, we have a disagreement going on here. Father Kuru, may he always be honored, believes that we could save a few days, perhaps a week, if we could detour into the lake country. Old Grigory agrees and has let us know in very certain terms that Kuru is right. He says that there are some roads that travel by the lakes, and there are villagers who would provide necessities, at a price of course. Kuru said he has done this before and that we should remember having done so too. We were very young at the time, but I remember our Persian masters haggling about this then."

Hazir and the Persians boys felt we should keep to our plans. However, I began to see how dominating their father could be. The fact that Grigory Yurevich agreed with Kuru added more weight to the possible change of plans. Nissim and I were somewhat ambivalent although as the discussion continued we began to agree with the older ones. The idea of saving considerable travel time was obviously appealing. It also meant a shorter trip through the eastern coast of Kalmykia rather than entering into the center. I told everybody that I would consider the question and make my decision tomorrow morning. Kuru was very apologetic, but I told him not to concern himself. It was obvious who was master of the camels.

I slept well that night. Lately I noticed that, perhaps because of the cold, Nissim did not go outside for prayers. Instead, well before dawn, I noticed, he would wake and light a candle—Father John had given him a bundle—and prayed silently on his knees before his icon. Little did he know how much I depended upon those prayers. I went back to sleep with no dreams.

We were awakened just after sunrise by my personal slave who had come into the tent with a steaming pitcher of water and a metal trough. Nissim's servant followed. My father had given one of his servants to Nissim who was greatly distressed by it.

"You will need him my son. He will take care of many details you have no time for. He has been with our household from his grandfather's time. Treat him kindly and honorably if that will lighten your conscience, but you *will* need a servant." And so Nissim humbly acquiesced.

We washed in the tipi trembling and shivering in the cold. Nissim never let his servant wash him, particularly his back. Even when we were bathing in the Volga in the autumn, he always wore something if there was any chance of exposing his scars. He preferred to bathe at night.

We ate in the tipi also even though the coals were dead. The old lady had baked a small loaf of bread for us, and we were warmed by a plate of kasha and onions she had prepared. I had pulled out some dried smoked billy goat and, without thinking, tossed some to Nissim who gave it to his servant. I was certainly not going to be outdone by Nissim and told both servants to sit and eat with us. I saw Nissim give his smile, and I wondered who had outdone whom.

"As long as we were traveling," I said, "we will have to be more casual. It's too cold to hold on to formalities."

Nissim tried to engage the servants in conversation, but they were somewhat reticent to be personal. This bothered my brother, and when I dismissed them, I said, "Servants do not usually talk to their masters. Surely you should know that. Besides, they may be put off at having to serve a former fellow slave." I realized that what I had said was somewhat harsh, and I asked him to forgive me for making him feel worse. "Listen, brother, you are a Nogay warrior. You are a nobleman. It is your responsibility to be served. Your saint Paul, if I have been told rightly, did not tell Philemon to release Onesimus but to treat him as a brother. Am I correct? Isn't that what you always told me?"

After a long pause, he reached over and held my knee. "You are right, brother. The days of universal freedom will be a longtime coming. It's my duty to be who I am, as I am." He paused. "Now to change the subject: we have to make a decision as to our route. What's the word, Lord Tambor?"

"I think Kuru and Grigory are right. It makes more sense. Hazir will just have to go along with it." Nissim nodded in agreement.

When we stepped out of the tent in the morning, the servants had already had the horses fed and ready. The sun was bright this morning and had brought some warmth with it. The servants were quick and silent. They rushed into the tipi, picked up what clothing we had discarded, and quickly folded up the tent. Nissim helped. I had no patience with tents. I was pleased, and if I allowed myself, I was impressed.

"Tell them, Tambor. Let them know how much you appreciate their efforts. They are human beings. You'll get a lot more from them if you give them some recognition. Try it."

I wondered how he could make me feel so guilty, but I tried it out. "Thanks, lads. I appreciate the extra effort."

The boys were fixing the tent along the side of one of the camels. They turned to me and said, "Tengri bless you, Master."

When they turned back to work, Nissim looked me straight in the eye and said with that smile of his, "See?"

I thought, since it was warmer in our tipi because of the coals, the servants should bunk with us. Those small tents which they used must have been very cold.

All Tatars, slave or free, are able to ride horses, and our servants were no exception. I had provided them with mounts, and they were told to attend us rather than fall back to the end with the other servants who rode on the carts. Everything being ready, we rode toward Grigory's house where I turned to face our company from the porch. I wondered where Grigory was. As the troop was gathering, I got a bit concerned and had my servant knock on the door. The old lady opened it and started rapidly talking, speech which not even Nissim could understand.

Then I could see why. From the back of the house where the shed was came a most marvelous spectacle. There, mounted on a splendid gray steed, sat a Russian military man wearing a full-length great coat, a bit shabby but draped over his steed's hind quarters. His head was topped with a lamb's fleece soldier's hat; he was saluting proudly.

"Greetings, Lord Tambor, Officer Grigory Yurevich Ureic is at your service!" He paused to see the effect on his audience and said, "Don't think you are going to get away without me." Nissim was the first to break the silence as he began to laugh. Hazir picked it up and began to clap rhythmically as we do when going into battle without drums. The whole troop joined him. What could I say? I had to take him seriously. Just looking at him, with his mustachios curled, proudly wearing his green uniform, it seemed to me he had shed ten years off his life. His wife looked at him and began another harangue, this time at him. He moved toward Nissim and spoke quietly.

Nissim interpreted, "Don't worry about the old lady, young fellers. I have two sons in the village who help out three or four times a week. They'll come and get her. You'll meet them in the village."

I looked around, wondering, *What village?*

He addressed me, although I didn't understand a word. "Lord Tambor, I've been dying. I felt that I would have died before the winter's out. Died of boredom, that is." He chuckled. "You boys have brought life back to me. Nothing would please me more than another adventure. An old soldier must die with his boots on, or he has little honor. And, young men, if God wishes to take my soul before I get home, bury me in an old churchyard and tell my sons I died in the call of duty." When Nissim finished interpreting, I was so moved I reached over and took the old officer's hand and welcomed him.

"Officer Grigory Yurevich Ureic, I am proud to welcome you to our company. As you once commanded men, you are now here under my command. We shall proceed through the lake country, and you shall be under the direct authority of Captain Hazir, the master of our troop."

"How will we talk to each other?" Hazir asked. "I don't know Russian, and he doesn't speak Tatar or even Turkish." Hazir spoke seriously and quietly.

I responded quietly. "Just keep an eye on him, but restore to him a sense of dignity. I know you can do it, Hazir, just give it a chance. You'll love the old man." And he did.

It all turned out that we were very close to a road that had been covered over by snow. It was not long before we saw a small light on the horizon. This turned out to be the sun shining on a newly coppered church dome, which dominated the bleak terrain. Of course this was the village Grigory talked about. We met his two sons who started at him rapidly and passionately. Obviously they were set to dissuading him from coming with us. The old man was undaunted and pulled himself up stiffly on his horse and gave a glare that would have melted ice. He said one thing: "I am still alive, sons, and I am still a soldier."

The lake country was amazing. Grigory told us how to avoid the marshes, which in any case, were iced over, so we swung back toward one of the small branches of the Volga. I was amazed at the population living there. The villages we entered and sometimes passed by were mostly Russian villages, but we also encountered a few Tatar and even Kalmyk settlements, sometimes with as little as six or seven yurts, hardly a tribe. Whenever Nissim could, he would try to enter some of the local churches to pray and venerate the icons. We also accepted hospitality of the Tatar people who were delighted to have us. Most of them knew of Akilli Khan and had heard of Lord Dalgali. That we were going to Georgia with Persian camels and a retired Russian officer, of course, mystified them. We told them we were going to find somebody in Turkish land, and Tbilisi was a stopover. The Kalmyks were not friendly, but they were not hostile.

One of the Tatar elders had two grandsons who were training as warriors and bowmen. He begged us to take them with us, saying that they needed the experience; most of all, they needed to see the world. I took them along under much pressure. I had to give in. When I thought about it, I realized that a warrior needs to encounter life outside his small world so as to face any challenge. So why should I deprive them of some training? Wasn't that after all what I was doing? Their grandfather was delirious with delight. Their names were Erali and Dilaver and were sixteen and nineteen respectively. They had three older brothers who of course stayed behind. I suspected that our boys were probably a liability for their tribe, which was little more than an extended family, so they now became my liability. The little settlement was gracious, and besides their steeds, they provided a mule to carry a yurt, some extra clothing, and some nonperishable food tied up in a canvas sack. One slave came along.

I knew the two would never return home, and I believe they also knew it. It was important that we keep active, so when we had some opportunity to rest, we played war games. The new men needed more training. They had little real concept of fighting and had never fought in any real way, so we were a little heavy handed with them. Eventually, it became evident that some bonding was needed; they needed to be made squires and be responsible to a single warrior. Erali had such an attachment to Nissim that he hung onto him like a puppy dog. I asked Hazir if he would take Dilaver, but he declined, saying that Kym was enough of a responsibility. So Dilaver fell to me. I found him methodical and very disciplined and very hard to get to know. Once after a very bad spill where he almost broke his neck, I saw him trying to hold back tears. I was gentle with him especially since this was the first evident sign of emotion I had seen, and he was in obvious pain. I took him aside.

"You didn't really want to come along, did you, my friend?" He tried to pull himself together, but the pain weakened his will. As I was rubbing his shoulders, I asked, "Why were you chosen to come with us?"

"I am in love with a girl from another village, and she is in love with me." He paused. "However she was promised to my eldest brother. I guess I was in the way. It is not that my elders do not love me, Sir Tambor. It's just that the community being so small, there would be no end of feuding and strife. My brother is a fine man. He will not be cruel to her. He may even love her." At this, the dam finally broke.

In order to spare him from embarrassment, I lifted him off the icy ground. "Here, let me appear to be supporting you." We walked together to the end of the field with his arm around my neck and shoulder. I envied the ease that Dilaver could burst into tears. What it did for me however was to ignite the flame of passion and longing I had for Katya, and in that, I recognized the real source of my former depression. It had been a long time since I allowed myself to think of her. As long as Father was around, I managed to put away my thoughts of her. It was a kind of loyalty to my father, but now that he was away from me, the feelings flooded back into my heart.

"I understand you, my friend. I suffer somewhat the same fate. What I do is work hard to develop my skills. You never get rid of the pain of love, but you can learn to ignore it. As you are my squire, I will work you hard, but that's because you need it. Your horsemanship is fine. I have no complaints. Your spear work is very good, and your archery could use some improvement. Your swordwork is poor. You would be knocked off your feet in a minute. Too bad my brother Chabuk wasn't able to come along. He is an incredible swordsman from a horse, but so is Nissim on his feet." By this time, Dilaver had pulled himself together. At least we were communicating. I felt that he was becoming somewhat more interested. All he needed was a little human compassion, and that was something I was being educated in that year, my dear spiritual Father.

I noticed Nissim and Erali coming toward us, so I inquired as to why Erali had been sent off too. Dilaver replied that it was purely economical as it was with him too. "It is a small tribe in a small community. They can't afford us. We are not marriageable, really not enough women of breeding around. We are Tengrist by faith, and one of the three family groups is Muslim. We call our community the Three Yurts. Erali and I are in the way. Amongst our people, it is customary to pay for the bride either in a year's work or, if affordable, to present the mother of the bride with the dowry. Fortunately we had only two sisters. But our father and grandfather would not have done this lightly. It is just that you were of the same people, and it was a step up for us."

I teased him, "Well, Dilaver, I expect you to make this worth my while." I'm not sure how he took it, but over the next few weeks, he improved amazingly.

It became a matter of talk among us as to why two slaves shared a heated tent with Nissim and me, while two Tatar warriors slept in an unheated tent. I loathed to throw my two servants back into a cold tent after serving us faithfully these weeks. Hazir came to the rescue. It turned out that he was an excellent tent maker, trained and talented. He managed to join the squires' tent with our tipi so that our two servants and the squires' servant could benefit from the coals at night while giving the free Tatars their proper status. These tents could be easily disassembled while traveling and set up easily at night.

One of the great advantages of taking the direct southern route was the availability of wildlife as a food source. Tetik's hawks found a constant source of ducks, hares, and rabbits. Tetik would release his hawks just after sunrise, and there would be sufficient fowl to be cooked for breakfast. Venison was a good source of meat in the lake country as well as wild boar. Herds of antelope were plentiful, even more abundant than home. They also provided good bow and spear practice. As we drew near to the sea, streams and tributaries teamed with fish. Nissim had been given a dispensation by Father John to eat fish during the fast. If we had taken the western route, fish would not have been so plentiful. Wildfowl teamed the shores of the Caspian and kept the hawks sleek and active. They were quicker than any arrow, and eventually they were used to hunt all day. It was normal to hear their shriek as a regular part of the daily sounds.

I had never seen a body of water whose other side I could not see. It was cold and gray, fed from the north by the Volga, but it was calm except during the frequent rainfalls. Snow was rare in this terrain, and it was getting warmer as we moved south into the Kalmykian eastern shore. We had passed by the lake country and were again into the flat lands of Kalmykia. We were not bothered by the Kalmyks themselves, but once or twice, we were questioned by a few bored Russian dispatches. The official documents that Father John had provided were sufficient to assure us of an uneventful trip.

Grigory advised us to enjoy the mild weather because it would not be quite as temperate as we drew nearer the Caucasus in southern Dagestan and Azerbaijan. Our pace was good. Kuru and Grigory assured us we were making good time. Northern Dagestan was fertile and even green, and for four or five days, we experienced balmy weather. We ended up in a bustling shipping town called Makhachkala in the foothills of the Caucasus. As we had little to sell and limited resources with which to purchase anything, our visit there was not commercial. We did however purchase a few trinkets and gifts for our loved ones at home from a sailing ship docked at the harbor. No one spoke Tatar. Turkish and Russian, and Persian were the only languages we could relate to. But Turkish and Tatar are much alike.

The mountains were clearly visible from the south side of Makhachkala. They were more than I could possibly have imagined. The first sighting of the sea was not nearly as powerful as the first view of mountains. I remember my father and the khan describing the mountains of the Kuban that they themselves could barely remember from childhood. Astrakhan's grassy rolling lands the old chief brought us to must have been an enormous shock to the forest-trained Kubanshyi.

We could not cross the mountains there. They were too thick for our caravan to pass. Instead we traveled south over a rocky and very windy shoreline to the town of Derbent and then made a long trek over some high country overlooking the sea and swooping inward to avoid the treacherous shoreline and then back to the sea to the city of Baku on a peninsula in Azerbaijan. In that beautiful city with its market places and palaces, we rested a few days before turning finally westward into the interior, into mountainous country. Grigory, Kuru and the Persians, and Nissim discussed what the best route was for us to take, with the natives and traders in the marketplace; I was there with them but unable to participate due to the fact there was no language I could speak. It was frustrating sitting silently by while the others made plans for us. Nissim was always translating for me, but I realized that he needed to be more involved than a mere translator. So I entrusted the whole issue into his hands. I could rely upon his judgment.

I was comforted by the company of Hazir whom I grew to know more intimately and took pleasure in the members of my own tribe. I was grateful for the Persians and Grigory but felt left out. It was a pleasure playing with Kiymetli and observing his education at the capable hand of Tetik and his father. They were a joy to me and, I believe, a consolation to Hazir. We had chosen an area to camp just outside the city. It was not as flat as we would have found at the Birches, but rolling and rocky. Basically it was a challenge. We were informed that from hereon, we would be traveling through mountains and passes to meet up with the Kura River in Azerbaijan, which would take us directly to Tbilisi. So the practice on this terrain was essential. Our archers were learning to shoot upward and downward rather than level. Our horses would have to get used to rocks and rubble rather than the soft and level plains of the steppe.

Hazir and I were relaxing on a couple of these rocks and watching the boys. The squires were doing quite well. I looked over at Hazir and noticed a look of worry—actually, a customary look of worry—come over his face. He saw me observe him and turned away slowly. After a few minutes he turned back and looked at me straight on.

"You have caught me thinking, my lord. It is a habit I do too often."

I responded, "Forgive me for intruding on your thoughts, Hazir." And trying to change the subject, I said, "Your lad, Kiymetli, is doing well. You must be proud of him."

"Yes, yes, he is. He is the only one I have left, and I am a bit fearful for him. I really wanted him to go back home with the caravan, but I hated to part from him. I would have gone back myself except for your father's insistence that I come with you. I was terrified for his life battling the Kalmyks, but he was wise and strong for a lad his age who had just lost his father."

"Did you never marry, Hazir?"

"Yes, my wife died in childbirth. The child did not survive."

I took a chance: "You seem to be surrounded by death, my friend."

He turned and gave me a soft and very sad smile. "You have caught exactly how I feel, my lord."

"Please call me Tambor when we talk privately. How did your parents die?"

"Mother died in the plague before you were born. My brother and his new bride took me in as a youth. However she is now a widow and has returned to her family leaving Kym with me." He paused as if he wanted to say more but was unsure.

"Is there something else?"

He took a deep sigh and looked straight at me. "Tambor, my father was one of the officers who had gone with Stenka Razin's first campaign against Cherny Yar. I watched him die. I believe your grandfather was also one of them."

"I too watched my grandfather die."

"I wasn't sure. You were much younger than I was, Tambor. It must have been painful."

Now I looked away. We never talked about it again, or rather not until many years had passed, but the shared knowledge forged a special bond between us. The only other one I had ever told was Nissim on one of those rare moments when we were alone. This occurred one night after one of my nightmares, at home, after our present campaign.

It was time to go. Nissim and the men had returned with an abundance of information. Kuru seemed to be correct. We should be taking the shore from Baku and then swinging west to Qarasu where we would then be able to take the caravan trail on the north shore of the Kura River. Centuries of travelers had made it easy, but there were still possible hazards to overcome. Highwaymen and robbers were not unusual in these parts, and we, being a small group of travelers, would be thought easy prey. We were advised to trust no one on the road. Setting up tents, such as we were used to, would be difficult as we would lack the wide spaces we needed for a typical campground until we got to the plains. We would have to be alert and easily adapt to the new terrain. Previous travelers, we were told, had cut out some open ground, which could be used for tenting, but there was no guarantee that others had not taken advantage of these valuable areas. Of course we were not really a caravan in the trading sense;

we were warriors ready to fight, expecting to fight, not just as a defense operation. But if another caravan were taking advantage of the space, we would not contest their rights.

We were also warned about the wildlife in the mountains. Packs of wolves inhabited the forests. We had always thought that wolves were dangerous and vicious creatures, and I suppose they could be; however travelers told us that they rarely attacked humans; what they would do is drag off our animals as prey. And at one time, this happened. It was after a particularly heavy snowfall. We camped down by a small river that night; I suppose we were a little nervous to sleep in the trails up in the mountains. The shore, while often rocky and icy, spread out along the shore line, giving us some flat ground to set up some tents and provide a fire to warm us and dry out some of our clothes. Tetik had not let the hawks out that day, fearing the swirling snow, but we had caught some hare, and Dilaver and Erali had actually shot down a mountain goat. During the day, it seemed we were not bothered, although we were told that there were leopards that would attack by day, unlike the wolves and the massive tigers who were night hunters dwelling in the forests. There was always a watch during the night to alert us of any danger. We knew we had been stalked by wolves for several days. We had sighted them on some of the crags, and sometimes they came so close we could see three or four of them together to our rear. At night they would serenade us to sleep with their wild vocalizing. While the songs seemed melancholy and mysterious, I rather welcomed the strange and mournful melody.

After the storm, however, they were hungry. We were hungry. We stripped the mountain goat and hung the meat and the coat to dry over the abundant rocks. The sky was gray, and that night, it was starless. We had set some torches around the camp as well as extra logs on the fire. The wind had died down, and strangely the serenade had ceased. Some of us thought it was a good sign; Grigory said it was not and that we should keep a greater watch.

Nissim and I kept watch that night with the two squires. Hazir and our Sopasi boys took another shift, and the Persians took theirs but this night it was our shift. At first, we heard the horses acting up, and one of the camels, normally sitting to sleep, was standing upright and nervous, gathering the colt to herself. I walked over to them with a ready spear in my right hand and my sword in the other, and tried to see what was disturbing them. There was even some fluttering in the cages although the birds were normally subdued. We made sure the camel colt was well protected. The meat was closer to the fire that was guarded by Nissim who was nodding a bit. As I turned, I saw in the pale shadows perhaps three wolves. I shrieked in surprise as I saw a huge wolf grabbing one of the cages by the jaw. As I shot the spear at the beast, I didn't take into account my rear. Something hit me between the shoulder blades and knocked me face forward on the icy snow. Whatever hit me now grabbed me by the neck. I tried to turn over; I felt the paws kicking me on the ribs and claws scraping my face. I couldn't even shout as panic grabbed me, but I did hear a loud shriek and the animal lay limp. I heard a swoosh not far away and realized that the boys were shooting their arrows, somewhat wildly in the dim light. Nissim turned me over, and I grabbed at him and started punching thinking him to be a wolf. But he took me by my head and pressed me to his breast until I calmed down.

When I regained my breath and composure, I could see Erali bringing a torch beside me. Nissim said, "Are you all right now? Can you move your neck?" I could see the fear in his eyes.

I shook myself and said, "I guess I am all right. It hurts, but I can move my neck." Nissim took some fresh snow and pressed it against the back of my neck. I had worn a woolen undershirt and a leather jacket which had covered my neck so that the fangs of the animal had only just penetrated the skin. One of the boys ripped a strip of linen from his shirt and gave it to Nissim to use as a bandage. Then I saw over at my left side the huge creature with Nissim's ax embedded in its back. I recoiled.

"You don't know how scared I was. I was afraid that I would ax you, my brother. But it was a chance I had to take. I could barely see in the dark. God was merciful!" Nissim slowly stood up. "Can you make it? Give me your hand." I reached out, and as he grasped my hand, Dilaver and Erali supported my shoulders.

"Thank you, my friends," I said. Nissim's eyes were still wide with anxiety. "I'm fine. I'm all right. Don't worry." I tried to say this with a smile. "God is merciful!"

By this time, almost the whole company was there and wide awake. Tetik and Kym were straightening the cages and trying to calm down the birds. In the moment of panic when I had first seen the wolf, I must have taken a wild thrust because the spear had gone through the animal's neck. One of the new boys had brought another down with an arrow. Three wolves had been killed. I was hurt but not damaged. I have borne a scar under my lip ever since where the wolf had clawed me, and there are still faint fang marks on my neck. Of course I cannot see them.

We dragged the corpses near the fire and put on more wood with the resolve that from here on, another fire would be lit at the farther end of our camps. In the morning, the beasts were stripped carefully by Hazir. His talents never ceased to amaze me. There was enough meat on the scrawny animals to make a stew. The wolves had stolen some of the strips of meat from the goat we had killed and spread out to cure on the rocks farther from the fire. Since wolves are basically afraid of fire, the wolves plundered only the poorer meat on the farther rocks. The wolves neither returned that night nor the following. However we noticed, as we drew nearer the plains, that the terrain was becoming gentler.

The wolf pelts were turned inside out near the fire for the morning, but when we moved out later on, they were hung on poles made from local tree branches and supported between two of the smaller camels. One was for Nissim, one for Dilaver, and the other for me, and from then on we were called the wolf slayers. In fact, I used mine after being cured, under the blanket on my horse's back, as did Nissim. Dilaver gave his to Erali, who seemed to be bothered by the cold, so he could sleep on it at night. It was obvious these two brothers loved each other.

Grigory commented, "It is very unusual for a wolf to attack from the rear. When they attack from the front as they usually do, they go for the throat. A man cannot resist the power of those wild beasts. You were lucky, Lord Tambor,"

"Not lucky, my friend." I nodded and smiled. "God is merciful!" And you know, Father, at that moment I almost believed it.

We were moving on. It was a slow ride in the mountains. The camels were a bit clumsy, especially the large desert ones. They were grumpy but obedient. I thought at times they might lose their grip in the narrow ledges and fall down the steep inclines. Fortunately the storm was over, and the wet snow was packed rather than filmed over with a crust of ice as we had experienced through the mountains. However we noticed some gradual changes in the terrain. The pine forests with their distinctive odors and fragrances were being left behind as we started descending. The peaks, which we had become used to, were no longer there. I would have to turn around and look behind to see the mountains we had traveled in. We could still hear the wolves howling in the distance, but we never had another visitation. I still loved their melodies. They were admirable warriors in themselves; I respected them.

The forests were now open with leafy trees although there were no leaves yet on them. The little stream that we followed or rather followed us gurgled more happily and frequently tripped down the hillside in rivulets and waterfalls. Many parts were still frozen over. Here was where the birch trees grew naturally. It was from forests like these that our forefathers brought our birches.

The white bark of these trees shone in the starkness of the winter woods. It was beautiful; I had to confess it.

We were descending hourly and daily and the smell of vegetation and rotting leaves was quickly replacing the heady odor of pine.

As we further descended, the snow melted into mud and mire and the camel-men dismounted to lead their beasts down the slippery slope. We left our little river at the advice of some of the villagers and goatherds we met on the way. The Azerbaijan people were friendly and generous and led us to a road that would bring us down to the Kura river which would eventually lead us to Tbilisi. They were a little puzzled as to why a caravan would be traveling to Georgia at this time of year. When we told them we were on a mission to bring some family members back with us, they were puzzled as to why so many of us had to come along. We left them puzzled. They did however welcome us to return by the same route; hopefully the weather would be more pleasant.

This was land for herding goats, and they had domesticated some of the mountain goats found there. There were pleasant hills and valleys. The woods were not as dense as the pine forests we had just traveled through. Nor was it so cold but rather crisp and damp. The villagers had gathered for us some dried sheep and goat dung, which made excellent fires; its coals kept warm our tents. There was not much talking through these hills. We plodded one by one through the leafless woods along the narrow but unambiguous track, hoping that the villagers had not led us astray.

They had warned us that we might encounter highwaymen and robbers. One time, a group of five attacked us by surprise. One of my cousins was wounded in the arm, but three of the robbers lay dead in the snowy puddles. The wound was not serious, and we had sufficient medicine, which Katya and Uyari had given to Tashi. Tashi thought we would need it more than

Dalgali's caravan would, so she gave it to us. My cousin healed quickly enough, and mercifully, no infection set in.

I missed the songs of the wolves, for we were now far away. There were more men about with their goats and mountain sheep, and the sound of goat bells was a regular sound. Even amid the snow, there were still twigs and berries and brush for the hardy hill creatures. Many of these men would not be home until the springtime when their animals could feast freely on the village vegetation, which was at that time still covered in snow. At night we were invited to share their fire and sing their songs sung in the sweet lilt of the Azerbaijan tongue. Some of the people held onto the old sky religion, but most of the people we met worshipped Allah. These were suspicious about our foods having some restrictions of their own.

The hawks were in heaven. We lacked nothing. Small animals and birds were regular fare. Shamefully the birds had no scruples about thieving poultry from the villagers. As we drove farther from the larger streams and rivers, fish was less available. We had hard cheese to chew on during the day and flesh during the night. Nissim continued his abstinence. We had run out of bread and were limited in terms of grains. Some kasha was left, and we made sure there was enough for him. That would all change once we hit the Kura. There were many villages on the way, and we could buy some supplies.

I awoke one morning to a warm dawn. We would never call it warm by our standards, but the dampness of the night seemed to lift. The mists, which we had become used to, every morning seemed to dissipate in the rising sun. My boys were already awake; they were boiling water. We had become lazy through the woods and not always could we wash in the morning. *But today*, I thought, *I shall stand in the fresh morning air and have my boys wash me down.* I lifted my hands to Koyash and praised the heaven and earth. Nissim joined me and smiled in the morning sun. He faced east and made the sign of the cross three times, touching the ground with his right hand. We smiled at each other in friendship. I was stripped to the waist when my boys came and washed my back and armpits with warm water, which contrasted to the chill of the morning air. Water was brought to Nissim, but the bucket was left on the ground.

I sent the servants away. I reached over to my brother and grabbed at his tunic and started to pull it off.

"What are you doing? Have you gone crazy?" He pushed me away, but I felt playful and jostled back. He saw me holding back laughter and began to play along with me but warily. We hadn't played with each other for a long time. Our boyhood was seeping away. Winter can be so inhibiting.

"I'm going to wash your back!"

He looked startled as I knew he would.

"Kubanshyi nobles do not wash warrior's backs," he retorted.

"I'm going to prove you wrong. Today, I am the servant!" Again I reached for his tunic, and he fought me. I could see Hazir looking our way as he was instructing the servants disassembling the tents.

"It's all right, friend!" I shouted. "Go back to work!"

He smiled and waved.

The distraction gave Nissim the advantage, and he stood ready for the attack. "You forget, brother, I was a wrestling champion at the academy. I'll wallop you, you know. You are not that big." He moved slowly and slyly, ready for my attack.

I noticed he had grown a half head taller than me over the year, but I was thick and solid as our people are, my father being an exception. Back and forth he moved, lithe and lean. I reached quickly, or what I thought was quickly, and he had me on the ground rolling in the snow with dead leaves flying around our heads. He may have been quick, but I was thick, and I easily pushed him off me, and in a moment, we were on our feet again, this time shoulder to shoulder, neck to neck in a bear hug. He tried to knock me off my feet by kicking me on the back of my heels, but I wouldn't budge. I knew that if I could just get him off balance, I would have him. All his fancy footwork is great with an ax and a sword, but in my grip he was just dancing. Finally with all my strength, I grabbed him by the waist and forced him face down in the snow with me straddling him.

Fortunately the bucket was close enough to us and not overturned although the chamois cloth had been knocked onto the snow. I pulled up his shirt and threw snow on his back and countered that with the now lukewarm water. We were both weak with fighting, and both broke into laughter. Then I washed his back. I hadn't really thought about the scars, but as my hands rubbed over those stripes, I realized how deep they were. I was angry. I wondered at what inner strength he must have had to have stayed alive.

As I got off his waist where I had straddled him, we both stood up quietly. Silently I scrubbed the snow and mud off his chest with the chamois. I was almost ashamed to look into his eyes.

He however caught my eye and said, "Had anyone else done that, Tambor, I would have killed him."

"Forgive me, Nissim," I said quietly still a little breathless. "I vowed to avenge those scars."

He put his hands on my shoulders. "It is enough that we are friends."

As we were dressing, we heard hoofbeats rapidly drawing near. I stood alert, ready to draw my sword. Nissim slid his silver ax from its saddle case.

It was Kiymetli riding at a pace. "Come, Lord Tambor, come quickly!"

" What's going on, Kymmy?"

His voice had been gradually deepening, but he still acted like a boy. "Oh, Lord Tambor, you should see what we saw!" He paused and stumbled off the pony Dilaver had given him having once been his own. "Forgive me, sir, I was rude. I wasn't thinking." He kissed my hand, realizing his breach of protocol and blushed looking ashamed. I looked stern. I tried to look mean in order to keep myself from laughing.

"I repeat: what is the meaning of this ruckus? I thought you were warning us of an attack."

His deep brown eyes doubled in size. "Oh no, my lord. Oh, I am so sorry, sir. Oh, but you must come, right now while Koyash is still low in the sky. Tetik said you would want to come right away."

Hazir was about to intervene, but I suppose he remembered *his* protocol and wisely let me deal with it.

"And what is it that I *must* do, young man?"

"Oh, please, sir, please don't be angry with me." He looked to his uncle for support, but Hazir smilingly looked away. "It's only that...well, oh, Lord Tambor, it will make you *so* happy."

"Well, I certainly want to be happy. I'll agree to that." Nissim buried his face in his saddle blanket to stifle his laughter. "Well, warriors of the Kubanshyi Nogay, what say you? Shall we obey the commands of this young upstart, or shall we tie him to the camel colt and have *him* walk for half a day?" It looked as though he just might protest but abruptly chose silence. We all feigned seriousness and severity, but it was old Grigory who, having heard from Nissim the proceedings of our council, broke the silence. Nissim translated, although by this time, Grigory understood a considerable amount of Tatar from us and some Turkish from the Persians both of which he confused.

"It seems to me, most noble Lord Tambor that, as the eldest of our honorable company, I should speak for the youngest, do you agree?" All hemmed and hawed with only apparent seriousness and came to a mutual agreement. "As I see it, if this young man is leading a rebellion, we have no choice but to fly off swiftly and crush it. Am I correct?" Everyone looked at each other and agreed. "Well then, let's be off!"

We all mounted ceremoniously and left the Persians and the slaves to clean up and follow. Kym looked visibly relieved. We didn't have far to go before we met up with Tetik who was watching his bird and Kym's, soaring in the shimmering sunlight, circling a small portion of the vast valley below. As we all drew up we sat on our mounts in silence overcome by the magnificence of the view. Kym stood up in his saddle flushed and smiling in triumph.

The day was incredible. It was still early in the morning, but the falconers were right in urging us to see this before Koyash would take his full position in the high heavens with Tengri his father. He shone right in our faces such that we had to shield our faces to get the full view. Nissim broke the silence.

> Bless the Lord O my soul.
> O Lord my God, you were greatly magnified.
> With acknowledgement and splendour you were clothed,
> wrapping yourself in light as in a garment, stretching out
> the sky like a skin.
> He who covers his upper stories with waters,
> He who makes cloud masses his step-up, he who walks
> about on wings of winds.
>
> Psalm 103: 1-3 (lxx nets)

Somehow, I thought, *this did not sound like Tengri or Koyash. Nissim seems to be talking about a great khan above the heavens, rather than being part of the whole world like our gods.* It unnerved me somewhat, but it also fascinated me. However I was not ready to pursue this God.

Nissim turned his speech from his God to me. "You know, Tambor, the Kurds never brought Timov and me to Astrakhan this way. We came up from Persia and then up the coast of the Caspian. I would have remembered this."

"I will never forget this view, brother," I grunted. "Now we have to think about getting down. It is very rocky on this precipice. I can't see how our steeds and camels can possibly descend from here."

"With your permission, Lord Tambor," Dilaver asked, "let us scout east and look for an opening. Perhaps, Hazir's boys or your cousins can veer west and report to you their findings."

Hazir read my thoughts and sent the lads off in pursuit of an opening. I was pleased at the way we all cooperated and followed orders. It seemed that everyone wanted to please me. In the meantime, Hazir, Nissim, and Grigory perused the situation. Although it was still winter, the Kura plains bristled with fields of soft green grass. Our horses grunted a response, obviously tired of scuffing over the sparse vegetation on the snowy hills. Off to the south, we could see the snowcapped mountains of Armenia though at a very great distance. Looking back to the high hilly country where we had just come from, we knew we were leaving winter behind, or at least until we arrived in Tbilisi.

From our perch, we could see to the southeast where the Kura river emptied into the Caspian well beyond our view. Our eyes turned westward following the river and the streams and rivulets, which attached themselves to its serpentine banks, sometimes hiding behind walls of rocks, sometimes disappearing entirely from view. The Volga was never so subtle. We knew the Kura would take us to Georgia, that ancient land, which was the first stop in our destination. Christmas was still more than a week away, and we still had a distance to travel. But traveling would be better. These plains would give us swift passage unless sudden winter storms were to hit our troop. We had been told that the plains were experiencing a mild winter; Kuru insisted we would move swiftly along the banks and plains, which hugged the winding river, and he said that caravans and travelers had beat out a straight and narrow trail the closer we got to Georgia. We would press on quickly and the camels, more sure of their footing in the plains, would keep up a steady and swift pace.

Villages and little towns dotted the countryside, and from where we were, we could see the town of Qarasu in the plain just below the hills. We needed some supplies badly. Although, as Tatars we could survive on a diet of meat, we could have used some bread and vegetables with our stews. Nissim was running very low on kasha. I'm sure he could have liked some more variety although he never complained about his rule. I found out later that the rule would normally be suspended for travelers, but I knew that Nissim had his reasons. However he never complained as I said.

In retrospect, Holy Father, I suspect he used this fast as an *epitimia* or penance for the years he felt he betrayed his God. That we were there to liberate his mother and sister provided an additional impetus to his fasting. We Nogay, who are not Muslim, never fast. Of course the Muslim Tatars, like my brother Dikkatli, keep Ramadan for a month. Our Persians commented that there was no need to fast if you are beloved of Ahura-Mazda, who provides all good things for his devotees. Even at that time, Holy Father, not knowing why, I respected Nissim's self-discipline and stamina. This was all part of the inner heroism I continue to recognize in him.

As I was pondering this, I began to hear the thick thud of horse hooves pushing through the thick woods and realized that our riders were returning with some information. My brother Tolga and my cousin Koray were the first to return. They informed us that there seemed to be no access down the mountain from the west.

"We found the stream we left back there, and it has become a waterfall pouring down the mountain and making a river down the hill toward the Kura. It is incredible, my lord!" Tolga said. "Look over there. You can see somewhat over the fields." It was not big, but it was impressive; it reminded me of our Sopasi River near our community though without the waterfall, which I could only hear but not see because of the trees.

Koray added, "If you look closely, my lord, it seems that the local inhabitants use it for irrigation. Look at that little community of yurts just west of the village, dotting both sides of the river. I wonder if they are our people." They were definitely yurts just as we make them, circular, with a domed roof with a hole in the middle. In the fields there were flocks of sheep and goats.

You know, Father, even then, the instinct to descend and raid the community was still alive in me. My father Dalgali would have been disappointed had we done so. He always said that we raid only when there was a desperate need or there was a need to uphold our honor. I know that that was not always the case in the old days. The Mongols drove us ahead of their armies, and we were used to clear paths for the troops; they depended on us to do the dirty work. We could be savage.

But these were peaceful people here, it seemed. We would have to ask rites of hospitality and do them no harm. But as I was wondering how we would get down, Erali and Dilaver returned flushed with excitement.

"We have found it, my lord," They were talking one over the other in their excitement. I clapped my hands over my head and demanded silence. "If you are to be warriors of the Nogay, you are to use self-control. Are you women? My mother and maybe yours can contain themselves better than you just did. I am ashamed to say this in front of your fellow warriors. How does this reflect on me? The great khan instructed his warriors to maintain a cold face. You will learn to do this too, for it may one day save your lives." They hung their heads in shame. I waited. It seems that the little community they came from hardly taught the basics. But I reflected upon Chabuk and his tendency to rage. He still struggled with it. I would make an effort to make solid warriors out of these two boys.

I resumed. "I want you to stop immediately this useless look of shame. Put on a cold face. Learn from what you are told. Be men of honor and discipline. Learn to take a rebuke well." I saw them pull themselves together as though they were putting on a new coat. "Now, Dilaver, what do you have to tell us?"

"Knyaz (This was the Russian word for Prince), we have found a sheep path a little east from here. Well, my lord, this sheep path was made by somebody. There are stone walls on either side sometimes as low as your waste and at times as high as your shoulders, and the path is made of stones shaped to fit together. Sometimes the path is made like a series of steps descending."

I addressed Erali. "Is there anything you have to add, Erali?"

"Yes, Knyaz!" I could hear him take some self-control. "We wondered if our steeds and camels could descend upon it, so we went more than half way down. Everything works just perfectly. It is unlikely that the camels will stumble. Perhaps you would like to see it now."

"So you went more than half way down, indeed? I trust that you did that because you were attempting to be thorough?" I was impressed.

"Yes, Knyaz," he answered that a little too quickly, but I let it go.

"Well, lads, show us the way!" Actually I was slightly amused. Nissim looked straight at me with that turned up twist of his lips, and although I felt justified, I also felt just a bit ashamed for teasing the squires so.

But what they had reported was, in fact, amazing. We pushed through a bit of a low-hanging brush, although the path was wide enough for us to move comfortably one by one. This path opened onto a larger path not far from the crest of the mountain. To the left, a larger cleared path came from the north, which made me wonder if the villagers had not misdirected us. To the right, there was a poorly kept stone wall, which gradually appeared next to us. This wall curved south and led down the hill, which seemed to have been paved with bricks like the waterfront at Mikhailov. This was the pathway down the hill. The sides of the descending path were bordered by a wall, and when things got steep, a series of wide steps kept us from descending abruptly.

"You are right, my lads. This is perfect." They were pleased at my approval although they kept their cold face. I sent Hazir down with Tolga and Koray. We had to make sure that the carts that carried the falcons would not slide down the paved path.

I instructed the servants to follow close to the carts and Vishtaspa got the brilliant idea of attaching the carts to the camels' necks. He lassoed one cart and attached the loose end to his saddle. He used his dromedary, the larger one-humped beast, and a few of the smaller two-humped ones. Mardunya did the same, and we formed a procession down the hill. The camels were thick and sure-footed, used to varieties of surfaces. Kura rode down first on his own. Nissim and I lingered to watch the procedure. Then we descended.

The town of Qarasu was pleasant but poor. The inhabitants were simple village folk, small merchants. There was a Russian center where we got some information. When we told the official, as we were showing our papers, that we had just come through the hills, he looked at us strangely commenting that it was a good trip through the summer months but dangerous during winter. We told him that we survived a band of bandits and a wolf pack, showing him our pelts.

"I shouldn't wonder," he said wryly. "You really didn't save much traveling time either. You'll never make it to Tbilisi by Christmas. Spend the feast at Saint Davit Gareji Monastery and enjoy Theophany at the capital when it will not be so crowded."

Nissim told him he was a Christian and asked him about Saint Davit Gareji.

"Georgia is a country divided. Persia has had its hands in the country for a long time from the south and the Turks from the west. We Russians have been trying to get our fingers into the stew too in order to keep the Orthodox faith stable there. The Georgians are Christians, and we intend to keep it that way. The

Persians divided the kingdom over a century ago, so as you leave Azerbaijan, you will be entering the Kingdom of Kakhetia.

"The first landmark will be the Cave Monastery of Saint Davit to your right. There will be a large tower perched on the hills. You can't miss it. The fathers are very welcoming, and most speak Azeri, so if you speak Turkish, you will have little trouble understanding them. There will be pilgrims of course, but not like Tbilisi, which is on the border of the Kingdom of Kartli the center of Georgian culture. Go to Tbilisi for the Lord's Baptism. It will be more peaceful at that time, and you won't have to rush to get there and find yourself late a day or two. Whoever told you to come over the mountains at this time of year misinformed you. Go back by the shores of the Caspian. The route over the mountains is beautiful but not in the winter." I could not have disagreed more, though I would not say so. I had been concerned however that because of it, we may have lost some time. Nevertheless we were grateful for his advice and hospitality.

Having refreshed ourselves for a day in which we replenished our stock of food items, we were ready to press on. We purchased a few sheep and enjoyed some mutton, which we had not had for some time. We purchased these at the little community of yurts that we had seen from the hills. It was a very poor village, and we didn't mind paying more than the animals were worth. The travel alongside the river was easier than we expected, and any time we may have lost in the mountains was made up for. It did seem however that we had underestimated the length of the trip and that the Russian official was quite right: we would not make it to Tbilisi for Nativity.

Azeri was the language of most of the people we met, and we could understand it for the most part. We also encountered a group of Kurds called Yezidis who actually turned out to be of a similar faith to our Persians. They both called their god "Mazda."

They were somewhat suspicious of us at first but after talking to the Persians they welcomed us heartily. These were a peaceful and independent people somewhat frowned upon by the larger Islamic and Christian population. Nissim confessed to me that meeting them and enjoying their hospitality somewhat cured him of his fear that all Kurds were thieves. In fact, we began to suspect that the ones who brought him and Timov to Astrakhan were not actually Kurds at all but renegade Turks. He said they had not spoken Kurdish but some Turkish dialect. Kurdish people are tall and pleasant to look upon. The men are handsome warriors, and their maidens are stunningly beautiful women. They did not cover themselves like the Muslim women do.

We also met two communities of Nogay Tatars who had also emigrated from the northwestern Caucasus about the same time that Khan Akilli's father went to Astrakhan. Both groups were friendly and still, like us, considered it a tradition to train warriors. They offered us some of their women, of course for a good bride price. We said that we would consider it on our way back. They probably had an excess of women, and I might challenge their price on our return trip, not for me, of course, but I did not want to insult them. This was not the way that the Nogay traditionally find mates, but we obviously have had to adapt to the fact that our communities were few and far between.

The old way was that the prospective groom would spend a year of service at the yurts of his desired bride. I believe we got this tradition from the Mongols since it is still done that way among the Kalmyks and the Jungar east of the Caspian. I believe that you Chuvash arrange marriages this way too. It is not done much these days though I suspect that that was the reason why Dilaver and Erali were among us. Perhaps if my boys wanted to marry I could consider providing them with wives. I could not do that with the others because they were the responsibility of their fathers and uncles. We didn't stay too long, and we didn't press rites of hospitality. They did want us to come back however, and we were even invited to send warriors for Saban-Tui at the summer solstice.

HOSPITALITY

I met my enemy when all were enemies to me.
A stranger I was and yet they took me in.
Despair engulfed me.
I had no life left, my manhood marred,
I was warrior without a war.
But my foe took me in and fed me.
He at whom I had hurled the lance
Gave me back my dignity when
My own had cast me out.
Can a man be more grateful?
A fool I would be to turn back!

—from Kokochu's acceptance speech

The Russian official was wrong. We arrived at Gardabani on the other side of the border five days before Christmas. The inhabitants told us that if we had pressed on, we might have made it to Tbilisi by Christmas, but everyone seemed to think, as the Russian had advised us to veer north somewhat away from the Kura, and that we should stay at Saint Davit Gareja Monastery, where we could not be bothered by an excess of pilgrims as in Tbilisi, for the Feast of the Nativity. If we wanted to make our confessions, the priests at the monastery spoke Azeri, whereas with the busyness at the capital, we would risk being unable to find one who could understand our tongues. Grigory asked if there were any priests up in the mountains who spoke Russian, so the pastor at the local church wrote a letter to the Abbot to provide a Russian-speaking Father. So it was settled. The priest took us up to the monastery, and we were given permission to camp outside the walls. This pleased us greatly. There was no snow there, and the grass thrilled our horses and camels.

The cave monastery was extraordinary. The cells had been hewn out of the rocky mountainside by monks about a thousand years ago. There were chapels and churches in the upper ridges and a huge tower on the ridge. The walls inside were covered with brightly colored icons, telling the life of Jesus and his mother and other saints.

Nissim and Grigory both confessed. We did not eat with the monks but were served at a separate table in a smaller guest room, also covered with paintings on the walls called frescos. One of the monks read from a book during the meal, which we could hear in the Azeri tongue. It was the life of some saint who had lost his life defending his faith. He was very brave and loyal, but I felt his death was somewhat unnecessary. We kept the fast at their table, simple but hearty.

We pitched our camp on a hill just beneath the mountain in full view of the tower. I still remember walking in the morning to see the mists moving around the tower swirling like a silent serpent. It would be quiet and still around the hill, but the mists were ever moving around the tower and the peaks wherein the monks dwelt. As the day warmed, the mists disappeared, and the sun shone brightly on the eastward facing hills. What a glorious location this was, and when we ascended to the top, which was quite a climb, and looked back over the Kura valley, we were astounded at the view, which was perhaps even more glorious than our first view of it above the village of Qarasu.

Just before Christmas Day, Nissim returned from the monastery after Vespers, the evening prayer service, with Erali and Dilaver, who had gone up out of curiosity, and Kymmy, who as usual, wanted to know everything. I had also seen Koray and Tolga once or twice at the back of the temple, and this time they joined us. We had a fire and a pot of tea and were relaxing. Grigory had gone to bed having trekked up the mountain earlier to make his confession. He told us he couldn't make another trip that day. I was curious though.

"Well, boys," I asked, "what do you say about the monastery and its services?"

"Knyaz Tambor," Dilaver began thoughtfully (the boys had been practicing restraint), "It is beautiful, and the chanting is awesome, like nothing we have ever heard even though we couldn't understand the Georgian tongue. I felt as though we had been brought somewhere else to another world."

Tolga said, "Sir Nissim's God is not like our gods. Our gods belong to the cycle of nature and the seasons, but this God seems to be outside of everything, like a mighty khan who oversees the whole world, as though Tengri and Koyash and Yer-Sub obey *his* will."

Nissim made no comment.

The silence was broken by Kiymetli, who asked, "May I say something, Lord Tambor?" (He too was learning restraint).

"Of course, my lad," I said affectionately.

"I was a bit afraid, my lord, not scared like facing an enemy, but like being watched by this khan-God who can look into my heart and know what I was thinking and feeling. The men in black all know him and talk to him, they told me, and more than that, they seem to love him. That's what was scary because I didn't know him. Do you know your God, Sir Nissim?"

"Yes, Kymmy, I know him and try to love him, and at all times, I need him."

"But if he knows you and sees you, why do you have to tell him your sins. Doesn't he know them already?"

"Oh, sure he does, but you and I don't always recognize sins for what they are, so confessing them helps us to understand ourselves and change our ways especially if a wise man witnesses our confession."

"That makes a little sense, I guess. Do you think I might get to know him some day?"

I was amazed at his questions.

"He knows you already, Kym," Nissim answered. "And more than that, he loves you and is waiting for you to ask." I could see the boy blush in the light of the fire. Nissim smiled and ruffled his hair. "In any case, my friend, you have nothing to fear from him. When you are ready for the Lord, he will be ready for you."

This was too much; I sometimes felt irritated at pious conversation. I had to change the subject. "What are these monks all about, Nissim?" I asked. I was curious. They were somewhat like Father John, but at the same time, they were very different.

"Do you mean what are monks?" He looked at me and pondered. Everyone sort of drew attention to him as he pondered.

Kym broke the silence by saying, "Yes, tell us all about them, Sir Nissim." Hazir grabbed him firmly by the knee, recognizing that he was out of order. I let it pass.

"Well, there have been monks around for a long time, for well over a thousand years, even more. There was a famous one in Egypt who was called Saint Anthony. He was one of the first monks although there may have been others before him. He lived around the time of Saint Constantine, the first Christian tsar of the Romans. His family was not poor, but his parents died when he was young, I guess at your age, Lord Tambor. They left him much property and a comfortable life for him and his younger sister. One day, while standing in church, Anthony heard the priest read from the Bible the words of Jesus, the Son of the Great Khan, who said, "Take no thought for tomorrow, for tomorrow will take care of itself." At that moment, he realized that he must sell all that he had, and so he gave all his riches to the poor. He put aside a small sum for his sister and left her with a community of holy women called nuns, or mothers, who lived like monks do now. He then went into the desert, which is like the steppes but with almost no grass or water. There he lived for twenty years battling the demons, evil spirits from the house of Erlick. He fought them all alone but was victorious only with the help of God, who kept him day by day until he attained peace. He was a mighty warrior.

"These men in black are also mighty warriors, though they do not fight physical enemies and they do not use weapons of steel and bone. But they fight with faith and hope and, more than that, with love. They do not run to a shaman and get a spell or talisman when they fear. These monks fight the spirits of Erlick by the name of Jesus, whose name they say continuously, and by the power of the cross whereon Christ died, and are helped by the mightiest warrior of all, Saint Michael and the armies of heaven. Toward the end of Saint Anthony's life, he was known to say, 'I no longer fear God, but I love him.' So, Kymmy, you may fear my God now"—Nissim gave me the briefest of glances—"but if you truly seek him, you will come to love him too."

"Maybe so," Kym said, with his great smile. "But I'd rather fight Kalmyks than Erlick's demons." They all laughed, even Nissim.

I was not so amused. I felt as though I had walked into a trap.

"Well, men, the evening seems to be getting cold. Why don't we retire now? I told Nissim and Father Ambrose that I would attend the Royal Hours tomorrow. Is that what you call them?"

Nissim nodded.

"Father Ambrose said that they would be reading some of the Christmas readings from the Bible in Azeri or maybe Turkish tomorrow in our honor and for the benefit of the Azeri pilgrims. The service starts before sunrise. Perhaps, Hazir, you could come with us this time and let my boys keep guard at the camp. I'm sure Kymmy wants to hear these words."

Mardunya and his brothers asked permission to come with us and, of course, I gave them permission.

As we moved toward our tents, Nissim tugged me by the elbow. "I hope I didn't offend you by anything I said tonight."

"Nothing you said could possibly have offended me!" I said this too abruptly and felt I had to laugh. With Nissim, it was impossible to keep a cool face. "Sorry, brother. But I confess I was somewhat disturbed by the conversation, though I really can't tell why. Sometimes I feel this God of yours gets just too close to me. However, that shouldn't bother me. I sort of like him. Hey now, let's just drop it. I should be grateful to have such a God on my side, and I am." I grabbed him by the arm, and we both laughed. "You'll be eating meat in a few days. You need to get some flesh on those bones."

I shall say but one thing, Holy Father, about the service that morning. All through the service, there was mention about Jesus being born in a cave. I have never thereafter been to a service of the Nativity Royal Hours, which has been so vivid as that one. There we were, a bunch of pagans standing in a cold and drafty cave in the Caucasian mountains hearing about the birth of the Son of a God into this world. I thought what an honor. However when the priests brought out a beautiful gilded icon showing a simple maiden lying in a cave adoring this little baby cradled in a feeding trough, a chill, a shiver actually, went through my body, not a cold chill, Father, although it was certainly cold, but a chill that had lain dormant in my being all my life that at that moment was finally released. I was then flooded with an unexplainable warmth. When I whispered to Nissim if I could kiss the icon like everyone else, he said, "Come." We both kissed the icon together. I noticed that Kymmy followed us without a trace of shyness. Tolga and Koray attended this service too quite on their own volition.

We left the temple about half an hour afterward. There was another service, and Nissim and Grigory wanted to stay. They would be staying all night and would be back about noon the following day. Kym begged his uncle to let him stay with Nissim and was granted permission. "After all," Kymmy reasoned, "Sir Nissim needs someone to attend to his needs, right?"

Nissim squeezed his shoulder and said, "Whoever desires to become great among you, let him be your servant. And whoever desires to be first among you let him be your slave—just as the Son of Man did not come to be served, but to serve, and to give his life as a ransom for many (Matt. 20:26–28, nkjv)."

I had, as usual, no idea what that meant, but it sounded good, perhaps even appropriate.

Nissim walked us to the entrance of the chapel. Still enrobed with the warmth I had experienced, I looked back at the beauty of the place and got a very strong impression. I thought of Father John telling us that when he had to speak, he had to speak. I drew Nissim close to me and whispered in his ear. "I feel some urgency, my brother. We must leave immediately. As soon as you come down from the mountain tomorrow, we leave. I'll have Erali and your servant get your things ready. Don't be concerned. Your God is with you. Have a glorious Christmas. I'll take care of everything."

There was a swarm of villagers coming up from Gardabani to visit the monastery the following day. Our plans for a hasty departure had been interrupted by the villagers and peasants bringing gifts of food and home-brewed brandy and vodka and bags of sheep dung so needed for our fires. When we inquired about their unexpected generosity, they told us that it was a custom to share food with the needy and with travelers at Christmastime because Persian kings, foreigners, came from the east with gifts for the Christ child, which sustained the little family on their flight into Egypt where *they* were strangers.

We were overwhelmed. We feasted now and had enough to keep us until we arrived in Tbilisi. They were a warm and wholesome people, not unlike our folk. After a while, I had little trouble understanding them. They did interrupt our packing, but there was no way we could stop the overflow of their generosity.

They of course were curious about the reason for our long journey, so I told them that Sir Nissim was a Christian, and we were going to the land of the Turks to rescue his mother and sister from slavery. Their response ranged from encouragement to downright fear for our safety. The women were most concerned and would make the sign of the cross over me, and the others would insist vehemently that they would pray for us. The men, on the other hand, examined our weapons and equipment and agreed that we were well equipped. One man, an old Azeri warrior, said that the Turks were not well disposed toward Christians, but that they would not be expecting foreigners of noble blood; that would be to our advantage.

He added, "When you have succeeded on your mission, flee quickly, for the retribution will be fierce. You will be safe when you get back to Georgia. The Lord will be with you and bless you for you will be doing a deed worthy of him."

All the while we were flooded by guests and well-wishers, there was constant activity around the Persians who kept talking to our visitors. Normally our Persians stuck to themselves and were quiet and respectful. It is not that I noticed any trouble; it was just that they seemed so out of character I needed to know what was going on. As I approached them, Mardunya, the talkative one, broke away from the group and came toward me, his face flushed with excitement.

"Lord Tambor, you know what we heard from the holy readings yesterday is true. Before the Arabs came to our land, we were governed by the Magi, a powerful and very wise group of people, who were councilors to the king. Our legends tell us that some Magi, maybe three, maybe more, were led by an unknown star westward. This star they had studied in the heavens. They were looking for a Priest King who would rule the world with peace and justice. They claimed to have found him in the land of Judea. These people tell us that Nissim's God, Jesus, was that very king and that they brought gifts to him."

I hardly knew what to say. I had heard the story myself and didn't know what to make of it. The only great world rulers I knew was Chinggis Khan and his grandson Qublai, and he certainly did not fit this description, nor was I aware of any place where there was any true peace and justice.

As I pondered this, I noticed Nissim, who was supporting Grigory, and Kiymetli descending the steps of the monastery a little ways off. When I saw them, I felt a little guilty that the day's activities had put us behind schedule. They were accompanied by three monks, two young ones and someone around our khan's age. The elder monk, Father Iskender, took me by the hand and kissed me in the cheeks three times saying "Christ is born!" to which the others responded, "Glorify him!"

"My dear Lord Tambor (He also called me Knyaz), it has been a special joy to have you here for this wonderful feast. We would never in all our days have expected to grant hospitality to an entourage of Tatars from the north. And you have brought us Nissim and Grigory and of course Kiymetli, the valued one." Kymmy blushed red like a Mongol. "I bring a message from the abbot. He is aware of your mission and sends you his blessing. We pray that you will accomplish what you have to do with very little bloodshed." After a pause, he smiled, I would say with some amusement, and continued, "We have also some gifts for you. The younger monks opened their bags and drew out two ornate boxes. He opened one and told us that it contained grains of jasmine-scented incense a visitor from Egypt had left. "Your father's concubine will enjoy this for her prayers." The second was a box of very pungent myrrh. "Hopefully you will not have to use this on your mission. However, if necessary, a little salve made from this will stave off some serious infections. It is mixed with camphor, aloes, wintergreen, and other healing herbs." I knew who would want this.

Father Iskender then drew from his robes a little bag of gold coins. "Use these well. They are given to you for a specific purpose, which shall be revealed to you in time. You have great wisdom, and you care for your people. Your Khan is well blessed to have you as a bondsman, and you are a pride to your father. But your life will be stormy, dear one. Justice is not an easy path to follow. In time you will find peace to your soul. Seek the wisdom of the Christ child. His peace will be your peace."

I must confess to you, Holy Father, that as grateful as I was, the incident actually irritated me. What was it these Christians had on me? Who needs Uyari or Lazim throwing their bones and stones? There on the mountain is a whole race of shamans only too willing to tell me my doom. It was the same with Father John and his warrior saints. No doubt Nissim told the monk about Natasha, that's why they gave incense, and Katya, that's why the myrrh, but why the gold? Gold, frankincense, and myrrh—so what's that got to do with me? And why gold? I had enough money, both some gold and a good bit of silver. But the way Father Iskender put it to me, it would have been disrespectful of me to refuse. There was this God, whom I didn't worship, always getting into my life. Tengri didn't bother me, why should *this one* interfere?

Nissim caught up with me after making his departure from the monks. He came at somewhat of a clip until I realized that I was walking unusually fast. I was a bit put off as he asked, "What's the rush? The servants have the horses ready. Look, Hazir and the boys are all prepared and the tents are pulled and the Persians are mounted." I almost snapped at him as though he were once again my slave, but I saw his happy face and heard the excitement in his voice, and I regretted my pique. Who was I to resent the favor of any God? If Jesus Khan wanted to care for me, I should be grateful for it, but at that moment, I felt he was becoming too close for comfort.

I deflected. "Yes, brother, but this morning I got the strongest sense of urgency, and I want to go right away. But you're right," I said realizing that the slaves had our garments and armor already to put on us. All we had to do was stand there and let them strap us up. I was glad to be on Onyx again, who was now well rested and fed, and I could see Cereyan almost leaping with anticipation. A feeling of satisfaction swept over me, and I dared to look at Nissim. What I saw was joy in his eyes. I was ready for a new adventure. The line was forming although the pilgrims were still about, and I felt I should say something before setting off.

"My friends and companions and my devoted and loyal servants, this, I believe, has been an eventful experience for all of us. Few of us have ever had the opportunity to celebrate Christmas, the feast of the birth of the Christian khan Jesus Christ. It was an event, which we were invited to partake of, and although we may not understand its real importance, we were nevertheless made a part of it. Normally we associate this feast with the Russians, whom we traditionally hold in contempt, but here we were made welcome by Georgian and Azeri Christians, at least one Russian, our comrade Officer Grigory, and one Macedonian Greek." I gave them permission to applaud and quieted them down quickly so as not to disturb the tranquility of the monastery, which loomed over us, its mists having been dispelled by the warm winter sun. "We are rested, our horses grazed, and our camels well fed. We are grateful for the break, but it is time to accomplish the task we set out to do. Let us hope that it will be done quickly."

I walked Onyx slowly next to the procession. Nissim and Hazir came on each side of me. I nodded to them lifting my right hand to my breast, and they did likewise. On one of the ledges which led up to the monastery, I could see Father Iskender and his monks looking back at the group waiting as it seemed to bless us on our departure.

"I feel it is time to tell all of you the mission we are on." I looked around to see if any of the pilgrims and village folk were listening, but apart from the monks' owl-like presence, we were alone. "This is a very secret mission. You may only suspect our destination, and we shall keep it that way until the time comes.

What I shall now tell you, you are to discuss with no one outside our company. If any one of you servants betrays us, I will have you killed, no matter how dear you are to our family. Any warrior who betrays us will leave our company. You may wend your way back to the Birches or become a vagabond or die in the wilderness." I let this sink in before continuing; I looked them all in the eye. "This mission goes with the blessing of my father, Lord Dalgali, who speaks on behalf of our noble Akilli Khan." I put up my hand to prevent a cheer. "We are to be entering Turkish territory, my friends, for the purpose of freeing Sir Nissim's mother and sister from slavery. You know our tradition: Our slaves are from generations of family slaves born and raised with our families. We also take slaves as spoils of war as was my brother Sir Nissim and Timov. But they and the rest of his family had already been made slaves in the empire because they refused to abandon their faith for another. Sir Nissim, I know for a fact, would refuse to tell you how much he had to suffer before he was sold to the treacherous Kurds who were probably not Kurds at all."

"We rarely ever buy slaves. The only reason we have our Persian camel masters is because they came with the camels and refused to be released." At this, Mardunya made a gesture of obedience to me and the others followed.

"I do not wish to have the reputation of being a slave freer. My purpose in this venture is to correct a great injustice, an injustice that was inflicted on my new brother Sir Nissim, who is now the adopted son of Lord Dalgali. If you remember, Sir Nissim saved my father's life during the recent battle with the Kalmyks.

"For myself, I am prepared to purchase the freedom of these women, but I do not think it will be that easy, as they are, we believe, in the household of the same person who abused Sir Nissim. We fear for his sister's chastity, something which is highly prized amongst the Christians." I turned back to the warriors, but made sure the Persians heard me. "You warriors were handpicked by Lord Dalgali for your trust, your skill, and your bravery, and you servants, for your longtime loyalty. I trust you are all with me." This time I let them raise their shields and their voices, but just for a moment. "Let us go, warriors. We will have one stop in Tbilisi before the final trek. We were called to be warriors, my brothers. Let's fulfill our destinies!"

As I headed the troop, Nissim pulled over to me. "You are beginning to sound like your father. I'm surprised you didn't bless us in the name of the One True God."

"I don't have to," I said, gesturing toward the hill. "They are doing it for me." One of the monks had pulled a pail of Holy Water from beneath his robe (it is amazing how much could be hidden under those robes), and Father Iskender was splashing it in our direction with a long brush. Nissim gave his special curled up smile at me. We were friends.

The Azeri warriors at Gardabani had given us a route we could follow into the Kingdom of Kartli, where Tbilisi was the capital. Because the north shore of the River Kura became rocky, and the large cliffs would force us to travel up around, it would be far favorable to travel on the south side of the river. There would not be a bridge for another two days' travel over rocky ground. But we could gain some time by crossing the river at a shallow place, a day's journeying hence. The water might come up to our knees, if we were walking, but it was the only shallow place, they said, to make the crossing. Markings on the trees would indicate where the passing was. Once on the other side of the cut over, traveling was somewhat smoother. It was however uphill all the way. The Kura River (*Mtkvari* in Georgian) ceased being the center of a lush valley but the seam of a large ravine. Rocky cliffs lined the north side although for long stretches, it occasionally narrowed out. Our side was obviously a traveling road, fairly broad for the most part and at times rather narrowed by thick pine woods. I loved the smell of these woods. The shore was relatively shallow so we could swim and bathe ourselves for some recreation. Practice was out of the question since there were no wide open spaces. There were some villages on the way, and the more we traveled, the harder it was to communicate. The Georgian language is quite different from the languages we had become accustomed to. They were not hostile people, just distant. There were small churches in every village. If we chose to stop, Nissim would enter the little temples to venerate the icons, usually accompanied by Grigory, if he were up to it, and Kiymetli, as an unofficial squire perhaps. Grigory seemed somewhat subdued these days; I fear the traveling was wearying him. I said nothing as I didn't want to wound his warrior's pride by noticing it. We had run out of kumis, all but a small flask, but we could buy vodka and another drink made from barley from the villagers. We enjoyed our talks around the fire.

Something had been happening for the past few days that began to cause me concern. We had, from time to time, passed travelers on their way east, and at first I presumed that there were likely travelers on the same route going west too, so I took little thought of it. However I had the strangest feeling we were being watched or even being followed. I said nothing, but I kept my eyes and ears open. Once in a while, I would watch Nissim get up from our fire and walk passed the servants sitting around their fire at the rear of the camp. I thought he merely wanted to relieve himself, but the fact that he went armed made me think he might be feeling the same way as I did. Neither of us said anything.

It was perhaps three or maybe four days after passing the cut over that we were startled. It was dusk; the sun had left an eerie light over the camp as we were settling to eat. Hazir and some of the servants were preparing a stew; we were quite excited about it as my brother Tolga had killed a wild boar he found trapped in a thicket, and we were going to make a feast out of it. Our visitor did not come from the rear but from near our part of the camp. By the time we noticed him and had drawn our weapons, he had put his own weapons on the ground and stood with his hands outstretched and his palms up. There was silence for a few minutes. He stood still and silent. We all started to put our weapons away except for Nissim, who had drawn his bow, and Grigory, whose rifle was cocked.

"Well, friend, speak," I ordered.

"I am unaccompanied—actually quite alone, Lord Tambor, and I beg your hospitality." His begging hospitality was a traditional greeting amongst the Tatars and the Mongols. We were bound to it. It also marked him as a man of lineage since a common person or slave would not be permitted to use it. He spoke in Tatar, not Turkish and not Azeri.

"You have it, sir. Nissim, Grigory, put down your weapons. Dilaver, gather those of our guest and bring them to me."

His features were dim in the waning light, but I could see he was a warrior. "You have been following us for at least three days. That is why you know my name, I presume. Tell us who you are so there is no disadvantage."

"My name is Kokochu, and I have actually been following your troop since Gardabani where the natives mistook me for one of your company. I took advantage of their hospitality, the hospitality due to you, to sustain myself."

"Come over to the fire, friend, where we can talk. Nissim, accompany me. Hazir, leave your work to the others and attend me, please. You others gather around the fire. Kokochu will eat with us. Dilaver and Kiymetli, you will serve us."

When they all started buzzing among themselves, one look from me brought silence. I motioned to our guest to sit and whispered to Dilaver to bring the flask of kumis. Kymmy was to bring cups of vodka and the native drink for our boys. Nissim motioned to Erali to help them. I open the flask and poured what was left of the clear liquid into the cups. Kokochu took two sips and looked up at me.

"This is good. This is very good."

"My mother brews it at our encampment at Sopasi."

"Sopasi? Akilli Khan?"

"He's my uncle."

"And Dalgali, the trader?"

"Dalgali is my father."

He jolted just a bit and tried to cover it up.

"So you know my family. What dealings do you have with them?" I asked.

"It would require some explanation," he said looking briefly around him at the others.

I instructed Koray, my cousin, to have the servants prepare another fire about a stone's throw away where the young warriors could socialize while Nissim and Hazir and I could question Kokochu further. Of course he would have a story; that was to be expected. In the meantime, we would all eat and refresh ourselves. After the meal, the boys retired to the new fire, and we talked.

"Again, it seems, Kokochu, you have the advantage over us for you know who we are and still we do not know who you are and why you are here. These two are my officers, my right and my left hand, Sir Nissim and Sir Hazir. You may speak freely and confidently. We shall treat you fairly and justly."

"Until this very evening, I did not have that information you just gave me. But before I tell you who I am, I shall tell you why I am here. In that way, who I am will have less importance. Until the eleventh month, I was the chief bondsman to a revered khan. My responsibility was to teach the art of war. I trained the sons of the khan and was in charge of the training field. Today I no longer exist. I have been banished from my tribe and am a vagabond with no place to go and no identity because I have no tribe. None of my people will have me, and all other tribes of our race are vowed to shun me because of my disgrace."

We waited.

"My crime was an indiscretion. I had an affair with the khan's third wife. She was very young and beautiful and very ignored.

You know how some minor brides of important men are little more than servants to the older wives. She and I loved each other. We both thought the old man knew about it and blinked his eye. Perhaps that may have been so, but one of the older women found out about it and spread nasty and jealous rumors. In order to defend his honor, we had to be punished. In front of my very eyes and everyone else's, the khan sliced off her head. He gave me somewhat of a chance, I suppose, because I was a warrior. He placed my horse at the end of a gauntlet where I was to be beaten with rods and whips. Even my closest friends were forced to beat me. But I made it through without stumbling, which would have ended my life, and managed, exhausted and in great pain, to mount my horse while the tribesmen attempted to chase me. My horse is the best and surest of foot, and we managed to escape the arrows.

"I was lost at first, begging and stealing all the way down here, thinking that if I offer my services to a caravan, I would end up in Turkish lands and offer my services in a land that didn't care about my disgrace. When I heard that you were traveling into the empire, I wondered if I could be of service to you until I arrive there. Begging is humiliating, and stealing is a disgrace."

"We are not a caravan. We are on a special task."

He responded, "If you need a fighter, I still have my weapons and have fought often."

"All right, Kokochu. You have told us why you are here. Now answer us: who are you?"

"My Lord Tambor, I am nobody. My life is in your hands. I used to be the chief bondsman to Khan Ubashi, and I fought against you at the Volga."

The three of us reached for our weapons, and his hands reached out to us empty. The others were immediately on alert.

He said very quietly and slowly: "Nobles, my life is in *your* hands. It would have been better had I died as a warrior at your hands. Yes, I would rather have died as a hero and not as a wretched vagabond. But please remember one thing: the Kalmyks have made me their enemy. Therefore whoever is enemy to the Kalmyks is a friend of mine. At least I shall have the honor of dying at the hands of a friend."

When I returned my silver dagger to its sheath, I said to him, "This dagger slew two Kalmyk boys by the hand of a woman—"

"Had those boys lived, they would have tried to kill me."

"We shall decide upon this tomorrow. You may travel with us as our guest. You will be expected to fight if you are needed. Tonight you shall sleep in my tent. Hazir, if you don't mind, could you spare some room in your tent for my servants? Have Dilaver stash the weapons with your belongings. I don't want to be murdered by a Kalmyk during the night."

As we stood up, I noticed that he was taller than me and well built. He was dark skinned. Thick black hair streaming down his neck and shoulders. His appearance suffered some neglect. His hair seemed to lack care. His eyes were black and partly hidden behind their slightly slanted lids. But even in his depressed state, he had managed to keep a noble appearance. He was about forty years of age.

In the morning, I sought Nissim's advice, and afterward, we returned Kokochu's weapons. "I am giving these back to you, my friend, as an act of trust. You could indeed kill me, but you would be run down by the others; that is, unless there is a troop of Kalmyks around the bend. Perhaps you have been setting us up for an ambush." I looked straight at him to see his reaction.

He shrugged his shoulders and replied, "Lord Tambor, I confess I would feel the same way myself. But knowing the hatred between our two tribes, I am certainly the one with the disadvantage."

I was probing. "It is curious that there should be such hostility between the Kalmyks and us, the Nogay. After all, Nogay Khan was Mongol, a grandson of the great khan Chinggis and cousin of Qublai Khan. Our own Khan Akilli is a direct descendant of Nogay, and you can see it in his features and even in my father's. That there was a breach between the Kalmyk and the Nogay, there is no doubt, and we each feel justified in defending ourselves, but we are not unalike and generally keep the same traditions. We fought wars alongside the Mongols and you alongside us. Why should we keep alive a gripe that means nothing to either of us now?"

He replied, "You know that Chinggis Khan put you Tatars in the front lines in order to kill you off. This was one of the few errors in judgment he made. Your people don't die off easily, and you breed like marmots. But you are right. The whole thing seems so petty.

"You don't know, Sir Tambor, how humiliated Khan Ubashi was by the battle at the Volga. Your father was absolutely right about the matter. While our khan did not authorize the battle, he was well aware it was happening. He did not expect it to fail so miserably and was grief-stricken at the loss of his sons. But it was Lord Dalgali's words that humiliated him most of all. I was there."

"So was I."

"Here's a twist, my lord. With his sons quite dead, the old man didn't have an heir. He was very clear about it: I was to be the next chief." He paused to let this piece of information sink in. "And now he has lost me. I have added grief and shame to his grief and shame."

Nissim at last spoke up. "The real shame is that forgiveness was never considered as an alternative."

He countered, "Forgiveness would have been considered a weakness and a breach of honor."

Nissim was not going to let this pass by. "Others would say that mercy and forgiveness is the mark of a truly wise man, for mercy blesses both him who gives it and him who receives it."

Kokochu looked at him for a long time, dropped his eyes, and said nothing.

A few days later, we entered the region of Kartli and approached Tbilisi from the opposite side of the river from the south. The journey was fairly easy in spite of a few minor delays.

We had been en route since dawn. Nissim hoped to be able to attend the first liturgy of Theophany, but we knew we wouldn't make it. However, as we approached, looking up at the great stone church, we saw people filing out of it; they seemed to be coming toward us. As the first comers saw us, they gruffly told us to push aside. We didn't understand them of course, but we got the idea. We were in the way of the procession. A bearded man, dressed in gold with a crown on his head and a heavy staff in his hand, was surrounded by beautifully dressed servants and a group of men chanting very loudly.

Nissim looked a little panicky for a minute. "Good heavens, they are coming to bless the water!" Nissim said to me, "Let's get out of their way." We began to pull back, stumbling away from the shore. "They are coming to the shore to bless the water! Move away please!" This time he called out to the men.

"Bless the water?" I remarked. I had always thought that Water (a god) was to bless us. Again I was to experience something new. It was hard for me to conceive of a God who made the things we took for gods. Does this mean he is going to bless Water? We came into order and let the worshippers crowd around the man in gold whom I was later told was a bishop or a high priest.

There were some long prayers in the Georgian tongue, which were incomprehensible to all of us. But at a certain point in the ceremonies, the bishop stopped praying and walked down toward the waters. He cast the metal cross in his hands into the waters. I didn't see it until then, but there was a cord around the cross for the bishop to pull it up. He then repeated the action two more times. I take it that this gesture was the thing that blessed the waters. Each time the crowd shouted out, "*Kyrie eleison! Kyrie eleison! Kyrie eleison!*" Nissim translated this as "Lord, have mercy!" in Greek. They then did it in Slavonic and the third time in Georgian. When the prayer ended, they all burst out in song. Nissim leaned over and said that this commemorates the Baptism of Jesus in the Jordan River in the Holy Land just before he began teaching. When this was over, some men of the congregation took silver buckets and pulled water out of the river. The bishop dipped a sprig of herbs bound by a cloth into one of the buckets and as people approached, he would splash them on their foreheads with the herbs. Nissim and Grigory dismounted and joined the crowds with Kiymetli following. There were ladles supplied, and the people would take a drink from the buckets. Others would take clay jars and fill them and take them home. Again, I experienced this sense of joy around the feast. People of the congregation who passed by smiled and greeted us in their tongue. Nissim and the others returned with their faces and hair all wet.

In a few hours, we went up to the monastery. We left our animals to graze outside the walls as there was no snow on the ground, unlike other years, we were told. I asked Hazir to accompany Nissim and me, as well as Officer Grigory. Of course, Kymmy had to come along. Then I noticed Kokochu standing by, wanting to catch my eye.

"Did you want to come?" I asked.

"With your permission, my lord."

"So be it."

Nissim had Father John's letter to Father Abo, hoping that it would introduce us to the monks. In fact it was an important letter. It was written in Russian so a Russian-speaking monk was summoned to read it. He was pleasant. Nissim told him that he could speak Greek or Turkish better than Russian. Officer Grigory knew nothing of Father John, so he could say little. The monk told us that they had a few Greeks at the monastery visiting from the Holy Mountain monastery of Iveron in Greece, if they were granted permission to speak to us. We waited at a comfortable room off to the side and eventually two black-bearded monks approached us and introduced themselves as Father Theodosius and Father Michaelangelos and bid us welcome. We came to an agreement that Turkish was the most common tongue, so that is what we would use.

They explained that Father Abo was painting a church up north and could not return in time. In fact, he probably would not return for a month and then only to pick up some supplies. He had advised the abbot of the monastery that we would visit but, expecting us for Christmas, when we did not come, they assumed we had bypassed them. But we were welcome to camp on the ground for a short time and worship with them and eat at their table. I thanked them for their hospitality. There was enough fresh grass for our horses in spite of the large clumps of snow that were not ready to thaw.

Nissim also told the monks that we had actually spent Christmas at Saint Davit Gareja cave monastery, they perked up instantly and plied us with questions. "How I would love to go there on a pilgrimage," Father Theodosius confessed.

Father Michaelangelos added, "Perhaps the Elder would let us go, but alas, it is too far. It would be a long walk. We have no horses."

"Well, if you can get your elder's permission," I said, "we could always take you with us on our way home, although I couldn't guarantee a return ride."

The food was excellent. The monks apologized that they would be fasting until three o'clock when they would have vespers. Then they would eat only simple food because the eve of the feast required a strict fast. We ate well, though. They offered to bed us for the night, but we said we should return to our men.

After the meal, we rested before seeing the abbot, who had requested a meeting. During the meeting in which the monks acted as interpreters, Kokochu was asked how he liked Saint Davit's. He replied that he had not joined us until later, but he was not unfamiliar with monasteries as he had been brought up at a lamasery in Kalmykia, something that all the boys of Kalmyk aristocracy were required to do.

"There we were educated in the arts and Buddhist philosophy until puberty arrived, and then we were sent home to learn the art of war. I find the way of life here not significantly different. It is quite pleasant. Perhaps at a future date I could spend some time here."

Kokochu had a question. "There is something I would like to know, however, about this feast in general. You talk about blessing the water. In which way is it blessed, and why is it blessed yearly?"

Father Theologos responded, having obtained the abbot's blessing. "One of the things about Christian feasts is that they are not based upon the agricultural cycle of nature. The gods of our Greek pagan ancestors were personifications of earth forces. Apollo was associated with the sun, his sister Diana with the moon, the cycle of seasons with Ceres, the goddess of agriculture, and her daughter Persephone, who was forced by the god of the underworld to stay below ground for half the year, obviously winter. So therefore, those deities were subject to the forces of nature, even victims of nature like dear old Persephone. If any of you are believers of many gods, perhaps you can relate to what I have just described.

"That is so," I responded. "Tengri is the sky, Koyash, the sun is his son."

"Even we who follow the Buddha, and are supposed to be atheist, recognize that godlike beings manipulate the forces of nature, even though nature is categorized as illusory." This came from Kokochu.

Father Theologos continued, "Some Christian feasts do, in fact, fall at the same time as pagan feasts. Our early fathers deliberately superimposed some Christian feasts on top of the old ones to draw their new converts away from the old practices, and for the most part, it worked. Some writers from western lands, I am told, use this to imply that our faith is artificial. We say that the faith is actually historical. Our feasts are based on events that actually happened in history. You were blessed to spend the Nativity at Saint Davit's and now you are here celebrating the Baptism of our Savior Jesus with us.

"Water has always been used for cleansing, and cleansing washes away dirt and diseases. Many years before Jesus, the holy prophet Elisha commanded the commander of the army of the king of Syria, who was a leper, to wash in the River Jordan seven times. By the seventh time, Naaman, that was his name, was cured. In that same river, many years later, Saint John the Baptist, another prophet, was approached by Jesus to baptize him, who created the water and who knew no sin. The Baptist hesitated, knowing who he was, but John was obedient. It was by this that Jesus took all the sins of humanity upon himself, washing them away. Even more, noble guests, the Holy Spirit took the form of a dove and hovered over him, while the Father's voice declared that this was his Son in whom he was well pleased. This is why we keep the feast. For Jesus, it was his commission to come here, to this earth, and wash away our sins in water and his own blood. That is why the bishop throws the cross in the water, for Jesus's blood was shed on the cross and blood and water flowed out of his pierced side. Now all water is blessed."

Father Michaelangelos added, "Now no doubt, some scholar or some historian or even some Englishman may well turn up some evidence that this was just a revival of some pagan water festival, but of course, they will have entirely missed the point."

Nissim and Grigory decided to stay the night with my consent, and Kymmy got his uncle's permission to remain with them. The abbot blessed us all and gave us a bottle of the blessed water to bring with us for the rest of our journey. Nissim brought some more the next day since there had been another blessing in Church.

We left shortly after noon the following day. The monks were not so abundant as the others in their gift-giving, but of course, it was not Christmas. They gave us a bundle of very fragrant beeswax candles and jar of olive oil. Again we were splashed with holy water, which turned out to be a tradition, but one which made a little more sense to us.

Again, we followed the Kura. We were told that we would be entering the woods again for the rest of the trip. The river again would turn west, and we would be, as before, on the south side. Cliffs would rise on either side of the river, and sometimes we would have to travel on top of the cliffs because they rose on both sides. It stormed only two separate days but mostly it rained. Other than that, the rest of the trip was relatively uneventful.

One moderately mild morning, we woke up to a warm sun. I felt I wanted to walk into the river and wash. Kokochu stopped me before I stripped and said, "I have been noticing how fussy you folks are about washing and bathing."

"I insist that my staff keep themselves clean. It was not always so amongst us, and there are still many who will not wash at all for fear of offending water. That superstition we got from the Mongols. Our Islamic Tatars actually changed all this by insisting upon physical cleansing."

"Not to wash is a practice, which we Kalmyks still observe. Some of us have developed serious rashes and even infections. Nevertheless it is still a custom. You know, Tambor, after hearing all that talk about water and its cleansing properties at the monastery, I have to rethink my position. I also will commend your discretion for not mentioning the odor I bring into your tent. We live with it, and it doesn't bother us, but I have overheard talk about how unpleasant it is. So if you don't mind, I shall join you this morning."

I think I laughed. "I don't mind at all, my friend, in fact, I welcome it. My servants will give you a good wash down."

It was amusing watching this dark-skinned, well-built man playing in the water like a boy, splashing and teasing the servants who were just trying to do their job. We needed a little laughter. Later on, he asked why Nissim did not join us, and I mentioned that he preferred to bathe at night as I often did. But it was warmer this morning; we were traveling south.

It was fortuitous that the road was well traveled, so we needn't have to guess where to go. But the river turned south into Turkey, and we wanted to cut through the woods and make our way down the coast of the Black Sea. We experienced no danger. The wolves merely sang us to sleep. Perhaps they smelled the wolf pelts we road on. We encountered no mountain lions, no Caucasian tigers, and no enemies—in fact, no trouble. We ate well. Our falcons were very busy. Deer were abundant, and our boys shot down some wild goats; we actually lacked nothing.

It was however slowgoing. The Kura at this point did not flow through wide and spacious plains as it had in Azerbaijan. It was rocky and occasionally snowy and often surrounded on both sides by enormous cliffs. We stopped at Mtskheta, which was the ancient capital of Kartli. Nissim and a few others visited some shrines and venerated some relics. The most important one was the robe of the master Jesus. I saw the robe but didn't know how to venerate. I remembered what Father Theodosius said about the importance of history in their faith, and I was coming to appreciate this. The last place we visited was the monastery at Khashuri. The Kura had sunk down into a ravine, so with some difficulty, we climbed over the cliffs above, irritating the camels and forcing the camel masters to lead their beasts on foot. Just a few hours after reaching the top, there ahead of us was a large and very imposing monastery. Only a few people spoke Turkish, but we were permitted to camp just off the grounds. I must say that these monasteries were very hospitable, but I'm sure that we must have been an intrusion to these men of prayer whose lives are devoted to silence.

We were advised that the terrain would become friendlier as we traveled south. As soon as we reached Akhaltsikhe, we were to leave the Kura and head across the rolling hills west until we arrived at Batumi on the Black Sea in the province of Ajaria. From there it was but a short distance south to Turkey. The whole trip from Tbilisi to Batumi took us several weeks, but the first sight of the Black Sea was overwhelming. We also appreciated the warm weather, which although far from hot, at the end of January, was much more comfortable than the mountains of Georgia. From here on it would be essential to appear as traders. Since we had nothing to sell we would have to be buyers. Fortunately there were enough of us who spoke Turkish to soften any suspicion and even my own Turkish was improving. I could now easily speak Turkish to my Persians though Nissim teased me that I spoke it with a Persian accent when talking to him.

As we were enjoying the weather, the sunshine and the wide blue skies along with the smell of the sea as the winds blew eastward, I felt it was time to consult with my officers about what we were going to do and how we were to do it. We realized that apart from Nissim and the Persians we were not familiar with the terrain and the layout of the towns and villages. I also needed to talk to all the warriors and especially the camel masters. We stayed at Batumi only two days. It was enough to replenish our stock of food necessities although as I said, we lacked no meat on our trip along the Kura.

Before gathering together my officers, I needed to talk to Kokochu to establish our relationship and future plans. "Well, Sir," I said, pulling him aside, "you have been quiet lately." I had been calling him sir for a while, recognizing that although we were of different races, we maintained the same rank, he being like me a bondsman to a khan. "What are you contemplating now that you are reaching your destination near the Turkish border?"

He looked at me for a moment and then dropped his eyes. "You are right, my friend, if you will permit me to call you that." I nodded assent, I hoped, in a friendly manner. "It has been much in my thoughts, and in actual fact, I am of two minds on the subject."

I needed to make this easy for him. "Up until now, you have been our guest under the terms of the rule of hospitality, which both our peoples respect. Of course you are free to go as of this moment." I paused. "If that is what you wish. We have fulfilled our duty according to our mutual arrangement."

"I thank you for that, Lord Tambor. My gratitude extends beyond the formalities of the situation. You and your men have helped me to restore my sense of dignity and self-respect. I feel a warrior once more. Should I leave you now, I become again a wanderer and a vagabond. The Turks may employ me as a laborer, but I shall be always a stranger in a foreign land."

"Would you consider remaining with us?"

He looked into my eyes as if to probe my thoughts. "Would you consider my remaining with you?"

"The terms of our relationship would have to change, of course. You are a man of rank and therefore you cannot be an unbonded warrior amongst us. As a Kalmyk, there would definitely be the question of loyalty. We have, after all, been enemies." He waited for me to continue. "I am bondsman to Akilli Khan. Nissim, who was once my squire is now bonded to my father Dalgali, but he will belong to the khan on our return to the Birches. Hazir is bondsman to Akilli Khan also. My brother Tolga and cousin Koray, still boys, are under my father Dalgali's command until they are older. Tetik is the son of my father's free servant Tutumlu and has been a warrior with us. The others are part of Hazir's clan. Dilaver is my squire, and Erali is Nissim's. I bought the Persians as slaves. They came with the camels." I chuckled. "No matter how often I have offered them their freedom, they choose to remain my servants. Presumably they are my bondsman even if they don't recognize it. Grigory, the Russian, has freely offered his service to me. I am in his mind his superior officer."

I let Kokochu have some time to think. "If you are willing," I continued after a time, "you may swear loyalty to me, and I would gladly accept you as bondsman. Your loyalty, like Nissim's, would go directly to Akilli Khan. What do you say?"

I saw that he was struggling to keep a cold face. (The Kalmyks perhaps value this more than we do. We allow ourselves some expressions of emotion.) I feigned to look elsewhere so as not to embarrass him.

Then he spoke. "My friend, I am honored to offer my service to you as a bondsman. With your permission, I will make a formal statement of loyalty before the others when we meet together tonight." I took him by the hand, and we held each other's arms.

"Please, Kokochu, go and help the others get ready for tomorrow's departure and ask Nissim and Hazir to attend me." I silently thanked God for our small fellowship and asked him to bless our enterprise. Even though I didn't know him and maybe even didn't believe in him, I knew it was he who was behind it all.

Nissim and Hazir joined me. Hazir seemed somewhat preoccupied.

"Forgive me, Hazir, for taking you away from your work. You do such a thorough job." He nodded respectfully and visibly relaxed. I continued. "Tonight the whole company of warriors will assemble to discuss a game plan. You and Nissim are both my right and left hand, and I need you at my side. I need your perceptiveness and insights. Kokochu has just sworn loyalty to the khan and has become my bondsman. He will publicly declare his loyalty before the others tonight. He is of the same rank as we are and is a skilled warrior in his own right, and I would like him to join us as officers. Do you have any objections?"

"None whatsoever, Sir," Nissim said and looked over to Hazir for agreement, which came typically with a nod.

He did say, with a smile, "It seems ironic that just three months back we were on the same field trying to kill each other and now he is taking part in our planning sessions. But I do bow to your wisdom, Sir Tambor. I will however keep an eye on him, my lord. Who knows what will happen should the winds change?"

"I appreciate your caution, my friend. And, Nissim, I thank you for your trust." I motioned to one of the boys nearby to get Kokochu, and while we waited, I complemented Hazir on the compact folding of the felt we used for the tents. "More than that," I added, "you have the slaves and the other warriors so thoroughly trained that all you have to do is watch."

"You know, my lord, it is my family that supervises the felting each spring. Everyone in the tribe works at felting because of the importance of the yurts. Even Nissim and Timov put in their hours when you were off training. That is because Lady Yerinde exempted you—you and Dikkatli, who was always away during the spring felting anyway. I've seen the khan on his hands and knees rolling out the felt. But your mother said, 'No! Tambor has other work.' So 'No!' it was."

I laughed. "That's ridiculous! You mean, Mother had enough clout to have me exempted? I'm going to have to do something about that. Hopefully we'll be home by then." We all laughed again until Kokochu joined us. I asked him. "Sir Kokochu, tell me in all your experience, have you ever done felting?"

He looked at me somewhat puzzled and said, "Everyone does the felting." We all laughed again, except for Kokochu, who had no idea what we were referring to. When we told him, he was astounded that I never had.

"Now, let's get serious, men. Kokochu, are you willing to participate in our planning sessions? Your training and experience will be very helpful to us." He bowed deeply.

We sat on the warm grass and basked in the breeze coming north eastward from over the sea, from Africa we were told. The air was dry and pleasant after having trekked through the damp and snowy mountains. The camels were already showing their approval of the climate.

"Vishtaspa and Mardunya should be in on this." Hazir offered to get them, and they returned with a pot of hot salted tea and a few pottery cups.

"Of course, you all know that Lord Dalgali has commissioned us to rescue Nissim's mother and virgin sister from their owners in the Trabzon area of Turkey. We won't have to travel much as Trabzon is the main city in the easternmost shores of the Black Sea. Nissim spent some time studying war at the small military academy there. It was in that city that Nissim and his family had been enslaved because it was found out that they were Christian. If you will pardon me, Nissim, the family was Turkish on the outside and Christian on the inside. Nissim and Timov were made slaves in the city, and Nissim believes that his mother and sister do their servitude at the country residence at the shore. That is our destination. We are also concerned that his younger sister may have been forced to be compromised since she is now fifteen, a year younger than Timov. We do not know where Nissim's father was taken, but that is for us to search out at some future date. Nissim, do you have something to add?"

Nissim looked a bit hesitant and said quietly, "I do. Kokochu, I've noticed that when you go into the water to bathe, your back is afflicted with many scars. These, as we have been told, occurred when you ran through the gauntlet at your camp a few months ago, and survived."

"They are still sore and a bit raw and sometimes painful. The sea water stings them, but they seem to be healing, perhaps because of it."

At this point Nissim slowly moved into a prostrate position and slowly pulled his silk shirt out of his leather trousers and, sliding it over his head, exposed the deep welts in his back. There was a sharp intake of breath even from me at his having finally exposing his secret.

He raised his body and looked around at us all. "That, my friends, is why I bathe in the moonlight. Up until now, I have been ashamed of my stripes, but when I saw Kokochu proudly enter the Kura with his bare back exposed, I was ashamed of my shame, for these stripes were suffered for the sake of Christ. Being beaten was an almost daily experience at the house of Mehmet Pasha. Timov was exempted because he was too young, and I'm sure they thought of other possible uses for the women. My father and I got it all." He put his shirt back on and stuffed it into his trousers. We were unable to say anything. "Tambor has known this all along and has vowed to find my father. I thank you all for your generous service. We should now listen to what Sir Tambor needs to say."

"Thank you, brother. I believe that the exposure of your sufferings gains for us some more commitment to this cause than before. I respect and honor the memory of your pain and wish to see justice done. I think we all feel that way, am I right?" We were in full agreement.

"When I first considered this plan of mine, it was shortly after our visit to Cherny Yar. I had envisioned some of us riding down to Trabzon, grabbing the women, and flying back home. I knew it was unrealistic. No doubt the Turkish army would be on our necks, we would be killed, and the women subjected to worse treatment. So I had to scrap that idea. But what was my alternative? I really didn't see it so clearly until the market place at Vetlyanka. I may have bought the camels on a whim, but I began to realize the real importance of the camels on this venture. This is the first time I have ever mentioned it, either to Dalgali or even to Nissim. Vishtaspa and Mardunya, you and our camels will play a major role in the release of these women. What I really need is a deception, a trick, you might say, or a deflection.

"Of course we will try diplomacy first. It may work, but I doubt it. I am not quite sure that Nissim should deal diplomatically because being a former slave, the Pasha may just doubt the legitimacy of your freedom." I said that turning to him. "It may be a little awkward saying: 'Mehmet Pasha, I am now a Nogay warrior from upper Astrakhan. I am now bondsman to Akilli Khan of Sopasi, and we would like to buy my mother and sister from you.' What kind of response do you think we'll get? I'll tell you: "Get out of here, Nissim. I sold them years ago. I neither know nor care what happened to them, and if you don't get off my property, I'll crush you personally. Get off and don't come back!"

"So you are expecting a fight, Sir Tambor?" Hazir questioned.

"Yes, very definitely!" I responded. "We shall obviously not let the Pasha get away with that. I have no doubt but that the two women are at the summer residence. I could be wrong, but I don't think so. We will make our respectful obeisances to the Pasha and apologize for inconveniencing him and then put the next plan into action, but that would depend on circumstances which we'll need to work on."

"So far so good, Sir Tambor," Kokochu said. "We would need a small distraction, but what are the details of the next plan which is presumably to remove the women?"

"That is where the camels come in. We shall have to find a place where the camels can hide. When we manage to get the women out we will rush to a meeting place and dress the women as Muslim women, entirely covered, and put them on the camels. You camel masters must be Muslim for a few days and these women your pious and obedient wives. You must be casual and not flee, for you are just merchants and haste might draw suspicion.

Should the militia be sent after us, and that is likely, of course, you must tell them that you did notice a band of ruffians heading in such-and-such a direction to make them chase us. We shall then ambush them, and with God's help, we'll destroy them."

"Ah! Brilliant!" They all responded.

"Of course after this encounter, you camel drivers must then fly as fast as you can back here to Batumi, where they cannot touch us. Before all this happens, we will have to find a place where we can store our gear. Only the most needful of servants are to come with us. The rest must stay here. Hazir, two of your men should stay behind so as to be ready for our return. Now I need your feedback. Perhaps there is something I have not foreseen. We shall discuss this tonight after the evening meal over a bottle of ouzo, a very potent Greek drink that Nissim and I bought in the village yesterday."

We talked for a little over an hour. The plans didn't change much, but we both questioned and added some details. We were all satisfied with the current plans and relaxed, ready to enjoy the dinner. After the meal, before any talk could start, I asked Kokochu to stand up before me. I explained to them that he had become my bondsman and was now willing to announce his loyalty to Akilli Khan in front of the whole company as witnesses. As he began to get on his knees, I lifted him and told him that we were of equal rank. He would bow before Akilli Khan in due time but not to me. But he did make an impressive and moving speech, some of which I have quoted at the beginning of this chapter.

That being done, we moved on to describe the game plan. The only objection came from Hazir's kinsmen, who really felt disappointed to have to stay behind to guard the camp. We could leave only two. Tetik and his father would stay behind also; hawks and falcons would be unnecessary baggage. Kiymetli would come too; it was Hazir's choice. Over the weeks and months, the boy had become an excellent archer. Since he was getting taller, he was to leave his pony behind and ride on his own horse, one of the horses left by the brigands in the woodlands. A few more suggestions were made, and a few scrapped, but there was a general realization that when all was said and done, only the scene itself would determine the action. We could plan all we want to, but we could not wield the future.

In the morning, Nissim joined us bathing in the sea. I washed his back, as a token of my commitment, and Nissim washed the back of Kokochu as a sign of identification. From then on, there would be no questions asked. Tetik had been teaching Kymmy how to cry like a hawk, and the hawks and falcons swirled around him as he splashed at them in the water. It was important to be light at this point for heavier times would be ahead of us.

As usual, we had inquired of the natives if anyone could direct us to the routes toward Trabzon. All were unanimous that the shoreline was the fastest and most pleasant way. This was the route for the camel masters. I had bought a half dozen burkas from a local market place and gave them to the Persians. Nissim had also thought of the kinds of wedding jewelry new brides would wear. All the camels and all the camel masters were to go. They were not to be very noisy, but they were to be visible. They were to be on their way to the market at Trabzon. Posing as Muslim, they were to use all the proper Islamic greetings and expressions. Their purpose obviously was to purchase wives.

The rest of us warriors were to take the more tedious and maybe more hazardous route through the hills, along the rivers, and over the plains. Lacking the camels, we would be able to move swiftly. Nissim said that the summer home was at a place called Yomra on the shore but that he had never visited there. Near Yomra was a small town called Arsin where the Persians should set up camp. There was a little village somewhat south whose name he could not remember where we could camp. We found out later that it was called Karaka and that there was a small Greek community there. Greeks and Armenians were accorded some independence in eastern Anatolia (which is the word Nissim used for Turkey).

The Persians would stay somewhat hidden if possible at Arsin until we located them and wait until the deed was done. We would swiftly leave the women with them and immediately rush toward Karaka where we would ambush any pursuers before they got there. The camel masters were to dress the women and leave immediately. If they were questioned, they were to say that they saw riders heading toward Karaka. Leave it to the Turks and Russians for a logical battlefront, we Tatars and Kalmyks preferred to use trickery. All were to be killed. "All but one," Nissim said.

And so, Reverend Father, we entered Turkish land. We traveled swiftly, making few stops and only once to ask for direction. At last we reached Karaka, which we hoped was the town where we were to camp. Wherever it was, that would be our place. We found exactly the right spot for the ambush. Nissim said, "We will have to trust God that he oversees our deliberations."

Apparently, the Persians encountered two different troops of soldiers on their trip on the south shore of the Black Sea, one in Rize east of Trabzon and another in the territory of Trabzon itself. The troop in Rize treated them routinely, but the one in Trabzon asked more questions. The men countered their questions lightly, complaining of the loneliness of the life of travel and flattering them on the beauty of the brides of Trabzon. It worked.

After arriving at Karaka, Nissim and Kokochu accompanied us to Arsin and found the Persians hidden in a copse of thick trees on the outskirts. This is where we would meet to drop off the women. Hazir had already laid out the camp when we got back, and we too were hidden. The only sound we could hear was the trickle and bubbling of the nearby stream and the tolling of the church bell, not too far away where there was a Christian quarter in the village on the north side, our side.

Perhaps it was the anticipation of a skirmish the following day, but I had a night of fitful dreams. Nissim woke me up when he returned from his prayers. I told him that they were the same old and familiar ones. He made the sign of the cross over me, and I remembered that Nissim's God was watching, so I slept peacefully for a few more hours.

Just in Time

Greater love has no one than this,
than to lay down one's life for his friends.

—John 15:13 (nkjv)

The chamberlain was obviously unnerved by our presence. As he stood on the top of the steps and looked down at our small group mounted in the courtyard, a thin layer of sweat formed on his forehead and upper lip. He was not an old man; he was well dressed in an embroidered rose-colored jacket with cream-colored pantaloons. He was fairly handsome. It was evident however that he was just unfamiliar with dealing with obvious foreigners. We spoke Turkish, but that still would not ease his consternation.

"Mehmet Pasha is not here…uh, gentlemen," he said for the second time. "The master is on a business trip in Izmit (which the Greeks call Nicomedia). He will not be back for two weeks." When we did not move, one of the two guards who stood at the entrance leaned over to him and said something in his ear. "Ah yes, gentlemen, I have been reminded that the master's son is home. Perhaps he will see you, if that is your desire."

"That would be well appreciated, sir. You may tell him that Sir Tambor, son of Lord Dalgali of Astrakhan, would like a few words with him, if he would be so gracious." I thought my accent would work well in my favor.

"Well, yes. Yes, of course, if you would be patient for a few moments. Young Fahesh Pasha was not expecting visitors from such a distance. Please allow him to get ready." By this time, he looked visibly relieved as he turned and entered the house.

Nissim leaned over and said quietly, "I think he recognized me. I certainly recognized him. His name is Yussef, and he was kind to me." Erali's horse stood to the left of Nissim's, and Kokochu was on my right. A servant girl offered us some fruit from a basket she was carrying while we were waiting. When Yussef reappeared, he announced Fahesh Pasha with a large flourish and stepped aside to let the young prince make his appearance.

"Welcome, Sir Tambor. Please accept our hospitality. I apologize for my father's absence and hope that I shall be a suitable substitute. Ibrahim, what an unexpected surprise." This he said, looking Nissim up and down with approval. "All of you, please dismount and join me on the veranda. You may leave your weapons with your horses." He motioned to a lad to lead our horses to the back.

"Thank you, Fahesh. To Sir Tambor's right is Sir Kokochu, a Kalmyk prince and to my left, my squire Erali."

"Squire? Indeed? So, Erali, you are learning the art of war from my old classmate Nissim, whom we used to call Ibrahim at the academy. He was the most successful of students and a master of weaponry."

"We have certainly benefited from that mastery to the extent that my father, Lord Dalgali, adopted Nissim as his son after he saved my father's life."

"Well, that is commendable." He clapped his hands, and servants appeared. "Do you gentlemen prefer cushions or chairs?"

We all agreed on cushions. He ordered the servants and turned to us. "I hope you will forgive me if I use my chair. Kava for our guests," he called to the servants. "Now let us talk comfortably." The café came quickly along with sweets. To all intents and purposes, Fahesh was the perfect host, handsome, well spoken, and gracious.

"I must say one thing, Ibrahim, or rather Nissim, I would never have thought to see you here again and certainly not as a free noble." And turning to me, he declared, "Of course, you are aware that Nissim was once a house slave here. He has indeed come into some good fortune. If I am not prying, gentlemen, you would surely understand my curiosity as to how this came to be. Did you purchase him from the Kurds?"

"If you don't mind my saying it, noble Fahesh, I believe you sold him and his brother to a group of disreputable Kurds, very unlike the others we have met since. When our noble Khan Akilli offered them hospitality by allowing their horses and livestock to graze on our land, they abused the privilege by stealing from us."

Nissim added, "They were a band of highway robbers posing as merchants. They stole horses and cattle and slaves. Timov and I must have gotten a good price because I never knew them to ever buy or breed anything. They were on their way to Kazan to sell their stolen goods."

"Well, if that is the case," he protested indignantly, "we shall have nothing more to do with them hereafter."

"That shouldn't be a problem," I added. "We slaughtered every last one of them!" I watched his eyes blink and cloud over, with perhaps just a trace of fear. "Nissim and his brother only narrowly escaped death because we Tatars do not kill children."

"Allah is merciful," he said quietly, bowing reverently.

I continued, "Only recently did I become aware of Nissim's origins, and when I realized that the servitude of my boys came about by no reason *we* would make them slaves, I presented Nissim to our most gracious khan to have him trained as a warrior. Of course, we are indebted to the Military Academy here for providing him with prior training and experience."

I paused just to let it sink in. "Timov, on the other hand, has talents of a very different sort, and I fully intend to exploit them. It is a blessing from Almighty God that they both came our way."

"Yes…well, umm. Have you warriors come our way for purposes of trade? With my father Mehmet Pasha away, unfortunately my devices are somewhat limited."

Nissim looked at me to go ahead and a slight lowering of my eyes indicated for him to proceed. "Actually, my dear Fahesh, we do want to make a purchase which we hope to pay for in gold coin. We are looking to buy back my mother Anna Maria and my sister Eleftheria. We would make it worth your while to dismiss them to us."

"My dear Nissim, I am *so very* sorry. We sold them a long time ago, well before we sold you to those Kurds. I have no idea where they would be now. We don't keep records, at least of women slaves."

"You *did* remember who bought Nissim and his brother?" I questioned.

"Yes, but women slaves are of little consequence. I am very sorry, gentlemen. If you have no further requests, I would like to retire. My morning prayers are soon to begin. Excuse me. You will find your horses and gear around back in the stable. The boy will take you."

We left quietly. We knew it would not be so easy. Nissim looked despondent. There was half a possibility that Fahesh was telling the truth. Our eyes met, and he allowed me to see the pain and doubt. I tried to look confident and positive. We didn't want to say anything in the presence of the young slave, but when he went away, Erali piped up.

"Forgive me, sir," he said to Nissim. "I don't think he is telling the truth. We have to stick to the plan, don't we, Sir Tambor?" He looked at me. "We have to trust in Nissim's God." But before any of us could respond, another voice came out of the shadows.

"The boy is absolutely correct, gentlemen." We all turned and saw someone coming out of the shadows. He startled me because even after he came into the light, his face was still covered in shadow. He was so dark I thought it was one of Erlick's demons. We drew our swords immediately. Kokochu had his bow drawn; he was very quick!

The man spoke quietly but firmly. "Spare me! Spare me! I am a friend, not a fiend. The master was lying, Nissim. Your mother and sister are not far away. I can take you to them. But it will have to be done secretly, or I shall lose my life. Do you not remember me, Nissim? I am Moussa, the steward at the summer residence. Maya and Livvy are there."

"Moussa, Moussa, of course. I never really knew you. You came here just for supplies."

"Just as I am doing now." He smiled, and a row of gleaming white teeth shone from his black face. "It will be dangerous to be seen leaving together. I shall meet you near a hill of rocks on the east road. We can then travel together. Your mother prays every day that you will come to rescue them, and at last here you are!" He gave a quiet and husky laugh and slapped Nissim's thigh. "I must go."

"Brothers, you can trust this man. He is an Ethiopian Christian."

Moussa mounted a mule and led another one burdened with supplies. He looked out of the stable to see if we were being watched and left. He whispered back at us, "The east road just past Cimenli at the hill of rocks. It will take me about an hour with these mules. Your horses will take you there in much less than that. Wait there for me. Trust me, this is no trick."

We left from the courtyard that we had come in from so as not to arouse suspicion. The chamberlain stood on the verandah looking fretful. We waved him a friendly good-bye and left quickly and quietly. Moussa left by another exit at the back of the estate.

We decided that we should trot comfortably along the shore road. After all we were but travelers—no need to draw attention to ourselves. We passed Cimenli, which was a small baked town on the south side of the road. A few dusty children paused in their play as we passed by. Nissim threw a few copper coins, which they eagerly swooped up like the screeching seagulls overhead.

The hill of rocks was just that. There were no cliffs leading to the beach, but these rocks looked as though they had tumbled down to the shore scores of generations ago. We were sitting on the rocks at the shoreline, washing hot feet in the still cool water, when Moussa turned up. He hid his mules discretely behind a few trees and came toward us. His dark color still unnerved me, but I put that aside, wanting to hear what he had to say. He went first to Nissim and kissed his hand and came then to me, perhaps a little hesitantly.

"You are the master?" he asked.

"I am Sir Tambor, the leader, but certainly not master."

"I knew Nissim many years ago, when he was a slave in our master's house." He turned to Nissim and then back to me. I had let my feet dry in the sun and was now putting on my boots.

"It would be proper to call him Sir Nissim for he is a Nogay warrior and my adopted brother."

"Forgive me, *effendi* (the Turkish word for *sir*). I did not know. I heard only part of the conversation between you and Fahesh Pasha. You want to liberate Nissim's, that is, Effendi Nissim's mother and sister? I can help you." He paused. I looked firmly at him. "I know where they are and how you can get there."

"Are they safe? Are they healthy?" Nissim was impassioned.

"Yes, effendi. They are safe and sound and have been waiting for you to return. God has answered their prayers." I did not want Nissim to lose control of himself, so I asked them both questions.

"Well, Moussa, what makes you think we can trust you?"

This question snapped Nissim back to himself.

"Effendi, we three are in charge of the slaves' quarters at the summer residence. We are actually getting the house ready for the master's return to Trabzon. This time of year, the mistress moves to the summer house until winter comes by. We live in the slaves' quarters closer to the shore. I would not suggest however that you come and steal the ladies. The master is a patron of the Military Academy, and Fahesh Pasha would have thirty men after you in an hour. Forgive me, effendi, surely you have a plan."

I relaxed and smiled. I was beginning to like this man. "We do." After a moment of ponderous silence, I asked him, "And what is there in it for you? Is it that you want some money?"

"Good Lord, no, effendi." He looked at Nissim and again at me. "I want you to take me with you. Sir Nissim, I wish you to take me with you as your slave and serve your mother as I have served her ever since you were taken away."

"Moussa, I don't need slaves. How could I possibly face myself taking you as slave when you have helped me free my mother and sister?"

"Effendi, freedom is no good to me. If I left your mother, they would hunt me down and kill me. I have served these women for years. I have often helped preserve your sister's virtue at the risk of my own life. Please take me with you." Nissim looked at me, pleading.

"All right, Moussa," I said. "We will work something out. We need details which you can provide on the way. We had better go. How long will it take to get us there?"

"These mules are slow. If I push them it will take an hour and a half."

"If we push them, it will take far less. Kokochu and Erali! Tie these lazy beasts to your mounts," I commanded. "Moussa, climb onto my horse, we'll ride together. Nissim, ride close by and help me with the details. Let's get going."

He talked. He gave such a clear description of the estate we lacked no details when we passed it. "You'll see. I'll show you when we get there. We are not alone effendi. There are six permanent guards there. They are not soldiers but the master's personal guards, all graduates of the academy. They live in an attachment to the west of the house. Mehmet Pasha is a patron of the academy and has special favors. That is why you were sent to him for discipline, Sir Nissim. Many Tatars, I am told, are Muslim." He hesitated but turned. "Is your tribe Muslim?"

"We hold the old faith although we have Muslims amongst us. There are also some Christians amongst us such as Sir Nissim and his brother." I could see visible relief come over his face. "We also have a stray Buddhist here, like Sir Kokochu. And you? Are you Christian?"

"Yes, effendi. I am from Ethiopia in the land of Africa far to the south, past Egypt. In these days, our people at home have a different understanding of who Jesus is, but I have been following the Greek faith for a few years with a priest's blessing. I am very devoted to your mother and sister. I was not enslaved for religious reasons but for an indiscretion committed many years ago."

"Do you have a wife and family?" I asked. When he nodded, albeit somewhat sadly, I continued, "Would freedom not allow you to return home to them, my friend?"

"Dear effendi," he replied, "I would not be of any use to my wife. Better she think me dead."

"Surely not, friend."

Nissim leaned over to me and said discretely, "The Kalmyks left Kokochu intact, Tambor. Moussa was not so fortunate. He is a eunuch."

"Forgive me for embarrassing you, my friend. That is not our custom."

"In some fashion, effendi, it has provided me with some status. I can move around at will and have some respect amongst the other slaves, and I have the supreme joy of serving your mother, Sir Nissim, to whom I am completely devoted. I have also been able to stave off some of the young master's advances toward your sister. He is a little afraid of me although I would never lay a hand on him. Should I catch him in the act, it would bring such a shame that his father would be able to provide only a lower status marriage. Sadly Fahesh would tire of Livvy and sell her to the slave market or to prostitution. I would never allow that. Of course *he* would never suffer the same fate as I have. The master needs heirs."

"All right, Moussa. You've won your case. You can come with us."

He gave us one of his glorious smiles and said, "Thank you, master." Needless to say he never called any of us *effendi* again.

We talked again of our plans. Moussa was still very concerned that we would be pursued and killed and the women sold as slaves on the market.

"Moussa, we have thought of that. Tonight we shall come just before midnight. Be ready. Be ready to fly. Erali here and his brother will take you to a designated location. A horse will be provided for you. There you will encounter my camel masters who will dress you in burkas. The three of you shall be Muslim brides until we get to Batumi in Georgia where we shall all be safe."

His smile was infectious. "Oho! This *will* be fun! What a good plan, master." I decided at this point that I truly liked this man. "But are you not coming with us?"

"No, we have business to do here. We intend to destroy the summer house. You will not recognize us. We shall be masked and in uniform. The Blue Raiders will be riding again. Do not look so wide-eyed, Moussa. Mehmet Pasha owes a long-standing debt to Sir Nissim. Tonight he shall pay for part of it. Tell the women to be ready. They shall not see Nissim in the confusion but do not tell them about the raid. It would frighten them. We shall join you in Batumi. Do not be afraid, but trust in your God. He is wise."

"Yes, master. But how will I convince the women that it is really you, Sir Nissim? Do you have anything to identify yourself by?"

Nissim thought for a moment. Although Nissim did not shave his hair as many of us do, letting the waves of his raven hair flow freely, he had been growing a braid down the back of his neck in our fashion. I could see him thinking. He bent his head forward and said, "Tambor, please cut it off." I took my silver knife from its scabbard, sliced it off, and gave it to him. Nissim took the braid, kissed it, and said to Moussa, "Take this, friend, and give it to my mother with all my love."

We were nearing the estate, which was perched on a hill a fair distance past the village of Yomra to the west of the estate. Fortunately we would not have to pass it to access the grounds. The estate was not made to be easily seen, but a stone ledge allowed its inhabitants to lean over to get a view of the sea. We could see the red roof of the house from the road but nothing else. A large road veered off to the right, on the approach, which Moussa said was the grand entrance to the estate.

"Don't come this way. Two of the guards stand at the top. If you want stealth, you will have better access to the grounds by the servants' entrance on the east side. It goes directly up the hill toward the servants' quarters. Normally it is unguarded because it is not easily seen. That is where we shall be waiting. If your boys should come first and leave immediately with us, all of we should be down below the grounds before anyone notices you. See where I am pointing, that's where you go up. I should take the mules up now." I helped him down. He added, "Hopefully no one from Trabzon will suspect you might be coming. Fortunately, Fahesh will be tied up with business for the next few days and is not expected here very soon."

I held his hand as he descended and said, "Thanks, friend. You have made this easier than we could have expected. I believe your God sent you to us." This time, his smile was quiet and peaceful. "Oh, and keep the mules in a safe place far from the fire. We will not be able to take them with us."

We continued at a leisurely pace toward Arsin where we made contact with Vishtaspa and Mardunya and the others. They were surprised to know that they would have another wife in their company. I explained that she would be a man and that they would have to use another burka and make sure the gold coins and baubles dangled over their brides' foreheads. Kuru offered to take the new wife, his gold teeth shining as he smiled. What I had thought to be intensely serious seemed to be greeted with light hearted humor by everyone except Nissim, who in spite of it all, managed a grin or two amidst his solemn frowns. They were to start slowly at dawn just a while after we would be passing by. They were expected to encounter the guard and say that a band of infidels rushed by up the road to Karaka and that they should follow them. We finally decided to drop that last phrase as it might sound a little too enthusiastic. If the guard didn't come, they were not to wait. They were to move leisurely until they encountered a small river that emptied into the sea under a bridge. After crossing the bridge, they were to continue at maximum pace until reaching the province of Rize, after which they could relax their speed. All agreed.

We then left to reach the rest of the company at our camp up the hill halfway to Karaka. We again examined the proposed site for the ambush just before we arrived. At camp, we were close enough to hear the Vesper bells chiming from the little temple near the village.

Nissim said he felt a little safer being near one of the Christian communities. He attended Vespers in the little Greek church dedicated to Saint Theodore the Commander. He had met the priest and had told him that we were here attempting to rescue a few Greek slaves and would be leaving shortly. The priest, Father Tryphon, was apparently a little suspicious and very cautious but gave him a blessing anyway.

We ate quietly. Even Officer Grigory, normally a source of entertainment, was quiet and perhaps prayerful even. Kiymetli was told he would be needed at the camp with his father and afterward would perch himself in a tree with a quiver full of new arrows. These he would use at the ambush. Dilaver and Erali were excellent fletchers, and we never lacked good arrows. This would be the first time Kym would enter into real combat. Even he was quiet and solemn.

After eating, we reviewed the plans together. Some of us rested; others talked quietly by the fire. Nissim stayed alone. An hour before midnight, Hazir doused the fire and put everything away. As I had learned to expect, he was well prepared for a hasty departure.

It was a full moon that night. The sea was calm, and the moonlight rippled on the surface. From the hill, we could see the light on the waters. Spring came early in Anatolia as usual, and the fragrance of fresh flowers mingled with the scent of the sea. I thought of Katya and deliberately forced her from my mind. I prayed to the Creator of heaven and earth and told him how impressed I was and humbly asked him to protect us in our mission. We slowly descended the hill with me in the lead. We would be easily seen if there had been any traffic on the road. There wasn't. Without a word, Erali and Dilaver moved ahead with the extra horse. Tolga carried the pot of coals, which would light our flaming arrows. Nissim followed with Kokochu, who was surprised at having to wear the garb of the Blue Raiders. He primped and preened himself like a bird.

"So you are the real Blue Raiders, after all." He chuckled quietly.

"Now you are one of us." I rubbed it in with a whisper and a finger to my lips. "The blue turban suits you. It is fortunate that we have an extra one to spare. However it means that neither Dilaver nor Erali have one to wear. These came from the dead and wounded bodies of the battle with your tribe. We washed the blood off in the Volga, and Dalgali's women mended them." He nodded his head and returned to silence.

Next came Koray with Hazir's two men. We were seven, and the guard was six. We depended on surprise to attain victory. As at Mikhailov, destruction was the goal. If Fahesh sent thirty men, we would be badly outnumbered. We had alerted the camel masters on our way past Arsin. No need to say how ready they were. "May God be with us," I said. "Now pull on your masks."

Erali had shown Dilaver the path where they were to pick up the women and paused to get my permission to proceed. I nodded, and the rest of us pressed against the wooded area to the south side of the road. The moonlight was now dazzling. We needed quietness and shadows to guarantee that the guards at the main entrance should not be alerted. I suspected that they were too high up the hill to be aware of our presence.

In a very short time, we could hear a scuffle in the bush, and the boys emerged with the women on their horses and Moussa on the third. They waved, but quietly, and Nissim whispered, "Kyrie eleison" under his breath.

Now it was our turn. Tolga was the first to go up with the pot of coals. Each of us had three or four arrows tipped in felt and soaked in animal fat. We were to be silent; there were to be no war cries. Up we went single file as light as a feather as only we knew how to be. The path was of plain earth unpaved, and at the top, we could see where the women had stood in the shadows. There was a large flat surface of polished stone slabs, which went up to the house and spread forward to a shallow stone wall where dwellers could walk out to see the sea. Tolga was in the shadows, but it was impossible for us all to be there. Two guards sat on stools at the spacious entrance to the house whose doors were closed and whose interior was dark. The servants quarters to our right provided the shadows we needed to hide us from the moonlight.

I dipped my arrow into the coals and a flame spurted up. One of the guards grunted and nodded in our direction. Before he could even react, my flame smashed through one of the upper windows. Nissim shot a normal arrow into the guard's throat. The other guard shouted, "Attack!" but he was silenced by my arrow in the head. In the meantime, the other warriors were shooting their flames at every corner of the house. The house was a lot smaller than we had expected. A pretty blaze was blowing inside the house where my first flame hit. We were still silent and masked. The other guards were running from both sides of the house with their sabers drawn. But they were panicking, looking in all directions, and rushing into the courtyard in full view of us. The arrows kept hitting, and the fire was now out of control.

Those three guards were hit: five out of six. That meant one of them was on his way to Trabzon.

We could hear some terrified horses at the back of the building, and Koray had the quick wit to go in their direction. He came back leading them and said they had been in a safe location. The two lazy mules followed blinking their eyes and braying.

"Bring the horses, Koray. Lead the mules down the hill and let them go free. They will slow us down." He tied a few of the horses together, but the others were only too happy to follow.

"Let's go!" I cried and grabbing Tolga's pot, I threw it into the servant's quarters. The coals mixed with the fat caused a fire to ignite immediately on whatever it landed on. There would be nothing left. Those house guards had been ready to react to thieves; they hadn't counted on an attack of Tatars intent on destruction. I couldn't help thinking of the good old days. We had been so silent that the inhabitants of Yomra or Arsin would not even know that there had been an attack. The smoke from the fire would be the only thing to alert them.

There was no need to rush. Reinforcements wouldn't arrive for an hour or more. I suppose it was the excitement that made us speed up. Kokochu noticed it first and reminded us we needed silence and suggested we slow down. When we arrived at Arsin, we were at a better pace; it was obvious that the camp was completely closed down, and the camel masters were ready to go.

I asked, looking around, "Where are the women?"

Dilaver was quick to answer. "They are in the woods."

I confess to being a little annoyed. "Well, what are they doing?"

"I don't know" was the response. Even in the moonlight I could see Dilaver reddening. "They're doing what women do, I guess, Knyaz."

"Oh. I see." I decided to take the situation more lightly. Nissim was beside me saying nothing, as usual. However when the bushes started to rustle and three covered figures emerged from the copse, we both dismounted and approached them respectfully.

Before we could say anything, Vishtaspa asked me, "Should we not leave right away, Sir Tambor? The women are ready."

"Hold off for a bit, boys. I want you to wait till the guard comes so you can tell them where we are. Tell them that a band of ruffians went up toward Karaka. Point to that hill over there. We want to encounter them."

I heard one of the women say, "Oh no! Please certainly not! We are terribly afraid. They will kill us, or worse!"

"Don't be anxious, Mother. This is well thought out, and your God is with us." I tried to reassure her respectfully.

"Mother?" she questioned. "You are not Nissim. I would know your voice."

"Nissim," I said. "Speak to your mother." It was as though he was in a daze. "Take off your mask." He did, but still he said nothing. But at the moment of recognition, both women rushed toward him and embraced him.

He then said quietly, "Mother...Livvy."

"Nissim, oh Nissim, my son. Almighty God bless you!" she spoke lovingly.

And Livvy cried out, "Oh Nissim! My brother. My big, beautiful, brother. I love you. God be praised!"

After the first few moments of recognition, Nissim's mother turned to me and asked, "Nissim, who is this man who calls me mother, my son?"

"Mother, this is my dearest friend and blood brother, Sir Tambor, prince of the Nogay warriors. Without this man, I would never have been able to see you again."

"My lord, I am so very grateful, indeed indebted to you. I am your humble handmaid, and I shall serve you as long as we both shall live."

"You certainly will not, madam," I said. "You will always be an honored guest in our tribe, and it is I who shall serve you as another mother. And you, young lady, for whose honor we have fought and will yet fight shall be as a sister. It is sad," I said with a smile, "you can see us, but we can't see you. In a few days, you can throw off those burkas. However for the time being, you shall pretend to be the Muslim brides of my camel masters. Do you think you can do that?"

"Lord Tambor, I think we have no choice."

"We shall have to leave you for perhaps a week. My men will show you the utmost respect. Moussa, of course, will take the same care for you as he always has, correct, friend? Of course, he is a bride himself! You must not worry, but as Nissim always says, dear lady, 'Trust God!'" Nissim embraced them once more and we mounted our steeds.

"One question more, my lord, where is Timov? He is not with you."

"Have no worry, Mother. Timov is safe and flourishing at our village. After we are safe and free again, we shall talk more about it. You shall have another reunion, in better circumstances. We must ride, and you must fly on the wings of a camel."

I could see that the moon, which had shone so brightly earlier on, was now slowly descending into the western waters of the Black Sea leaving a pinkish green film over the western horizon, and a gray-blue light to the east was promising a welcome dawn in an hour or so. We had work to do. Hazir and his group would be waiting for us. Of course there was always the possibility that no one would come after us, but that seemed unlikely.

As we approached the ambush area we slowed down. Dilaver gave a kind of recognizing bird call, and we could hear Kiymetli respond. Hazir stepped cautiously from behind a tree, and we hailed him and told him our mission at the estate was successful. I was perhaps a little nervous that the guard would not take the Persians seriously, but I could only see that that was the only way to deflect them from the Persians and the women. If they didn't chase us, they would surely question them and that would defeat the purpose. Hazir and Kokochu agreed. I knew Nissim was too nervous to comment. I couldn't imagine all that was going on inside him. While we were away, Hazir had prepared some traps which would trip the horses. Grigory and Hazir were ready.

When quiet resumed, I leaned over to Nissim and said, "Now it's time for me to tell *you* to trust your God, my brother. In a few brief hours it will be all over."

He smiled, "You are such a good friend, Tambor. But I will not feel safe until I see them safe in Batumi."

I rubbed the braidless back of his neck and agreed, "I know, I know."

No sooner had I said this than we could hear the guards and horses down the hill. We took our positions, some of us on horses, and others perched in the trees. Again, silence and shadow was essential. It was not yet dawn, but the sky was becoming light. Grigory was not to use his firearms but only his sword. We were concerned that they might have guns, but we took our chance. The sound of hooves grew louder. Obviously, our ruse worked, and the Persians, we surmised, were flying toward Rize. It was fairly warm weather, so they could push the camels without much objection.

Now we could make out their voices. If they were smart, they would have used silence. But of course, they were expecting to pursue us, not to encounter us. Hazir, who had come to know the area better than we did, had suggested that since the road was narrow, we should let some of the guard through so as to assess what we were up against. Five or six guardsmen passed by us, and Hazir, who was the farthest south, shot the first arrow, hitting the first of the guards in the side. When he swerved but didn't fall, Kymmy shot him in the neck. The guard was almost directly in front of him and below him so Kymmy's shot killed him. At that point, the traps were pulled and four or five horses came tumbling down and caused another three or four to fall into them. At once, Nissim was on the ground with his topor in his right hand and his saber in his other. He slashed and axed at least three people to their deaths before they could do anything to resist him.

Then Grigory led a charge down the hill swinging his sword. The guards had been thrown totally off guard. There were only about a dozen of them—young men like ourselves, students at the academy, probably just pulled out of bed for the occasion. Obviously Fahesh Pasha had enough pull to get the academy to let them go. When I saw Grigory and two warriors descend the hill on the west side, I took Tolga and Koray down the east side. Of course I did not expect to have something coming from behind, but it seemed that one of the guardsmen who had been trying to escape downhill took advantage of seeing Tolga just ahead of him. I saw an arrow strike my brother in the back just below the shoulder blades, and another one pierced his side. I thrust forward toward the guard and sliced off his head. Dilaver and Erali were already down the hill, making sure no one was going to escape, and when one of the guards attempted to cross the field Erali pursued him and shot him with two arrows. I was proud at how he had perfected this skill. I turned and again ascended the hill. Bodies were strewn all over the road. No one was fighting. No one escaped. The boys were mercifully killing the wounded. All but one had been killed, and Nissim had him defenseless against a tree. I saw at once that it was Fahesh, as though Nissim had been searching him out.

He was pathetically pleading for his life, and Nissim had his dagger to Fahesh's throat. Nissim was talking to him. "Fahesh Pasha, I will spare you only because your father spared my life once. We are almost even now. Tell your father that I came back only to get what was duly mine. He cannot pay me back enough for the years he abused me. But it is paid back today. There is only one debt left, the life of my father."

"Nissim," Fahesh gasped, "I lied about your mother and sister, but I will tell the truth about your father. He was taken to trial at Izmit. He saw the judge only once. I was there as a witness. But during the night, some Christians managed to cause him to escape. No one has heard from him since."

"If he is dead, Fahesh, one way or the other, your father will pay." At this point, Nissim released him.

"You walk!" I said. Then I cried to them all: "Anyone who sees him take a horse, strike him down!"

As he walked away, he turned back and cried out, "Allah's curse on you, Nissim. I hate you, you uncircumcised bastard, and curse your infidel religion. I hate your resurrected Jesus and your so-called martyrs and your filthy Tatar friends." Stumbling and falling, he ran down the hill. All was silent after that. The sun was up.

But the silence was not to last too long. Koray came running up to me with Dilaver on his heels.

"Sir Tambor, Tolga is badly hurt. Please come and see him. Sir Hazir is with him."

Nissim and I who had been enjoying the momentary silence snapped to attention. I told Nissim that I had seen him hit. We both rushed down to him. Hazir had turned him over on his side. Both arrows had snapped when Tolga fell on his back. Hazir had pulled off his leather jacket and with it the shaft that had hit his side. Because of the leather armor and padding it had not deeply penetrated Tolga's body. The other one was a different matter. The arrow seemed to have slid past the armor through one of the leather ties and pressed deeply into the back. It was broken off, but I could still grasp it in my hand.

"Are you in pain, my brother?"

"No, Tambor, I feel nothing at all, at least from my chest down. Worse than that, I cannot move my body. It feels dead."

In my heart, I knew he would not come out of this. It sickened me. I had heard about warriors hit in the backbone who became paralyzed. Sadly most of them died; others lived on like dead men wishing to die. Hazir looked at me as though he also knew the young warrior's fate. I grasped the shaft of the arrow firmly but gently. I could see the end of the point lodged in bone. I took my knife and opened the wound so as to let out the arrowhead easily, but as soon as I put any pressure on the arrow, the lower part of Tolga's body began twitching and jerking. I stopped. I had seen enough to know that the backbone had been penetrated.

Tolga said, "I felt nothing, Tambor. I am going to die, my brother, isn't that so? I'm already half dead."

I said nothing.

He was not whining and fearful but rather confident and peaceful.

"Move him up the hill in the field above the trees," I said quietly to Hazir and Koray. They took a blanket from one of the horses and laid Tolga on his back. With help from Nissim and me, we managed to lift him up onto the blanket and brought him to a secluded area beside a grassy field. We laid him down and gave him what was left of the vodka.

To comfort him, I spoke gently but reassuringly to him, "I am proud of you, my brother. You have fought well and are ready to die honorably. Father will be pleased with you as a son and honored that you died as a warrior. You shall go with dignity to the halls of Erlick."

He grabbed my hand and said seriously, "Tambor, I do not want to enter the halls of Erlick. I desire with all my heart to enter the kingdom of heaven where Khan Jesus reigns." He turned to Nissim and said, "Tell me, Nissim, how do I get there? Help me please. I refuse to die until he takes me." At that very moment, I thought, *just by chance*, we heard the church bell toll.

Nissim almost commanded, "All of you stay here and pray. Kymmy and Grigory come with me. We are going to get this man baptized!"

He whistled for Cereyan who drew up immediately. Our eldest and our youngest found their horses and went off after him. You know, Father, I actually did pray. It was the first time in my life I prayed, and it was actually out loud in front of Tolga and the other warriors.

"Jesus Khan, you have no reason to listen to me, for I am stubborn and unbelieving, but I am obeying my brother Nissim and pleading for my other brother Tolga, who wants to travel to your house. Please make it so. I love my brother Tolga and want him to leave this life happy and in peace. Don't you think he is a great warrior too, Jesus Khan? I know that you love him too." I realized that Tolga was still holding my wrist and rather tightly.

He said quietly, "Amen, Amen, Amen!" Then he turned to Koray who was struggling to keep a cool face but whose eyes were full of tears. "Do not grieve for me, dear cousin. We have talked about this many times. You will join me when the right time comes, and we shall fly like eagles in God's kingdom. Be happy that we have set these women free." That was too much for Koray whose tears burst forth as he embraced Tolga's broken body, which began to tremble but without twitching as before.

When he came out of his embrace, he quickly pulled himself together and said, "Tolga, it is you who is being set free. Look, here is Sir Nissim with the priest."

The black-bearded priest came walking alongside Nissim who was leading Cereyan. A middle-aged man with a long twisted mustache and two young boys Kymmy's age walked alongside the priest. The boys carried long poles with candles on top, and the man carried a bundle and some books and a table that could be folded. In the priest's hand was a small box and a cloth bag. Nissim introduced me to the priest.

"It is good of you to come to us, Father Tryphon. We probably interrupted your service. This is an act of mercy, and I am sure it will please your God."

He looked at me for a time and asked, "You talk to me of my God. Is he not your God too?"

"Our tribe believes in many gods, but I cannot say I really believe in any. Whatever is reasonable, that is what I believe. What is reasonable at this point is that my brother is dying, and he refuses to go until he has been blessed by Khan Jesus. If you must baptized him, I would humbly ask you to do so. My blood brother Nissim is a Christian and my half brother Tolga wishes to become one before he dies."

"Before we do that, Lord Tambor, I will have to speak to the young man alone in order to ask if he has anything on his conscience. I have brought along my chanter and two acolytes or altar boys. They will prepare for the ceremony, and if any of you can help, it would be most appreciated.

"Nissim, you will need to find a place in the stream where you can immerse the body. I cannot go in with my robes. Officer Grigory, I shall appoint you as godfather to Tolga."

I had been noticing that Kiymetli seemed disturbed, and I thought that he was merely mourning, but at this point, he shouted out in his newly broken voice, "Father, please baptize me too. Tolga won't mind. I have wanted to be a Christian since Christmas when we were at the Monastery of Saint Davit Gareji. Even Tolga and Koray talked about it at that time."

"Who are the boy's parents?" the priest questioned.

Hazir responded, "I am Kiymetli's uncle. My name is Hazir. Kiymetli's mother died in a plague when he was but a baby. His father died in battle not a year ago."

"Would you object to his baptism, Hazir?"

"Not at all. Is this really what you want, Kymmy?" The boy beamed.

"Nissim, I shall appoint you as his godfather. He will need some instruction in the faith. Right now I need to talk to Tolga. I have also brought the Lord's body and blood for Tolga."

"Yanni," he said, turning to one of the acolytes, "you will need to give up your stycharion for today. Kymmy will need a white robe for his baptism. Now I would appreciate it if all of you can leave me alone with Tolga." Immediately everyone began pitching in.

Nissim went to the stream, and Hazir approached the chanter. I was left with Kymmy, so we decided to go over to where the acolytes were. Yanni was pulling off his robe when we approached them. The other boy, Christo, looked shy and perhaps afraid, after all some of us actually had blood on our clothing. Kymmy thanked him for lending him his robe.

Yanni began speaking to him in Greek and realized that we spoke like the Turks. "Were you never baptized? We were baptized as babies. Why don't you speak Greek?"

"Except for Sir Nissim and his brother, there are no Greeks where we live. We are Tatar and our village is Falaka Sopasi."

Both boys turned as white as their stycharia when Kym said that he was Tatar, and then they looked at me even more suspiciously.

Yanni was still brave. He leaned over to Kymmy and asked him so I could just barely hear him, "Did you ever kill anyone?"

"Just last night, two or maybe three." He said casually, "They were Turks. But that was the first time for me."

"Turks?" they both said in amazement. "You killed Turks?" Their horror turned to profound admiration. "We have never heard of anyone killing Turks!"

It was my turn. "I would suggest that you boys say nothing about this to anyone. It could get your priest into a lot of trouble."

"Oh yes, sir—oh, I mean, no, sir! We shall never say anything to anybody."

Somehow I doubted that this promise would last very long.

Father Tryphon was now calling for Kymmy. I went to check on what Nissim was doing. He was standing in the middle of the stream up to his waist. He waived at me with a wide smile. I was glad to see his normally good mood return. He shouted, "This stream is mighty cold."

I went back to Tolga, who was resting peacefully. The vodka must have worked. I didn't want to think that he was genuinely happy. It was unnatural. Koray was at his side, not quite so resigned. Then it was time. Father asked that Tolga be taken to the rocky shore.

"I will be reading the prayers in Greek, my friends. I do not have a book in Turkish. I shall try to explain what I am doing whenever possible. Our faith tells us that when one is baptized he becomes a new creation. This does not mean that Tolga and Kymmy become someone else but that they have put on Christ as a new garment. Old garments must come off, at least for the baptism. So I will ask Nissim to help Kymmy to disrobe, and I will ask Sir Tambor and Koray to take Tolga's clothes off. You will have to take him into the river. Nissim will cover the boy's body with the oil I have brought, and Grigory will anoint Tolga. This oil represents the grace of the Holy Spirit, and during a smaller anointing later on, we shall pray that the Holy Spirit come upon them both. This whole service is a burial. It will be as though they will leave their sins in the river and will be cleansed and brought back to life again, which will be their destiny. Tolga, by the grace of God, will pass into the kingdom of God sooner than the rest of us, but he will not be dead, for his soul remains forever. I am trying to make this simple.

"One more thing before we start, and that is they will take a new name. Our tradition is that the new name resemble the old name because we don't stop being the same person. Tolga will be called Theodore, after the saint to whom our temple is dedicated, Saint Theodore the Commander. My son," he said to Tolga, "you shall meet him soon along with your guardian angel, who will bring you to the Lord Jesus.

"Kiymetli, God took your physical mother many years ago. Only he knows where she is now. But he is now giving you another mother, his very own mother, Mary, whom you heard so much about at Christmas time at Saint Davit's. Your new name will resemble the feast of her own departure to the heavenly kingdom, which we call in Greek 'Kimisis tis Theotokou' or the falling asleep of the Mother of God. You shall be called Kimisis. Your godfather Nissim will tell you all about it.

"Now let us begin. Right now, Tolga and Kymmy will turn their back on Satan, the evil one, and spit on him and all his wicked works." He said something in Greek and, when the time came, Nissim told them to turn and spit on Erlick. Kym did it with his usual vigor and enthusiasm. It was harder to get Tolga into position, and although he felt no pain, I could see that he was weakening by the minute. Kymmy was shivering, almost naked in the morning cold. Then they had to confess their faith in the Father, Son, and Holy Spirit. Nissim said the creed in Greek, trying to interpret phrase by phrase. Grigory said it in Slavonic and Nissim again in Greek.

Then Nissim and Grigory started to cover them with olive oil, and when they were finished, Nissim went into the water again. He motioned to Kymmy to come in and, taking him by the neck and legs, he lowered him into the water three times while the priest and the chanter sang sweetly.

Then it was Tolga's turn. Koray, Hazir, and I gently lifted the limp body of my brother and placed him in Nissim's arms. He also was dipped three times like Kymmy. When Tolga came up his hands, the only limbs he could move, were raised high, and he cried with tears, "Thank you, Jesus Khan! Thank you, Jesus Khan! Thank you, Jesus Khan!" I, who supported his shoulders, could barely hold him for his excitement and because of the oil on his body, he nearly slipped out of Nissim's arms. When we got to shore, Kymmy embraced him heartily and Grigory kissed him.

However it was not over. The priest paused and told us to lay him down. They were to be wiped down and dressed in their white robes. Apparently they were now born again. (I must say, Holy Father, I approached the whole thing rather cynically.) Father Tryphon had a small table in front of him on which there was a lit candle and nearby a stand where an incense burner was hanging, making the air fragrant. Father Tryphon gave Grigory four lit candles—one for Tolga, one for Nissim, who was emerging soaking wet from the stream, one for Kiymetli, and one for himself. The priest had only one cross, so the chanter gave his up for Tolga, though it seemed he did this with much regret.

"Now, beloved ones, it is customary to walk three times around the table. Grigory shall walk on Tolga's behalf. This symbolizes their first steps into the world as Christians, for this will be a walk with hazards and joys, defeats and triumphs, pain and consolation, until they make their final steps into the kingdom of heaven. I would like that all of you should make this journey, and and believe me, I shall pray for you each day that you join us in this walk."

I looked at Tolga, who wouldn't have much walking to do and saw streams of tears on a face shining with joy. I had to turn away and turn back to the solemn procession and sweet and heavenly music. Father led, swinging the censer, followed by Kymmy with Grigory and Nissim behind, and the chanter and the acolytes at the rear, one of whom lacked a white robe. Both were smiling. After that, they were anointed with oil on various parts of the body. The priest went over to Tolga, now Theodore, and fed him something from the golden box.

I was too upset to pay much attention. Everyone, beginning with the priest, kissed Kymmy and Tolga. I was the last. I could not understand why, but I felt angry, not at anyone, not at anything, after all everyone was happy. Perhaps I was angry with myself.

I found myself standing next to Nissim and Kymmy, who was taking off his white robe. Nissim, beautifully peaceful, was helping him to dress. Yanni and Christo came running toward us.

Kymmy said, "Thank you for your robe, Yanni. I hope it isn't too stained."

"It belongs to you now, Tatar boy. You will need it for your first communion. My *yaya* will make me a new one. Anyhow now you are Greek."

"No, I'm not." Kymmy responded, a little piqued. "Now I'm a Christian!"

"Yes, Tatar boy, you are a Christian!" Yanni said and hugged him affectionately. The boys pulled him away from us, playfully pushing and pulling.

Nissim laughed. I suppose I did too. "Our boy Kymmy has a special charisma. It will carry him a long way."

"A Greek word?" I asked.

"*Charisma*? Yes, it is. It means *graced* in Greek. I guess it would refer to a special touch from God that enables a person to attract and influence people. Tambor, you may not be aware of it, but you are such a person yourself. But let us go to Tolga, or rather to Theodore."

We saw the priest sitting on a horse blanket near my brother. He raised his hand to us to hold us back from approaching too fast. Obviously he wanted to talk to us before we got there. He arose quickly and came our way.

"Beloved ones," Father Tryphon began, "forgive me for failing to use the proper formalities. Forgive me most of all for treating you so suspiciously from the start."

"Father, you have no need to apologize to us," I said. "We are strangers and foreigners. We still have blood on our clothes from a battle last night. If we tell you what happened, you will not be able to lie to the authorities. That will get you into trouble. If you know nothing, you can plead ignorance. It would not please me to be the source of trouble to your wonderful community, who has shown such hospitality."

"Thank you, Lord Tambor, I appreciate your concern. When you see Theodore, do not be surprised at how altered he has become since his baptism. An infection from his wound has sent him into a fever as to be expected. I spend much of my life and ministry sitting beside the dying. I can recognize the symptoms. It is somewhat afternoon now. I will give him perhaps an hour or at the most two. He is already weak and refuses to eat, though he takes a bit of wine because his mouth is dry. Do not be concerned about what he says. He is in a state of grace, as we say, and is quite prepared to meet the Lord. He may seem to experience things, which we, in our rational mind, do not see. I know, sir, that you are a man of reason and would, of course, attribute whatever he is saying to his delirium. But they are very real to him and may in fact be very real. Our eyes and ears in this imperfect world often are blinded by the touch and feel of everyday life. But there are places in God's kingdom that we know not of. Listen to him, my sons. Open your hearts to what Theodore has to say, and you will share in his passing. Would you respect this?"

Nissim, of course, immediately agreed. I, on the other hand, hesitated to give my full assent, but after a little thought, I said that I would not judge.

Father Tryphon continued, "Then there is the matter of the burial, dear ones. We shall have to take care of that. Already our grave diggers are at work. Cremation is forbidden in our faith. But you will want to be away before the sun goes down and in haste lest the authorities pay an untimely visit. This will give you a good head start. You came in over the fields and paths. Go back the same way. I would suggest you stay clear of the larger roads. We shall do the funeral as soon as possible, but it is crucial that you be gone by then. Then we shall have no cause to tell lies. The newly baptized Theodore is one of our flock."

I was not pleased, but I recognized the wisdom in what he said. I said that I would take his weapons and armor. If he wanted the horse, he could keep it. I also offered him some gold, but he refused it without hesitation.

He did agree, however, to take the horse. "I know someone whose horse has died just recently. He needs one badly and I would give it to him."

Koray and Hazir beckoned us. Grigory was talking to Tolga in broken Tatar, but apparently we were the ones needed. Tolga interrupted Grigory, who made way for me. Koray was on Tolga's left, and Nissim and I knelt on the right. Tolga's face was covered in a thin film of sweat. He was hot to the touch. I wished Katya were here. He was trembling as though he were cold but only from the upper side which had not yet died.

"Oh, Tambor, my brother, please tell Father that I won't be home tonight. Mamma will miss me, but give her a kiss. I can't fight anymore. I'm too tired. No, I'm dying. Thank you, Tambor, for everything. Tell Chabuk he was a great sword master. And thank Bashina for teaching me well." I saw his eyes glaze over. "Who is that warrior over there?" he said, looking to where no one was.

Before I could say something stupid, Nissim asked quite seriously, "Could he be Saint Theodore, do you think?"

He *was* actually thinking. "Oh yes, he says he has come to take me home. No, not to Sopasi. Oh, he says he will bring me to the heavenly kingdom." I told the priest I would not judge, so I decided to treat it as though it were actually happening. Tolga continued. "Please some wine. I can hardly talk." Kymmy brought a cup to his lips. Tolga smiled and said to him, "We were baptized together today, weren't we? But you can't come with me for a long while yet." Again his eyes glazed over. "Who is that man with the flaming sword? Oh! That…that must be my angel? He is fighting some dark shadows."

He seemed to be able to talk to these visions without having to speak. He closed his eyes for a moment as though asleep and breathed heavily. When he opened his eyes, he said to Kymmy. "Mother Mary is sitting here. I don't think you can see her. She is very beautiful." At that point, he turned to me and said, "Thank you, brother. You have saved my soul." After a moment, he looked steadily ahead and declared, "She wants me to come to her. See? The Lady beckons me." And, raising both his hands, he exclaimed, "Please, warriors, help me to get out of this body." His arms immediately went limp, and his eyes no longer focused.

Koray brought Tolga's lifeless left hand to his lips and wept unabashedly. Tears streamed down Kymmy's face, and Nissim, who did not cry, put his arm around the boy to comfort him.

Grigory began to mumble prayers in Russian, and the priest, swinging incense, and his chanter began their solemn dirge while the boys with candles stood dutifully by. After the prayers were finished, the chanter went over to a large canvas bag and removed a bucket full of boiled wheat grains and a large loaf of bread. Everyone took a handful of wheat and some bread broken from the loaf and ate it quietly sitting on the grass.

That being done, the priest started packing up his gear. He again approached me and Nissim, with Hazir and Kokochu close by, and said, "We shall put a cross at the head of Tolga's grave and an inscription which will say: 'Theodore, a Christian, known as Tolga, a beloved brother and a mighty warrior. Memory eternal!' If some of your warriors can carry the body to the church, we would appreciate it. It is customary to have a prayer service on the eighth day and on the fortieth You must also remember the departed on the following year. We will do the services here, but if you are near a church, you can ask the priest to perform it. I will send your men back with a note that Kymmy was duly baptized and that he needs Holy Communion. I'm sorry, but it will be written in Greek. Come, lads," he said to Yanni and Christo, but they looked pleadingly at him. "Oh, all right, but be kind to Kymmy. Remember, he has lost a friend." They were kind. Seeing Koray alone, they went to him and kissed his hand. When they approached us, they kissed our hands also.

"Too bad we live so far away, lads. I would like to train you as warriors." I ruffled their hair and sent them away.

I turned to Hazir and Kokochu and asked them to be ready for a hasty departure. It then came to my mind that during all this activity, Kokochu had held back and participated little. I sort of knew that death might mean something different to Buddhists. I knew that funerals for them are long drawn-out events. Their burial customs as I mentioned before are very different. Perhaps we would talk about it later. I myself had much to ponder. Myself, I barely knew what had happened.

Our men returned with haste. I think the priest told them there was some urgency, so they obeyed. I was glad. I wanted to move on. The thought of those dead soldiers down the hill weighed on me. We were warriors; we needed to get back into shape. Eight or nine horses were added to our lot; the others had likely wandered off. I wouldn't complain, however. They had to stay with us and run. Erali and Dilaver said they were good at herding horses, and two of Hazir's boys joined them. I wanted Koray close to us; I needed to keep my eye on him. Of course, Nissim was at my side, but I asked Hazir and Kokochu to ride with Grigory. He had been quiet these days, and I wondered if he was feeling tired.

Just as we came, we were to fly back. I estimated we would ride the rest of the day and sleep tonight, merely because we had not slept at all last night. Then we would travel for two days, making sure we were well out of Trabzon territory. I was sure that we could be well into Rize before the authorities in Trabzon could alert the militia there.

After that, we would ride nonstop for two days, provided the moon would provide us adequate light at night. It would not be such a hazardous journey. You might find this remarkable, Father, perhaps unbelievable, but we are skilled horsemen, and in the old days, Tatar warriors could make more lengthy rides than that without food or sleep. But tonight, we would sleep.

I did not sleep well. I had a strange dream. Tonight, I saw three women sitting in front of a wide yurt, not close to each other. I did not approach them but stood back, wondering who they were. They were all holding bundles of rolled up felt. When Uyari saw me, she stood up and pointed her finger at me, and as the bundle fell to the ground, it unwound. My mother was the next to notice my presence. She stood up and held out her arms for me to rush into them, dropping her bundle. It did not unwind, and I did not run to her. Katya was the third. She stood up, still holding her bundle close to her breast. She walked slowly toward me and clasped my hand. However, she turned toward the east and a light shone on her face. I turned to see the source of the light and saw a beautiful gentle-featured woman holding my brother Tolga with her right hand, quietly leading him toward a shining disk of light. Tolga turned just for a moment and smiled at me and walked with the lady into the disc of light. Katya let go of my hand and walked back to where she had been sitting. Then I awoke. For a moment I almost believed I had seen Tolga entering the heavenly kingdom.

Koray lay to my right and Nissim to my left. The nights could be cold and somewhat damp, and since we slept in the open, we lay close together to maintain body heat. From the sound of Koray's breathing, I knew he was asleep; by the same reasoning, I suspected Nissim had awakened. He started to get up and touched me on the shoulder and went toward some trees to relieve himself. I joined him. We still spoke quietly so as not to disturb the others.

"Dreaming?" he asked.

"Not the same old ones. The old ones are almost old familiar friends. They still wake me up, but they don't cause so much fear. This one was different." I described it to him and ended up almost embarrassed. "You know I almost believed it."

"Why not? You told Father Tryphon you would keep an open mind and not judge. Why can't you accept this dream in the same way? Suppose it were true, brother, wouldn't you be happy for Tolga? Just think, you happened to be the one to whom he gave his last smile. Doesn't that touch you?"

"Yes! Yes! It makes a kind of sense, in a perverted way of course. But what about the women? What do they have to do with it?"

He gave his little crooked grin. "They're women," he said quietly, and I could see the twinkle in his eyes enhanced by the moonlight.

"What? What are you suggesting?"

"Look, Uyari has been hot for you for a long time. You're the only one who hasn't noticed it. She's not old, probably your mother's age."

"She's a mule bitten by a hornet!"

"But she's a woman. Then there's your mother. She reaches out but can't give you the kind of loving you need."

"The kind of loving I need? What makes you think I need woman's loving?" I was a little irritated.

"I suppose because I long for it myself. You don't know how I long for it."

"You'll be married to Mehtap within a year, brother, and in no time, you'll be rolling in pups. But there is no one waiting for me, Nissim. Katya is my father's concubine. Do you want me to end up like Kokochu barely escaping for my life?" I paused to think. "But you're right about one thing. There is a burning in my loins, a hunger which cannot be filled."

"Perhaps Dalgali will have prepared something or rather someone for you by the time you get back, after all he provided Marwa for Dikkatli. You are next in line."

"Well, Sir Wisdom, you didn't tell me about the other woman."

"Tambor, she is the true love of your life. Like Theodore, she will take you to your God. But she did not look at you, did she? That is because you have not yet abandoned your faulty wit and thrown yourself into the arms of faith as your brother did. But you did get a glimpse of her beauty, true?"

"Yes, well, the sky is now gray, but I don't know about you, I am looking forward to a taste of bread soaking up those greasy anchovies." The priest's wife had given some victuals to the men who brought Tolga's body to the church-yard for burial.

We could hear a cock crowing in the distance and saw Hazir and Kymmy stirring.

"All right, men. Let's get going. We won't be eating or sleeping for the next few days, so let's have a good breakfast, one which God has unexpectedly provided for us." I bent down to Grigory and shook him. "You are tired, my friend. I'm sorry to put you through this last ordeal."

"My dear son, whether I live or die, it's all in God's hands. What is important to me, young Tambor, is that I have never been so much alive as I have been these past few months. And I love you for it! Let's be on our way. Good morning, Sir Nissim, could you give me a hand with my things? I could do with some breakfast." Nissim reached down and gave him his hand to help him up.

Hazir came over. "Shall I make some tea, Tambor?"

"I think not, Hazir. Let's have some wine or ouzo. That will brace us for the trip back to Georgia." I said to all of them, "We'll ease off in a few days, men, and celebrate in Batumi, maybe before the camels come in." I saw a good challenge in their eyes and a hearty appetite. I was proud of them.

We rode and we rode, over the hills and valleys, across the streams, through the brush, six hours of the ride in the soaking rain. We didn't let up for almost two days and only then to revive our horses. There was little talk as we passed the jug of wine and then were on our way again. In eastern Rize, we stopped at a little town called Kukunat and found we were nearing the shore road, so we swooped a little farther south, hoping to reach Artvin, the main city in the province of the same name. This time, we didn't rush so heartily; I suppose we were tired, and we didn't want to overtax our steeds.

By that time, we were not so concerned about being followed, so we took some of the trails and roads and slept on the ground every night. We were not stopped by any military or policing troops; obviously strangers never posed a problem in these mountainous areas. But the hills were nothing like the mountains we traveled in coming here. When we got to the small city of Artvin, we rested half a day after a good night's sleep and pushed on alongside a river that led into Georgia directly to Batumi. We had made the trip in just over five days. There was a joyous welcome at our camp in the late afternoon after what the church calls the ninth hour. The camels would not arrive for another three days. Those we had left behind had prepared a grand feast.

It was not that they were completely ready for us, but they were prepared for the event. What *we* really wanted to do was sleep. The food was welcome though. The men had dug a pit and reserved a sheep at a local butcher for cooking over the coals. We were completely out of food although there was one jug of wine left. It had turned sweet and syrupy, I suppose because of being jostled around on the ride, but it was relaxing and was a pleasure to share with the others. Of course they demanded to hear all about the venture or mission, as Nissim called it. Of course they were deeply sorry for the death of Tolga and thoroughly amazed at the account of Tolga's baptism and funeral.

Kiymetli had his story to tell, and he did it with much fervor. It was also the first time he had actively engaged in battle and actually killed a few Turks. He said "three," so we gave him the silent benefit of the doubt. He would tell his version of the subsequent events when the camels came in, obviously wanting to impress the women. Yet in spite of his spirited story, he looked tired. After eating only a little, he fell asleep before the sun went down and, having been put in Hazir's small tent, didn't wake up until after noon. I insisted that Hazir indulge him. Hazir was pleased at seeing how much I loved the boy. I felt that because of Kymmy, Hazir's loyalty to me increased, and of course there was now a legitimate bond between Kymmy and Nissim, his godfather. Hazir confided in me somewhat later that he now felt that his sense of belonging had returned even if it was to a rag-tag troop of boys such as we were. I could see at the same time that he and Kokochu were building a friendship; of course they were about the same age. They were often engaged in congenial conversation

Old Grigory Yurevich Ureic caused me some concern. He was quiet; I found myself having to wake him up in the mornings.

He used to be one of the first ones up, imitating the sound of a Russian bugle's wake up call. I know that his venture into Turkish lands was tiring, but, although he had seemed enthusiastic by the battle, I surmised that the ride home must have exhausted him. He was not young, nor was he a Tatar, for we are accustomed to such rides, and I regretted that I didn't leave him with the camp at Batumi, though if I had but suggested it, I would never have heard the end of it. No, it was what he had wanted, and I could not have deprived him of the excitement. I came to love the old man. He had a true warrior spirit, which surprised me for a Russian soldier who would normally have to be paid for his military services. I would keep my eye on him.

We rested. It didn't take us long to recover. Good food, local wine, sunshine and water made us again active, and in no time, we were practicing our war games again. Erali and Dilaver were particularly anxious to train. They had also learned to respect Nissim and me. I could see that they were already becoming fine warriors. The Turkish incident made them a little more serious. I told them that they would probably never see their family again; however, they seemed only slightly sad. What I was surprised to discover was that they were much more excited about the trip to Falaka Sopasi. I knew that I would have to provide for them of course. Koray spent some time with them also, helping to train them and, no doubt, attempting to heal his loneliness although he had many younger brothers. I no longer felt the need to watch him so closely although I had likewise become genuinely fond of him.

Among us all, we had developed a true bond, one which really has never been broken. Even to this day, Reverend Father, sitting here in my novice's robes, any one of these men would respond to any call or request I might make, and I am sure they would find the same ease to confide in me as they did in those days.

Even Hazir's men would sit down around the fire and feel free to laugh and joke and rehash the events of our escapades.

I had been just a bit concerned that I was putting too much responsibility on him. On the contrary, Hazir told me later, my dependence on him was a great honor and increased his sense of belonging. His boys at first seemed somewhat stand-offish, but there was a reason for that: they assumed that I was a snob and that was because I didn't do the felting. After all, Hazir's tribe was in charge of the yearly event.

I was so embarrassed when this slipped out that I swore they were all going to have to train *me*, though I doubted we would be back in time since the felting would have been done well before we returned for Saban-Tui. Hazir explained Lady Yerinde's involvement in these arrangements. They were very good-natured about it, and the laughter eased the tension between our two clans and affirmed the bond. I had to congratulate the young warrior who had the daring to bring it up. (Of course Mother would hear of it.)

The one person I really worried about was Nissim. I had never seen Nissim fret before. He was always the model of patience and faith. Nissim, I noticed, was most himself when he was with Kymmy instructing him in the faith, which he said was his job.

When Nissim was not with Kymmy he made himself useful by demonstrating the use of the topor, promising that he would get one for anyone who was interested in being trained. It was at mealtimes and especially in the evenings when his mood was most obvious; even the others noticed it and tried to bring him out of it. He would smile and laugh a bit and perhaps even joke, but then he would sink again into silence. He would constantly look toward the south and for any sign of camel travel. An occasional caravan would immediately catch his attention, leaving him disappointed. His eyes were on the shore road, and his ears were on our little roadway. These were the longest three days we had ever experienced especially since, for all that we knew at the time, it could have lasted up to a week.

On the morning of the third day after eating, I pulled Nissim aside and told Kymmy that he would not have lessons on faith this morning. We walked down toward the marshes where we were surrounded by the sounds of spring wildlife, hoping that the pleasantness would open him up. He knew that I was concerned about him.

"Well, where are they, Tambor? What if they've been captured and taken? How would we ever know? We could wait here for days for a word, and then we would have to go back and try to find out what happened for ourselves. That would open us to investigation, don't you see? Then everyone would be in trouble, and it would have been my fault."

"You don't think these thoughts haven't crossed my mind too, except for being *your* fault? I would have blamed myself for bad planning. But I have to tell you, my brother, since we started this mission, I have trusted your God to take care of all the details. Tengri couldn't do it. Somehow this venture would have been too personal for him. But your God, your Jesus Khan, follows us around and won't let us out of his sight. Isn't he with your mother even now? Isn't he guiding the Persians at this moment wherever they are? He's not my God, Nissim. I trust him because you trust him!"

He actually laughed. He laughed that low, soft, deep laugh, which revealed much more than humor. "Tambor, you should be the theologian"—a word I didn't understand—"and the one teaching Kymmy. But you know, my friend, I am going to make my confession to you right now, and I am going to depend on you to pray for me for God's mercy."

"So now I shall be your Father confessor, is that it?"

"Yes...will you? I feel so far away from God and that grieves me more than anything else."

"Well, go on."

He was now the shy Nissim I used to know. He looked at me once and looked down. He looked so ashamed I was astounded.

"Tambor, I have sinned. It is true that I was glad that Mother and Livvy were freed, and indeed I glorified God for it. However, when I look back at the ambush on the hill, it shames me to think how vengeful I was. I did not want to kill Fahesh. That would have been too just and right, too easy. I wanted him to walk home exhausted just to have to wait for his father to return from Nicomedia. I enjoyed basking in his fear and the loneliness of the house as he waited. I gloated over imagining his father's face and the rage the affair would produce. Oh yes, there would be hatred for me, I would enjoy that too. But what really teased my imagination would be enjoying the thought of his father's anger and disdain for Fahesh, for letting me get away with it. Maybe I even added a beating! I gloated over the curses he shouted that would damn him, when I should have taken pity him and prayed for him. To have killed him would have been merciful!

"I am so ashamed, so ashamed even to be Kiymetli's godfather with this stain on my soul. Oh how I want to be purified and cleansed from this sin. How I want to start anew. It will be weeks before I can see a priest. You are the only one whom I trust enough to hear this."

All of a sudden, it was silent. He was silent. I was silent. I didn't know what to say. I lifted my finger to my lips to advise him to say no more while I took some time to think. All this would never have occurred to me. We had wrought a deed of justice. All the feelings he described would never have bothered me. But they made sense to *him*, and actually they made sense to me, at least for the moment, in the silence of the morning. It then came to my mind what Father John had once said as we were meditating on the warrior icons in his home. He was like Saint George; Nissim was battling the dragon within his own soul, and I was seeing him struggle with it. I had done my part in dealing with the injustice without. My part was almost over; all we needed was for the Persians to return with the women, and I would have done what I was destined to do. I was being like Saint

Demetrius. I couldn't believe it! But Nissim needed a priest; it was not me that he needed. Nevertheless I had to reassure him. I couldn't let him stay in this state.

I turned to Nissim and put my hands on his shoulders and stared up into his huge doleful brown eyes and said, "My brother and my friend, Nissim, if there is one thing, and one thing alone, that you have taught me about your Khan Jesus Christ is that he is always merciful and will forgive your sins—shh, shh, don't say anything yet. It seems to me that all you need is to recognize your sin and confess it before him. Isn't that what you have always told me? Let him provide the priest. He's the khan. True, you were not merciful to Fahesh, but he will still be merciful to you. If I, an arrogant pagan, can trust him, surely you can trust him."

Then I began to pray. I wasn't even serious; it was almost just a tease, but what came out of my mouth scared me. "Oh Great Khan Jesus Christ, you know I don't pray, but Nissim needs some help, and I am the only one here to do it. Please forgive him his sin just as you forgave him once before when he needed it and I forgave him. And if he needs help forgiving Fahesh, I will pray for Fahesh, after all he's just a silly boy. I am being selfish about this, but I really don't want to see Nissim suffering like this, for no other reason but that he loves you and he wants to do right… and…he is my friend." I then looked at him and asked, "Did I do it right? Do you think he heard me?" And then I felt stupid.

He was grinning at me, that silly crooked smile of his. He said, "You couldn't have done better, my brother. I love you, Tambor. I will always be loyal to you." Nothing more was said, and as the sounds of the marshlands returned, we could hear the screech of Tetik's beautiful falcon over our heads.

REUNION

For whoever does the will of my Father in heaven
is my brother and sister and mother.

—Matthew 12:50 (NKJV)

We had barely stopped talking when the beauty of the scene was interrupted by a kerfuffle coming, it seemed, from the top of the hill. At first, I thought the camp was under siege. Since we were both unarmed, in the panic of the moment, we cautiously slid into the underbrush in order to figure out what was going on without being seen.

Surely the camels have not arrived, I thought.

I was not expecting them for two or three more days. Of course, they had a day's head start on us and we had been here three days now. But I was splendidly wrong. Through the brush, we could see the camels and the camel masters greeting and laughing with our men. I had not realized how knit a group we had become, and I was pleased at our camaraderie. I waved Nissim over to me with a hush just to observe the goings-on. I knew Nissim wanted to rush out and join them. The ladies had dismounted but were still in their burkas. One was looking around frantically, and I presumed that she was Nissim's mother, Anna Maria. Moussa was also still in his burka and was helping Koray with some of the supplies.

"Let's go!" I said and walked out into the clearing.

Livvy was the first to notice us and cried out. "Nissim! Oh, Mother, here he is. Nissim!" At this encounter, she was actually shy as she saw her handsome brother standing before her. I could not see her face for the veils, but she drew her hand modestly toward her breast.

"He's so tall, Mother, and so strong-looking. And this must be Sir Tambor his friend…our friend." She then addressed me, "Sir Tambor, may we greet my brother?"

I smiled. "Only if you let Nissim take off those dreadful burkas."

"Mother," Nissim said quietly. He lifted the veil from her face. I was astounded at how beautiful she was. She was much younger than I had expected although I should have realized that she would have been my mother's age or Tashi's. Her raven black hair fell down her back and her deep blue eyes rivaled the color of the sea. She said nothing but kissed him on both cheeks. She turned to me and bowed to me, kissing my hand.

Livvy was about to throw hers off, but Nissim stopped her. He lifted her burka slowly and let it slide down her back. Livvy was no less beautiful with dark brown wavy hair the color of her eyes. At fifteen years of age, she had a maturity about her which she had earned by much suffering. But I could also see the sparkle in her eyes and sensed that touch of playfulness I could see in Timov. Nissim was serious like his mother. *What a beautiful family*, I thought. They were a different people, a different race.

Livvy approached and kissed me as she had kissed Nissim.

"Forgive me, Sir Tambor. You do not know how grateful we are, and…how much we love you."

I was touched and a little embarrassed, and I realized we had an audience. Everyone was looking on.

"And who is this sweet damsel hiding behind her curtain?" I addressed Moussa. Not even the Trabzon boys knew what to expect.

With a great flourish, Moussa threw off his burka and made a deep bow and came up with a huge smile. "Greetings, warriors! Pleased to be at your service." He was greeted with astonishment and a few even reached for their weapons.

I intervened of course. "This, my friends, is Moussa, who is servant to the ladies. We came to rescue Sir Nissim's family, and we have rescued him too. Bid everyone welcome, brothers!"

They were greeted with a cheer.

"Now let's eat!"

Anna Maria approached and modestly asked me if there were a place where they could freshen up. (I had never heard the phrase before.) Nissim took them to the nearby stream where there was a shallow pool with icy water where they could bathe and change their clothes. I knew that with the presence of women, our life would begin to change. I hoped that the camaraderie I had been observing would not become strained. In spite of their years of slavery and subservience, these were ladies of refinement. They could, like Katya, probably read and write. I always experienced some envy in the presence of this kind of advantage, and as with most negative feelings, I forced myself to conquer them or suppress them.

Now we were going home. For myself, I was enormously excited. We all were. The ladies would come to a new home far away from the pain and grief they had experienced over the past few years. They had been reunited to their long lost son and brother Nissim, a daily more joyful experience. Nissim and Anna Maria's natural reserve were breaking down, and laughter came from all quarters. Of course we were aware that they were yet to be reunited with Timov, and we were all very much aware that one, very important person, was missing.

The men, of course, had to curb their tongues at times and refrain from off-color comments. They were lonely for the presence of women; the months of all male companionship had been wearying them. I had known it for a long time.

Grigory Yurevich, with all his apparent disdain for his old woman, was an absolute charmer with the ladies. I could see that Moussa was somewhat put off at Grigory's attention. I spoke to Moussa about it and urged him not to make a fuss. I explained my concern about the old officer's possible health problems, and I pointed out that the ladies' presence had renewed some of his vigor. I asked him to accept the fact that he too would be having a new way of life with us and gave him the option to make his own way if he should so choose. At this he grew sullen, and I had to assure him that he would always have a family with us. He was of the same generation as Hazir and Kokochu, and I would often see them seeking each other's companionship. This included sharing recipes, and the three of them made it quite clear to Anna Maria that *they* were in charge of food.

This gave Livvy and Anna Maria a good opportunity to get to know Nissim again and me for the first time. Of course Kiymetli took his godson's rights to include himself in the family. This boy could charm a mountain lion. His rendition of the events at Trabzon—we now called it the mission—was fascinating to the women, perhaps even horrifying to them.

"Just imagine," they would say, "a twelve-year-old Tatar boy killing all those Turks! Incredible!"

Of course, Nissim would gently give a perhaps more accurate rendition of the events at the estate without diminishing the great heroics of the boy warrior. But Kymmy's account of the baptism was touchingly beautiful. He saw so much more in the ceremony than I could have imagined. His account of Tolga's, or rather Theodore's passing and funeral was extraordinary. It was so perceptive that it brought the women to tears. Even I almost believed it.

Even the telling of the event was not exactly without humor.

"Can you imagine that when my godfather lowered me into the water three times, all my sins came out of me and flowed down the stream and into the sea. I hope they didn't kill too many of the fish!"

I loved that boy. I couldn't imagine him having enough sins to kill a fly let alone a school of fish. But we all laughed, including old Grigory Yurevich, who needed a little translation.

Kiymetli figured out that since Grigory was Theodore's godfather for the Baptism, "That must make you my god uncle!"

"That's true, my lad. That's true!" I was glad to see him happy.

"I must tell you something too," Anna Maria said, "and I do hope Moussa doesn't mind, but I have recently become a godmother. Two years ago, wasn't it, Moussa?" He nodded. "When I could get away, Moussa used to take me to Saint Theodore's Church for liturgy since it was so close by. I know Father Tryphon and confess to him. Well, he baptized Moussa across the road from the house and in the sea. It was Yanni's father, Tasso, who oiled Moussa since it would not have been proper for a woman to do so."

"I was brought up as a Christian in Ethiopia," Moussa explained, "but I had turned my back on my faith although I absolutely refused to accept Islam. While the Ethiopian Church is similar to the Greek Orthodox, they fail in one thing. They do not believe that Jesus Christ was fully man. According to them, Jesus took flesh of the Virgin Mary, but he never took upon himself human nature. We Orthodox believe that Jesus is fully God and fully man, one person with two natures. The Armenians who live just south of here believe like the Ethiopians. We call them monophysites. The Greeks, the Georgians, and the Russians all believe in the two natures of the Lord and belong to the same church."

"So when I wanted to make my confession, Father Tryphon said I needed baptism. Since I had been so bitter toward the Turks for having mutilated me, I thought I could never be saved." Moussa then turned to Nissim and said, "It was your mother and sister who brought me to repentance. When I saw how patiently and faithfully they endured their humiliation, I became ashamed of my hatred and bitterness. I am convinced that neither of these two remarkable women bore a trace of anger or malice toward their oppressors, nor was there a touch of resentment in their souls. Your mother would often urge me to turn to God and ask for forgiveness and urge me to forgive Mehmet Pasha who, she said, was doing only what was required of him to do by Turkish custom. So after a year or so of your mother's gentle urgings, I was baptized in the Black Sea. My sins were so foul and smelled so rotten they must have sunk a few battleships before they could get to harbor." He slapped Kymmy playfully on the back of the neck, and everyone laughed except Kymmy.

After a pause, the young warrior looked up at Moussa and asked, "What do you mean by the Turks mutilating you? You don't look mutilated."

"Well, friends, how do I answer this lad's question?" Moussa looked around for advice.

I caught Hazir's eye before I attempted to answer Kymmy's question. After a brief moment, Hazir raised an eyebrow in assent.

"If we are concerned about our companion's youth," I said, "we will have to consider that Kymmy has had his first experience as a warrior and has killed a few enemies. Perhaps he is not too young to know the truth. Moussa, if you are willing to speak, then go ahead. I appreciate your discretion however. I must say that in our land, such an offence would end in death rather than mutilation. That is an unlikely punishment for a crime."

"Well, young Kymmy, I told you that I was a great sinner. I was a governmental official to my emperor and frequently made trips to Trabzon, which is located on what many people are calling the Silk Road the one on which the camel masters have brought me and the ladies, on the north shore of Anatolia. I used to stay at the home of Mehmet Pasha as a businessman and a guest in his house. While there, I had an affair with one of his relatives, his wife's niece, who attended her at the summer estate. When we were found out, she was sent back to her father in disgrace, with no opportunity of landing a husband. As for me, the Pasha removed from my loins the twin emblems of my sex and fed them to his dogs in my presence. I was then retained as his slave and eventually the steward of the summer estate. Word was sent back to my family that I was dead, and as far as I am concerned, I was. But I am no longer in despair, for I have been devoted to Lady Anna, as I call her. Livvy was like my little girl although she is now a beautiful young lady now." And turning to Nissim, he added, "I also remember you and Timov as boy slaves in Trabzon. It was well known how abusive the Pasha was toward you. Of course, I could never tell you where the ladies were, and I avoided any opportunity to get into trouble lest what I knew might accidentally slip out. However, mercifully, because of Lady Anna and Livvy's prayers, I have once again been given a chance to find my soul. And I have been blessed to be able to help them escape."

Kymmy held him by the arm and said quite simply, "Then I shall pray for you too."

That being said, we discussed our trip home. Hazir, with his incredible efficiency, informed the company how long it would take to disassemble the camp and presented us with what we would be requiring. We discussed what route to take back and whether we would go back to Astrakhan in the hopes of rejoining Dalgali. I suspected that my father had found this year's trip quite profitable and would likely have made his way home a little earlier, having spent the winter in Astrakhan and not in frosty Kazan as in other years. We had started the trip a month later this year because of the Mikhailov incident, so it was a shorter trip for him. The Kalmyk situation also put a wedge in his normal activities. No, my father would be long gone if we made our way to the city of Astrakhan. It seemed sensible to travel along the Kura River into Azerbaijan all the way to the Caspian Sea and avoid the mountain pass that we had come through. It might be a somewhat longer route, but it would be easier considering there were women with us.

Nissim had informed me privately that the great forty-day fast preceding Pascha (Easter) would be beginning soon and that, although he would love to stay in the capital for the feast with Father John, he preferred to be well on his way home before the fast. Pascha would be late that year, he informed me. He knew that his family would want to fast. Father John had told him that, according to the rules of the Church, travelers need not fast, but he suspected his mother would anyway. He decided that it would impose too much of a burden on the company if he fasted. We really didn't have enough grain products stored to be able to do it. There would not be crops enough to trade as the inhabitants of the land would also be low at this time. He hoped that he would be able to make his confession at Saint Davit's Monastery. It was like making a request, but of course I would never deny him; besides, Kymmy needed to make his first communion. I also wanted to make a stop at Tbilisi.

It was also important to be home well before Saban-Tui in June. We warriors needed much practice. We could fight, that's true, but we needed practice in our technique. Dilaver and Erali needed to see a real Saban-Tui. Apparently their communities got together for the sacrifices and the party, but the games were mostly for the young folk and were not taken too seriously. Nissim would be entering for the first time this year, that is if the khan approved. I was amazed at how far away last year's celebration was. Last year, he carried my gear to the fields; this year he would enter as a fully equipped warrior. We had both changed. I think that in that year, both of us grew up. We had lost our boyhood; we were both men.

Amid all the excitement, there was one person who lacked much enthusiasm. I suppose that the reality of going back north had finally hit Kokochu. Nissim and I made a point of walking with him one evening by the sea. He liked to bathe his back in the salt water as he felt that it was beneficial to his wounds, which had basically healed. He said that his wounds no longer stung, which was a good sign. These days, whenever I felt the need to be personal with any of the company, Nissim accompanied me. The reason for this was that Nissim often had a lot of insight, and besides, it covered me against being misquoted or even misunderstood.

"This is something you are going to miss, my friend. Of course the Caspian is somewhat salty although not so much in Astrakhan or Kalmykia. The Volga was not salty." I was only quoting my father. I had no direct knowledge of this or much of anything else, to be quite honest. But I was learning.

"It seems I don't really need it so much," he said. "I feel that I have been healed."

"Yes, it looks like the scars have healed over," Nissim said, rubbing a hand over his back. "You are blessed that an infection never set in. Perhaps the sea water attended to that."

I risked being blunt. "Forgive me for intruding in your private thoughts, but you seem a little withdrawn these days. I take it you are a little anxious about the trip home. You seem to lack the enthusiasm of the rest of us."

"Forgive me for sounding patronizing, my young leader," he remarked. "But what makes you such a good leader, among other things, is your awareness of the personal needs of your men. I am sure Nissim will agree with me. But you are right. Your arrow has struck the heart. You don't know how much I have enjoyed these past few months. The experience has renewed my manhood. Being amongst you young warriors has reminded me of the innocence of my own youth when I used to make raids on your people." He laughed. "The Nogay and the Kalmyks may be enemies, but we are much the same. We are dwellers of the steppes, we live on our horses, we fight fiercely, our language is much the same, and we both bear the heritage of the great khan from whom both our leaders are descended."

We all agreed. He went on. "But of our whole troop, I am the only one who has to deal with enemies. I am a stranger to lower Kalmykia, so that does not worry me, but we can't avoid my people along the Volga. Then after that ordeal, I will have to bow my head to a suspicious and perhaps hostile Akilli Khan."

I interrupted, "My friend, I put no chains on you. You offered yourself as bondsman freely. You have fought with us, even for us, and we have shared much together. But you may leave us if you wish. I can release you from your bonds—"

"No no no no! That's not what I mean. What could I do here? I do not know the Georgian tongue. Even if I went back to the Turks, what would I do there? I could become a blacksmith. I could work in the fields. No, that is not what I want. I am a warrior, brothers. The Turks do not need warriors. They have soldiers and military academies. You can see that I am better off with you. Our way of life is the same. But I am a nobody, an enemy to my own people and an enemy to my friends. Don't misunderstand me, I am not wallowing in self-pity. I am merely facing reality and taking my chances."

"I understand you, my friend. But I want you to take your chances with a lighter heart. None of your people will challenge you while under the protection of the sons of Dalgali. Dalgali, my father, would see that his promises to the Chief Ubashi would be fulfilled, and you and your Khan know that. As for Akilli Khan, no one can tell what he would do, but he will be just. That is for certain."

Nissim spoke. "You have no idea how terrified I was when Tambor brought me to the khan for the first time. I was a slave, a Greek, a total stranger. By rights, Tambor could free me, but only the khan had the right to accept me amongst his warriors. But he did, Kokochu. He is a most remarkable man. Don't fret. Be at peace. Be happy with us and consider, like my own family, that you are going home."

"That I will," he said, "with my deepest gratitude. But what I will probably do is fret perhaps a little more cheerfully."

There had not been much time or even opportunity to buy gifts for my family, but now that we were at leisure, I decided to go into the city of Batumi. I thought I would ask Nissim and Livvy to go with me .

There were a few city folk in the shop, called Aristides, when we arrived, and we endured their recognition that we were strangers. Xenophon, the owner, was a round fellow, slightly balding but with a short wiry beard. He was delighted when Nissim and Livvy spoke to him in Greek. Xenophon explained to Nissim that every month, ships come in from Istanbul and even as far away as Venice with many items from the west. The shop had recently received a shipment from Venice, a city in Italy, containing many items from Europe.

Xenophon showed me something from France; I had no idea what he was talking about or where these places were. The object seemed like a silver plate, which was carved with two birds called peacocks. There were small green, blue, and yellow stones placed in the enormous tails of these birds. There was a handle attached to it also made of carved silver.

When I asked him what it was used for, he looked somewhat confused, and handing it to me, he turned it over. I saw myself in a mirror for the second time in my life. It took me by such surprise that I almost dropped it. The mirrors at home were of polished brass, so I had never really seen myself so clearly. I smashed the last mirror I saw at Mikhailov, but this time I looked at myself with fascination. I had always made jokes about how handsome I was, but I never really knew whether I was or not. Seeing such a clear reflection caused me to question how much I felt I was a stranger to myself. I was a handsome man, a typical Tatar, I suppose. I could see some resemblance to Chabuk and much more to my mother. I was wide of brow narrowing to a beardless chin with a small growth of hair over my lip. There were also the scars left by the wolf attack. I had always pulled my black hair back straight and had it tied in a braid down my back. I didn't cut my hair or shave my head as seemed to be the going fashion; Nissim or Timov had always braided it for me and kept it even. But what really took my attention, as you can well imagine, were my green eyes. They were intense, deep green, and unnerving. I had never seen anything like them. I wanted to turn away.

Nissim saw my reaction and responded immediately. "This would make a beautiful gift for your mother." He took it from me.

That made me snap out of the spell immediately. "You're right," I said exhaling slowly. I realized I had been holding my breath. "What about you, Nissim? Take a look at that beard of yours. It needs a trim."

"Moussa can do that," Livvy said. "He was the Pasha's barber at the summer house."

"I have a fine set of scissors and comb with a razor," Xenophon piped up. "It is very fashionable to shave the face in Europe. Maybe you would like to see it."

"Well maybe. I'll take the mirror if I can get a good price." I had no idea what Europe was all about but was too embarrassed to confess it because the others obviously did.

When the shopkeeper made his offer, I commented, "At a price like that that's just about all I could buy. You would make more of a profit to lower the price and interest me in some other items as well."

Xenophon smiled and nodded. "Perhaps, you should make your choices, master, and then we shall discuss price." I also smiled and nodded.

I finally decided on a silver locket for Natasha in which there was an icon of the Virgin Mary. Although I would have bought the world for Katya, I decided upon something in keeping for my father's concubine, namely a pair of carnelian earrings set in filigree and a matching pendant. I felt that the carnelian (that's what they called it) would perfectly set off her golden red hair. Nissim nodded his approval.

Nissim saw something he wanted for Mehtap. It was a natural white dress made out of a fabric called Egyptian cotton. It was not as fibrous as the wool we were famous for and not as smooth as silk. But it was soft and supple. It had full sleeves tied tightly together at the wrists by a strip of what was called crochet in intricate patterns. The same pattern was repeated by a belt around the waist and for about two measures from the floor. The collar had the same crochet pattern in a bib at the neck. Livvy said it was a Greek garment and that the crochet was excellent.

On the wall, I saw a musical stringed instrument. It was different from any of the local village instruments I was used to. Seeing my interest, Livvy asked to see it. It had a round pear-shaped back in dark-colored wood and the front was a flat piece of pale wood with a hole in the middle. Apparently it was called an *oud* and was from southern Turkey. Livvy strummed upon it and quietly sung a strain of melody. We had plucking instruments similar to it back home, but the oud was soft and deep. It could be loud, but it never lost its softness.

"It's a good one, Tambor. It is well tuned and has been played before," Livvy concluded. "Do you know anyone who can play it?"

"Yes, my brother Dalgin. I doubt that he as ever heard of an oud, but he can pick up anything and turn it into music."

We bought a few other things for a few other people until we were satisfied. In the long run, our purchases were successful. We haggled a bit over the total price but finally came to a reasonable settlement. Xenophon was ecstatic and begged us to come back to Batumi. Actually I was pleased that there was enough money left for Nissim to purchase a topor for Chabuk and for me a beautifully embroidered leather pouch for Dalgali from the storehouse at Cherny Yar where we stopped on our way home. Konstantine Alexandrovich was away at the time, but Captain Yakov Varisovich was delighted to open the weapons room.

I did not want to use any of the money the monks gave me since I had a special purpose for it. Yet even at that, I still had enough left over. I had entrusted Hazir with the money for the supplies, and it seemed he was scrupulous with it. He preferred that we hunt or hawk for our meat. This also provided a diversion for our boys. But we splurged on some of the tropical fruits that

Batumi offered, like dates and figs. We bought a small barrel of black olives and almost a dozen large fruits called coconuts which came from those strangely shaped trees called palm trees, which grow all their branches and leaves at the top. These coconuts contain a sweet and succulent milk. They were all eaten up by the time we reached home, so no one believed us when we told the tribe about them except Katya and Dalgali. We left the city with mixed feelings; we were on our way home with anticipation, but we were also saying good-bye to an exciting experience and a successful sojourn.

While we enjoyed the warm spring-like weather on the coast, once we got into the mountains, we hit dark clouds and cold rain for much of the trip to Tbilisi. There was even some snow on the hills, and I think I remember some snowfall. We did not stay at the mountain monastery of Khashuri for more than a day but pressed on. Nor did we intend to visit the sacred city of Mtskheta except for the fact that Grigory took ill. We made our camp near a little village on the outskirts of the city. This just confirmed my suspicion that he had been ailing for quite some time. The trip through the mountains and the wet weather finally weakened him, and he succumbed to a fever. The ladies opened their yurt to him, and Anna Maria tried to communicate with him in their language which she knew better than Nissim did. Kym stayed with him and slept next to him, trying to comfort him. Grigory was the closest thing he had to a grandfather. I was concerned that whatever illness the old man had would affect Kymmy, but he was a strong boy and resisted any infection.

The women had some knowledge of herbs and remedies and scoured the mountains and fields looking for familiar plants in an unfamiliar terrain. Nissim thought that we should search out a priest and went to the local church, hoping for someone who could speak Russian or Farsi. The priest at the local church spoke some church Greek and directed Nissim and Erali to another church where they found a priest named Father Yaroslav who was actually Russian. He was part of the Russian mission to Georgia, basically a political ruse. Though the priest was encumbered with many duties and complained about them all the way to our camp, he was very consoling to Grigory and heard his confession. After praying for Grigory and making sure he was rested, he confided in us that he felt the old man would not pull through.

"Give him some sweet red wine to kill the pain and help him breathe. Vodka will cause him to choke. I will make some preparations to bury him in our churchyard."

"That is awfully kind of you, Father," Nissim said. "All this will take a lot of time away from your burdensome schedule."

"Ach! My son, it's no trouble at all. It is a joy to send such a repentant soul to his Heavenly Father. He will die with a heart full of love for you his companions and especially for you Knyaz Tambor. Next to God, he respects you. He has forgiven everyone who has wronged him and wants to see his Theodore."

"Oh, yes. That is his godson recently baptized."

"He will not need to see me from here on, but I shall likely see him within a week. His grandson will take this hard. He stayed by the old man during the confession. I let him stay since he told me he didn't speak Russian."

"It's true," Nissim said. "He is *my* godson."

I took it hard. As soon as the priest started to leave, I said to Nissim, "See if you can get some wine from the village on your way back. Dilaver, go with Erali and Sir Nissim. You should be back by nightfall."

I didn't want to see anyone, but I didn't want it to be so noticeable. I mounted Onyx and went in the opposite direction, not looking back. I rode along the river for about half an hour and turned up a side road away from the river into a wooded area. I passed some farm houses and paused to let a flock of sheep, a shepherdess, and her children pass by. I rode on but more slowly. I realized that I was basically unarmed with only a short sword at my thigh and my dagger in my belt. It would not be wise to get lost.

A little farther ahead, I came upon a little shrine in the woods. There was a life-size wooden crucifix in front of the shrine with what looked to be a roof perched upon it. The shrine itself behind the cross looked like a half a hut with one wooden wall. The wall and its little roof supported three icons. In the middle was the Virgin Mary, perhaps a little more severe-looking than others I had seen. The icon on the right depicted an older man with gray hair and a red robe which, in retrospect, I would identify as Saint Nicholas. The one on the other side of the Virgin was definitely Saint George. No one needed to tell me that. I dismounted.

I walked over to the icon and started talking to him. Afterward I felt like an idiot, but at that moment, it seemed the most natural thing to do.

I said, "What is it with you, people? You just don't take death seriously. The old man is at the point of death, and the damn priest treats it like a wonderful experience, an enviable experience." I was angry. "Look at you and your friend Demetrius. Both of you are murdered, and everyone celebrates it. The priest says Kymmy will take it hard, but give the boy a few hours, and he will be seeing a vision of Grigory being dragged off by angels. Just where are you coming from? Death is a serious business. It is the end of everything. You can go to the house of Erlick to see your ancestors, but it's *not* pleasant! Once you're there, that's it, nothing else! I don't want it, nor do I want any dreamy delusion about going to a place far beyond Tengri, and I'm not sure that Tengri even exists except as an idea."

The evening mist was swirling around my feet, which were already dampened by the wet grass. I could smell some fragrant flowers somewhere and a few squirrels chased each other up a tree, interrupting the sweet song of some lovely evening songbird. I did not feel alone although there was no physical presence nearby. I walked over to the cross, and as I looked up to the figure upon it, a cold chill ran up my back. There, juxtaposed upon the figure of Jesus, was my grandfather looking upon me. I must have been dreaming! I could hear him saying, "Avenge me, Tambor! Avenge me!" But as the true figure on the cross came back into my view, I also heard the words of Jesus, saying, "Forgive them, Father, for they don't know what they are doing." Nissim told me once that Jesus said these words on the cross

Fear! That's what it was. Not fear of the Kalmyks or Turks. Not fear of battle or blood. It was fear of something nameless and unidentifiable. My grandfather's face was familiar, not friendly; in fact, it was hostile and demanding. But the face of Jesus was full of compassion and grief, a sadness that I seemed to know deep down inside of me. It too was familiar. As in my dream, I imagined I was struck by that arrow. I was falling, falling, falling! I called out, "Nissim! Nissim!" But I had sent him miles away, and I was alone.

I had to get back to camp. I turned from the scene shaken. Onyx, who was grazing in the lush moist growth, lifted his head and looked at me, wisely inviting me to mount him. I took one more look at the face of Jesus and turned around. I needed to go home.

The sun was setting behind my back, and I could see my shadow, long and drawn, ahead of me. The sky had cleared; the sun was red. It would be a good day tomorrow, at least in terms of the weather. Nissim and the squires had returned, and there was a bustle around the yurt where Grigory was lying. The women were in and out fussing over the old man. Nissim had brought back some wine, and the old man was sitting up and talking to Kuru and Vishtaspa. I was too tired and overwrought to bother about the fuss although I would normally try to keep order.

"Ah, there you are, my knyaz. No one seemed to know where you were." Grigory had been speaking Tatar for quite some time.

"You look like you are feeling better, Officer Grigory." I did not want him asking questions.

"I had a good rest after the priest left and woke up feeling much better. I am sorry to have slowed you down."

"Think nothing of it, my friend. If you need the rest, you deserve it. I see Kymmy has been taking good care if you."

"He keeps me warm when the chill comes upon me, Knyaz. He's a good boy. There, lad, thank you." Kymmy had handed him a glass of wine. "Nissim traveled far to get this excellent brew. I feel so much better, my captain. Pour a glass for Sir Tambor, Kymmy."

Grigory died that night in his sleep. Anna Maria woke Kymmy up in the morning to find Grigory Yurevich lying there motionless. Kymmy cried openly and without restraint upon the body of the old soldier until Anna Maria took him in her arms and let him cry it out.

There was no party this time. We were all saddened; few words passed our lips except those necessary. Hazir came to Nissim and me and asked how far away Father Yaroslav's church was and suggested that we break camp, take Grigory to the temple to have the old soldier buried, and from there, move on. Nissim said that the parish church was close enough to the countryside that our company would not be a large intrusion.

Father Yaroslav was prepared for us and showed us where the grave had been dug. We all paid our respects to Captain Grigory Yurevich Ureic and prepared to leave. Father suggested that we remove his shoes and hat, but I told him that Grigory wanted to be buried with his boots on. I did take his gray lambskin hat and his weapons, however, which I would take to his sons. Father Yaroslov refused to take any money for his services but suggested that we give alms to the poor. We had many opportunities on our way home. The congregation fed us before we left with the traditional pancakes called *bliny* that the Russian associate with funerals and Kolyva or boiled wheat with honey, the same food which had been offered at Tolga's funeral. The Russian services were very solemn, and the music was, at times, somewhat mournful. I felt satisfied that, finally, Saint George had given me some satisfaction.

There were three things I felt I must do on our way home. First thing was that we stopped at the monastery in Tbilisi to visit with Father Abo, the iconographer, Father John's friend. He greeted us warmly, and having some authority, we were able again to visit with Father Theodosius and Father Michaelangelos. I again offered to take them with us to Saint Davit's. I told Father Abo that we could actually spare a couple of extra horses and leave them should they want to return to Tbilisi. Father Abo spoke to the abbot, who gave his approval.

We set out the following morning. The monastery had provided enough vegetable and grain products for the monks to eat their food. They could eat fish, which we were able to provide, but no meat. They also fasted on Wednesday and Friday. These two monks were so loving and affectionate toward each other that I almost suspected an unseemly relationship, considering that they had chosen a life without women, but I soon discarded the thought. These men were too pure of character for me to suspect anything strange. The trip to Saint Davit's took less than a week, and the monks chanted a service called compline every night of the journey. Their cheerfulness of attitude brought us out of our gloom, and by the time we got to Saint Davit's, we were all communicating again and in good spirits.

Nissim had prepared Kiymetli for his first communion, and the two monks had taught him his prayers. Again we attended the one chapel that conducted parts of the service in Azeri on request. Kymmy took communion three days in a row, and his grief over the death of Grigory Yurevich was lightened. So was mine. We stayed until the fortieth day after Tolga's death, and we chanted a panahida for him there. Again we feasted, but it was not so offensive to me.

I must confess, Holy Father, how much I loved that place. My feeling of having to go home was not so intense there as when we were on the road. I certainly love our monastery here, Father, please don't misunderstand, but I felt a peace there that I have felt nowhere else on this earth, not even my secret place along the Sopasi river. We stayed a week there, contrary to my original plans, and I attended some services every day, Nissim and Kymmy being my constant companions. Koray also came with us here and there and stayed in the porch at the back called the narthex. When we had the panahida for Theodore, however, he came right in with us.

He confided with us that day that it was not his time to make a commitment to the faith yet. He knew that Tolga, or Theodore, would have wanted him to be baptized, but he was not ready. Nissim told him it was not something he should rush into because it would be worse for him to take the faith and then turn back on it afterward.

"Right, Kymmy?"

"Right, Noune." (The Greek word for godfather)

Somehow or other, Father, I knew that they were referring to me. It was just enough to be there for me, and I was genuinely sad to leave. I found out later that Kokochu had also been spending much time at the monastery. He had been pursuing a relationship with Father Theodosius and Father Michaelangelos and sought out their company. I didn't probe. Kokochu needed his own life. Anna Maria and Livvy attended also but had to stand behind a screen where they could see but not be seen.

We left pleased at having come there, and again we left with a bundle of food. I have not mentioned that the two donkeys that we had abandoned had not abandoned us. Apparently their attachment to Moussa was such that they followed the camels all the way to Batumi and managed to keep up the pace. As a reward, they were now chosen to carry the food products. The Lenten fast was coming, and since our Christians were travelers, the monks encouraged only those who could to keep it. They were told to try to fast the first week at least and the week before

Pascha called Holy Week. However, we would likely be home before Pascha anyway.

There were two other errands, which I had kept in mind. As we left the Kingdom of Kakhetia, we descended into the plains of Azerbaijan once again. The spring weather had swelled the banks of the Kura, which proceeded at its leisurely pace toward the sea, only slightly flooding in places. I kept my eyes open for the landmarks that would lead us to both the Nogay communities and the Yezidis tribe. I finally had to tell Nissim what I had in mind especially since I couldn't find the tribes and I needed some help. Nissim, of course, grinned and shook his head.

"You mean for Dilaver and Erali? I suppose this is an act of gratitude on your part. Do you consider finding them wives a responsibility of yours? Dilaver is your squire. Do you think Erali can handle a woman?"

"Oh, come on, Nissim. Do you think I can provide a wife for Dilaver and deprive Erali of the same privilege?"

"I suppose this is your way of asking my permission. Erali is my squire, after all, and I do not have a bride price."

"Do you think I have?" I pulled a leather bag out of my belt and asked, "You didn't forget this, did you? Remember? The frankincense is for Tashi, the myrrh is for Katya, and the gold is sufficient, or almost sufficient, for our boys and, if we can find the Yezidis, we'll have a couple of brides for Vishtaspa and Mardunya. This may dip into my personal cash, but I think of it as alms in memory of my brother Tolga and old Grigory. I like some of your Christian customs. Alms for the dead: unique!" There was a moment of silence. "Well?" I said. "Why are you looking at me like that?" Nissim smiled and shook his mane in the wind.

"I suppose there is no harm in asking the men if those arrangements would suit them."

"You're right, Nissim. I really never thought of it."

Of course they were excited when we approached them, privately just after the evening meal. Erali and Dilaver flushed in the excitement. They turned as red as Kalmyks. They were not a particularly handsome pair, at least from a man's point of view. They were stocky and muscular, lean of body, but thick boned. They were warrior types and used to steppe horses. They were obviously brothers, dark eyed with typically round features. Both had thick matted hair and full lips. The Mongol heritage was apparent. Bathing was new to them, but they kept the rules and even learned to swim or at least enjoy the water. Dilaver was a serious lad maybe a year younger than me. Although he, like Erali, didn't shave his head, he kept a tight braid from the top of his head down the back of his neck. Erali kept his hair short, but it was becoming unkempt from lack of care. He had a quick and sometimes caustic sense of humor. I had to separate him from Kymmy occasionally because the banter occasionally became annoying.

My gift of barbering tools to Moussa paid off. He was only too glad to barber the men and was skilled in beautifying the women.

Of course we had to approach Kuru about his sons, but since they had to translate for the elder, it would have been very hard for him to refuse. He seemed pleased in the long run. Vishtaspa broke into a jaunty melody in Farsi, which caused the boys to laugh and Kuru to frown. I knew it was hard for these lusty young men, especially in the presence of two beautiful women. The Persians were a handsome lot in a very hairy way. All of them had beards, even the younger men. They were dark skinned and fine featured and kept their hair tied up in white turbans. They were scrupulously clean and constantly laundered their clothes in whatever water was available. I felt sorry that Naveed, the youngest of Kuru's sons, who had just turned fifteen, was left out, but I couldn't manage it. I promised that I would try to find someone among our people.

I had to explain to Koray that his father was the only one with the authority to make such plans for him. Besides, I reminded him that he was in mourning, and it wouldn't be fitting for him to take a wife at this time. He agreed of course though he admitted that he was somewhat hot at times. He said this with a bit of a snort and a grin. I told him I would speak with his father.

I had nothing to say for Hazir's men. His family was responsible for them. "What about you, my friend?" I asked him. "Just speak the word, and I'll make some provisions."

He gave me one of his long, gentle, but also sad smiles. "Perhaps I'll take you up on that some time in the future."

Later on that evening, just before going to sleep, Nissim confessed, "You were right, Tambor. I have to admit you were right. I admire that amazing foresight you have. Do you realize how many eyes are now peeled for these tribes?"

"I guess so." The answer was simple.

Within a few weeks, we found them. One of the Nogay tribes had left completely, we were told. They went into Armenia just after the felting, as they apparently did every year to trade in the south. Both were small groups, and when they traveled, the whole tribe went together unlike our village at Sopasi. We were too big for that; of course that is why my father's role was so important.

The other band had moved on. We were told they had moved in the direction we were heading, and so traveling lightly, we caught up with them in a few days. Their felting had been completed just before the move, and even then, one could still smell the fresh felt. They greeted us warmly. Hazir expressed admiration at the results of the felting. He and their felters talked on and on, sharing valuable ideas.

I gathered with the same elders we had talked to before and expressed my needs. Nissim, Hazir, and I introduced the boys to them, and we told them the women would be treated well. After that, we dismissed the young men. We advised the elders that the boys were healthy and had come from a good Tatar family. We told them that they had experienced firsthand combat and were loyal warriors. I felt that we were selling horses rather that procuring wives.

I told the elders that since we were paying in gold, we would prefer to take two women from poorer and less fortunate families, provided that they were not from people who beat them. They were not to be sisters since our boys were brothers, and it would not be good for breeding. The women were to be healthy and hard working and that they should have good teeth. Now we were buying cattle, it seemed to me. But that's the way things have always been among us. Besides the girls themselves, we wanted to meet their parents. Their folks were old, older than my father; they were respectful, though one of them questioned my authority.

"I have gold, sir. That is my authority."

His wife was pleasant, round, and healthy, with bright eyes, which gave her husband a threatening look. She, of course, took the bag of money as was the custom. Her daughter was equally bright eyed and cheerful and looked as though she were holding back laughter. Her name was Burca. She would adjust easily.

There was no father in the next family but only a poor widow. She had three daughters and offered the youngest one who was modest, shy, and fearful of her mother. She was called Kelebek and was as gentle as a butterfly. I thought she would be perfect for Erali since he could cheer her up, and she could calm him down. She might feel some homesickness. The old woman obviously needed the two older girls to care for her. I had asked Anna Maria to examine the girls, and she advised us that they were both in the bloom of health, though a little hungry and that they had good teeth and bones. Both were virgins, both were fifteen, both were friends, both were pleasant-looking. Neither of them were beauties.

When we introduced the young men to them, there was blushing all around, but I admired our boys for keeping a cold face. The price of course was too high, and we had to whittle it down to something reasonable. All were happy in the end. The snappy man was apologetic, and the widow was very pleased. My bag of gold was lighter. The women fussed.

There was not much of a ceremony, nothing at all resembling the Christian marriages I would witness in the future. The shaman danced and sang and shook rattles and burned fragrant wood. After dancing and drinking a lot of kumis, which was a good brew, Dilaver and Erali with their new brides were ushered off to a small but pleasant yurt. Evidences of the girls' former virginity were left outside the yurt for the morning. We stayed an extra day. From here on, I would no longer think of them as boys.

Proceedings were not so easy with the Yezidis. We caught up with them a few weeks later just in time, for they were about to head south along the Caspian shore into Persia. They were also not prepared for our request as we had not discussed it at our previous encounter. I had discussed with Kuru and his sons that they must not be considered as slaves. They were to be considered my bondsmen, a relationship the young ones had gotten used to, but was still alien to Kuru's thinking. I was quite relieved to have this clarified, and it made negotiations a little easier. While the Yezidis had more or less the same religion, they were Kurds and a tribe, which had been despised by both other Kurds and Persians. The tribal chieftains admitted that they were too inbred, and it was hard to find suitable mates. They were appalled that we offered gold for the women, but we explained that while our tribe was rich in horses, sheep, and cattle, we were not on a trade mission and all we had was money. Nor could we possibly comply with their betrothal ceremonies. We insisted that we wanted women from poor families.

Eventually, after much discussion, the chieftains proposed that there was a woman who had been widowed a few years back with a seventeen-year-old daughter and a thirteen-year-old son and a paternal female cousin, an orphan also living with them. She was fifteen years old. The mother was still young in her mid-forties. They advised us that we could have the whole family. Of course, I thought the price would be out of our range, but I was quite surprised when they asked for much less than what I had. I feigned that it was too much, and they actually dropped the price further. I asked to meet them and realized that they were very poor and probably a liability to the tribe. But the girls were beautiful. All they needed was some good food and a bit of happiness, and they would glow. Besides, the boy would be a good companion to Kymmy and would keep him out of Erali's hair. Of course, the boy would have to learn our language, but young people find that easier to do. I expected that all of us would be speaking our dialect of Tatar before long. I noticed that Vishtaspa and Mardunya already were talking like us.

I consulted with Nissim and Kuru, who needed his sons to interpret, and he agreed, adding that he wanted nothing to do with the mother and that his days with women were finished. He was very insistent about this. I had in mind that Hazir might succumb to her charms. She was a strict woman, attractive, and maybe a little strong-willed. After all she had to be. Besides the boys themselves, Kuru was the only one permitted to attend the proceedings, which took almost a week. They had to have formal betrothals and gatherings, the less religious ones we could attend. We grew impatient. Finally they were done, and we were a week behind schedule. However, everyone was happy. What more could we ask for? Kurds and Persians do not live in yurts as we know them, so the tribe provided the kind of tents they used. Then we were back on the road.

I felt the need to make up for those two weeks, yet I didn't want to press our men and cause our women anxiety. We took the Kura almost all the way to the Caspian even though it took us somewhat south. I was tempted to go through the mountains when we reached Qarasu but changed my mind on the advice of Hazir and Nissim. I knew Nissim would have liked to pay a visit to Father John in Astrakhan but never said so. He knew I could never deny him, so he said nothing. He seemed, like me, to sense the need to go home.

We made an inquiry at a small city called Ali Bayramli. The dwellers were friendly enough and told us that, rather than following the river south, we should follow the river until we met the Chalovly road going north. We would follow that road until we passed the village of the same name, which would take us directly north to Baku. We took their advice. Once there, we rested and enjoyed the pleasant climate. The women needed rest, and the married men needed time again with their wives. I could spare only three days at the most. I didn't know why, but I needed to get home.

I had asked Anna Maria to take charge of the women, knowing her to have a quiet authority. Nissim and I asked how the women were making out. She said that the girls were adjusting well. Since she spoke Turkish, she had no trouble communicating with the Tatar girls who could speak the Azeri tongue. The girls respected her. The two Kurdish brides were pleasant and humble and spoke some Azeri but kept to each other. They were helpful and didn't shirk their work. Ruxsar, the mother, however was not so respectful and seemed to want to take over the women's quarters. I asked Anna Maria if she were causing trouble.

"Not exactly trouble, Tambor." I allowed her to drop the *sir*. "It just seems that she wants to keep the Kurds separate from the rest of us. Fortunately, she speaks Azeri. I have tried to explain that we are all together and that I need to control the chores and that once we arrive at Sopasi, your mother runs the household. Do you know how she answered that?"

"Tell me."

"She said, 'We'll see!'"

"I'll talk to her tomorrow. I want you, Nissim, and Vishtaspa present with me. We'll give him a first taste of a mother-in-law."

The Persians had not finished their wedding celebrations, so on the third night, we pulled out the wine and the jug of kumis the Nogays gave us. What a treat. I suppose I wanted to enjoy the celebrations too. Vishtaspa had a beautiful voice, sweet and clear. He had sung before for us on occasion, and Mardunya also played a string instrument. Someone had a drum; I think it was Naveed. Ruxsar, the girls' mother, danced with her daughter, Hana, who was Vishtaspa's wife, and Meraz, who was spouse to Mardunya. Ruxsar seemed happy enough. The Tatar men, of course, danced together. Then there was a demand.

"Sir Tambor, up and dance for us," they called out. I made the excuse that I was in mourning.

Livvy approached me, "If I can play your brother's oud, I shall sing you a mourning song."

"If I dance to a mourning song, the night's festivities will be over." I warned them.

"So be it!" they all said.

After Livvy made a few strums on the oud, Mardunya caught the melody and rhythm and accompanied her on the strings. She had a soft and deep voice, and at first, she sang wordlessly. Then she sang in Greek; the beautiful words I couldn't understand drifted over the pleasant evening air. Koray pushed me up, and I moved to the mounting melody. It was too serious for anyone to cheer. I could see out of the corner of my eye Anna Maria pushing Nissim and giving him one of her scarves. As he stood up, he swung the scarf a couple of times, and I caught it. Here we were, the two of us dancing opposite each other, two very different men, brothers—he, intense and so unafraid of his feelings, and me, with my cold face—both of us dancing together. At one point, he looked straight at me and, passing my ear, told me that Livvy was singing for their father. Slowly the music ebbed to the sounds of the night beside the wash of the sea. That night, we rested well.

First thing in the morning, I called Nissim and asked Hazir to summon Vishtaspa, briefing him on what I need to do. Vishtaspa, who was less communicative with me at that time, looked a bit worried. I tried to relax him by telling him there was a job for him to do. We entered the women's yurt, small for six women, and dismissed the brides. It was almost a social event, and salted tea was served. I was a little unsure how I would approach the subject, but Anna Maria was quick to provoke it. As she was serving, she made a point of asking Ruxsar to do something, a chore of some sort, which I cannot now remember. The Yezidi woman gave her a long hesitant look, which Anna Maria countered with a pleasant smile. She went and did what she was asked but with a somewhat put-upon attitude. Anna Maria repeated this exercise a couple of times such that no one, not even Ruxsar herself, had any doubt as to its intention.

I asked, "Ruxsar, are you happy here? Do you think you could be happy with us?"

"Which question do you want me to answer?" I was appalled at her audacity.

"Let's try both."

She paused and thought. "I can't remember being happy for many years, certainly not since my husband died and maybe not even before. My husband's brother also died and left me with another girl to raise, that's Meraz, whom I treat like a daughter. Now beside my own son, I have two sons-in-law to serve and these other women." She spit that last phrase out.

"Suppose you had your choice, Ruxsar. How would you have it?" She paused. She was aware she was being put under observation. She just shrugged her shoulders and feigned doing something.

I continued. "You came with us of your own free will. No one is insisting that you stay. I can spare a horse, Ruxsar, and you can go wherever you want. I did not take you as a slave. You know, I thought that being with your family would have made you happy. Now you have sons-in-law. If you are happy to be amongst us, then you will have to cooperate with the people I put in charge. If you choose to oppose us, then I insist you go. I will force you to go."

"But my daughters are now married. I cannot take them with me."

"With you?" I responded. "With you? There is not a possibility in the world that I will let them go with you. Are you mad?"

I let this sink in. She was quiet. I might have expected rage. Instead I saw tears, which she strove to cover up.

Anna Maria was quick to respond. "Ruxsar, you know that I have treated you with dignity and respect, but you have refused my friendship. If you are nursing some grief or sorrow, perhaps we could talk. I've had my own share of grief as everyone knows. I need you to help me, work with me, and not oppose me. Both of us are looking toward a wonderful life ahead, aren't we?"

She took Ruxsar's hand. There was a brief pause. Ruxsar looked at her and lifted Anna Maria's hand to her breast.

"Forgive me…sister. I have been so hurt. I am so afraid that all of you will treat me badly too. I just needed to cling on to the only things I had left, my daughters. I'm sorry." She looked at me. "Lord Tambor, I know you mean well for me. You took me in when no one wanted me. I will be happy. I want to be happy."

Vishtaspa quietly said, "Mama, we love you. We boys now have a mama to love. We shall make you happy."

"You have, my son, you have." She almost gasped this phrase as the tears flowed.

"Do you want us to leave you alone for a while?" I inquired.

"No, no," she said. "I haven't wept for years. Just give me a moment." She wiped her face and adjusted the scarf around her hair and sighing deeply she proceeded. "My husband, and to a certain extent, his brother were renegades of the tribe. Many people, the Muslims and the Christians in Armenia, call us devil worshippers, and I'll tell you why although it is not true. Like the Christians and Muslims, oh yes and also the Yehudi, we believe in one God. We the Yezidis call him Mazda like the ancient Persians, like you Persians. We all believe that a powerful angel caused evil to come into the world God created. Christians call him Satan. Persians call him Ahriman. Whatever he is called, he caused the trouble. What made the Yezidis different is that they believe that God pardoned Satan and accepted him back into the council.

"My husband didn't agree with that and tried to convince our people that it was not true. He reasoned that the presence of evil in this world and suffering and sin showed that Satan had not repented of this evil and was still causing grief. My husband did not go so far as to say that God had not forgiven him, but he insisted that Satan had never really repented and was still the source of the world's trouble. The elders violently opposed him, almost physically. But he persisted in this thought. Since the Yezidis are numerous in Armenia, he inquired as to what the Christians thought. All said that God had not forgiven Satan because he could not repent."

"That is what we believe, as Christians, Ruxsar," Nissim said. "We say that it is impossible for Satan to repent. Humans can repent and be forgiven because we were created in God's image and likeness. Jesus, God's Son, after his crucifixion, entered into death, the realm of the enemy and rescued and freed the righteous believers that Satan had imprisoned until that time, and all who believe in him are no longer under Satan's spell and are given the grace to escape death."

"I must think on that, Sir Nissim. However my husband became like a foul stench to the tribe, along with his brother who supported him. They were ignored. They wouldn't let us starve, but we were unable to work and so lived on what they left over. Meraz's father died first, and we took responsibility for his daughter and wife, who died of grief and shame a few months later, to be followed by my husband who had caught a fever. I was alone with three children whom I could never marry off."

She began laughing. "How stupid I've been. My two daughters are now married, and my son Zargo is still with me. Here I am still complaining. Instead of being grateful, I am still grasping and fretful. Forgive me, young lord. I shall be happy and grateful for the rest of my days here. And may my daughters increase your tribe with many sons."

"And I hope a few beautiful daughters also," I added. She leaned over and kissed me on the hand, imitating Anna Maria.

It was not long before we left Baku wending our way up the coast. It was somewhat mountainous up the coast until we reached Makhachkala, in the Russian province of Dagestan, where we stayed only a day, no more. The rest of the way was much easier, the land being flatter and the roads being closer to the shore and less forested. I had one more stop to make once we got into Astrakhan.

There was another I could have made but decided against it. I took Dilaver and Erali aside, thinking that they might have wanted to visit their family. This would have pulled us too far west. But time and travel were not my main concerns. These young men, our squires, had become identifiably part of the fabric of our lives. Now having wives, they were quite eager to settle in Sopasi, the Birches, and benefit from the training provided there. They anticipated and even feared meeting Akilli Khan whom they had heard so much about. But I needed to tell them they would not be visiting home.

"I suppose," Erali said, "that it would be a bit of a laugh flaunting our wives and good fortune in front of them who found it so easy to send us away. But, Sir Nissim, you have always taught us that forgiveness demonstrates nobility of character. No, I don't want to go home. Home is where you are, Knyazi."

Dilaver, who was a more serious man, said, "Perhaps many years from now, we could visit them. The elders are so stuck in

their ways and so unwilling to change they would be offended
if we should return home now. Let them forget us and we them
until we have established ourselves. Then we may be able to visit
them with no bad feelings."

"Thank you, men. I can see you have grown in wisdom over
the past few months. I am proud of you, and I am sure you can
tell how much Sir Nissim and I appreciate your fine work. I do
have one more stop to make. I must inform Grigory Yurevich's
sons that the old man has died. Maybe the four of us can ride
together. We'll take Kymmy along too. He loved the old man.
The rest can stay and take some leisure. I think I know how to
get there."

When we got into Astrakhan, we veered inward toward the
lake country. It was spring, and now I could see why the land
was considered a swamp. It was wet and soggy, the snow and
ice having melted some time ago. We camped just outside of
Nikolayevska, and our people and servants were told to relax
and enjoy the pleasant weather. Hazir, ever the cautious one,
permitted Kymmy to come along with our small delegation.

The women were getting along wonderfully. Ruxsar and Anna
Maria were becoming friends. Anna Maria confided in me that
they both had let it all out. She said it had been somewhat a
cleansing for her as well. The married girls however teased Livvy
about being single. When I found out the reason they giggled
every time I passed them, I put a stop to it. Nissim told me that
Livvy found it embarrassing. Apparently they continued, though
not within earshot of me. Moussa was always there to restore
calmness, so he and the two women kept the ladies' yurt in order.
By the time we got back the women had moved into one of
the tents and Moussa, Kokochu, and Koray were using another
for themselves.

These were happy times. Tetik and Kymmy had renewed their
friendship. Kymmy, in his winning way, tried to include Zargo in
all his activities. The boy was, at first, sullen and incommunicative

because, of course, he did not speak our language. He used a few Turkish words, which had crept into the Kurdish vocabulary of their tribe. Kymmy seemed totally unaware of any problem and talked to Zargo incessantly as though he were able to understand him. What I observed was his incredible ability to understand and make himself understood so much that, after a short while, both boys were talking in a mixture of both languages. Fortunately Farsi, the language of Zargo's Persian brothers-in-law, is related to Kurdish especially the Yezidi dialect, so Kymmy was picking up Farsi and Yezidi and Zargo was learning Tatar and Turkish. Because of this, both boys were becoming friends. They were inseparable, and hawking was their primary interest. This allowed Hazir and Nissim a little more free time, although Nissim still insisted on Kymmy's morning prayers and religious instruction. Zargo usually sat with them.

After a few days, our little group left camp to find Grigory's village. We had passed through Nikolayevska on our way down, and this made it easier for us to locate the village where Grigory's sons lived. It was in fact heading toward the route home, and that meant we had to backtrack to pick up the rest of our company. After all we had first run into Grigory but half a day's journey from the Volga after saying farewell to my father. It was in my mind that bringing the whole troop to Grigory's farm was not in our best interests. I also thought it a great opportunity to ride like the wind over the open plains toward the village where Grigory's sons lived. But that was not as easy as I had expected because those plains, which had seemed so vacant when covered in snow were, in fact, farmlands which we could hardly trample over. By the time we reached the village, we had to stick to the roads, and the road did lead to the village. When we arrived, we were told that his sons and their mother were at the farmstead. By that time, we remembered how to get there.

We approached the homestead quietly and solemnly. We could see some men and boys working in the fields, plowing and planting. The fields were alive with the activity of spring farming. A few children were playing around the farmhouse, which looked tidy and well kept, and they stopped in their play to study us strangers. One little girl banged on the door saying, "Babushka! Babushka!" until the old lady came out. She said something to the children and sounded annoyed. Slowly sweeping her eyes over our group, I saw that she recognized me and Nissim but couldn't find what she was looking for.

Nissim attempted to speak Russian to her. "Greetings, Gospozha! Forgive us for bothering you, but may we speak to your sons?"

She hesitated but told a boy a little younger than Kymmy to go fetch the men. She was quiet and thoughtful and took her apron into her hands, squeezing it nervously. We could see the boy talking to one man, presumably his father, who motioned to his brother and pointed toward us. They came quickly though not really in haste, resting their tools on the side of the house. They seemed no friendlier than they were before when Grigory Yurevich left them.

"Well, what do you want?" the elder of the two said.

Nissim looked over to me for the go-ahead and solemnly said, "I regret to inform you, Gospoda and Gospozha, that your father Grigory Yurevich Ureic is dead. He was confessed and had a Christian funeral. He is buried in a churchyard in Mtskheta, Georgia."

The younger of the two said something, which I was told was "The old idiot serves him right! Going out to war at his age. The old fool!"

The older one asked, "Who killed him? Was he drunk?"

Nissim turned to me and translated. I said to him, "Translate for me, Nissim." I said to them. "It has been a special honor for me, as a warrior prince of the Nogay Tatars, to have under my command the very brave and honorable officer Grigory Yurevich Ureic. He was the oldest member of our troop, and I have with me the youngest member, Kiymetli, a brave Nogay warrior who thought of Grigory Yurevich as his grandfather. Your father fought with us in the Turkish lands, freeing two noble Christian ladies from slavery to the Turks. Your father was a man of courtesy and kindness, and all of us loved him. He was also made godfather to my brother, Theodore, just before he died.

"Grigory fought, but he did not perish in battle. After an exhausting ride and some ill weather, Grigory took a fever and died. He died during the night, lying beside our Kymmy here, who was trying to keep him warm. I speak to you about Grigory Yurevich as a gentleman whom you obviously do not know. We came looking for his sons, but we have not found them. There is not a man here I would think of calling his son."

I was about to turn and leave when the widow descended the steps and came over to me. She looked straight at me and said, "Knyaz." I looked at her. "Knyaz, did you bury my husband with his boots on?"

"Gospozha, Grigory died with his boots on as he wished, and they are still on his body to this day."

She made the sign of the cross and with a big sigh she said, "I give glory to God. He was a good man and never beat me." She brought her apron to her face and sobbed a little but quickly pulled herself together.

"I have brought his hat back to you and the weapons that he used."

"The weapons you can keep. Give them to his grandson here. You will stay with me, and I make some bliny and drink some of Grigory's vodka. You are my honored guests." Then turning to his sons, she spat, "Go back to work!" They hesitated for a moment, looking rather sheepish and turned away.

Kymmy wasn't loud, but he spoke clearly, "Shame! Shame! Shame!" This he said in Russian. I suspect the old man might have disciplined him with this word. Kymmy continued, "Old Grigory is in heaven with Jesus, no thanks to your prayers. You will not go to heaven unless you have a panahida for him, for you must honor your father and mother." The younger one turned back, and to my surprise, he made the sign of the cross and wiped his eye. Later both came home to eat. They were quiet and perhaps repentant. Verusha, their mother, served them the traditional bliny but refused them vodka. They drank tea.

We left only a few hours later amidst protestation from Verusha. We explained that the rest of our company was at Nikolayevska, and we wanted to be there by nightfall. The elder of the two sons said that if we stick to the roads, we would arrive safely but after sundown. As we mounted our horses, the two came toward me and offered their apologies. The young one attempted to speak in Tatar and went to Kymmy. "Thank you, *vnook*," he said. "I do want to go to heaven so we shall have a panahida next Saturday and a requiem every year. Pray for me. My name is Sergei Grigorievich, and my brother is Pavel. Pray especially for him," he whispered, "for he is very bitter. When you get older, maybe you could visit us, do you think?"

Kymmy said simply, "I would like that. My name is Kymmy. You could pray for me too."

"Good-bye, vnook," he said affectionately, squeezing his knee.

As we turned to depart, I saw Verusha standing on the step making the sign of the cross over us just as the monks had done on our departure from Saint Davit's. I felt comforted by that. After we were out of earshot, I asked Nissim, "What is this 'vnook' business?"

Nissim grinned. "It means grandson. It looks like Kymmy has become part of the family."

Kymmy said, "Thank you, Lord Tambor, for letting me come. I feel now that I have put Dedushka Grigory to rest in my mind. I think his sons are sorry for what they said about him. Maybe they will learn to love him because of your words."

Erali and Dilaver were anxious to get back to camp in the hopes of spending some time with their brides before having to move on. But they did express their appreciation for being asked to come along.

Nissim told me he had had a long talk with Verusha. "Half of what she said I didn't understand, but I did glean some information from her. Apparently they came from somewhere on the Dnieper, which would have made them Cossacks, likely. He was always off to war, and that made her lonely and the boys estranged from their father. The farm was originally her father's, but when he died, Grigory bought it from her older brother. He never farmed it though, even after his retirement from the army, so the boys had to do all the work. That's why they called him lazy. He had other vnooki, but all he would do was just play with them. Who knows? He did run the still on the side and made fairly good vodka. I have a jar hidden away." He grinned. "The farm, she told me, was fairly successful, however. Now that Grigory is dead, his sons will probably split the land although that would be a shame in my opinion."

"Yes." What more could I say?

All of a sudden, I felt melancholy. Kymmy and Erali were having a race and were in high humor ahead of us. Dilaver, always more serious, rode with us quietly. I had come to appreciate this solemn quality, and he gradually became closer to Nissim and me. So I was somewhat at ease expressing myself.

"Do you remember, Nissim, when we started this journey how gloomy I was? I thought it was leaving my father or perhaps feeling a little homesick, but I feel the same way now."

"Perhaps," he replied, "it's the flatness of the land, the long stretches of land with nothing on it but farmhouses scattered here and there and yurts. You are used to rolling hills."

"Maybe. It's certainly a possibility. But you would think I would be happy and satisfied. After all, we accomplished what we set out to do, and I have been able to keep the vows I had made to myself, all of them. Your mother and sister seem to be very happy. I've been able to find wives for most of my men. I have lost a brother of course, but even he died content, and Grigory is lying in his grave with his boots on. The two fathers are in their monastery praying for us. I've finally freed and bonded my Persians. And Kokochu has recovered his manhood and dignity. What more can I ask? And yet I feel sad, maybe empty. My purse is empty." I had to laugh. "But we are well fed so that is no problem. And we are going home. I should be thrilled!"

"Knyaz," Dilaver said, "those of us who have been brought up on the plains often feel this way. It's the wind, my lord, the wind. It comes from somewhere you don't know, and it blows toward another place where you can't go. It doesn't want to stay, and it pays no mind to the cheek it brushes against. In the deep hours of the night, it cries out in its loneliness because it can't find what it is looking for.

"But you, my knyaz, came in with the wind and followed after it, and you would not let it go, and you took us along with you. It flew up the mountains and through icy forests, and you chased it. It swooped over the valleys, and you caught it by the tail, and we followed you out of breath. Isn't that so, Sir Nissim?"

"I could never have expressed it better, Dilaver."

"You can't imagine how grateful I am, sir, and I am sure it's true of the rest of us. You never thought about yourself once, isn't that true, Sir Nissim? Be at peace, my lord. I beg you. Do you not know how much you are appreciated?"

"Enough of that, my friend. Thank you for your words, Dilaver. Listen, you have all played your parts. What could I have done without all of you? Isn't that right, Nissim? You men and, yes, even the women, you all cooperated and gave your best. I am grateful for that."

Nissim looked at me with that smirk on his face. Frankly, Holy Father, I was embarrassed. "Come on! Let's catch up with the others!"

We rode with the wind, just as Dilaver said. But my mood had lifted. I had become genuinely fond of this young man and his brother who was just a little older than Kymmy and needed to play. At first I thought of them as a liability; now I recognized their loyalty and appreciated it. I had once thought Dilaver to be sullen and gloomy, but now I saw him as a man of deep thought and intense feeling. It was time for me to talk.

We arrived at camp just a little after sundown as we had been told, and supper was ready for us. Not having stopped, we were quite hungry. I complimented Hazir and his crew on the fine stew he had made only to find out that Anna Maria had prepared it. Hazir took up the compliment and passed it on.

"This woman and the other have created a kitchen from which I have been banned."

"What else would we do, Sir Hazir, if we were not busy? Women spend too much time in foolish gossiping when they are idle. We need to work."

"No complaints!" Hazir said. "One of my boys shot down a small deer, and the falcon and the hawks have also been doing their jobs."

Tetik said, "We have a bit of news. But Zargo wants to tell you about it."

The boy blushed a bit, but not enough to deter him. Kymmy of course sat beside him. He spoke in Tatar. "The new hawk, which Tutumlu captured in Batumi, now sits on Tetik's shoulder. At first we thought she was uh, attacking him, but she sat on his shoulder. Tetik wears…" He turned to Tetik, who whispered the words, "thick leather shoulder pads so the claws don't…hurt him. We call the bird Banu, which means Lady. Tetik gave me one of the…uh…chicks. But they don't fly!"

"Hey! Hey!" everyone cried.

Vishtaspa said, "He practiced all day. He'll be talking Tatar before we get to Sopasi Falaka, and so will I."

Kymmy sat there open-mouthed.

Now it was time for me to speak. "Hazir, can you gather together the whole company, including all the servants?"

In no time, no doubt due to Hazir's abilities, all were gathered around the fire. Nissim brought out the glass jar of vodka, and Hazir, some wine, and everyone had a taste of one or the other.

"My friends," I began, "for I think I can call you all friends, we have come to the end of our mission, and we are on our way home. For some of you, it will be a new home, and I trust you will all feel welcome, especially you women. For some of us, it will be a reunion with friends and family, with those we love. I believe however that *we* have formed a special bond amongst us. We have been successful. We have done what we set out to do. Anna Maria and Livvy are amongst us, and we mustn't forget Moussa, who helped it to happen.

"We all worked together, and I am no less grateful to those of you who stayed behind in Batumi and kept camp for us. You warriors fought bravely and if we lack one who died from the fight, he was a hero. We must also not forget that Captain Grigory Yurevich died with his boots on, and he is still wearing them." All cheered. "His wife treated us warmly today. She was proud of him. His sons have a little more to think about."

"You Persians were indispensable to this mission, carrying the jewels at great risk. You managed to dodge the Turkish militia three times, I am told, by your cleverness and wit. My gratitude to you. I am also pleased that you are now my bondsmen and no longer my slaves."

"It would be unfair to single out one person in our company lest we leave someone out, but I will express my deepest compliments to Sir Hazir, whose ability to organize us riffraff into a manageable body has been unquestioned. Once again, tomorrow we will be on our way, and we will all be prepared because of him. My personal thanks to you, my friend. My appreciations to Sir Kokochu, a mighty warrior, who has proven that enemies can become friends.

"Behind all this is a group of people who helped all this to happen. These are our personal servants who have done all those other important things that make our lives manageable.

You have been handpicked by my father, Lord Dalgali, and Sir Hazir since all of you have been with our families ever since we can remember. Some young and some old, you are part of our families, and I want to express my appreciation." Everyone stood up, turned toward them standing in the shadows and cheered.

"There is also one other who has guided us and directed us throughout this entire venture, and this is Nissim's God, Khan Jesus. There was never a moment when I was not aware of him. It was as though we had been asked to do a job for him, and he has helped us see it through. It would seem that he took both Tolga, that is Theodore, and Grigory Yurevich for himself. May it not be that I would object to his ways and bring a curse on myself. Better it is that we thank him. May his name be praised!" Everyone was quiet and reverent. "May his name be praised!"

"Let us celebrate, friends, for tomorrow we begin our long trek home. I don't know about you, but I long to see the Volga!"